MID-CONTINENT PUBLIC LIBRARY
15616 E. 24 HWY
INDEPENDENCE, MO 64050

3 0 0 0 4 0 0 1 2 8 5 1 4 3

WITHDRAWN
FROM THE RECORDS OF THE
MID-CONTINENT PUBLIC LIBRARY

D1507201

PROMISE TO CHERISH

This Large Print Book carries the
Seal of Approval of N.A.V.H.

PROMISE TO CHERISH

ELIZABETH BYLER YOUNTS

THORNDIKE PRESS

A part of Gale, Cengage Learning

GALE
CENGAGE Learning·

Farmington Hills, Mich • San Francisco • New York • Waterville, Maine
Meriden, Conn • Mason, Ohio • Chicago

GALE
CENGAGE Learning®

Copyright © 2014 by Elizabeth Ruth Younts.
The Promise of Sunrise #2.
Thorndike Press, a part of Gale, Cengage Learning.

ALL RIGHTS RESERVED
This book is a work of fiction. Any references to historical events, real people, or real places are used fictitiously. Other names, characters, places, and events are products of the author's imagination, and any resemblance to actual events or places or persons, living or dead, is entirely coincidental.

Thorndike Press® Large Print Christian Romance.
The text of this Large Print edition is unabridged.
Other aspects of the book may vary from the original edition.
Set in 16 pt. Plantin.

LIBRARY OF CONGRESS CATALOGING-IN-PUBLICATION DATA

Younts, Elizabeth Byler.
  Promise to cherish / by Elizabeth Byler Younts. — Large print edition.
    pages cm. — (Thorndike Press large print Christian romance) (The promise of sunrise ; #2)
  ISBN 978-1-4104-7767-5 (hardcover) — ISBN 1-4104-7767-3 (hardcover)
  1. Nurses—Fiction. 2. Amish—Fiction. 3. Civilian Public Service—Fiction. 4. Large type books. I. Title.
  PS3625.O983P75 2015
  813'.6—dc23   2014049299

Published in 2015 by arrangement with Howard Books, a division of Simon & Schuster, Inc.

Printed in Mexico
1 2 3 4 5 6 7 19 18 17 16 15

To my daudy, *Freeman Coblentz.*
You've been gone for many years, but
your service and stories live on.

To all the Americans who served in the
Civilian Public Service,
your stories matter.

LETTER TO THE READER

Dear Friend,

I first want to thank you for picking up this book. We all have a long list of wonderful books to read and *what to read next* is a big decision. So, thank you.

Promise to Cherish is the second book in *The Promise of Sunrise* series. The first in the series only briefly spoke about the Civilian Public Service, while this book focuses heavily on the camps and life.

I took the creative liberty to change names, scenarios, and facts to best suit the novel while still keeping with the spirit of the era. I wanted to handle this history with sensitivity, and I pray I honor our country's history. I'm a proud military wife with an ancestral line of Amish conscientious objectors. I truly respect both. This is only a snapshot of one scenario.

I'd also like to clarify that the terminology used in the book with regards to Down's Syndrome is based on historical language, and is only used to remain accurate to the era. I have a very strong love and kinship with these very special people, having grown up with a cousin and aunt with Down's.

Back in the 1940s my *daudy* was among the many young Amish men drafted to fight in World War II. Since he was a conscientious objector, however, he was sent to work at the Civilian Public Service labor camps and mental hospital units with over twelve thousand others. Though this unique service is braided together with the history and politics of our country, it has been largely overlooked.

From my earliest memories of our horse and buggy and kerosene lamp-lit home, to our braided and pulled back hair and the best baking in the world, my whole life has been enmeshed with the Amish, and this story comes from the front lines of my heart. From my very family roots comes the story of Eli Brenneman and Christine Freeman.

Until next time,
Elizabeth

PROLOGUE

1944

The sudden grip on Eli Brenneman's arm brought him back to his surroundings. He looked down and found the probing eyes of Matilda Miller on him.

"Hi, Eli." Matilda smiled and tilted her head as she looked up at him.

Eli and his friends used to call her *Fatty Matty* in grade school. She wasn't Fatty Matty anymore. She was petite and even pretty, in a simple sort of way. Matilda, who hated being called Matty, was a few years younger than him and one of the few older girls who still attended Singings.

He looked around. He had not been paying attention for the last few minutes. The Singing was nearly over and a yellow-faced moon had just replaced the quiet November sunset. A bit of light cascaded from the golden windows from the king's house they'd just exited. A few flashlight beams flickered on as they all congregated outside. The brisk autumn air was nice after the stuffiness of inside.

"Hi, Matilda," he said, giving her his full attention.

"Rufus just called out Walk-a-Mile. Girls choose partners," she told him. He'd never noticed before but her voice reminded him of a mouse — high pitched and squeaky.

This was his last Singing before he left for the Civilian Public Service camp for conscientious objectors in Hagerstown, Maryland. Shouldn't he be sad to leave his home? Going to the Sunday evening Singings with the young people from his district had been his routine since he started his *rumschpringa* at sixteen.

He'd always teased and toyed with the girls, so finally being allowed to date had just added to the fun all those years ago. But now after more than ten years of Singings and so many girls, he was ready for a change. The day his draft notice came, it struck him that he was in the same place in life now that he had been in when he started managing the farm at twenty. Nothing had changed.

Eli hadn't, however, wanted to go to a labor camp in order to make a change. He managed his father's farm, and his abilities would be wasted working in the backwoods of Maryland digging ditches. But it would be his way out — for now. He didn't want to leave the Amish for good, but he did need to get away, even if just for a short spell of time.

As the couples lined up, Matilda pulled Eli to the back of the line. He'd played this game many times, and if you were lagging in the back there would be no one behind you to tap your shoulder and force all the men of the group to move forward one girl. If you were steady with a girl, you didn't want to be in the middle of the pack where the lousy fellow behind you would end up walking with your girl. You'd have to tap a lot of shoulders to get back around to her. That was how Walk-a-Mile was played.

"I wanted to talk to you before you leave this week." She smiled as she spoke. Her brown eyes batted in the moonlight. She made him curious.

Matilda wasn't the kind of girl that usually flirted with him. She was more of a *straight-and-narrow* kind of girl. People called Eli *vilt*. He knew he should want to tame his wild ways. His gaze fell on his brother Mark and his new girlfriend, Sylvia, a short distance ahead of them. Mark had wanted to date Sylvia for years. During

11

those years, however, Sylvia wanted Eli instead of Mark. In his usual thoughtlessness, Eli had dated her out of a competitive spirit and had only split with her because of his draft notice. He didn't want her to wait for him. She'd run straight into Mark's arms.

"A fine pair," Matilda spoke up.

Apparently she'd seen where his eyes had landed. She was right. Eli and Sylvia had never been right for each other anyway. Mark was ready to settle down, and Eli suspected they'd be married by spring. The fall wedding season was coming to an end.

"They'll probably be married by spring." Matilda echoed his thoughts. She paused briefly.

"So, you're going to be a camper in Hagerstown? Leaving in a few days?" She took his arm again. Her touch shouldn't have annoyed him. It was part of the *game.*

He nodded and imagined the long bus ride away from home.

"The Singings won't be the same without you."

"Oh, I reckon you'll still have a *gut zeit.* You always seem to, anyway."

"A good time without you? You're funniest of the *yungeh,* Eli. You always keep everyone entertained."

12

He smiled at her compliment, but her calling him one of the young people — at his age — grated. Since receiving his draft notice and taking stock of his life, he realized he was nearly the only twenty-five-year-old man still unmarried and without any real prospects. He wasn't the model of a well-brought-up Amishman. Most men four and five years younger weren't just married but were already fathers.

"I'd like to write you while you're away."

"Yah?" His head twitched with surprise. In the dim light he could see that her cheeks had grown rosier from the cold air and that she never ceased to smile.

"*Mem* and *Dat* said that as a community we should support you boys who get drafted. Especially after what happened with Henry Mast."

She was right. No one wanted any other Amish boy leaving the CPS to enlist in the army. The whole idea of the camps was to provide a place for conscientious objectors — the *conscies,* as they sometimes called the campers — to serve peacefully in the midst of the war. The only other options were noncombative roles or ending up in prison. Defying the Amish standards and the options the government offered was not their way. Eli was not going to enlist like his best friend Henry had. He would serve out his time and return to his farm work, but he would not return to *this.* The idea of returning to Singings and playing games with many who were only sixteen and seventeen years old made him see clearly how childish he'd been for so long.

He let out an audible sigh. Maybe Matilda was right. Getting letters from home would help him through what he expected to be mundane and unsatisfying work.

"Sure, you can write," he said. "I can't promise you'll get many letters back. I'm not very good at *breevah schravah.*" He couldn't remember the last time he'd written a letter.

He laughed.

"Maybe you can just drive me home sometime when you get back as a thank-you." Suggestion filled her high-pitched voice reminding him of the udder of a cow that'd missed a milking.

Eli cleared his throat in order to push away a chuckle. Then he stopped walking and turned to look at her. She bit her lower lip and her intentions, amidst her nervousness, were clear. He had to defuse this. He gripped the curl of his hat, forcing her hand to drop from his arm.

"Matilda, it's nice of you to want to write

me, but it has to be just as a friend."

Matilda didn't move for several long moments. Finally, she nodded and her eyes lowered to the cold ground in front of them. The group finished Walk-a-Mile, and the couples headed toward the buggies and their horses that were loosely tethered to the hitching post. Eli wasn't in the mood to say a lot of good-byes to the group, so he decided to crack a few jokes instead.

"Just wanted to say *bis schpatah.*" He gave a quick wave as he said he'd see them later.

"*Blap rahs druvel.* We'll miss you, Eli," someone yelled out. Several more agreed that he should stay out of trouble.

"Too bad I won't miss you," he yelled back, getting a hearty laugh.

Everyone's eyes were still on Eli even as the laughter died down.

"You know, I thought at first that I'd take some books with me, to pass the *zeit.* Maybe some westerns, but I heard I might not have much time to read with all the ditches I'll be digging." A few laughs filtered through the group. "So I decided to take with me the shortest book ever written. You know what it's called?"

The curiosity in the group was palpable.

"Amish War Heroes."

Laughter erupted as everyone waved and

he waved back. A few of the boys gave him a hearty handshake or a slap on the arm as they walked by. As the group cleared Matilda still stood there.

"You're always so funny, Eli," she said, walking up to him. She looked around. "Well, I better go. I've got three miles to walk before I get home. I'll get your address from your *mem.*"

Eli watched her walk away and couldn't help but release a sigh. He never could say no to a pretty girl, even if he had no real intentions with her.

"Wait, Matilda."

She turned, and the moon's glow was like a spotlight on her.

"Hop in," he said. As he said it he had a feeling he would regret this decision. When they were both in the darkness of the buggy with only the moon to light their way he spoke. "I know we're just friends, but you shouldn't have to walk home alone."

"*Jah,* friends," Matilda said with a soft and breathy voice.

CHAPTER 1

1945

January sunlight spilled onto Christine Freeman's face and reflected off her glasses. She closed her eyes in the white light and pretended she wasn't just standing in front of a window in the drab hospital hall. She had always loved mornings. And she would continue to find beauty in her mornings even while she worked at the dreary Hudson River State Hospital as a nurse for the mad. With almost no budget, the hospital was nothing more than a primitive asylum. Had it ever truly been an *asylum* for its patients? A sanctuary? A protection? A refuge?

She opened her eyes. Across the wintry lawn at the top of the hill stood the gothic Victorian Kirkbride structure. It was the hospital's main structure and stood like a palace against the washed-out sky. Its green hoods pointed to the heavens. Its wards stretched in opposite directions like wings

17

of an eagle, one for men and one for women. It was also where she lived, in one of the small apartments on the top floor. Though the Kirkbride building was designed to be a comfortable setting for the patients, giving them jobs and a purpose, during these bleak years of war many of those ideals were lost. The palatial building was more prisonlike than ever.

Edgewood, the two-story building Christine worked in, was dwarfish and rough by comparison. Being from nearby Poughkeepsie, she'd often viewed the hospital from the outside. How many times had she and her friends ridden their bikes out to the edge of town where the timeworn Victorian buildings stood, hoping to catch a glimpse of the lunatics. She had never imagined that she would work there someday.

Christine wanted to run down the path and away from this place. But there was no point entertaining such notions. Her family needed her to work. End of discussion. Their very survival depended on it.

A mournful cry from the nearby dorm room infiltrated her thoughts. She released a long exhale, then moved away from the window. She pulled at the tarnished gold chain from under her Peter Pan collar. The small cream-faced watch at the end of the necklace ticked almost soundlessly in her hand. Her twelve-hour day couldn't wait any longer. After tucking the watch back beneath her pale blue and white uniform, she stepped inside the thirty-bed dorm that then slept over forty-five men. She scanned the room to find the moaning patient. The paint-chipped iron beds were crammed so tightly it was difficult to see. The few who refused to leave their beds or had been sedated during the night shift were the only rounded figures atop the cots.

Christine walked to the second row and went sideways through the narrow aisle to check on the noisy patient. Wally. Electro-convulsive therapy usually caused gas-trointestinal and abdominal discomfort, but Wally's always lasted longer than a typical patient's. Christine didn't have any medications with her but knew Dr. Franklin had a standing order of hyoscine to treat Wally's nausea. Confirming his temperature was normal, she left the room.

She passed several of the rooms with two beds and a few with only one, usually retained for contagious patients. She would have to visit each as soon as she spoke with the night nurse to assess how her shift had gone.

Christine passed another dorm room with

nearly fifty beds and let out a sigh, noticing how few of the beds had sheets. Even the mattresses themselves were thin and flimsy, covered in shabby vinyl and incapable of adding any warmth to their inhabitants. Though she'd gone through three years of nursing school at this very hospital, she had a difficult time growing accustomed to how little bedding and clothing the patients received. It was not as tragic in the summer — save for the patients' modesty — but when the autumn breezes brought in winter storms, a sense of failure came over her.

The Kirkbride patients were supposed to make clothing for everyone, but with dwindling supplies and money everything was at a minimum or a standstill. The state only provided one sheet and one set of clothing per patient. If they were soiled, the patient would have to go without. Her efforts to co-ordinate a clothing drive had been thwarted. The town wanted little to do with the institution. Outside of some extraordinary donation, the funding they needed would have to come from the state alone.

As she moved on, Christine dreaded the scent of urine that lived in the very concrete blocks of the building's walls. The smell in the day room heightened. The odor in the hallway was mild by comparison.

"Remember, Christine," she said quietly to herself as she pulled open the door. "This is the day the Lord has made. I will rejoice and be glad."

Rejoice. Be glad. Rejoice. Be glad.

In order to accept the difficulties, she focused on the good she wanted to do for her patients and her family. With her brothers dead and buried half a world away in a war-torn country, her parents needed her income. That thought alone gave her the encouragement she needed to continue.

Christine's lips stretched into a forced smile, she pushed her glasses up on the bridge of her nose, and walked into the day room. Every corner of the large, square, gray room was filled. The windows let the light pour in, though darkness would have been preferred. Nearly a hundred men were walking in circles, hugging themselves, leaning their heads against the walls, sitting in the corners, and only a small handful congregated and interacted with one another. There were a few metal chairs, three rickety tables, and one bedbug-infested davenport. The tables usually held a few boxes of mismatched puzzles, several checker boards, tattered newspapers, and outdated magazines.

The night-shift staff gave Christine's day-shift attendants a rundown of how their night had gone. Todd Adkins, the most experienced attendant, listened carefully to what the other attendants said. A loud crash came from the far right corner of the day room and the attendants jumped into action. Christine couldn't see what the problem was in the sea of bodies but knew Adkins could handle it.

What would she have done in her first month as an official nurse in Ward 71 if it hadn't been for Adkins? Of course, Christine wasn't alone. Nurse Minton was the experienced nurse in her ward. How the two of them managed to keep track of over a hundred men with only two aides, she didn't know.

Christine said good morning to a few of the nearby patients. None of them even looked in her direction, except for Floyd, the only mentally retarded mongol patient in their ward. He was secretly her favorite patient. It was one thing to study Dr. John Langdon Down's work, which clinically described the syndrome in the mid-1800s, but to interact and observe Floyd was far better than learning from a textbook. He was sensitive, funny, and by far smarter than anyone gave him credit for. He bore no resemblance to the term *mongoloid idiot* used to describe his condition.

Floyd's small, almond-shaped eyes, like slits in his puffy face, sparkled. He smiled at her, with more gums than teeth, and then returned to tapping two old checker pieces together. She patted his head as she passed him. Christine walked over to the office in the corner of the room where she would prepare to hand out the morning round of medications.

"We had to restrain Rodney a few hours after our shift started. He went after Floyd." Millicent Smythe, one of the ward's night-shift nurses, was writing in the patient log-book in the office. Her lips were pasty and unpainted, though twelve hours ago they'd been as red as Christine's. Dark circles framed her brown eyes and her voice carried a hint of exhaustion.

"What? Floyd? He wouldn't hurt a flea." Christine said.

"Rodney said that Floyd was cussing at him. Rodney had all of them riled up — acting like the big cheese. It put a wrench in the whole night. Mr. Pricket even had a difficult time with him."

Mr. Pricket was one of the oldest and most experienced attendants in all of Hudson River. Surely Rodney's latest outburst would finally get him transferred to Ryan

Hall, where the truly violent and disturbed patients were kept.

"I know what you're thinking." Millicent looked over at her and raised a dark brown eyebrow. "Ryan Hall."

"Aren't you?"

The other nurse shrugged. "They are even more crowded than we are and there are injuries weekly — both the patients and the staff. If anyone needs more help instead of more patients, it's them."

Just before Millicent left she called over her shoulder. "Have an attendant check on Wayne and Sonny when you get a minute. Wayne was agitated last night. Oh, and the laundry is behind — again."

Christine nodded and hustled to get started handing out medications. The patients who were able lined up for their medications, which she handed through the open Dutch door. The attendants helped the less competent patients line up. She took a tray of medications out to the remaining patients who weren't able to form a line or were bedridden. This took some time, since each had to drink down the medications in front of her so she could check inside their mouths — under their tongues and in the pockets of their cheeks.

When she was nearly half through with

administering the medications, the attendants began taking the patients in shifts to the cafeteria to eat breakfast. When a patient in the other hall needed an unscheduled electroconvulsive therapy, often referred to as shock therapy, she was pulled in to assist since Nurse Minton was busy with an ill patient who had pulled his IV from his arm.

When she finally returned to the corner office in the day room her logbook was still open. Quickly Christine documented the lethargy of one patient she'd noticed earlier in the day and the aggressiveness of another. She reviewed the schedule for the rest of the day: more shock therapy, hydrotherapy for calming a few patients, and numerous catheterizations for the patients who refused to use the toilet. How would she keep up with it all?

She didn't have time to dwell and carefully picked up the tray of medications she needed to finish. Christine was only a step out of the office when Wally approached her.

"Hey, nurse, have a smoke for me? Have a smoke for me?" Though his words were still slurred she was glad he had come out of his stupor from earlier that morning. "Come on, have a smoke for me?"

"Wally, you know I'm not going to give

you any cigarettes." She smiled at him. It was difficult to have a conversation with the men when they stood nude in front of her. She had trained herself to treat them as if they were fully clothed individuals and would look them directly in their eyes.

"Aw, come on, nurse, I know where you keep 'em," he whispered loudly, stepping closer to her as she closed and locked the Dutch door. "What if I tell ya you've got some nice gams? You're a real Queen 'o Sheba! Prettiest nurse here."

"I don't smoke, Wally." It was only a half lie; she did smoke on occasion, but would never give a cigarette to a patient. "Now go back and play checkers before you get beat."

"No one ever beats me. You know that. Never." He repeated *never* over and over as he walked away.

The door to the day room swung open and hit the wall behind it. Adkins jogged in. His eyes were round and his face was as colorless as his starched attendant's jacket.

"Nurse Freeman," he said, breathless and shaky.

"What is it?" She'd never seen Adkins rattled before.

"I went to take some breakfast to Wayne and Sonny."

"Just now?" She sighed heavily. "Adkins,

this isn't like —"

"While you were in shock therapy I had to pull Rodney into solitary and this is the first chance I've — it doesn't matter now." Adkins breathed heavy and shook his head. He stopped long enough to look into Christine's eyes. "Wayne and Sonny are dead."

"Dead? What do you mean they're dead? From influenza?" They'd been sequestered to a private room for contagion for the last forty-eight hours.

He shook his head and grabbed her arm, making the small cups of pills on her tray rattle. "Froze to death."

Numbness fixed her where she stood. Christine wasn't sure she would be able to move from that spot. Had she heard him properly? It was her fault. She should've sent Adkins to check on them as soon as Millicent mentioned it. How long had it been since they'd been checked on? Her heart bemoaned that she had not insisted Adkins or even an attendant from Minton's hall check on them immediately. She took a deep breath and the stench of guilt filled her lungs.

"Nurse Freeman?" His grip tightened on her arm.

"Yes." She returned to the corner office behind her and calmly put the tray of meds

27

on the counter. Then, with Adkins on her heels, she jogged to the last room in the hall.

Christine pushed her way through the crowd of patients gawking at the unclothed bodies that lay frozen. She wrapped her arms around herself, partly for warmth and partly for a sense of security. Her breath puffed white as her breathing quickened. Snow piled in small mounds on the floor and the walls were frosted around the two sets of open windows.

"Get everyone out," she said rigidly to Adkins, who obeyed immediately.

Once the room was empty she had Adkins call for the administrator, Jolene Phancock. Christine also wanted to make sure Minton had heard the news. Once the two veteran staff members arrived they could instruct her on what to do next. Perhaps all that needed to be done was to call the morgue on the grounds to come pick the bodies up. They would hand them over to the state and have them buried in some unmarked plot for no one to grieve over.

"Good morning, Nurse Freeman," Ms. Phancock said in an even and pleasant voice as she walked in. She was too friendly not to give a proper greeting, but her voice carried the bitterness of the morning's events.

"Not a very good morning, unfortunately."

28

Christine tiptoed around the snow to the open windows and closed them. "Wayne is — was — always opening windows. We should've found a way to bolt the windows shut in here. I never thought this could happen. I feel responsible."

Like a hollow cavern, Christine's voice echoed in her own ears. Reality and dream crossed each other and she wasn't sure what was true anymore. Wayne's naked body, in the fetal position, was blue, and his bedsores were flaky. A shudder shook her body. Sonny, also blue, was long and skinny, and his toes were curled. He lay flat otherwise and had not even curled around himself to conserve heat. Guilt filled her empty heart.

She picked up Sonny's chalk and slate on the floor next to his bed. As a young boy, deaf and dumb, he was sent to the Children's Ward. There he'd been taught to write a few simple words in order to communicate. She blinked back hot tears when she saw what was scratched onto the slate.

Cold.

"Let me assure you that you are not to blame." Ms. Phancock released such a heavy sigh Christine could feel the weight of it around her. The administrator made a fist with her hand and pursed her lips.

"Ma'am?" She laid the slate back down

on the frozen floor.

"We need more workers." Ms. Phancock's fist pulsed up and down with each word. "You and the rest of the staff cannot possibly do more than you already are."

Christine agreed, of course, as she looked at the tragedy before her.

She found herself sorry that Sonny's nakedness was so visible, more than Wayne's. Of course, they often had more naked patients than clothed ones. Keeping patients clothed was difficult if they were incontinent or when they displayed erratic behavior. But this time it seemed worse. He wasn't just asleep or behaving dangerously. He was a human being who was lying naked in front of everyone coming in or near the room. She untied her apron and draped it over his lower body.

"What are you doing?" Nurse Minton asked as she strode in. Christine looked up at the older nurse. Her hair was already coming out of her severe bun, as if she'd been working all day instead of only a few hours.

"He deserves some dignity." Christine turned to her superior.

"Thank you, Nurse Freeman," Ms. Phancock said. "You're right."

Nurse Minton remained quiet.

"Can we tell the state what's happening here? Maybe they will find a way to get us the help we need."

"That sounds about as likely as a pot of gold at the end of the rainbow." Ms. Phancock sighed as she spoke. She patted Christine on the shoulder and told her that Gibson from the morgue would be there soon, then she left.

The two nurses remained in the room, silently together for several pregnant moments.

"Did you record Rodney's insulin shock therapy today?" Nurse Minton finally broke the quiet.

"Nurse Minton, we have a real tragedy here, and you want to talk about insulin treatment?"

"We are nurses, Freeman. This is our job." Her voice came out harshly, and even the old, jaded nurse seemed to realize it and cleared her throat. "I've been around long enough to know this is part of the job — though terrible, I understand. I also know that we have to keep the ward running regardless; otherwise another tragedy will be right around the corner."

Christine nodded. Minton was right. She turned toward the older nurse and stifled a loud sigh. "Yes, Rodney got his insulin treatment."

"Did his anxiety and aggressiveness subside? I was dealing with the other hall and haven't checked on him yet."

"Yes, ma'am." Subsided was putting it mildly. Rodney had gone into a coma from the massive dose of insulin. He had lost all control several hours earlier when the doctor had come to see him about his outburst the night before. Like a frayed rope under too much strain, he snapped. "Tonic-clonic seizures continued for several minutes post therapy. He's being observed for any aftershocks now."

"Fine." Nurse Minton looked at Christine out of the bottoms of her eyes, with her chin up and nose in the air. The older nurse was no taller than the younger, but looked down at her in any way she could find. Tall women were typically placed on men's wards with the expectation that they would be able to better handle the larger male patients.

"Dr. Franklin has a standing order of barbital for him. If he wakes up agitated I will administer it. Dr. Franklin said to keep him in the restraints until he returns." The use of the sleeping drug was a mainstay in the hospital.

"I'll leave you to deal with Gibson and

the morgue; I'll get back to the patients. We still have a full day." The older nurse started walking out of the room.

"Nurse Minton, don't you wish there was more we could do? You've been here for years and I'm new, but I already feel so helpless."

"Adkins said you were idealistic." The older nurse's mouth curled into an unfriendly and mocking smile. "Idealism doesn't work in a place like this. Look around, Freeman. This facility is its own town, with its own community. You know that. Do you think the state is going to listen to you, a woman just barely a nurse? Your very meals depend on the garden the patients maintain and their harvest and canning in the fall. Why do you think it's like that?" She paused for a minuscule moment, appearing not to want an answer from Christine. "Because no one wants to bother with the patients. No one wants to even believe they exist, including the families that drop them off. They want to go on with their nice simple lives behind their picket fences and pretend this beautiful building isn't more prison than hospital. Besides, even if we had more clothing for the patients, what we really need are workers. There's just too many patients and not enough of us."

They'd been over capacity for a long time without any help in sight. The war had taken so many of their staff away while an excessive number of patients poured in — some of them soldiers returning from the war and unable to cope.

Without another word, Nurse Minton walked away but turned back after several steps.

"Adkins says you sing hymns to your patients." One of her eyebrows arched and a crooked smirk shifted across her lips.

"I think it helps their nerves," she said pushing up her glasses though they had not slipped down her nose.

"Sing all you want, as long as you're getting your work finished." The nurse turned and walked away.

"S'cuse me, ma'am," a deep voice said a few moments later.

Christine's eyes caught Gibson's. He was holding one end of a canvas stretcher and a younger man held the other. Gibson was a tall, brawny colored man with a voice that was gravelly yet still somehow kind. His cottony hair and eyebrows reminded Christine of summer clouds. His eyes, on the other hand, haunted her.

Gibson's job was to gather the deceased

and take them across the hospital grounds to the morgue. If warranted, a doctor would perform an autopsy before the patient was prepared for burial. In that brief moment she returned to a hot August day when she had observed an autopsy. Half her class fainted. Christine nearly had herself. The odor, sight, and sounds, mixed with the humidity, made her fantasize about running away from the school.

Now, in the frozen days of winter, Christine wanted to pretend she was somewhere else. She shuffled awkwardly back toward the wall near the windows, her knees locked. She could not watch them take the bodies away, not like this. Without a word, she pushed past them and left the room. She ran to the opposite end of the hall and leaned against the stairwell door.

Chapter 2

Eli Brenneman blew warmth into his hands. They were chapped and calloused. He and several other Civilian Public Service campers had been digging fence posts for what seemed like a month. How this satisfied the government was beyond him. Requiring hard labor from thousands of men, without paying them a dime, had nothing to do with the war effort — but there were worse options for him. Several inches of wet snow had fallen while they worked. The rubber boots he wore sunk into the slush along the ditch. He wiggled his toes, trying to keep them from going numb. He would have to write to his *mem* for another pair of socks.

The sun settled deeper into the sky. It was late afternoon but he wasn't sure what day of the week it was. Days rose and fell, one after another, and were each the same except Sundays. Since they didn't work on Sundays, it was the slowest day of the week.

The dark winter evenings seemed to last an eternity — it made him so stir crazy he couldn't even sit still to read a book. Sundays made him miss the comfort of his Amish settlement in Sunrise, Delaware. He'd been away for several months and missed the steady lifestyle of his community. The world beyond his home was not as wonderful as he'd imagined, especially as a conscientious objector living in a country at war. Going into town wasn't even allowed because of the dangers. Conscientious objectors were not liked.

The relief he'd experienced when his draft appointment had arrived pricked his heart. He had wanted to leave his community — his family, even. But when he arrived at the camp he realized what he really wanted to leave behind was himself. He dug the posthole digger harder and deeper thinking about his disloyalty to those who depended on and loved him. He had taken up with the Civilian Public Service almost joyfully, even making jokes about it. He had gotten himself in too deep back home — with girls, his influence, his lack of responsibility. The one thing he was good at was running the farm. But still, he left without a care.

He yanked his hat off and wiped away the sweat. The dampness around his head made

37

him colder. Eli pulled the hat deep onto his head. The labor camp work was more draining than anything he'd ever done. Being raised on a dairy farm had always been demanding, but the rewards of the labor made it worth the effort. Here he was working merely to pacify the government. It was just work to keep them busy and away from home. Surely there was more meaningful work they could do.

"Brenneman," a loud voice called from a short distance away.

Eli turned to see one of the camp directors waving him into the administrative building.

"You in trouble again?" one of his fellow campers said with a chuckle as Eli ran in.

Eli didn't feel much warmer once inside the administrative building but was glad to be out of the wind. He went into the office and waited for the director to acknowledge him before he sat down. Stewart Blunt was a nice man, older with deep lines in his brow. He was thorough and friendly, but there was always a measure of sadness around his eyes. Eli watched as Stewart looked over a document with a grimaced face, mumbling as he read the words. It sounded like a buzzing bee. Eli had to keep himself from laughing. Mr. Blunt cleared his throat as he stacked the documents against the desk and then looked up at Eli with a smile.

"Eli, please, have a seat." He gestured to the seat in front of the organized aluminum desk.

Eli sat and his mind spun. Why was he called into the office this time? He'd been in there often. It was a running joke among the other campers that he was always in trouble, but he never was. In reality he hadn't done anything to get himself into trouble, but the idea usually followed him regardless. He'd once been asked to keep morale up when there had been some unrest regarding the campers in the nearby communities. Another time the director asked Eli to manage the crew building a new chicken house. Yet another time to head up the building of a new fence.

"We have an opportunity and I think you're perfect for it." He paused. "There's a unit being detached to Poughkeepsie, New York. Thirty men. You'd be thirty-one." He paused and looked back at the document. His mouth moved while he mumbled what he read. The buzzing returned.

"What's in Poughkeepsie?"

"Hudson River State Hospital. It's for the mentally unstable, the insane, the feeble-minded. They are over capacity and under-manned."

"I don't know. I'm not sure I'd be any good working in a hospital."

"Well, these jobs usually are a mite more specialized. Many of the men in the unit have some college education or experience working in hospitals before. But I think you'll catch on. So you're being transferred."

"How would I even fit into this group? I only have an eighth-grade education."

"You'll receive training and attend classes once you arrive at the hospital. And, let me assure you, this unit will be there to enrich the lives of the patients and offer custodial care. You'll bathe them and help them eat — keep them corralled, so to speak. I don't think you need anything more than human kindness to do this kind of work." The man grinned a little. "We have detached units all over the country working in hospitals like this and reports are saying that not only are the hospitals appreciative of the service, but the campers are feeling useful. They say that the job is very rewarding. This is an all-Mennonite unit, so you'll be fine in that regard. You have proven yourself here and you are a very strong young man."

"Strong?"

"Yes, apparently they are really looking for people who are tall and strong to help with the unruly patients. When I read that, I instantly thought of you." As if handing Eli a compliment, his smile grew wider.

Eli's shoulders sagged. They only needed his brute strength? Was that all he was good for? The fact that he'd been asked to head up some of the building projects came to mind. He inhaled, and for the first time in his life he found his mind and heart longing and praying for God's peace.

"When do I leave?" he sighed.

"April." The director stood and put a hand out to Eli.

Eli shook the director's hand and after signing a form turned to leave.

"Oh, Eli, here's a letter for you. It was missed earlier." The older man's furrow lifted momentarily as he smiled and handed Eli the envelope. "Looks like pretty handwriting — sugar report?"

Eli nearly rolled his eyes at the mention of *sugar report*. Simply any letter from a girl did not make it a sugar report, which, in the CPS, were letters from wives and girlfriends. Matilda did not fit into these descriptions.

"Not quite," he answered back as he grabbed the letter and stuffed it into his

41

back pocket. "Matilda's just a friend."

After his duties and their evening meal, he retreated to the barracks. There were several conscies setting up a Monopoly board and a few others writing letters or reading. He went to the sink in the corner of the room and washed his face and hair. The cool wind that coursed through the broken window nearby chilled him. His wet hair was icy.

"Hey, Eli, you coming?" One of the men he worked with held up some Monopoly money.

He shook his head. "Not tonight."

The group moved on with the game without him.

He reached his bottom bunk and pulled out Matilda's letter. She'd been true to her word and written him faithfully. He'd also been true to his word and barely wrote her back; in both letters he'd written in the two months he'd been away he closed it with *Your Friend* hoping it would remind her that there was nothing special between them. Her letters always covered all the district's news. One letter even described his brother Mark and Sylvia's wedding down to the sliced almonds that decorated their cake. It wasn't a month after he left for the CPS that they were quickly married. He'd always known that Sylvia wasn't the girl for him, but dating her made Mark angry. Why had he done that? Of course Mark hated him.

February 4, 1945

Dear Eli,

Hello in the Name of our Lord! How is the camp treating you? I wish you could visit home. I saw your mom at church and she said they all miss you. Norman Hershberger came home this week from your camp. His mother already looks healthier now that he's home. Norman said you are well-liked there. I am not surprised. He also said that letters from girls are called sugar reports. How sweet. I think I quite like that.

Your brother and Sylvia look real happy and their little house is so nice. They make such a nice pair, don't you think?

Eli stopped reading and stuffed the letter back in the envelope. He did not want to read about Sylvia and Mark. He'd gotten his fill of hearing about his brother after his mother first wrote him about their wedding. A wedding after the fall wedding season came as a shock. When it was clear the families rushed the wedding because of an expectant child, the awkward timing became understood.

CHAPTER 3

The winter passed in slow motion. By the time April arrived, the nurses became restless and the patients were antsy. Keeping them cooped up in the ward for so many months made everyone feel sufficiently crazy. At least once the warmer weather came the attendants would be able to take the patients out walking.

"My favorite dresses to dance in are my spring dresses, not my boring winter ones," Millicent Smythe said on a slow Sunday afternoon as several of the nurses spent time together in the day room at the top floor of the Kirkbride. She perked up. "Let's go dancing on Saturday night."

Everyone quickly agreed, even Jeanne. She was a nurse in the Children's Ward and Christine's best friend from high school. She'd been widowed several years earlier. Her husband, Paul, had died only days after landing in Europe. They'd only been married for a few months when he left for overseas. The stress of his death had forced Jeanne to also lose the baby she had been carrying. She usually avoided all festivities.

By that Saturday six of the nurses squeezed into Millicent's powder-blue Mercury Eight — borrowed from her older brother — and giggled the whole way to the dance hall. They shed their winter blues as quickly as they could drive out of the hospital lot. The hall was as busy as ever. Christine didn't often go dancing, not wanting to spend any extra money. But with the stresses of her job weighing her down, she decided she needed the fun. If it meant she would have to wait a smidgen longer for her new nursing shoes — so be it.

The dance hall reminded Christine of the high school dances her mother had forced her to attend in the school gymnasium. She suddenly had the urge to shrink away into a corner as she had years ago, but when her group found a table near the wooden dance floor and bar, it was clear that retreating wouldn't be possible. They pulled chairs over for everyone and took in the excitement of their surroundings. The ceiling rafters were lined with streamers, the band's loud music and the chatter of the crowd around her set a happy scene in motion.

"Look at all the men," Millicent said, elbowing Christine. Millicent put special emphasis on the word *men* and with it brought giggles and agreement from the other nurses. Away from the hospital, the serious nurse became a gregarious young woman. Her curly hair, usually tamed beneath her nurse's cap, was styled to perfection tonight with pin curls framing her heart-shaped face. She took a pull from the cold drink in front of her and slammed it down against the wooden table.

"Take a look at that fella," Gussie, another nurse, said, tilting her head over. "The one with the cocky grin."

Christine blinked to see who Gussie was talking about.

"He reminds me of Errol Flynn in *Robin Hood.*" Nearly every statement Gussie made was in reference to some picture show or Hollywood star. Her own fire-red hair had the waves of a starlet. She wore an emerald-green dress with a low-cut neckline and a full skirt that would twirl better than anything else on the dance floor. Her strong New York accent made Christine smile. Her own eastern accent, barely noticeable, was nothing like Gussie's, who had grown up very close to New York City. "Ain't he a looker. Not so handsome as Clark Gable, but he is something else."

Everyone but Jeanne agreed whole-heartedly. From Christine's vantage point, the tall man had a strong, chiseled face and broad shoulders. His greased hair gleamed under the lights. A few moments later, the man came into full view, displaying the loss of an arm. All of the ladies' eyes diverted quickly.

"Hey, Bette Davis — er, I mean, Jeanne — you a nun or something?" Gussie asked, breaking the uncomfortable silence that hovered over the women.

"A nun? No, it's just that —" Jeanne began.

"Jeanne's just a bit of a wallflower, is all. But she was a cheerleader in high school, and homecoming queen," Christine interrupted.

Christine didn't want her friend to talk about being a widow when they were out to have fun. It was the same reason she rarely spoke of her dead brothers. Everyone knew someone who had died. No family was exempt. At this point, however, no one wanted to talk about it at every turn since the signs of the war were everywhere regardless — the one-armed man, men still in uniform, and empty chairs around the dinner table.

"What about you, Christine, you're tall and curvy — you really don't got a fella?" Millicent piped up again. Every sip of drink brought out more of her eastern accent.

She shook her head. The conversation moved on without her before she could think of anything to contribute. Her thoughts lingered on being called *curvy.* Christine wondered if she really meant *fat?* No one had ever called her fat, though she'd never been willowy thin like Jeanne. Her hands smoothed down the length of her flat abdomen, then she straightened her glasses, and exhaled. And if curvy was really a positive, it had never worked for her. She was known as the smart girl in high school and she hadn't dated much. She'd stood in Jeanne's shadow as she floated around with her boyfriend Paul, the football player.

"Hey, Christine, anyone ever tell you that you look kinda like Vivien Leigh with lighter hair?" Gussie broke into her thoughts.

Christine rolled her eyes. "Gussie, please," she laughed, then threw back her head and put the back of her hand against her forehead. "Kiss me, Rhett."

The group of ladies laughed and collectively said, "Frankly, my dear, I don't —"

"Remember, we are ladies." Jeanne piped up. "Nice girls do not cuss."

"Oh, fiddle-dee-dee." Christine elbowed her friend.

They all laughed.

"Enough talk." Gussie stood from the table. "Let's dance. Who's with me?"

They all danced through several songs. Christine found that the one-armed man had a lot of rhythm and he took turns dancing with nearly all of them. They all had to remind Gussie not to twirl too fast otherwise her garter and panties were on display, but other than that, they all had a smashing time. After several laughable efforts at an East Coast Swing and the Jitterbug, Christine needed a break. She and Jeanne each ordered another Coca-Cola and sat down. Their friends continued spinning on the dance floor.

"Don't look now, but I think I just saw Jack Delano." Jeanne elbowed Christine and pointed with her pinky as she sipped her soda.

She peeked over carefully, then looked back at Jeanne. It was him. She'd know that face anywhere.

"Is it true that Sandy Jordan split with him?" she asked Jeanne. Christine couldn't imagine why.

"Yes, she wrote him saying that she wouldn't wait for him when he wasn't even halfway over the Atlantic. She started dating Tim Crandal who returned injured from the war shortly after."

She just couldn't imagine why anyone would leave Jack Delano. They'd gone to high school together. He was handsome, smart, a football and basketball star, and everyone seemed to want to be his friend. After all, their high school had voted Jack most popular. His father died when he was a boy, but she did not know many other personal things about him. He and his mother came to church some Sundays. She also heard they occasionally visited Jack's well-to-do grandfather in New York City on the weekends.

Christine tempted another glance. Jack's black hair was slicked to perfection. His Italian roots made his skin tan enough to make him stand out in a crowd. She bit her bottom lip at his handsome, chiseled face when suddenly Jack looked over. Their eyes met for a moment before she turned away. How long had she been staring?

"I think he saw me looking," Christine said to Jeanne. "Please tell me he's not coming over here."

When she saw her friend smile and wave over her shoulder, she immediately grew warm.

"Jeanne?" Jack's voice, deep and sharp, came from behind her.

Christine squeezed her eyes shut for a few moments and did not turn around.

"Jack, you're back!" Jeanne stood and hugged him. Jeanne's husband, Paul, and Jack had been good friends. "And how dapper you look in your uniform. Who would've thought you were over there for so many years. You don't look a day older than when you left."

A distinct pause filled their conversation.

"I was sorry to hear about Paul." Jack's soft voice could barely be heard over the ruckus around them.

Christine sensed Jeanne nodding her head — she usually did when people brought him up.

"Who's your friend?" Jack's voice resonated against her back.

Christine wondered how her hairstyle looked from behind. Her caramel-colored hair was in the usual victory rolls on top, but she'd left her length to cascade in waves past her shoulders. Usually the back of her hair was in a snood or rolled up when she was working. Why worry over it? It wasn't as if he was looking at her.

"You remember Christine Freeman?" Jeanne grabbed Christine's shoulders and pulled her up. "Christine, say hello to Jack."

After that awkward introduction, Christine couldn't do much more than nod. She may have waved a few fingers in his direction also. His dark eyes met hers and her knees wobbled.

"Sure I do." He smiled and nodded.

"You do?" Christine hadn't meant to say that. She pushed her glasses up and began pulling at the skirt of her dress then moved to the neckline of her dress — or rather, Millicent's dress. She had insisted it was perfect for Christine's shape. It was much lower cut in the front than what she usually wore. Why couldn't she just have worn something more sensible? She imagined her cleavage getting more obvious by the moment.

"You're Pete's kid sister, right?" Jack took a long drink from his cup, and then smiled at her. "I guess not so much of a kid anymore." He winked at Jeanne and chuckled.

Pete was her brother, the oldest of the four of them, and had died a few years earlier. All through school she had always been known as Pete or Nathaniel's sister. They were special and popular. She had not proven the same.

"Pete's dead," she blurted out. "I mean, yes, I'm Pete's sister."

Jack nodded. "I hadn't heard. I'm sorry."

Christine nodded back, feeling a lot like Jeanne, only less sympathetic in her awkwardness.

"Wanna dance?" He looked at Jeanne.

"Oh no." She waved her hands. "I'm beat. But you and Christine should dance."

His eyes went slowly back to Christine, who held her breath. What had Jeanne just said? He put his glass down on their table and lifted his eyebrows at her.

"How 'bout it?" His hand extended toward her.

Jeanne nudged her.

"Okay," was all she could say and she took his hand. The warmth of his hand made her entire spine tingle. She was holding Jack Delano's hand and he was about to dance with her. She had been in the Math Club and had worked at the YMCA locker room since age fourteen, when all her popular classmates were playing sports and spending time together. She'd never held a pompom or gone to a homecoming dance with a boy. She and Jack had nothing in common, but here they were hand in hand.

As soon as they stepped foot on the dance floor the big band music shifted from a lively tune to something slow and soft.

"Fellas, why don't you hold those pretty

dolls a tad closer for this next number." A man's warm, soft voice came through the stage's microphone.

Jack pulled her closer than she expected and she could smell the slight scent of alcohol on his breath. It heightened her sense of his nearness and she let her rigidity go. Christine's body grew warm. She'd never had a man press his hand against the small of her back and draw her in. All the boys she'd grown up with had been off to war for so many years, and the ones who hadn't gone to fight usually weren't worth dancing with.

"So are you a nurse like Jeanne?"

She nodded, not able to find her voice.

He nodded back.

"Do you like it?"

She imagined herself only nodding and not saying a word. That question was not easy to answer. Before she knew what to say, her mouth opened and she spoke.

"I had been interested in nursing for a while when the war started," she began. "I knew nurses would be needed."

"But you stayed here. You didn't go over there or work at a military hospital?"

"My ma didn't want me to go far away, like my brothers," she said and shook her head. "I needed to be here to help support the family. Hudson River was short-staffed because of the war and my ma had me enrolled in their nursing program before I even had a chance to say no."

"Sounds like my mother," Jack said.

"Really?"

Jack narrowed his eyes. "She always tries to make plans for me. Her and my grandfather, that is." He smiled down at her for a moment. "How's your father? I remember Pete telling me about your father. A hero of the First World War. Has a bad leg because of an injury, right?"

Christine nodded. He was shot in the leg during the war and had walked with a significant limp up until a few years ago.

"Just as my brothers left for the war, right after Pearl Harbor, he lost his ability to walk. His knee never really recovered fully from his injury, but now, nearly twenty years later, he . . ." She wasn't sure how to finish. He's an invalid? He's unemployed? He won't even try to find a job? "No one wants to hire someone who can't walk."

"Surely a seated job for a war hero can be found."

"Not when your only credentials are door-to-door sales before the war. Afterward he worked in a factory, but he had to stand for hours . . . besides, all sorts of younger

soldiers returning are looking for work, too."
She winced at the edge in her voice. This
topic made her uncomfortable — all of it
leading to how poor they had become. She
didn't know him well enough to know if he
was judging her or not.

They danced in silence for a short time. It
was an easy silence, but Christine was eager
to get to know him better.

"What are your plans now that you're
home?"

"Well, Columbia next semester, and living
with my grandfather in the city. I'll have to
take a few extra summer courses, but then
I'll graduate." He looked so handsome when
he smiled. "You know, Christine, I always
wondered about Pete's quiet little sister.
Neither of your brothers were very quiet."

He was right about that.

His head tilted as he looked at her and he
smiled as he spoke. "I always knew you were
smart, but now I can see you're also pretty."

Her face grew warm and her entire body
matched the heat. Had he really just called
her pretty? The words from "I Don't Want
to Set the World on Fire" filled her ears and
their bodies swayed until it was through.
Jack Delano had just set a fire in her, like
the song said. A new fire that she'd never
experienced before.

The next day Christine went to church with her family. Though her family's home was only a few bus stops away from the hospital, the transformation from the grim and prisonlike hospital to small, cottagelike homes and steeple churches always brought her a sense of peace.

Their church, Pine Hill Community Church, was just down the street, and they'd been going there for as long as she could remember. Nothing had changed much in all her years there. The church still had the bell that rang at sunrise and sunset on Sunday. They still had the annual Sunday School picnic where they'd bake pies and sweet breads to sell for the hungry kids in Africa. Preacher Mabry still turned red about halfway through his sermon. And everyone still called Mrs. Nellis *Mrs. Cupcake* because the scent of cupcakes always wafted around her.

A few hours later, she sat at her family's kitchen table, just as she had in her youth. Her father, Harold, had always been quiet, especially now that his two boys were gone. Doris, her sister, wasn't much different — often being scolded for bringing novels to the table. An awkward yet smart girl, Doris didn't care about popularity in school. She worked at the local bank as a secretary.

While Christine had also not been popular she was outgoing enough to make friends. She had been the captain of the Math Club, and when the science teacher had gotten ill in the middle of class, she'd taught the rest of the lesson. She tutored other students, which was how she and Jeanne had become friends.

Christine's mother, Margie, was a busybody and pretended better than anyone that their family wasn't in a near-poverty state and completely dependent on Christine's and Doris's incomes. Margie had only been speechless once in Christine's memory. The haunting quiet had consumed the house in the weeks after the telegram came telling them that Peter had been killed in action. Only weeks later another telegram came saying that Nathaniel had died also. Margie was never really the same after that, though she hid it well, most of the time.

"Do you want my help?" Christine asked this every Sunday when she went home after attending church with her family. Her mother always said no, especially on days she'd prepared chicken.

No one would ever forget how Margie had

gone into a near-catatonic state after the deaths of Peter and Nathaniel. She could do nothing, which left Christine to cook for the family for the first time in her life while balancing the added responsibility with nursing school. A full week into her new duty, she'd burned everything except the chicken. It was undercooked. This forced her mother back into reality. Putting the chicken back into the oven was Margie's first sign of life.

"It's chicken, honey," her mother said with a sigh hugging her words. She cleared her throat then put a smile on her lips that reminded Christine of a mannequin in the window from the dress shop downtown. Fake.

"Any job interviews this week, Dad?"

Sometimes asking poured salt in the wound of unemployment, but her concern was genuine. Her dad inhaled and the muscles in his neck grew tight.

"Doris got me an interview at the bank, but it didn't work out." His voice was devoid of emotion and his face remained placid. "They said there might be duties I cannot do because of this." He gestured to his wheelchair. "When I asked them what those duties were, since the job was for a teller, they just said it required standing for long hours."

He shrugged.

"I think I'll join Doris in the living room and read the paper until dinner's ready," he said, without looking at either her or his wife.

Christine grimaced as he wheeled himself against the table leg, then the corner of the cabinet, before he was able to get out of the kitchen. After using his cane for church, his body was too exhausted to do anything but sit in his wheelchair.

"Maybe you should move the cabinet into another room, so dad could get in and out of the kitchen better."

Her mother cleared her throat before she answered. "Your father won't let me. He said I've already sacrificed enough."

Christine didn't respond but let her mother's words rest between them for several moments.

"Didn't Jack Delano look handsome at church today?" Her mother looked knowingly over her shoulder at Christine.

Christine nodded and silently prayed that her face wasn't turning red. It had only been the night before that they'd danced, not just one but three dances. But today at church when they locked eyes across the sanctuary, he nodded at her like he had at everyone else. She replayed the previous night in her head through the pastor's sermon. Had she read too much into their time together? Maybe dancing for three songs in a row with the same girl was normal for him. Maybe it wasn't as special as she thought.

"He looked so handsome sitting there next to his mother." Margie blinked awkwardly and rapidly as she spoke. Then as she continued it was almost as if she spoke to no one but herself. "He's a good boy and so much like Peter, except Jack has never been half the size of my Peter and Nathaniel. How can it be that a tall and narrow boy like Jack could've made it through a whole war when my big, strong boys . . ." her voice faded away and she shook her head and turned back around toward the sink.

There were several minutes of heavy silence in the kitchen and the mood remained low for the rest of lunch. Christine was heading out the door when her mother lingered there while saying good-bye.

"This is for you and Dad." Christine waited until the last moment to hand an envelope of cash to her mother. Giving her family most of her paycheck had become a regular routine, but she still didn't like to do it in front of her dad or Doris.

Her mother took it and tucked it into the pocket of her apron — the same one she'd had since Christine's childhood. It was white with bright red and pink flowers and had wide straps over her shoulders that crisscrossed in the back. Margie took such good care; it didn't look half its age.

"I'll see you next Sunday," Christine said and started turning away.

"Wait, honey." Her mother bit her lower lip. What was she up to? "I know you keep telling me not to, but I couldn't help myself."

"Mother, what did you do?" Christine squared her shoulders and imagined the worst. Surely this wasn't about that greasy car salesman Roy Brown. Their mothers were on the Sunday School committee together and had been trying to pair them up for ages.

"Don't worry, it's not Roy. He has a steady girl now." Margie waved a hand at her. "But, it is about another young man."

"Mother." She groaned. "Why don't you work on Doris instead of me?"

"Oh, Christine, you know better than that. Doris doesn't have your spirit. Besides, I just really want you to be happy." She sighed. "You've done a lot for us — don't think we don't appreciate it. I know Hudson

River isn't the future you wanted for your-self. Every girl dreams about marriage and a family."

She'd heard all of this before as her mom went on for another minute about her own dreams of getting married and becoming a mother since she was five. Christine dropped her gaze onto the wooden slats she stood on — she, too, had once dreamed of marriage and family. Behind her were the stairs that led up to the small platform in front of the door. How long would it be before her father could no longer take stairs at all? She pushed her glasses up.

"Christine? Are you listening?"

"What?"

"Don't you want your own family some-day?" Her mother untied her apron and roughly hung it over her shoulder. "You should be thankful that I have an eye out for you."

"Mother, please. I've already told you *no blind dates.*"

"This wouldn't exactly be a blind date. You already know Jack Delano."

"Jack Delano?"

What was her mother talking about? Who told her about last night?

"Mother, did you say something to him?" Is that why Jack had danced with her the night before? Was it just an obligation? She hadn't told her mother about going out dancing with her friends, had she? How could she have even known?

"Don't worry, honey, I haven't said anything to anyone." Margie leaned against the doorframe and crossed her arms. "Elsie Delano and I were both at the Missionary Brunch a few days ago and she and I sat at the same table. I overheard her telling Carol Strand that Jack is definitely ready to find a nice girl and settle down. He does have to finish college first, his grandfather's orders, but I think you two could be a fine match."

All the way to the bus stop and then during the drive out to the hospital, she thought about Jack and her mother's comment. What if she was right?

CHAPTER 4

Relief washed over Eli as he stepped into his private room on the hospital grounds. He had no idea before arriving that he would get his own room. At least that was one consolation after not having a choice whether or not to come. He knew how to build, dig, and pal around with other men. He did not know how to work with sick people. He wasn't sure he could do this job.

The room was small, but it didn't matter. The bed was just in front of him, and a small sink with a shaving mirror was on the wall behind the door. His mother had sent him a yarn knotted comforter, and before he unpacked anything he put it over the army blanket that was tucked around the small cot. He'd never thought that the look and feel of a brightly colored blanket would ever comfort him as much as it did in that moment.

There was a contentment that surrounded

him as he stood in the middle of his new room. A sense of peace washed over him as he unpacked his few belongings and settled in. When he pulled out his Bible he paused. It was new to him, but it was used and worn around the edges. Some passages were underlined, and he'd written his name below the first owner of the sacred book. Since his family only had one Bible, he was not able to bring one with him to the CPS. A visiting Mennonite preacher had given the donated Bible to Eli soon after he arrived in Hagerstown.

The man had preached a sermon on accepting God's gifts of grace and forgiveness for past sins. The preacher spoke about Jesus with such familiarity that at the start made Eli uncomfortable. But week after week he wanted to learn more about living with such fervor that was alternative to the stoic nature he was accustomed to. Living that kind of life, however, made him nervous.

The next morning arrived early. Even though his first shift at the hospital wasn't until eight, the C.O.'s had breakfast together, followed by prayer and a meeting where they learned their ward assignments. He was placed in the all-male Ward 71, along with three other C.O.'s he'd met the night before: DeWayne, James, and Freddy.

"Think we'll be working with any lookers?" Freddy asked as they went up the stairwell steps.

"Freddy doesn't think about too much other than playing cards and girls," DeWayne told Eli.

"Don't you get me in trouble, Freddy." James pointed at him. "My girlfriend is volunteering here. She'll whip me if she thinks I'm getting fresh with the nurses, or playing cards for that matter."

"So, does your girl Lisa have any friends?" Freddy looked hopeful.

Freddy and James walked ahead, talking loudly about a few of the other girls who volunteered their time with the CPS unit.

"Hosh en frau?" DeWayne asked Eli if he had a wife.

"Nay." He shook his head *no* but smiled at hearing his dialect. Most of the Mennonites he'd come in contact with either didn't like to speak Pennsylvania Dutch or didn't know it. It comforted him to hear his tongue.

"Girlfriend?" Freddy asked.

"No, not anymore."

"Well, there go my chances," Freddy yelled back at them, his shoulders slumped.

"What do you mean?" Eli asked as he pulled the collar of the white attendant shirt

68

he'd been issued. He would have to get used to being so buttoned up.

"None of the nurses are going to be interested in scrawny me if you're around. You're four times my size." Freddy was a mite puny.

Eli learned that everyone else in his new unit had experience in a mental hospital setting, including Freddy. He'd gained a reputation that despite his short stature he was still able to get the patients to do what he needed — as long as he wasn't in an aggressive ward.

The four men laughed as they made their way through the door that led to their ward. The laughter died quickly when they saw the stern face of a man standing there waiting for them. This must be the attendant that would be training them. The four men stood in silence in front of him for several long moments before DeWayne broke the ice and introduced himself, leading the others to do the same.

"My name is Todd Adkins, and I'll be showing you around the ward." He had a full head of gray hair and Eli guessed he was nearly sixty. The attendant spoke with an accent Eli hadn't heard before. He held a clipboard out in front of him and ticked a pen against the side of it. "Have any of you worked in a hospital before?"

The other three all answered yes. Adkins gave Eli a look and pursed his lips. Eli's body grew warm despite the drafty gray hallway — he was nervous. Groans from the open doors of the rooms around him were getting louder. A distant bawling met his ears and he winced.

"If you think this is bad, you'll never make it here," he said, still glaring at Eli. "Which one are you again?"

"Eli Brenneman."

The attendant marked something on the clipboard.

"At least you're brawny. As long as you can follow directions, you'll work out okay."

Was his size all he would ever be good for? Eli sated his annoyance by remembering what the director of the hospital detachment had said just that morning in prayer. He said that the weak and foolish responded in anger but a wise man had self-control. He gritted his teeth in his attempt to be a wise man and not a fool.

"For your benefit," Adkins continued, "I will explain to you what your duties are. You will be working forty-eight hours weekly. That equals eight-hour shifts, six days a week. Over two hundred fifty attendant jobs have gone unfilled for several years, so you will need to learn quickly and pull your weight. We need you to learn efficiently since there aren't enough of us to babysit you. You will be responsible for what we call *custodial care.* This means you will keep the patients clean and do your best to keep them from injuring one another and themselves. If they get violent, be ready to restrain them and yell — and I mean *yell* — for a nurse to bring a sedative. If they soil themselves, shower them and have their clothing laundered. If they refuse to eat, throw their food away — they won't starve before they learn their lesson. We only have two nurses on this ward and you will be assisting them in handing out medications and when the patients need hydro or electroshock therapy. Also, we actively use straitjackets, bed restraints, and we have one padded room on this floor. Any questions?"

He raised his eyebrow at Eli.

Adkins walked them around and pointed out some of the patient rooms without taking them inside, telling them that they were mostly empty at the moment and that several contained contagious patients. He showed them where they would be showering the patients in groups. Eli subtly nodded when it appeared necessary but otherwise kept quiet. With each minute passing, each instruction given, his lungs grew overfilled with too much air and the beats of his heart pressed against his chest painfully. Would he ever learn to work with these patients in these conditions?

Eli estimated one of the rooms at having over forty beds. A few patients lay flat on their beds and many of the beds had no sheets. There was an undercurrent of stench that spun around him. He would have to get used to that.

His eyes fell on the patients but none of their eyes met his. The state of the patients disturbed him. Now he better understood his director's advice — offer to do any duty, no matter how abject. He impelled them to do everything with graciousness and with the patient's dignity at the forefront. He reminded them that no matter their mental condition, all of them were created by God and were not less important to Him, no matter what society believed.

"This is the day room where the patients spend most of their time," Adkins said to them. "This is where you will also spend your day when you aren't cleaning the dorm rooms, showering the patients, or helping with treatments." He opened the door and waved them inside.

The odor of the room hit Eli before he

was completely through the doorway. The acrid scent of urine was so overwhelming he began gagging. He pivoted and walked back into the hallway, gasping for air. He didn't know how DeWayne, Freddy, and James could stand the stench as they remained inside. He walked to an open window in the hall to catch his breath.

"Here," a voice came from a few paces away.

He looked up and saw a nurse pushing a white handkerchief into his face.

"It'll help with the smell. Adkins probably doesn't remember how bad it can be the first time." The nurse stood there with a raised eyebrow. Her rapid speech carried a slightly nasal tone.

"Thank you." His eyes met her chocolate-brown ones as he took the handkerchief from her. The kindness in her gaze couldn't be hidden behind her glasses.

"Put it up to your nose when you go in. You'll get used to the smell soon. Your eyes will stop burning so badly, too."

"We're waiting, Brenneman," Adkins walked back through the door, the smell trailed into the hallway with him. He looked at the nurse and smiled. "You playing babysitter, Nurse Freeman?"

"Be nice, Adkins," the nurse said over her

shoulder as she began walking away. "The first time is the worst. I heard you vomited."

The other three men stood behind Adkins, with furrowed, sympathetic brows as they looked at Eli. He recalled their warnings about the stench but hadn't taken it to heart. Now he understood.

Adkins let out a heavy sigh. An honest smile warmed his face by degrees as he looked up at Eli.

"She's right," he said and chuckled. His mannerisms shifted and he smiled at Eli. He sighed then asked kindly, "Are you ready to try again?"

Eli nodded, holding up his handkerchief.

"You'll love the smell of that hanky, lucky fella," Adkins said, waving them to follow him again. "Nurse Freeman wears nice perfumes."

Eli couldn't help but look back again to see if he could catch sight of the beautiful nurse again, but the feel of the handkerchief between his fingers reminded him he had to focus on the task at hand. He turned back around and followed the other three into the room. Adkins was right, he thought, as he breathed in the delicate, rosy scent of the perfume-doused handkerchief. The act of kindness not only calmed his nerves, but the sight of the patients and the state they were in triggered his need to help.

This time he was able to take in the room as he walked through the doorway. The bland, overcast sky tempted more gray into the room. The cold, sticky air chilled him to the bone even though it was already April. The hum of moaning seemed to come from the room itself. A man across the room opened and shut the windows repetitively. Eli diverted his eyes from the patient's nakedness but looked back as an attendant began trying to turn him around to clothe him. The man put his hands over his head and began spinning and yelling.

Was this what the CPS director meant by mingling with the patients and being a friend to them? How was that even possible? The lack of sanitation in the room turned his stomach.

"Our idea of a good patient is one who minds his own business. It would be great if they would just sit still and keep their hands to themselves, wouldn't it?" Adkins's words were insensitive, but by the way he patted certain patients as he passed and even ruffled the hair of a few, Eli could see he was kind to the men he worked with. "We don't have a lot of talking on the ward. As I said before, you just need to make sure you get them to the toilet, get their baths, clean up the floor from all their incontinence, and generally keep them from hurting themselves and others. It might seem like a short list of duties, but once you've started you'll realize that you won't stop working through your entire shift. There is always more to do."

Adkins told them to spend some time walking around and getting to know the different patients. Eli, still holding the hankie to his nose off and on, had to keep his emotions in check. He'd never been a crying man, but there was something so desperately sad about the men in this room.

He saw a man reading a seven-year-old newspaper. Several were moving puzzle pieces, not actually putting any together. One patient typed on a typewriter with no ink or paper. Then there were the dozens and dozens who just stood around. So many of them didn't move a muscle his entire time in the day room.

After winding between the men, he began noticing someone following him. He turned around to find a mongoloid man standing there, smiling at him.

"Hello," Eli said and waved.

The man's eyes nearly vanished into his round, chubby cheeks as he displayed a gummy smile. His chubby hand moved up, and he waved at Eli.

He pointed at himself and spoke. "Fouyd."

Eli looked around to see if anyone could understand what the man said, but he was in a sea of patients — no attendants or nurses near him.

"Fouyd." The man smiled and repeated himself several times.

Was he trying to say his name?

"I'm Eli," he said loudly.

"He's not deaf," the beautiful nurse from before said as she walked up. She lifted an eyebrow, chilling him. She walked toward the office in the corner and unlocked the door using a small key tied inside her apron pocket.

He followed her, partially curious over what the mongol man was trying to say and wanting to thank her for the handkerchief he still held loosely in his hand. He stood in the doorway of the small corner office that appeared to store the medications. The nurse wrote in a book, appearing to log information as she glanced from her watch to the medication bottles, then back to the book, scratching quickly with a dull pencil.

"I didn't mean to —" he started then stopped. "I've been around *special* people like him in my church, but I couldn't understand him." His last few words faded some.

Her head snapped up from the book. Their eyes fixed on the others before she spoke.

"Special?" Her voice was breathy before she cleared her throat and looked away.

"That's what we call them in my community." He shrugged. "I know that's not what they are usually called."

"No, it's not," she said with nonchalance as she pulled out trays of small cups from the cupboard, each holding medication. Without a word she shut the bottom of the Dutch door he stood near. Patients began lining up almost immediately. Eli's heart rate increased, unsure of what he was supposed to do.

"They are special though," Christine said and handed a patient a cup. He threw the pills into the back of his mouth without any water. He opened his mouth for the nurse and she checked his cheeks with a flat stick.

"What's your name?" she asked Eli while handing out the next cup of medication.

"Eli," he said. Then, realizing no one seemed to go by their first name, he corrected himself. "Eli Brenneman."

Her eyes looked back at him and sized him up. She was tall and had a presence about her that intimidated him.

"I'm Nurse Freeman." She nodded toward the mongol man. "His name is Floyd."

"Oh, Floyd, of course," he said.

A man came up to the Dutch door and started pounding his head with the heel of his hand. A distinct, growly moan came from the patient whose agitation grew.

"Wally," Nurse Freeman said sternly. "You're all right."

Wally twitched and ground his teeth together. He looked in Eli's direction but their eyes didn't meet.

Eli inhaled and glanced over at Nurse Freeman.

"He heard who you are — what you are." Her voice was so monotone it was like a slap against his cheek.

"What?"

"We have a patient, Rodney, who likes to stir up trouble. He told Wally that your group was coming."

Eli didn't understand.

"Wally was a soldier — and tortured before being rescued. He went to war and did his duty but returned only a shell of a man." She paused for a moment and looked at him. "You should've seen his parents when they brought him here. Wally lost his mind and they lost their son. But he still knows what kind of man you are and the others in your unit. He knows only cowards duck out of duty and leave the brave to be wounded, if not killed."

Eli swallowed. He had no comment.

The nurse's breathing sped up and her lips, which came together, began to tremble. Her eyes did not waver as they locked on Eli's.

"What have you lost?" Her voice softened but her words dug deeply. She walked through the Dutch door with another tray of medication in her hand, handing them out to the patients who hadn't lined up.

He wanted to look away from her, but the battle that waged inside between retaliating against her and accepting her argument wouldn't let him. His anger was so great he wasn't sure he could work with her. On the other hand, his ache and sadness for Wally made his chest constrict and it hurt to breathe. She was wrong *and* she was right.

"You okay?" DeWayne said, standing next to him.

He inhaled, his nostrils flaring, and with long strides he walked out of the day room. He didn't hear the door slam behind him and turned to find that DeWayne had followed him out. He unbuttoned the top collar of the white, stiff jacket. He leaned his hands against the concrete windowsill in the hall.

"I don't think I can do this," he said. He backed up a few steps, agitated, and ran a hand through his hair. The shortness startled him for a moment. He'd gotten a crew cut only the night before. "I don't think I can work here. It's too . . . They hate us. They hate what we stand for. How can we work with and for these people? And the patients are — it's just too terrible to see every day."

DeWayne didn't say a word, which also made Eli angry.

"How didn't you just completely lose yourself in your last hospital?" Eli asked.

"If you know who you are, you can't ever really lose yourself. You might stray a measure from time to time but you don't lose yourself — unless you just don't know who you are." DeWayne patted his arm then motioned for him to follow. It was time for them to shower their first group of patients.

Nurse Freeman's and DeWayne's words weighed on him for the rest of the day and by the time the thirty-one men sat before the director of their unit after supper, all he could do was listen.

"Ryan Hall is considerably worse than the last ward I worked in." One man stood.

"Here the patients are hit with billy-clubs and barely fed. They have sores all over their bodies and don't have proper medical attention. It's no wonder they continue to be so violent. The attendants laugh like it's a joke."

Another six men stood with fists pounding the air in front of them as they spoke loudly. The room filled quickly with angry voices. Eli noticed instantly that everyone's anger was over the patient care, and not over how they were being judged for their C.O. status. His own frustrations had more to do with *Nurse Freeman's* opinion of him than anything else. He didn't like someone putting him down, even if it was a pretty girl.

"Listen, listen, calm down." The director gestured for them to sit. He patiently waited for each of them to comply before he went on. "I know it's bad — very bad. That's why we're here. You have to remember that both the patients and the staff aren't being treated properly. Yes, the patients are not being taken care of at a level even close to humane in some instances, but the staff has been grossly overworked for a very long time." When the round of voices grew louder again, he put a palm up. "I'm not done. That does not give them an excuse; it just gives us a reason to minister to them as well as the patients."

Many of the men agreed and nodded their heads. The righteous uproar over the situation at the hospital twisted around them like twine and gathered them together with one clear mission.

Well, most of them. Eli was still unsure if he could handle working in these conditions. It seemed a strange sort of hell on earth, if he was being honest. There were several moments with no one talking before the director asked DeWayne to close their meeting in prayer.

The only sound that could be heard was the rustling of everyone kneeling at chairs, the couch, or where they stood near one another. Though this was more commonly an Amish exercise, they had decided early on to do this in order to truly be humbled before the Lord.

As DeWayne began to pray, Eli opened his eyes and stared at his tightly folded hands.

"We've no right to judge them. Even if they judge us," DeWayne said.

Eli's jaw tightened.

"Let us partner with the staff, let us befriend and love our patients. Let us be Your light — a salve of healing — for all the broken here . . . not just the patients. Remind us to decrease so that you may increase."

DeWayne's prayer brought a familiar prick into his heart and he pushed it away. Wasn't it time that people accept the work of the CPS camps? The camps had been serving the country for several years and yet there was still such unrest regarding the C.O.'s. He and the others who served were still Americans, yet they were working without pay, with the exception of the little money from the churches that supported them. That money barely covered their basic needs. As a detached unit, the hospital would pay them another fifteen dollars a month, but how much less was that than the other attendants?

"Move us — use our hands and feet. Let the words from our mouths be like sweet honey to *all whom we serve.* Humble us. Remove our egos and break our hearts to prove that all of Your creation deserves dignity and respect. You love them all. The senile, the simple, the invalid, and even the cruel."

For the next few mornings Eli only followed through with his duties half-heartedly. He was kind and followed instructions to the letter. Nurse Freeman avoided him but was as friendly with DeWayne and James as they were with her. When she told him to hold Rodney down for his insulin injection after an outburst he did so. When she could've asked — told, rather — any of the attendants to mop up the disgusting mess on the floor from a patient who had gotten sick and vomited several times, she asked him. He even thought she had a smile on her face as she did so.

He bit the inside of his cheek when the bucket sloshed over the edges and his pants and shoes were splashed. He wanted to spew a curse but the room wasn't empty and DeWayne might walk in any moment. The C.O. was quite like having a preacher following him around. He wasn't altogether sure he liked him.

He pushed the sopped mop against the filthy floor and considered how he'd rather be mucking out barn stalls.

"Seems like women's work to me." Wally plopped down on the moth-eaten couch nearby.

Eli paused. "Why don't you —" he stopped just in time. He cleared his throat and went on with his mopping with his back to the patient. Wally was right. It was women's work.

"You let that nurse boss you around like a cheap floozy."

It took all of Eli's strength to keep quiet after that remark.

"At least you got a nice, pretty one. That Minton in the other hall's a battleax."

Eli raised an eyebrow and turned to face Wally. "Yeah?"

"You wanna smoke?" Wally handed him a cigarette.

Eli shook his head. He'd tried cigarettes years earlier, soon after he started his *rumschpringa*. He'd pretended to like them for a few weeks before making up a story about his parents finding out so he could quit. He hated smoking.

"Nah."

Wally shrugged his shoulders and stuffed his pack away in the front pocket of the coat he wore over his patient uniform.

Eli worked in silence for several minutes and the floor looked as clean as he thought was possible and he pushed the mop back into the bucket. He sighed.

"Gum?" Wally offered Eli. He blinked rapidly and coughed loudly. Eli started to realize this was one of Wally's usual ticks.

Eli chuckled. "What else do you have in your pocket?"

"Oh, smokes, gum, a few pieces of peppermint candy. My mom sends them in every so often. She sent me this coat. Nurse Eager Beaver always makes sure I get my mail but I'm not supposed to have them at all."

Eli nodded. "Why are you being nice to me? Nurse Freeman told me that —"

He waved a hand at him.

"I was drugged up the day you came. I tricked the good nurse today. My lunacy isn't as bad as they think." Wally's eyebrow raised and reminded Eli of his hard-as-nails brother Mark.

"What?"

"I don't need those pills." He leaned forward on his knees as if trying to hide his twitch with a gesture for Eli to sit. He did, glad for a short break.

"Nurse Freeman said you had a breakdown after you came back from . . ." Eli stuttered when he spoke. He'd never really talked about the war or breakdowns.

He nodded a confirmation. "Still get these sort of — *memories.*" *Twitch.* "Almost seems like I'm still over there. But the drugs make it worse."

"Why are you telling me all of this?" Eli leaned forward and asked in a loud whisper. It almost infuriated him. He didn't want to get personal with the patients, or the staff, for that matter. He just wanted to do his job and leave. "I thought you hated me because I'm a C.O."

"Come on, man, you're like me." His smile was part humorous and part cynical. "Angry all the time. You hate your life as much as I do. You're not like the other C.O. do-gooders."

Eli sloshed around the mop and bucket. He swallowed hard. Wally spoke the truth. He did hate working there and couldn't easily fake a smile.

"Why don't you just go home? You can leave, can't you, if your parents take you? Maybe there's —" He kept his eyes far away from Wally.

He shook his head rapidly. "Can't do that. All my friends are dead. My mom dotes over me like I'm a child. I'm —"

"Afraid?"

Wally's eyes sharpened before they softened but stayed diverted from Eli's.

"Brenneman," Nurse Freeman's voice interrupted the two men. "Don't put that away. There's another mess in the hall."

Wally elbowed Eli. "Go on, little miss maid."

Eli laughed as he got up.

"What's that?" Wally grabbed the magazine from Eli's back pocket. He flipped through it and looked up at him.

"Oh. Pulp fiction. Do you mind?" Wally raised his eyebrows.

"Brenneman," the nurse called out, sharper this time.

"Go ahead." Wally nodded to him.

Their interlude rolled around his thoughts for the rest of the day. Wally had seemed so normal and real. He'd seemed almost like Eli himself. A grown man afraid of his past and unsure of how to move forward.

Hours later, as he lay on the cot in his room, Wally's situation and DeWayne's prayed words from earlier in the week pressed against him. Sleep had run far away from his busy mind. Praying wasn't something he was good at, but he began breathing heated words from his mind to God. He told God how unfair this was, that it was too hard. He didn't deserve to be treated this way. Without warning, he began weeping. Embarrassed by himself, he got up and turned on his light to wash his face with cold water. He caught his image in the small shaving mirror that was attached to the wall and wondered when he'd grown so angry. His face declared it with a furrowed brow and a set jaw. Was this his face now?

DeWayne's prayer poured into his mind with the verse he'd referenced.

He must increase, but I must decrease.

In the silence of his room he pictured Floyd and the soldier Wally. Nurse Freeman's words plagued his memory. Before the hospital, before his draft, for as long as he could remember, he always made sure he won — every last word, every bit of attention, and especially every girl. Pushing his ego ahead of everyone else, proving his masculinity, his popularity, to anyone willing, or unwilling, to hear and watch him. Who was he without this arrogance?

He would have to lose himself here in the filth of the hospital in order to find himself — to become the person God wanted him to be.

Usually he only knelt in prayer out of obedience to the church and his *dat.* But tonight his knees fell onto the concrete floor harder than he expected, and yet it was trivial to wince when there was so much greater pain surrounding him. He rubbed away the furrow on his brow and laid his head in his hands, his back hunched over his bed. The realization dawned that he knew he could do nothing truly good on his own — not with the patients, not with the staff, and not with his life — without Him. Why hadn't he realized this of himself when he was at home?

Lord, help me decrease.

CHAPTER 5

As Christine walked to Edgewood from her apartment in the Kirkbride building, she noticed a commotion at Ryan Hall. Jeanne caught up with her and linked her arm through Christine's.

"Are they really getting fired and arrested?" Jeanne questioned. "I knew Ryan Hall was bad, but I never expected this."

Christine vacillated between frustration with the C.O.'s for having gotten the attendants at Ryan Hall fired to being glad that the four regular attendants were gone — arrested even. The patients didn't deserve to be abused.

"How are the C.O.'s in your ward?" Jeanne asked.

Christine shrugged. "Well, if any of them try this with my crew, they'll have another thing coming."

"But your staff isn't anything like the Ryan Hall staff."

That was true.

"Are they nice?"

"I have to admit, they are nice and fine workers. The patients like them and they've been a huge help, even if they're cowards."

"Hear from Jack?"

Christine raised an eyebrow as she looked over at her best friend.

"When are you going to stop asking, Jeanne? It's been weeks. He hasn't even acknowledged me the few times he's been to church. It was just a few fun dances, that's all." Christine hoped she had convinced her friend. She'd secretly hoped on a daily basis that Jack would seek her out and ask her on a real date, but so far — nothing.

Only ten minutes later Christine was in the corner office in the day room. Brenneman's loud whoop caught her attention as she prepared the medications for the day. He had the patients more engaged in a fake game of checkers than she'd seen them in all of her time there. Wally laughed out loud and it annoyed her that he had chuckled.

His shoulders barely fit into his starched attendant jacket. His white-blond hair and icy blue eyes made him striking. He was handsome, in an unrefined, rustic sort of way — nothing like Jack. Eli had avoided personal conversations with her since that first day when she'd let him have it. He seemed to have gotten over the verbal slapping she'd administered and had been cordial ever since. His easygoing manner had deflated her. His special attention to Wally forced a knot in her stomach as tight as her clasped hands. She cleared her throat and lifted her chin. She would not be remorseful for the truth she'd spoken to him.

Eli even took five or ten minutes to sit next to Wally and read novels about some amazing adventure or tell him about the green farmlands he came from. At first she wanted to tell him there wasn't time for sitting and reading, but it calmed the patients, like reading a child a bedtime story. In the end, it was worth his time. The patients loved the colorful covers and even the less-than-intricate line drawings inside. He'd taken to the job quicker than expected and even Adkins complimented his work.

Brenneman began doing a magic trick — a rather poor one, too. He then pointed in her direction and the patients near him began lining up for their meds.

He stood by the Dutch door to ensure that everyone took their medications by checking their mouths. Without being asked, he'd started taking on this responsibility his first week of work.

"What do you think about what your pals in Ryan Hall did to get the regulars fired? Now we have four fewer workers." Christine hadn't expected to go at him like that, but being around him made her feel defensive.

Eli inhaled and then he cleared his throat. "I'm sorry that it happened. Honestly."

"Which part?"

"All of it," he stated simply, checking a patient's mouth for pills with the tongue depressor. "We don't want to cause problems, just help."

His calm and collected attitude deflated her. She handed a patient the mini cup of medications, and she and Eli watched as he swallowed them down. She watched as Eli used the depressor with slow, careful movements, knowing that the patient had mouth sores from his latest electroshock therapy. He impressed her.

"You're good with the patients."

Eli's head snapped to look at her. A wide smile crossed over his face. Christine turned away from him and looked back at the next patient in line, handing him his medications. She wouldn't give him the satisfaction of recognizing any admiration on her part.

"And you really don't have previous experience?" She sighed as she resigned herself to compliment him, knowing it was the right thing to do, though it hurt her ego to do so.

She handed Wally his meds.

"No, but I come from a large family. I've watched my mom take care of us." He shrugged.

Wally smiled at Eli and opened his mouth wide.

"I'm going to beat you at cards later," Wally said. He twitched some as he spoke but his voice was clear and not slurred.

"You'll never win, buddy," Eli said, patting the patient's back as he walked away.

"What about the magic trick?" She noted in her logbook that Wally was alert and attentive today. This was not his usual way. While she wanted to challenge Brenneman more, she found it difficult to do so when his actions were so helpful and his demeanor so polite.

He turned again and smirked. "You saw that?"

"Yes, it was awful." Christine handed out the next medication. The patient took it and Eli checked his mouth.

"Rodney," Eli said, his voice firm. "Take a drink."

Rodney crossed his arms.

"No," Rodney said. His eyes narrowed.

Eli took a step toward Rodney and his chest puffed. "Take a drink, Rodney. If you don't, you know what will happen."

"I'm not afraid of restraints or of you." Rodney grabbed a small cup of water and drank it. Eli checked again, using the tongue depressor to push away the pockets of his cheek.

Eli didn't seem to be concerned about Rodney's distaste for him. His size alone was imposing and he seemed to take on the same no-nonsense attitude as Adkins — just enough power to remind the patient that they could be dominated.

He nodded his head to move on.

"Better than yesterday," Eli commented under his breath. Christine just barely heard him.

"You sure push your weight around. I thought you didn't believe in fighting." She baited him.

"I'm not fighting," he said simply, but Christine could see his jaw clench and relax back and forth.

"But you were intimidating him. What if he'd refused to take his meds, then what? Would you get physical?"

"I wouldn't hurt him. If I have to hold

him down in order to restrain him, I will, but I will not harm him — or any of the patients. That's what Adkins has instructed us to do."

She held in a huffy sigh.

"So, you said you have a big family." Christine tried to keep the sharpness out of her voice as she moved on to the patients who weren't able to line up. Eli continued to assist.

"Five brothers and two sisters," he said while checking the next mouth.

There was a short pause in conversation.

"Wow, five brothers." She paused. "My two brothers were killed in the war. You know, the one that you're skipping out on." She looked at him and their eyes met. She couldn't let it go. He was a coward. She was getting to him. His mouth was tight and his face was becoming redder with the passing moments.

Eli checked another mouth, gave the patient a look, and handed him a second water cup. The patient drank the water and pills down and Eli checked again. He patted him on the arm but the patient scowled as he pulled his arm away.

"I'm sorry to hear that." His voice was so soft that Christine could barely hear him.

Christine stopped passing the medications

until Eli looked at her.

"Are you sorry?" Her heart pounded faster by degrees as she spoke. "While you and your people refuse to fight I have two brothers dead in Europe out of loyalty and service. I just don't understand." She sated her building passion by biting the inside of her cheek and fiddling with her glasses.

"I'm not surprised you don't understand it, or the rest of the country, for that matter. I don't think I understood until my draft notice came. Listen, I've made bad decisions in my life, fighting and that sort of thing. It's not something I'm proud of, but still, it's not the same thing as killing someone — and forcing him into eternity — when he might not be prepared. My conscience won't allow it."

He shook his head and cleared his throat.

Christine found his explanation honest but didn't agree. Couldn't agree. As a Christian she naturally believed in God and the Devil, and heaven and hell, too, for that matter. But wasn't everyone accountable for themselves? If they headed into war, they should expect they might die and be prepared.

"Since when are you responsible for their hearts? And what about defending freedom and being loyal to our country? Righting wrongs? I mean, what about Pearl Harbor?"

"It's terrible and —"

"But you're not going to do anything about it, are you?" She interrupted.

Eli sighed and pursed his lips.

"I don't believe Jesus himself would ever kill or hurt anyone. The Amish church chooses to follow his example and —"

"So why did his disciples carry swords? Didn't Peter strike a Roman soldier and cut off his ear?"

"Sure, but Jesus then told him not to strike and he miraculously healed the soldier."

"So, he wanted peace — we all do. Isn't there a difference between seeking peace and avoiding even defending our freedoms?"

His eyes glanced over to Wally. "The cost is too high for war. Too many people are wounded. Too many die."

"What about the Old Testament? There were so many wars." She had stopped passing out the medications already and she didn't waiver from his eyes as she spoke.

"And what about the commandment not to murder?" he countered, and he stood straight but his voice remained cool and collected.

Though Christine's mind wasn't changed, she couldn't help but see a small glimpse of his point of view.

"Jesus told us to turn the other cheek and love our enemies, to do good to those who hate you. The Bible gives us plenty of reasons not to agree with war."

"What if your family was going to be harmed? Would you just let it happen? Didn't Jesus also teach to always be prepared to defend your faith — to defend our right for freedom to choose our own faith?"

"What do you think I'm doing here?" His voice was quiet but deliberate and passionate.

Christine winced. He had indeed just, in part, proved his faith through his actions.

CHAPTER 6

July Fourth fireworks had put half the patients into panic attacks, and the rest had clamored to open the windows to catch a glimpse. If that wasn't bad enough a few neighborhood boys had set off some firecrackers next to their building just an hour before Christine's shift, rousing them all into further fits of shock and confusion. It had taken Christine still another hour to get the patients calmed down enough to give them their medications.

She was walking down the hall toward the day room to start handing out medications when she saw Eli cleaning up another mess in the hall. Wally barely gave him enough room to use the mop. He hadn't left his side since she arrived. If it wasn't for Eli she was sure Wally would've needed a sedative. Loud sounds always affected soldiers more than anyone else.

A loud scream came from down the hall

behind her.

"Get out of —" The screechy voice was cut off by the sounds of a slamming door.

"That's Gov. I'll go," Brenneman said to her as he rushed by with Wally at his heels.

"Albert, get out of bed before you soil it," Nurse Minton's voice carried through the now open door. Albert was Gov's real name. Minton didn't cater to his belief that he was the governor of New York.

Curiosity drove Christine to the doorway of the room. Instantly she surveyed the situation in the opposite corner of the five-bed room. Both the nurse and patient were in their forties and both had tall, angular faces and bony elbows. From her vantage point both the patient and the nurse looked crazy. She hated referring to people as crazy, but with Minton yelling and Gov wailing, it was all she could see. Eli stood off to the side with Wally next to him.

"Get up!" Nurse Minton's pale face was turning a bright shade of red.

"I can't. Snakes under my bed," Gov cried. His gray and brown hair always looked as if he'd been electrocuted. His skin was an ashen hue, with entire sections that seemed reptilian and other sections that were scabbed over from his own picking.

"There aren't any snakes under your bed."

103

The nurse rolled her eyes and groaned. She grabbed his arm and pulled him harshly. Gov's other hand gripped onto the metal bed frame, and the bed shifted from the wall, clambering against the concrete floor, but Gov remained firmly on top.

"Nurse Minton, let me." Eli stood next to Minton. Their eyes met.

"You think you can do better?" The woman's eyes narrowed.

"He was left in the woods for two full nights as a child. By the time they found him he was covered in snake bites." His voice was calm and cool.

"He's all yours." Nurse Minton walked off.

Her shoulder purposely hit Christine's on her way out of the doorway.

Christine watched in amazement as Eli handled the situation. His voice sounded gentle and almost songlike, like he was talking to a child. His eyebrows rose with an excited expression on his face.

"Look Gov, I'm getting all the snakes and I'm throwing them out the window," Eli began saying as he smiled.

Eli opened the window and began picking up imaginary snakes and tossing them outside.

"Don't let them bite you." Gov sat up in

bed and watched.

"If they do, I'll just bite them back." Eli bared his teeth, making Gov laugh.

Christine put a hand in front of her smile and a flutter rose in her chest. There was something about Eli; she couldn't understand it, but she was drawn to him.

CHAPTER 7

December 2, 1945

Dear Son,

Blessings in the Name of our Lord Jesus Christ. May you seek to follow His Holy Word and not stray with the worldliness around you.

Our weather has been just fine this fall and winter. We are having a typical December. I'm sure Mem told you how Mark is doing managing the farm. He comes over every morning — sometimes Sylvia and the twins come also. Mem enjoys having company. Your Mem's Aunt Annie will be coming to live here, her husband Simon recently died. Since she doesn't have any children to take care of her we offered. She'll be living in the small cottage on the other side of the field. No one's lived there since Ault Daudy Mark died years ago.

I got your letter a few weeks ago and have been thinking long and hard about what to write. I am glad that you've decided to come to me and apologize for the *vilteh vehya* from your younger years.

You've been away for over a year now. That's a long time to be away from the church and our ways. Now that Norman's home from the CPS he has talked some about the life in the camps. The world is a dangerous place. Resist its temporal whims and remember what you've learned in church. The world will toss you about like a pebble on the beach. You're not an easily tempted boy anymore, you're a man now. Put those old things behind you and remember that you are Amish. The world will not understand you and God's ways.

In His Holy Name,
Dat

Eli sat alone in his room and relished a few moments in the quiet. His *dat*'s letter had given him some things to think about. It was the only letter he'd gotten from his *dat*. His *mem* wrote nearly every week, though never very personal it kept him updated on the family news. Matilda wrote about twice a week with news from their district, the neighboring districts, and of all the Amish in the greater northeastern area.

He looked at the sock he'd been darning before he read the letter. It was December now, and warm socks were a must — but he didn't have the energy to finish it. His fingers were calloused and pinpricked from all the socks he'd darned for himself and the others in the unit. It was slow and cumbersome work, but there were fewer lady volunteers than there were through the summer, so they all had to pull their weight. He'd been gone for over a year now; though he'd followed the list he'd been given and arrived at the camp with everything required, his possessions had slowly dwindled as clothes wore out without being replaced. His towels were ragged. His hygienic needs didn't account for much and all he had for reading was his Bible and a few magazines. He'd just run out of stationery and stamps. He didn't know when he would get more, so he asked his mother to send some. Sometimes Matilda would put an extra stamp in her envelope for him to write her back and his instinct told him the right thing to do was to use it to write her back — though he didn't want to.

"You coming for some crud?" Freddy

opened Eli's door and popped his head in.

It had taken some time to get used to the idea of calling food *crud.* He would never refer to his mother's cooking that way and could imagine the stern look from his father if he ever did. The mere thought of them made him wonder what it would be like when he returned home.

"Let me finish this sock." Eli concentrated on the last few stitches in the toe of a too-thin sock. After a quick inspection, he tossed it in his pile and stood. "I won't miss this at all."

"You'll be darning your own socks forever — well, unless you find a wife good enough for you," Freddy reminded.

"Bish du mai mem?" Eli asked Freddy if he was his mother and gave him a spirited shove as they walked out of his room. "Besides, you're only a year younger than me, and you're not married either."

"I think Marlene Miller likes me." He winked at Eli.

Marlene was here with her brother while he served. She helped in the laundry room and did some odds and ends for the C.O.'s. She was a nice girl and Eli hoped that Freddy was right.

"So, what did Matilda say in her sugar report?" Freddy asked.

"It was from my *dat.*"

"But Matilda's still writing you, right?" Freddy asked.

Eli nodded and sighed.

"You're a lucky fella. What's the matter with you?"

Eli's gaze narrowed on his friend. "I told her before I left for the camp and in my first letter back that we are only friends. I have a feeling she thinks we are more than that."

"Well, why not? She's cute, right? Good cook?" Freddy rubbed his belly, reminding Eli of a character in a comic strip.

"Sure, she's cute, but I'm just not interested in her that way." Eli remembered how Matilda looked up at him that last Singing. He should've noticed the stars in her eyes and never agreed to allow her to write him, but that seemed awfully harsh.

"Surely there's another girl?"

"Not for now. If you knew my reputation back home, you'd understand. I have to stay on the straight and narrow."

For several long strides the two men walked on toward the cafeteria in a neighboring building.

"I know you've said you plan to stay with the church but I have to say, buddy, I'm surprised. You don't seem the type to stay."

"What do you mean by that?"

"Aw, come on, you know the type. Dependable. Follows the rules." Freddy elbowed Eli. "A lot more like DeWayne than you. Surprises me that DeWayne doesn't actually leave the Mennonites to go Amish." Freddy chuckled then waved at some of the other C.O.'s and jogged toward the cafeteria. He didn't even realize Eli didn't follow him.

Eli had been kicked in the stomach by a cow before. The blow had caused several broken ribs and a bit of a bruised ego. Freddy's words hit him harder. Freddy had seen his dedication to the hospital, the way he stood up for the patients. Eli had even become one of the men to help lead the singing for their self-made church services. Why did Freddy think he wasn't a solid, committed man?

During the summer he'd retreated back a few acres to the gardens and often helped with it after his shift. He enjoyed working the soil and working with his hands. But the ground was hard and cold in December and his breath in front of his face made his irritation grow.

"What's gotten into you?"

A familiar voice broke into his thoughts and he stopped to look for it.

"Nurse Freeman?" A smile landed easily on his lips but was wiped away when he saw the cigarette between her fingers.

"Brenneman." She nodded. She puffed and blew the smoke away then moved in step with him.

"I didn't know you smoked." He tried to keep his tone light but he fought his instinct to pick on her. They were always half arguing with each other, though it had calmed some in the last few months.

"I don't," she responded as the last pull of smoke blew out as she spoke. She looked at the cigarette between her fingers. She threw it on the ground and twisted a black shoe over it on the cold ground.

He raised his eyebrows.

"What? Why was I smoking if I don't smoke?"

He stifled a chuckle.

"Milli— Nurse Smythe, the night nurse, gave it to me. She said it calms her. I've smoked a few cigarettes in my time but it's not something I do often."

"It doesn't seem like you," he said.

"And what's that supposed to mean?" Christine's eastern accent stretched like taffy from her mouth when she got riled up. Her hands went on her hips as she stopped and waited for an answer.

Eli stopped and turned to look at her. She wasn't wearing her nursing cap. He didn't often see her without it. She was awfully pretty. Her hair moved in the winter breeze. Her eyes squinted against the cold and her face reminded him of the smoothness of fresh milk when it was poured in the large canisters — smooth as silk.

"I'm sorry, that didn't come out the right way."

She started walking and he fell into step with her. They were silent for a long minute and only wind through the dead tree limbs could be heard.

"You're right," she said. "I hate it, actually. Always makes my lungs feel like they are about to start their own fire."

"Why are you out here?" He changed the subject.

"Just needed some air. Everyone else went out dancing tonight."

"You don't like dancing?" Eli had never danced in his life but suddenly wondered what it would be like to dance with her.

Eli gestured to sit at the bench near the dry, cold garden. They both sat. He blew into his hands, trying to warm them. He wished he'd brought his *szitbahkapp* with him. His mother never let him go outside this time of year without a stocking cap —

even at his age.

"Sure, I love dancing. You?"

He shook his head. "I've never danced." He peeked at her through the side of his eyes and chuckled.

"Of course. How dumb of me to ask." Christine put her hand in front of her mouth as if to stifle a laugh. She cleared her throat before beginning again. "So, what do you and the others usually do on a Saturday night?"

He shrugged. Another smile wanted to curl around his mouth but he resisted. He didn't want to give her the impression he was flirting with her. He wanted to though. Flirt, that is.

"It's not much different from any other day since we have to work anyway. I guess we usually make sure we are ready for service on Sunday morning."

"What about at home?"

" 'Bout the same as any other day. Milk the cows, keep the pasture and stalls cleaned up, get the milk ready for the milk truck, get ready for Sunday service. A few times a week we have families come who can't afford to buy milk and we make sure there's enough to give away."

"That's nice of you."

He shrugged. "It's just how things should

be. Some families never bounced back from the Depression."

In his peripheral vision he looked at Christine. Her expression was distant and she only nodded slightly at his comment.

"I usually try to write my letters also," he added.

Christine looked up at the sky and pointed. "Look."

Dark clouds had been hovering all day and were growing blacker. A winter storm was on its way. Suddenly, in the next moment, they were being pelted with hail and sleet.

"Come on." Eli pulled Nurse Freeman toward the greenhouse awning. They both laughed like children the whole way and were out of breath by the time they stopped running. Eli noticed she continued to hold on to the side of his coat as they caught their breath. Her cheeks had turned rosy and her rich brown eyes sparkled, even in the darkness that was passing over them. They were silent for a while before Christine finally spoke.

"I don't know how you do it," she said between breaths.

"What's that?"

"You've taken everything in stride at the hospital. You put me to shame. My nerves are always twisted in a knot."

"What do you worry about?" he said seriously while keeping a friendly smile on his face.

Her hand released from his coat and she looked away, over his shoulder, and as she breathed deeply, her smile faded. She pulled out a bottle of soda from her coat pocket and tried in vain to open it. Eli took it from her, opened it, and handed it back.

"Thanks." She took a long drink before she spoke again. "What if I told you that the only reason I work here is because I need to support my parents. My father's crippled — practically — and my ma would never get a job because it wouldn't look *respectable* in front of all the committees she volunteers at. My brothers are dead, so it's just me and my sister — we're all they have."

There was a bitter tone in her words. He leaned against the outside of the greenhouse.

"I'd say that you're a daughter who loves her family."

She shrugged and handed him the soda bottle. Her lost expression, like a stamp, embedded itself in his memory. He knew he wanted to do everything to bring a smile to her face.

"It doesn't matter why you're here, you're

still a caring and capable nurse," he repeated. He took a drink and enjoyed the fizz. It had been a while with his limited income.

Christine chuckled a bit as he handed the bottle back. "Thanks. I know that must be hard for you to say."

"Why do you say that?" Eli smiled at her.

"Well, I haven't made things exactly easy for you, Brenneman."

"Will you please call me Eli?"

Christine laughed at his request.

"What's so funny?" he said as they continued to cordially share the bottle of soda.

She shook her head. "When you first arrived I never thought I'd like you or any of you C.O.'s and I have to say, I'm glad you're here, Brenneman." She cleared her throat and fiddled with her glasses.

"You've dashed my hopes." Eli pretended being struck in the heart for her using his last name instead of his first.

"Okay, *Eli*," she shoved him playfully. "But only if you'll call me Christine. That would be a nice change around here."

"You've got yourself a deal, *Christine*." He nodded.

"But not when we're on duty." She wagged her finger at him.

"Of course," he said, imagining when else

they are even around each other to use their first names. This conversation was a first.

She offered the last of the soda to him and he shook his head. She finished it as they stood together in silence.

"You know, I thought you stayed at the hospital because I was so ruggedly handsome."

She slapped his arm. Eli feigned injury and they both laughed. Her mood appeared different from when they first met up. His heart tugged at her closeness, though he quickly pushed it away. She could be his friend. He could not allow his feelings to get wrapped up any more than that.

"Are we friends now?" He gave her his best smile.

Christine bit her lower lip.

"Friends," she said.

December 17, 1945

Dear Eli,

The Lord's blessing on you and on this holy season of Christmas. I wish you could come home. I've enclosed an extra stamp as a gift.

Is New York white with snow? Sunrise is and it feels colder than ever even though I know it isn't. Our new schoolteacher, Alberta Glick, is probably getting married to Reuben Esch this spring. Can you believe that? She moved to Sunrise from Lancaster to teach and now the school's going to have to find a new teacher already.

A few people have asked me if I'd be interested. I told them I doubt it. It's not something I could see myself being able to do very long anyway. Don't you think you'll be coming home soon? This spring maybe?

Sylvia and Mark's twins sure are cute. Sylvia and I have become good friends and I have gone over several times to help her out since I live so close to her. It's less than a mile between our houses. She and I are almost like sisters. Can you believe that?

I better go. Sorry to cut this letter short. I know the mailman will be here soon and I want to make sure the letter gets out today so that you have it by Christmas.

Yours truly,
Matilda

Eli received the letter from Matilda just before Christmas. Her simple gift reminded him of the year when his parents couldn't afford more than an orange and homemade pretend shotguns made with dried corncobs and wooden spools for each child. He and his brothers pretended to shoot birds and squirrels for months. It wasn't until years later that Eli realized what a humble Christmas that was. The fruit had been given to them by English neighbors, along with their Christmas dinner. Matilda's family was still in much financial distress and the gift of a stamp touched him.

Eli left his room after he wrote Matilda back, and he found everyone in high spirits. The lady volunteers made spiced cider and apple pie for everyone along with a traditional turkey and potato lunch. Just as he sat among his friends, the harmonicas started. Larry and his sister, Mira, who volunteered, stood tapping their toes as they played one Christmas tune after another. Eli didn't even know the words to all of them but he couldn't remember such a festive Christmas Day in his life. The food and the sounds of the harmonicas made Eli think of home — his family — but the longer he was away the more he knew he would never fit in again at home. He thought of Wally and their friendship, and he thought of Christine.

CHAPTER 8

Christine looked out the bedroom window of her girlhood home onto the snow-covered street. Byron's black Ford truck slid into her driveway. The horn sounded a few moments later and Christine gathered her things. Since she'd worked on Christmas Day, she'd gotten all of New Year's Eve off and she, Jeanne and Byron were headed to a party.

She took a deep breath as she looked in the mirror. The New Year's Eve party was being thrown by some high school friends and Christine was only going because of Jeanne's invite. They were her friends more than Christine's. Jeanne had been a popular cheerleader, after all. She'd only agreed to go after Jeanne begged her.

After repainting her lips red, she patted her hair, making sure it would stay. Ever since Gussie's comment about Vivien Leigh, she'd been trying to style her hair just like she'd seen the star do in the pictures. She moved her side part down the middle and smoothed it out on top, making sure the curls around her neck were shaped perfectly.

Though she could only see from the waist up in her mirror, the image that returned surprised her. Millicent had lent her a dress again — too cheeky for her — but she had nothing else to wear. The neckline was lower than what she usually wore, but she had to admit, she did feel beautiful and shapely in it. It perfectly hugged her curvaceous chest and waist. She blushed in her own presence for thinking such thoughts. Her curves always made her self-conscious. She was glad her nursing uniform, with its apron, hid her figure better than most dresses. At five-foot-nine, her chest wasn't the only thing that made her feel out of place with other women. She left the bathroom pleased with her appearance and grabbed her purse and coat off the davenport.

"Have a good time, Christine. You tell Cody and Darlene I said hello. Are you coming here after or going back to your apartment at the hospital?"

"Hospital. I need to work in the morning." She hugged her mother and waved at Doris and her father, who sat on the couch reading.

Her sister waved at her without looking up from *The Saturday Evening Post.* Her father at least looked up when he waved.

They all wished each other a Happy New Year, and she left the house.

With difficulty, she kept her feet steady against the ice-covered, snowy ground. Once she made it to the truck, Jeanne beamed at her; her smile as warm as the sun. Christine closed the door behind her and settled in next to Jeanne, who was sitting in the middle.

"It's freezing," she said, rubbing her gloved hands together.

"Happy New Year," Jeanne kissed Christine's cold cheek and kept talking. "I am so glad you're coming. I heard that *everyone* is going to be there."

"Most of them probably won't even remember me," Christine balked. Then she leaned over to Byron. "Hi there. Thanks for picking me up on your date."

He smiled and nodded.

"But look at you, Christine. You're not the same girl you used to be in high school."

"Thanks a lot," Christine elbowed Jeanne.

"You know what I mean. You have always been pretty, but with the dress Millicent gave you and your hair so stylish, now everyone will notice how beautiful you are.

And, I heard a little rumor."

Jeanne's eyes twinkled.

Christine looked at Jeanne out of the corner of her eye. "What?"

"I heard Jack Delano is going to be there."

Christine waved a hand at her.

"I've seen him off and on since we danced and he hasn't even once spoken to me."

"Yes, but I heard he was dating a girl at Columbia."

"It doesn't matter. He's not interested in me."

"Who's Jack Delano?" Byron asked.

"Only the most popular guy from school, and he danced nonstop with Christine last April after he came back from the war."

"You like him?" Byron asked Christine, peeking over at her for a brief moment.

Of course she liked him, but she couldn't let on.

Christine shrugged. "I really don't know him that well."

They arrived at the party, which was in a rented building behind a restaurant. Christine had never been invited to such an extravagant party and tried not to look ridiculous as she looked at the fancy sparkling décor and the unbelievable amount of food. Darlene, the hostess, greeted them and told them to help themselves to the drinks and food. Christine could hardly believe it. After the skimpiest Christmas meal they'd ever had this year, this reminded her how little money her family had. Doris made less than Christine, and with her father's medical bills mounting again, they were going backwards. She pushed away the thought quickly and decided to focus on having fun tonight.

Byron pulled Jeanne onto the small dance floor and Christine stood alone. It instantly made her feel like she was in high school all over again — except then Jeanne would've danced with Paul. She leaned against the wall and looked around the room. Christine giggled quietly when she heard Ricky Dilbert still laughing like a goose and Lois Marks and Lisa Craig were in the corner still whispering behind their hands and pointing at people — some things never changed. Suzie Lincoln had actually married Nelson Johnson. Suzie looked uncomfortable sitting at a table with a belly full of baby that couldn't be hidden. Nelson, on the other hand, looked happily dazed with a beer in his grip. Golden-blond hair caught her eye, and before she saw her face she recognized Sandy Jordan. She and Jack had been the couple that everyone thought would marry right out of high school, but she split with him as soon as he left for overseas. She was on the arm of a tall young man with the same chiseled features as Jack, only he had sandy brown hair. He wasn't nearly as handsome as Jack.

Only a few steps over she saw Jack. In an instant heat rushed to her face and the thudding of her heart sounded in her ears, drowning out the party. He gazed in Sandy's direction. Was he still hurt? It had been several years, surely they were both over the ordeal. She sympathized with Jack. How awful for him to receive a letter telling him she didn't want to marry him while he was fighting for freedom and to stay alive. Cody, who was hosting the party, patted Jack on the shoulder.

"What are you looking at?" Jeanne returned out of breath. Byron had been sent to get drinks.

She nodded in Jack and Sandy's direction.

"Oh, I did hear that Sandy was spreading nasty things about Jack."

"Like what?"

Jeanne whispered in her ear. "She said he hit her."

"What?" Christine said too loudly.

"I know, can you believe that?"

"Well, I think she must be mad about something. Maybe she didn't split with him at all. Maybe he split with her and he wasn't here to set it straight. No wonder he's upset."

For the next few hours Jeanne and Byron danced, and Christine mostly picked at the meatballs, and chips with dip. As she sat near the entrance, she watched her surroundings and wondered how it was that some people fit in and some just didn't. She never had.

Jack rushed by her and slammed the door behind him. He was upset, probably over rumors that wouldn't die. Without a thought, she grabbed her coat and purse and walked out after him.

"Jack?" she said as she watched him stomp down the sidewalk. What was she doing? Why did she think she could help him?

Jack turned at her voice. His face was worn with burden and he inhaled deeply. His hair had come loose from his slick pomaded style.

"Are you okay?"

"She's lying." He pointed at the hall where music filtered through and the windows glowed yellow. "That little hussy is lying."

Christine inhaled, recoiling at his words.

Jack exhaled slowly and took a step toward Christine. "I'm sorry. I know I shouldn't use bad language in front of a woman."

She shook her head and stuttered that it was okay. "I just wanted to check on you." She paused, unsure of what to say. "And — I believe you."

Their eyes met briefly but he remained silent.

When he didn't say anything she started turning around, but then his hand took her arm. The warmth from his grasp reminded her of the night on the dance floor and she stopped walking. He didn't let go when she turned. Their breaths, miniature puffy clouds, mingled in the air between them.

"Do you wanna get outa here — with me?" He nodded toward the parking lot. "I can take you anywhere."

"But it's not midnight yet."

He let go of her arm and checked his watch. "We've got about twenty minutes. Let's go greet the new year ourselves?"

Christine couldn't believe her ears. Had she heard him correctly? She bit her lower lip then looked back at the hall.

"But Jeanne — she and Byron brought me," she said.

"Why don't I just tell her that I'll take you home." He smiled. Her heart melted. "I need to get my coat anyway."

"All right." She smiled back, shivering from the inside out. Was this really happening to her? But if he was fond of her, why hadn't he talked to her since April? He had been busy and spent most of his time at Columbia. Right?

In a few minutes Jack returned, wearing his overcoat and hat. His hands were stuffed into pockets that looked full of something. He gave her his arm and she took it as he led her to his shiny Cadillac. She'd never ridden in a car so new before, and when she slid onto the seat she thought it even smelled new. Her glasses fogged up as soon as the door closed and she did her best to wipe them clean before he noticed.

Jack didn't say a word as he started the car and drove around until they got to a hill where they could look out over Pough-keepsie. She'd never been there before but knew many couples would go out there to neck. They were too adult for that kind of behavior, but it was still romantic. There were several other cars there, windows fogged up, and the idea of what was happening in their automobiles embarrassed her.

"It's beautiful," she said, looking out at the city. "All the lights twinkling. And the snow."

Jack smiled at her instead of the view. Her insides melted.

"You sure are pretty. Why haven't I asked you on a date yet?"

Jack winked at her and pulled out a beer bottle from each overcoat pocket. He opened one and handed it to her. She took it. He opened his own and raised it to hers. They tapped them together in a toast.

"We danced last spring," she reminded him, sounding stupid to her ears. She took a swig of the beer and grimaced. She'd never liked beer, only having had it once. Even wine never tasted quite right to her. She didn't have the money to buy anything extra anyway, so she was glad she didn't have a taste for it. But it would be rude not to drink it now, since he'd gotten it for her.

He took a pull from his own beer and nodded. "You're right. I got pretty busy with school after that." He shook his head and wiped his mouth with the back of his hand. "I'm an idiot apparently. Because you're beautiful."

She took a long gulp from the bottle, and the cold drink mixed with the heat that stirred inside of her, disorienting her thoughts. A chuckle escaped her lips at his words and she nervously took another drink.

"Try this," he said, and handed her a silver flask.

Christine opened her mouth to ask what

it was but he answered her first.

"Just a little whiskey I brought from home. Can't celebrate the new year without a little whiskey, right?"

"I don't know, I've never had any."

"Never had any."

Jack scooted over to the middle of the seat and put the flask to her lips and nodded for her to tip her head back. She obeyed, and the drink passed through her lips onto her tongue and burned her throat. Instantly she began coughing and sputtering. The two laughed companionably.

"I guess you're not ready for it. Why don't you stick with the beer."

She thought she saw a look of annoyance in his eyes and didn't want him to think she wasn't as sophisticated as any other woman.

"No, I like it. Can I have another taste?"

He looked over at her and smiled. He threw his head back for a taste and then handed it to her. She took it and looked at the small spout. Her lips would touch where his lips had just been. The mouthful of liquor didn't make her cough this time. She washed down the terrible tang with the slightly less awful beer.

She lowered the bottle and found Jack had slid a measure closer to her. He put his arm around her shoulders and his face close to hers.

"So, you came to the party with Jeanne?"

She nodded.

"She's doing okay? You know, since Paul and all."

Christine nodded again, focusing on trying to find her voice. The beer smell on their breath floated between them and her senses went wild.

"Jeanne's wonderful with the children in her ward. She and Byron are real keen on each other also." She paused. "It's nice to see her happy."

"He's not one of those *campers,* is he?" His face was still incredibly close and his voice husky.

"No, Byron is part of the regular staff." Her voice faded as she spoke. She didn't want to talk about the C.O.'s. Eli's face came to mind. She didn't want to think about Eli right now. She leaned her head back and took a long drink from the bottle, realizing that it was almost gone.

"Cowards." Jack sat up straighter and finished off his beer and took his coat off. "Aren't you hot?"

She nodded.

"Let me help you." He peeled off her coat and when his hand brushed against the back of her neck and hair a flood of heat rushed up her spine. She finished off the rest of her beer, thinking it would combat her physical reaction, but it only heightened it.

Jack looked at his watch.

"Looks like it's midnight," he said, smiling. His face was so close, all she could smell was beer and the slight scent of sweat on them both. The car was already steamed up from talking. He whispered, "Happy New Year, Christine."

CHAPTER 9

When his lips touched hers it wasn't at all what she'd expected. Christine had been kissed before, but only twice. The first time was when she was nine and a neighbor boy had been dared to kiss her. He'd leaned forward and gave her a sloppy kiss. The only other time was when she was on her first date. A high school boy took her to the soda shop in town when they were both seventeen. Dave Munson had kissed her as gently as a summer breeze. Then his dad lost his job and they moved away and they never got to have another date.

This was different. Jack kissed more like the men she read about in the trashy novels she wasn't supposed to read. Not like a nine-year-old or a seventeen-year-old. His mouth was hot, hotter than hers. He rushed at her and his hands pulled her neck closer to him. Christine could feel strength in his touch and passion in the way his mouth moved. She gave in to her desire for him and pushed away any memory of being told what a girl should or shouldn't let a boy do. Jack's hands went from her neck to her back. Still he kissed her. Her eyes opened for a moment and saw that Jack's eyes were tightly shut. She closed hers again and kept kissing him.

Christine was sad when he stopped kissing her but in the next moment his warm, soft lips found her earlobe and then traveled down the side of her neck to her collarbone. His hand was on her shoulder and gently pulled at her dress. He kissed the newly revealed skin.

"Okay, okay," she said, and pulled her dress back up.

He smiled at her. His dreamy eyes finding hers. He was so handsome. His hand caressed her cheekbone and their eyes locked. His fingers traveled down the side of her neck he'd kissed, the warmth still lingering, and down her arm and locked their fingers together.

He was falling for her, wasn't he? She was falling for him. The attraction didn't require much more than his eyes on her. His other hand tugged at the back of her neck, drawing her closer. If she leaned any farther her dress would reveal the soft curve of her bosom. But if she resisted she would spoil the night with Jack . . . *Jack Delano,* she reminded herself.

"Christine," he whispered. "Come here."

The huskiness in his voice was soft like butter melting on toast, steamy like a summer rain against hot pavement. She leaned toward him and his arms wrapped around her. She let him kiss her collarbone and her neck and giggled when he nibbled her earlobe.

Without realizing it, she found that he'd leaned into her and he was on top of her in the long front seat of his car. As much as she liked him she wasn't ready for this. She pulled her mouth from his. Jack's breath was hungry and deep.

"Jack," she said, "I can't do this."

"But, don't you like me?"

"Oh, I do, I promise. But . . ." Her voice faded. "I'm not that kind of girl."

Christine said it and as she did she wished she hadn't. Jack pulled himself back into a seated position in front of the steering wheel and without a word started the car. She was embarrassed with herself as he drove out of the beautiful clearing. After a few minutes, she could see that they were heading toward the hospital.

"I'm sorry, Jack, I didn't mean to ruin the night."

"It doesn't have to end right now. I really like you, Christine." He peeked over from the road. His smile was shier than before, like he couldn't stand to be turned down.

Considering fickle Sandy, she leaned toward him and squeezed his hand. He smiled and kept her hand in his. Her head tilted and a quiet smile formed on her lips. She wondered if they were still as red as before. Christine wanted to spend more time with him.

"I have until one," she said.

He suddenly turned against the gravel and ice onto the road ahead of the long drive up to the Kirkbride building. Her grip tightened around the door handle as they slid and swerved before he righted the automobile again. Finally he pulled over to the side of the road.

"Sorry," he said, looking at her pale-knuckled hand on the door handle. "I didn't mean to drive like that. It's icy."

"It's okay." She let go of the handle and shrugged off her fear.

He looked at her. "I don't want you to feel uncomfortable being alone with me."

"No, no, it's nothing like that," she lied. Of course, she was uncomfortable. A man had never touched, kissed, or desired her like that. But she didn't want him to think she wasn't interested. Her head swam in the too-warm air of the car. She blinked hard to clear her wooziness.

"Can I have some more?" She pointed to his flask.

Jack smiled as he handed it to her.

Christine took several tastes, more than before. It was starting to taste palatable to her. She handed him the flask as she dropped her head into her hands. It was heavy and light all at once.

"Are you okay?"

Christine nodded and would have shrugged her shoulders if only they weren't so heavy. "Light-headed," was all she could say.

She wasn't used to alcohol. Is this how she should feel after only one beer? She'd only had a few swallows of the whiskey. Oh, she did not want this feeling to ruin her night.

"Do you want me to take you back to your apartment?"

"No," she said suddenly. "I want to stay — with you."

Jack smiled at her then took a quick drink from his flask. He scooted toward her and spun her golden hair between his fingers.

"Do you mind if I kiss you again?"

He asked so politely, how could she turn him down? Her chest rose and fell deeply. Was she supposed to answer him? In the small moments that she considered all of this her mouth found his and she let all of the loneliness and anguish fall away. His kisses were unrestricted and her hunger matched his. Her mind emptied of all reservations.

It was only a few minutes, but time seemed to move slower. Her hands moved slower, like she was moving through water. But she liked kissing him. His hands cupped her face. She'd seen this in the pictures before and imagined her and Jack getting married. When he took her glasses off and put them on the dashboard his touch grew more eager, and her entire body grew softer and almost pliable.

Her body grew hot but she was confused when a chill danced against her skin. Christine opened her eyes and realized that not only was she lying back on the front seat but her dress had been pulled from her shoulders. Her arms didn't move quickly. She wanted to right her dress but when she tried her hand was like lead.

"Jack." She pushed him away from her collarbone. The clumsy move didn't work.

"Jack, I can't."

"Christine, just kiss me. Don't worry about it." His hand slowly slid down her leg and up under her dress.

This was going too far. Christine hadn't wanted this to happen. This was not what she expected.

"Jack, stop." She pushed him harder.

"Christine, I've wanted you ever since that night we danced," he whispered in her ear. "Don't you want me to hold you? Don't you want us to be — close."

What exactly did he mean? The weight of Jack's body alerted her senses. Christine pulled her face away and pushed against his chest, forcing him to sit up. She sat up and looked down. Her top three buttons were undone. She pulled at the dress to cover herself.

"What time is it?" Her voice was raspy.

Jack sighed deeply and looked at his watch and told her the time. It was only a quarter after twelve.

"See, nothing to worry about." He smiled at her as he moved closer and put an arm around her shoulders.

Christine leaned away from him, her chin dipping against her chest. He was getting the wrong impression of her.

"Don't do that," Jack said it sweetly, enticing her. "Just one more kiss — it's New Year's."

He was right, it *was* New Year's; just one more kiss.

She leaned forward and his warm lips melded into hers. Once the passion of the kiss abated she began pulling away and he leaned forward.

"Jack," she said, giggling. "We agreed, one more."

"I can't have just one. Surely you can see that."

He pushed her down and he was heavy on top of her. His mouth was at her neck, her collarbone, then he went lower. She pushed at him.

"Jack, stop it," she scolded seriously but was afraid of embarrassing him. Christine knew she'd led him to this point. She heard her mother reprimanding her in her mind — she should never have flirted so seductively with him.

"Christine, come on." He was breathless now and was fiddling with his belt.

Any trace of lightheartedness she had remaining left. She couldn't catch his eyes — they were wild. Jack pulled the skirt of her dress up again. She pushed it down. He pulled it back up, more roughly the second time. She was losing the battle.

141

"Jack, stop it right now," she said with a growl. "This is not happening!"

He didn't respond. His weight was getting heavier on her. Kicking didn't help, it only nestled him even closer to her. Her lungs tightened. She only had use of one hand; her other arm was pinned between the seat and Jack. Should she slap him, pull his hair? Scratch him?

Christine hit the side of his head with the heel of her hand. His eyes flashed anger as she looked up at him in terror.

"Jack, stop it!"

"What is wrong with you, Christine?" he barked at her. There were several moments of silence where only their breathlessness could be heard. "You can't tell me that you don't want this. You've been flirting like a floozy all night. This is what you've been asking for since we danced at the club."

"Get off me!" Her voice worked against her throat like clothing against a washboard. She tried to knee him.

"Oh no you don't." A sadistic smile crossed his lips. "You're not just going to be a big flirt and lead me on and get away with it."

Christine wiggled her other arm free and she began clawing at him. He grabbed one of her wrists and with the other hand she brought a fist to his ear.

Jack cursed at her.

How she longed for a syringe filled with a double dose of insulin. She imagined plunging the sedative into his neck. She cocked her fist back for another blow. He blocked it and grabbed her second wrist, trapping both with one hand. The strength in his grip made her lose hope. Was he really going to do this? Was he really going to violate her? Hurt her? She should've made him take her home right away. Why hadn't she?

Jack's other hand hurriedly finished undoing his pants and she had to look away as she screamed his name again and pleaded for him to stop. Christine screamed louder when he continued. Part physical pain and part complete horror over what was happening overcame her.

She sobbed in the fetal position when he was done. She wasn't sure what hurt worse, the pain of his violation or the ache in her heart for having lost her innocence — or the fact that she was to blame. That was what had happened. She'd given away her innocence.

Christine gathered the top of her dress together and with shaky hands tried to button it. By the time she looked over at him she couldn't believe what she saw. Jack had already buttoned up his pants and tucked in his shirt. He'd even tried to smooth his hair back in place. Looking straight ahead through the steamy windows, Jack took a swig from a flask from under his seat.

"Don't cry, darling. You'll see that everything's fine. If you didn't want it, you shouldn't have tempted me like you did. You wanted this to happen and now you're just pretending it's entirely my fault so you don't have to take any of the blame. You're the one who ran after me, remember?"

"Not so you could take advantage of me." She pushed her glasses back on her face.

"Don't make it a big deal. No one needs to know. I'm only sorry you didn't enjoy it as much as I did. We'll go slower next time. I couldn't stop myself. You were —" As Christine grabbed for the door handle and tried to open it he stopped talking.

The door was locked and she fumbled to unlock it. When she finally did, she grabbed her purse and stood outside the car.

"Hey, hey, hey. Christine, what are you doing?" He appeared genuinely surprised by her reaction.

"Whatever this was, it's never going to happen again. Do you hear me? We are over!"

Jack shook his head and laughed weakly.

"We? There's never been a *we*. Listen, are you going to get back in so I can drive you home or what?" Jack's breath turned white as he spoke.

"I'm not going anywhere with you."

Jack rolled his eyes. When he got out of the car and walked toward her, Christine started backing away. Her legs were shaking, she couldn't move fast enough. "Christine, stop talking like this," he said with lightheartedness in his voice. He pulled her close to him and his gentle touch broke Christine's reserve strength to fight and she wept. He put the coat on her like a gentleman would. When he bent to kiss her cheek she slapped him.

Jack pursed his lips and set his jaw.

"Now that was uncalled for." His voice was stern. "Listen, it wasn't like I'm the only one who got a little out of control in there. But it's happened now and we don't have to go about it like that again."

"It'll never happen again, Jack," Christine screamed at him. "Don't you get it? You raped me. I told you no."

"The girls always say no, Christine. It doesn't really mean no."

"The girls?" Was she just another one of his conquests?

He tilted his head at her. "It's different for

men," he appealed to her.

"Was Sandy telling —" She couldn't put a complete thought together. Maybe Sandy was actually telling the truth. Maybe he had raped her as well. The alcohol she'd consumed surfaced and she swallowed down the sour taste rising in her throat. The road looked long, then wide, and spun.

"Let's just forget that it happened. Maybe we can take a step back and go on a real date, soon." He patted her shoulder like a pet dog and gave her one of his winning smiles. "Now, pull yourself together and get back in the car. I'll drive you up to the hospital. At least try to act civilized."

Some of Jack's words made sense to her. Christine guessed they were at least a half-mile away from the hospital. She didn't want to walk the rest of the way in the icy cold.

Pulling her coat closer, she took a step on wobbly legs toward his car. Her ankles turned in and Jack grabbed her arm to help right her. As soon as he touched her she had the urge to vomit. How could she have let him kiss her like that and touch her? She'd told him to stop — right?

When she got in the car, she leaned hard against the closed door. She wanted to be as far away from Jack as possible. When they

146

got to the parking lot there were several other nurses arriving home. The last thing she wanted was for anyone to find out what had just happened to her. That would be the ultimate humiliation.

"I'll see you sometime at church and we can talk about a real date. Don't be so hard on yourself. It's 1945 — er, '46 — you're a modern woman now." He winked at her then reached over to the passenger door and pulled it closed from the inside. Jack drove off before she could say a word about his idea of her being a modern woman.

It was easy to be invisible. Christine had mastered it in high school. She didn't say anything to the other workers who were making their way from the parking lot to the Kirkbride building and up to the apartments. A prayer escaped her mind that Jeanne wasn't among them. How would she explain this to her best friend?

She wouldn't. That's all. She would keep this awful secret deep inside of herself and never let anyone ever know what Jack had done to her — especially the fact she led him to it. Christine lagged behind the larger group of giggling women and once she was in her hall she pulled out her keys. They dropped to the floor with a clang. Several nurses turned.

She bent down to pick up her keys and realized how desperately her hands shook.

"Christine, you all right?" one of the nurses said.

Christine nodded, her eyes welled up.

Don't cry. Don't cry.

"You don't look so good," said another in a thick accent. "You're about as pasty as my Grandma Rose, and she's eighty-two. You sure you're all right?"

Christine willed her knees not to buckle. Her leg muscles reminded her of how her patients were after hydrotherapy — wobbly, like they were made of rubber.

"Sure," she said. "Just tired. I think I might be coming down with something."

She didn't wait for another query but focused carefully on unlocking her door and then slipped inside without another glance at the other nurses. Once inside, she realized how her body ached. Carefully she walked to the small vanity and collapsed onto the chair. She found her reflection frightening. Her Vivien Leigh victory rolls she'd been so proud of were flattened and ruined. Her wrists ached from how tightly he'd held them. Her glasses were crooked.

Christine peeled off her dress down to her garter, and kicked everything under her bed in disgust. She pulled her housecoat off the back of the chair and wrapped herself inside the warmth. She tiptoed quickly down the hall to the bathroom and shower. Breath quickening, heart interrogating her chest. She could hear voices from the day room. She quickly slipped into the bathroom without being seen.

The hot water pelted her body. Her soreness was quickly getting worse. Surely the hot water would help. The water poured on her back and her chest for a while before she put her face in the flowing heat. Her tears mixed with the hot water. She wanted to wash everything away. She grabbed her washcloth and lathered it with soap. She began scrubbing every part of her body. Her skin turned red with the effort. Though they had been repeatedly asked not to take long showers, and especially not hot ones, she didn't care, not this time. Christine let the hot water wash over her until she couldn't stand the heat any longer. When she finally got out the cold air forced her into reality. Christine towel dried and pulled on her housecoat. She couldn't even look at herself in the out-of-focus image in the mirror.

She returned to her room and locked the door behind her. She didn't bother combing her hair or putting on any more clothes, just huddled under the heavy quilt on her bed in her housecoat. Her body couldn't relax. Christine knew her adrenaline was still racing through her veins. Shivers rocked her to the core. Why had Jack lost such control? Why had he forced himself on her? She shook her head trying to erase the images from her mind. Was he right though? Had she led him on like a common tramp? She had let him kiss her long and deeply. She'd let his hands roam the length of her back and around her waist and hadn't pushed him away quickly enough when his hands had begun to wander.

The only person she could blame for this awful night was herself.

CHAPTER 10

A loud knock at Christine's door startled her awake.

Her eyes opened wide and sunlight streamed through the gap between the curtains. Was it morning already?

"Christine." Jeanne's voice was calling. She pounded a few more times.

"Jeanne?" she called back.

Christine looked at the clock. It was nearly seven. The last time she looked it was three a.m. She scooted herself to the edge of the bed and winced. Her hands kneaded her achiness and her eyes squeezed shut.

Her body moved slowly to the door and unlocked it, opening it only a crack. Jeanne's bright eyes looked concerned.

"Christine, what's going on? Do you know how long I've been pounding on your door? Why aren't you up and ready? Is something wrong?" She paused for a brief moment. "I know you were out late — are you ill? I thought maybe you'd come to my room last night and tell me about how it went with Jack." Her voice went up and down excitedly. "Well, say something."

Christine shook her head. She was saying too many words. Asking too many questions. Questions she couldn't answer. She rested her head on the doorframe and squeezed her eyes shut.

"I'm fine." Her throat was dry and her voice hoarse. "My alarm just didn't sound. I'll have to skip breakfast and just get to work. I'll meet you later?"

She didn't want to give any clues to her best friend about how her night had gone. Jeanne would figure things out too quickly.

"You've never woken up late. What's really the matter? Was it Jack?" Jeanne pushed the door a bit.

Christine turned but didn't open the door any farther. Her dress and undergarments from the night before peeked out from beneath the bed.

"He's not interested? Did he hurt your feelings? He can be very coarse at times, Christine."

"No. Nothing like that." She shook her head. "He brought me home and I just forgot to set my alarm. That's all."

Did Jeanne buy her lie? Christine's friend

bit her lower lip and squinted her eyes. After a long exhale she agreed and told her to find her later. Christine locked the door again and sunk down to the floor with her back against the door. She couldn't stop crying. Her physical pain was minimal compared to remembering the feeling of Jack's body holding her down. That would stay with her forever. The sense of his probing, violent touch filled her with fear and humiliation. She hated him. She hated herself.

Memories of seeing her brother Peter and Jack joshing around in the halls at school came to mind. The way Christine would walk by and pretend not to hang on Jack's every word. Peter was always sweet and would wave and say hello, but Jack never paid her any mind. Now that he had, she wished Jack had died in the war instead of Peter.

Christine ran into work looking unusually ashen and feeble. After working nearly nine months at the hospital, Eli found himself assessing people's physical appearance and mental stability in an instant. It wasn't like he was always correct, but usually Christine was on the ward before him with a smile and rosy cheeks. Today her uniform was a touch wrinkled and her cap crooked. Her hair was combed into a simple Amish-looking bun at the nape of her neck and not in the usual intricate rolls and waves that he'd come to appreciate.

"There you are," Eli heard Nurse Smythe say to Christine. "I was about ready to call Phancock and see where you were. Minton didn't know either."

"Sorry," Christine said breathlessly. "I think my alarm is broken or something."

"You sure it wasn't your date last night?" Nurse Smythe winked at her and nudged her as they stood next to each other hovering over the nurse's log. "Word travels fast around here, Christine."

As the color washed from Christine's face a stab pushed against Eli's gut. She'd had a date? He'd always wondered why she was working at all and not married. She was by far the most interesting woman he'd ever met, and the most beautiful. But she never talked about any man in her life. As much as he'd urged himself not to get attached to her, there was a part of him that was bothered by hearing she had a date last night.

"Wish I could've had a hot date last night instead of getting stuck here."

"Well, next New Year's I'll work instead of you. It wasn't a big deal. Now, what's all this about Wally?"

Eli's ears perked again, hearing something about Wally.

"Something happened to Wally?" Eli turned around from pretending to help Floyd and another patient play checkers. He didn't want them to know he was eavesdropping, but he and Wally had become friends in his time there.

"No, nothing happened," the nurse said. "He's going home. Can you believe it?"

Eli's and Christine's eyes met. It was as if they were both remembering their first awkward conversation that happened over Wally's discomfort with him working there. Wally had improved greatly in the last nine months, Eli had noticed. Wally had become much more than a patient — he was a friend, and Eli would miss him.

"His parents visited during the day shift yesterday," the nurse went on.

"Looks like we both missed a lot on our day off, Brenneman," Christine smiled with her mouth, but not with her heart.

With the thoughts of Wally going home and receiving a letter from his mother at the end of his shift, it made his desire to return home all the stronger. If Wally could find the strength to return home, maybe, when the time came, he could, too.

December 22, 1945

Dear Eli,

Blessings to you in the name of our Lord Jesus. We are praying that you are well and healthy. Merry Christmas to you and I hope the new shirt fits you well. I know it's going to get to you too late. I am sorry about that. You probably won't get it before New Year's now.

Our weather here has been damp and cold. Uncle Rufus says we're due for some warmer weather in a few days. You know how he's always right and we're ready for it. I s'pose you might be getting about the same in New York. I hope the comforter is keeping you warm enough.

Betty and Emmy each colored you a picture. They ask about you almost every day now. We are all ready for you to come home. Are they feeding you enough? Mark's twins are growing so fast. Junior is just like Sylvia and little Lindy is just like Mark. They are as funny as can be. Your sisters try to boss them around. Mark says that Sylvia seems some better after a difficult autumn. I can tell Mark worries sorely over her.

Your dad hurt his back. That old bull pinned him against the wall and he didn't get out until David heard him. He's okay, but he's thinking of asking your cousin Andrew to board with us in your room until you come home. Aunt Annie is doing well in our small cottage. She's quiet though, probably misses Holmes County. She'll get used to living here soon enough.

Well, I best be off. David has been dating Amanda Fisher and the young people went to a Christmas Singing tonight. Moses still isn't interested in any of the girls, you know how shy he is.

God's Blessings be on you,
Mom

Eli stared at his mother's words for several long minutes. Though he was nervous to return, he was hungering for home. So many things were happening with his family — things he used to take for granted and even considered trivial. Now he knew that his growing little twin sisters and a twin niece and nephew were the important things. His brother dating a girl seriously might not be big news, but it was to Eli. It wasn't as if David would ask Eli for advice though. No one ever did. Eli had done just about everything wrong.

He leaned back on the cot and let the letter rest on his chest. He refolded the letter and stuffed it back in the envelope and added it to his small box of letters. The pictures his twin sisters colored for him made him chuckle. One was a simple drawing of a horse and buggy and the other was a pasture with cows. He knew his mother had drawn them. She had been drawing pictures for them since he was just a boy. The colorful scribble marks atop the drawing were his sisters' handiwork, he knew. There was a lot of pink.

Over the next few days Eli battled with the recurrence of missing home and his emotional attachment to Wally as he helped him prepare to reenter life with his parents. He lived out in the country in upstate New York. Eli would likely never see him again.

"Thank you, Eli," Wally said to him as he was ready to leave. His parents stood behind him with hope in their eyes. His dad held Wally's small suitcase with white knuckles and his eyes glistening with unshed tears. Wally clapped Eli on the shoulder and then the two men hugged briefly.

"I'm glad you're going home," Eli said.

Eli was glad that Wally was able to meet his eyes. That had taken months to do comfortably. After their first conversation over mopping, Eli continued to talk with Wally like he would talk with any of his friends — simple conversations, as well as deeper thoughts on his faith and life at home.

Wally waved at the other staff. Christine stood on the bottom step, wiping her eyes. Floyd patted her shoulder in sympathy. He understood more than most people gave him credit for.

"You better vote for me when you get out there," Gov yelled over to Wally.

Wally turned and nodded at Gov. "You betcha, Gov," he said. Then he was gone. In the nine months that Eli had been there Wally was the only one to leave. He wasn't perfectly *healed* or *cured,* but he'd found his way out of the storm that raged inside and was ready to start his life again.

There was only another hour left in Eli's shift after Wally left. Everyone had eaten their suppers and the ward was unnaturally quiet. It was as if every patient had seen what the possibilities could be and those who had greater control of their actions and minds were on their best behavior. Even Rodney was polite and careful.

Early the next morning, one of the other

C.O.'s yelled down the hall. "Eli, call for you."

He looked at the clock. It was just after six o'clock in the morning. Eli woke muddled but instantly concerned. He pulled himself from bed and quickly trotted to where the only phone was attached to the wall. He'd never gotten a call at the hospital before. Eli himself had called his family only once because it cost so much money. Another C.O. held the receiver for him. Concern wrapped around his body, making him feel as if he was moving in slow motion. The phone was cold in his hand; the shiny blackness seemed too unworn, too simple to be allowed to carry the weight of his world on the other end. He had the receiver to his ear for several long moments before he could say anything. He heard someone sniff on the other side, jarring him into reality.

"Hello?"

"Eli?" It was his brother, David. Had something happened to his parents? His sisters?

"David, *vass ist letz*?" He instantly asked his brother what was wrong.

"*Mem* said I should call you. Thought you should know."

There was heaviness in David's voice. He

160

was usually one of the jokers of the family. Eli's heart rammed against his chest and he inhaled, holding his breath.

"Is it *Dat*? The *szfiling*?" What if the call was about his twin sisters?

"No, it's Mark and Syl. Their *haus* burned down last night."

"Nay. Sis net wah." This wasn't happening. His chin fell to his chest. "Are they okay? Is anyone hurt?"

"They all made it out, but just barely. Mark has some problems with his lungs. He's a little weak, but the doctor says he'll be fine. Sylvia is just beside herself. No one can get her to sleep. She's having a hard time. She feels guilty because they think it might have started because of a candle she forgot to put out. Mark isn't overly down, but you know Mark. He's just that way. Doesn't let anything get him down."

That wasn't what Eli was thinking at all. David had it all wrong. Mark was the most serious of all his brothers, not lighthearted in the least.

"You tell Mark they can rebuild. It'll be okay. I'll help him however I can — when I get home."

"When will that be? Everybody sure wants you home. I think that's why *Mem* wanted me to tell you. Maybe something like this will make a difference to your CPS director or someone. Because we need you."

Eli could almost have handled those words better if they'd come laced with anger or bitterness. The words, however, dropped so heavy into his ears with such a sadness his eyes burned instantly. He cleared his throat and turned toward the wall. He stood and straightened his shoulders, inhaling deeply.

"Don't know yet." He cleared his throat again. "I'll write if I learn anything. Thanks for calling, David. It was nice to hear from you, even though it was bad news."

"Better go, *Dat* won't like this phone bill and the neighbor *frau* is watching me and checking the clock about every five seconds." The two men chuckled a bit, glad that they could speak without the neighbor lady understanding them. They'd always paid for their phone calls, but the farmer's wife about three-quarter miles away was always unsure of letting them borrow the phone.

"*Ja, ich veis.* Tell *Mem* I'll write soon."

"Will do."

The phone clicked off, but Eli waited for a few moments just to be sure. He took the phone from his ear and then found himself looking at it. It was as if he was expecting to see the answers he needed inside some-how.

By the time he got to the ward his shoulders were weighed heavily with the news. It didn't help that the patients had left their more calm selves from the day before by the wayside. While some were simply ungainly, there were others who were being purposely difficult. Eli's patience was wearing thinner as the day progressed.

Adkins and DeWayne were helping Minton with shock therapy most of the day and he was with the patients by himself in the shower room. Freddy was in the other hall and James was in hydrotherapy. Not a single moment could be wasted on a day like this.

After lunch he was showering a room full of patients and Rodney grabbed the showerhead from his hand and sprayed it back at Eli. The water burst into his face and eyes. The taste of water was like metal in his mouth and he pinched his lips together. He scrambled to retrieve the showerhead from Rodney, who was cackling as he continued his wild antics.

"Rod, give it back." He finally grabbed it. "Now, grab a towel, dry off, and line up."

Rodney, who had become much more compliant than when he'd first arrived, reared up and pulled the showerhead back out of Eli's hands. His face was red and his eyes grew wilder by the moment. Eli ducked when the showerhead came at him but then let instinct take over. He barreled into Rodney's chest with his head and arms, taking them both down. The showerhead snapped from its place on the wall.

Rodney was yelling like a stuck pig and before Eli could even get off of him Christine ran into the shower room.

"What's going on? Eli — Brenneman — what happened?" Christine's face was instantly angry and she practically shoved Eli off of Rodney. "You've hurt him! Look at his arm."

Eli looked down at Rodney. Sure enough, Rodney held an arm that was bent awkwardly. Clearly it was broken.

"He was trying to hit me with the showerhead. He nearly got me, too."

"And you weren't prepared for Rodney to act up? Come on, Eli, you know better than to let your guard down with him."

Eli stood dumbfounded as he watched Christine gently help Rodney up. She picked up a wet and dirty towel from the floor and wrapped it around his bare waist. She didn't look back at him as she walked out with Rodney, who was wailing loudly and cursing. He was left in the shower room alone with his guilt. How quickly his old self came back when the stresses around him pressed on him. Now he'd hurt a patient, would likely get reprimanded, and, worse, he'd probably lost Christine's respect.

Eli was still breathing heavily when he left the shower room. He went about his work waiting for Adkins or the ward administrator or the CPS unit director to call him to answer for his actions, but after several hours none of them came. The other attendants were too busy to stop and ask him about what had happened, but he could glean from their expressions that they heard that he'd lost his temper. Christine avoided him for the rest of her shift, but when he left their building she was standing out front.

"What were you thinking, Eli?" she spat her words at him, getting close to his face. She was only a few inches shorter than him.

He exhaled and pursed his lips. "I know. I lost my temper when he came at me. I should've tried to calm him down before I pinned him."

"I would say so." Christine let out an angry groan. "You're lucky that Rodney isn't going to say anything. I told him that if he does he'll end up in solitary anyway, since he also lost his cool."

"You're not going to say anything?" Mostly Eli was relieved, but there was part of him that wanted to be punished. Wasn't it flagellation that brought righteousness and purification from sin? He'd already pleaded with God for forgiveness over his temper.

"Not this time. But if it happens again, I will." Christine's gaze pierced Eli's. "I was able to smooth it over with the doc while Rod's arm was set. The doc knows Rod's behavior and that he's not unaccustomed to injuries, so he didn't ask a lot of questions."

Eli sighed and looked at his feet.

"Thank you," he said quietly.

"What got into you? You're always so collected and at ease with the patients. This isn't like you." Christine's eyes were wide as she spoke to him but her face was drawn.

Eli shrugged. He rubbed a hand down his face and stifled a groan that was growing inside. "Actually, this is more like me. I'm not as fine a person as you think I am."

"I think you're wrong, Eli." Her voice grew softer and her head tilted. "Just don't lose your temper again, all right?"

Suddenly he had the urge to grab Christine, pull her close, and kiss her soundly on the mouth. But unlike the urge he had to take down Rodney, he didn't fall to this temptation. He couldn't. All week he'd seen a change in her. She was working more slowly and would stare off into space like he'd never seen her do before.

"What about you?" he said quietly as other nurses and attendants were walking past, coming and going from their shifts. "You haven't been yourself this week either, Christine."

She let out a loud sigh and looked away. "This isn't about me, Eli. Don't change the subject."

"Well, if you're not going to talk, then I won't either."

"How mature of you," she said, putting her hands on her hips.

"Christine," another nurse said, bounding up to them. He recognized the woman as one of Christine's friends. "You've been avoiding me all week, what's going on with you? You haven't even told me if you had a hot time on your date with Jack."

"Jeanne," Christine scolded and her eyes shot back and forth from Eli to Jeanne.

"Oops," Jeanne said.

Eli raised his eyebrows. "See, I'm not the only one who's noticed."

Christine didn't meet his eyes before he walked away. Eli admitted to himself that he wished he could overhear the whispering between the two nurses. He wanted to know what secret she was keeping and why. Was it something to do with her family and the strain of their dependence on her, or was it about this *Jack* fellow and their date? He was uncomfortable with how much it bothered him to learn that she had gone out on a date.

"I heard about Rodney," DeWayne said as he and Freddy fell into step with Eli. "Are you okay?"

Eli shrugged. He didn't want to keep talking about it.

"You're a lucky fella that Nurse Freeman's got a shine for you, otherwise you'd be toast, buddy." Freddy spoke too loudly, making the others near them turn around as they walked back to their dormitory. DeWayne shoved Freddy and put a finger to his lips, telling him to keep quiet.

"She does not," Eli said in a loud whisper. "Christine's just a friend."

"If that's the truth, then I'd make sure to call her Nurse Freeman from now on." DeWayne said, eyeing him.

CHAPTER 11

"So, what happened on New Year's Eve?" Jeanne pressed Christine as they walked up the hill to the Kirkbride building.

"He drove me home." Christine made sure to keep her eyes diverted from Jeanne's.

"Come on, there's no way that's it. You sure were pretty forward to go after him. I saw you leave and then watched you talk outside. I saw the way he looked at you."

Christine's face burned. She couldn't ever tell anyone about that night. It was too humiliating to even think of, let alone say out loud.

"He drove me home and we said good-bye. I'm fine with it, really."

"Oh, here I'd been hoping he asked you for a real date." Jeanne frowned. "Well, maybe it's not too late. Or what do you think? Maybe he's just distracted with school and with those awful rumors Sandy started. Did he talk about it?"

Christine shook her head. The lump in her throat kept her from being able to speak. Her knees grew weaker with each step, partly from the escalating hill but mostly because of the strength that left her any time the memory of that night took over her mind.

"Jeanne, I can't —" her voice broke. Her eyes filled with tears. She wiped a hand against a cold cheek but Jeanne noticed them anyway.

"Oh, my darling." Jeanne took her hands as they stood at the base of the Kirkbride building. Several nurses went by and Jeanne pulled her away from them, hiding Christine's emotion from curious eyes. "I didn't mean to make you feel worse about it. I'm sure if Jack gets to know you better he'll ask you out."

"Jeanne, I don't want him to ask me out. I don't want anything to do with him." She got the words out between reluctant sobs.

"What? I thought you liked Jack?"

Christine held back more sobs, trying to regain her composure. In the few minutes they'd talked her growing need to confess what had happened overwhelmed her. Finally she broke.

"He raped me, Jeanne. Jack raped me."

■ ■ ■ ■

A week later, the ground everywhere was covered like powdered sugar. Christine walked up to the white steepled church that was so familiar. She was helped up the icy steps by a red-cheeked deacon with a wink and a grin. Once she was inside she couldn't bear to see the smile on her mother's face without giving one in return. Smiling, however, was the last thing she wanted to do. She'd had constant nightmares and couldn't close her eyes where she didn't see either Jack's face or the image of herself throwing her innocence away.

Her mother gathered her into her arms as she arrived at their pew in church. How Christine wanted to stay safely in her mother's hold. How she longed to tell her of the turmoil in her heart. That for the past several weeks she had hidden the worst of all secrets.

"Oh, you're so cold, Christy," Margie rubbed her daughter's arms. "I just heard the most interesting news and I cannot believe that you didn't stop by this week to tell me. I was just talking with Mrs. Cupcake about our next Sunday School committee meeting and she said that her niece Wilma's daughter Helen was at the New Year's party, and she insists that Jack Delano took you home."

Christine imagined watching the color drain from her face. Of course, Mrs. Cupcake had connections everywhere.

"Christy? What's wrong? Oh, I was afraid it wasn't true. I told Mrs. Cupcake that —" Her mother continued to talk as if to herself then looked back at Christine and stopped. "I'm sorry, I didn't mean to upset you, dear. I didn't think it could be true."

"It's true." Christine's words barely escaped her lips before she wished she'd let her mother believe that what she'd heard was all a rumor.

"It is? Then why do you look like a pillar of salt? Tell me everything. Will you be spending more time together?" Her mother elbowed her and batted her eyes.

"You heard it all, Ma," she said, starting toward the sanctuary with her mother at her side. "It was nothing. I was ready to go home and he was leaving so he took me. Nothing more."

She waved at several people to keep the conversation light as they walked down the blue-carpeted aisle. Christine was always struck by the church's natural wood against the beautiful stained glass picture of a cross.

Here was where she'd learned nearly everything she knew about the Bible. Where she'd decided to follow Christ and believed God was calling her to care for her family no matter what it took.

Given all of her history with the church, she expected to feel some measure of comfort at being here. There was none. Her heart was still heavy and her burden weighed on her shoulders. Now that her mother knew Jack had driven her home after the New Year's party, her countenance stooped further.

The head deacon greeted everyone from the pulpit and offered a prayer.

"Why didn't you tell me the instant you walked into this church or stop by since New Years? This is big news," her mother whispered to her during the deacon's lengthy prayer.

"I didn't think it was important," she whispered back. Would her mother believe the lie?

"Not important. This could be it, Christy. Jack would be the perfect gentleman for you to marry."

The prayer was through and the organ began to sound the first hymn and all Christine could think of was that she needed to leave. Her mother's questions, the purity of the church, all of it was too much for her. She wasn't pure. She wasn't good and she couldn't answer her mother's questions without lying. Her mother and Doris stood. Her father remained seated for the first hymn.

"Christine, stand," her mother scolded quietly. "What's the matter with you? You're so pale."

She obeyed and stood but then her guilt wrapped around so tightly it took all her strength to not run from the church and hide away forever. Christine quietly sang the first verse of "I Know Who Holds Tomorrow," but the words mocked her. Did she even believe the poetry expressed in the lines of the song? No. She did worry about her future. She didn't feel anyone's hand in her own. Her mind only took her back to the weight of Jack's body holding her down.

She realized that morning as she sang in the church full of memories that she would never be free of the memory of Jack and her own sin.

Several weeks went by. February ushered in another round of winter storms, and Christine was growing used to the idea that her life was different now. Her confession to Jeanne about what had happened between her and Jack hadn't helped anything. She'd explained to Jeanne how things had happened and when her friend wasn't able to give her any words of wisdom or healing, she'd taken it even harder. Her guilt grew. It really had been her fault. Jeanne promised not to tell a soul and hugged her and told her everything would be fine. Christine knew better than that though. Of course, nothing would be fine. Nothing would ever be okay. She was a dirtied girl, never to be pure and clean again. Her life was over.

Her work kept her busy, but even work couldn't distract her from the pain in her soul. But it was all she had now — despite the bouquet of flowers Jack had sent to her. She'd thrown them in the trash, but not before reading the small card attached.

I'm coming home next Friday. Let's go dancing!

His address was on the back, but she wouldn't write him back. How could he say that? She ripped it into the smallest pieces she could.

Focusing on recording all the needs and happenings of the ward patients — from hydrotherapy for calming to hyoscine for nausea — in the logbook took all her energy.

"You didn't vote for me," Gov yelled from the opposite corner. His voice was loud and reverberated around the cold, square room.

Christine looked around. Eli was the only attendant in the room. Where was everyone else? She saw Eli crane his head from the mopping up he was doing. The two of them hadn't spoken much since the incident with Rodney. He had guilt in his eyes anytime they were together, and he was growing more despondent every day.

"Did you vote for me? You? And you?" Gov was pointing at the patients around him and stirring up discord.

Christine walked through the doorway. Eli leaned the mop against the wall and began walking over.

"You did not vote for me!" He put his finger in a typically quiet patient's face.

At Gov's accusation the patient began pulling his hair and spinning. His mumbling was getting louder by the moment.

"You did not vote for me!"

"Come on, Gov, let's put this puzzle together." Eli took him gently by the arm.

Before Christine could react, Gov socked Eli in the side of the head. As she ran she saw Eli falling. His body fell against a nearby table, then onto the floor.

"Eli," she yelled.

She pulled a drawer open and took out a readied high dose of insulin in case Gov

176

didn't calm down. Her eyes glanced toward the door — as usual it was closed. No one was going to hear her if she needed help. Gov hugged himself and walked in tight circles. These habits indicated that he was calm for the moment though still highly agitated. She would have to write his behavior down; he'd had more outbursts lately — the doctor might have to reevaluate his treatment plan. Her eyes diverted from Gov to where Eli lay. She weaved through the patients and by the time she got to Eli he was wincing as he rubbed the side of his head.

"Are you all right, Eli?" Christine bent down and turned his head to see where he'd been hit, then lifted his eyelids and checked his pupils. "You might have a concussion."

"I don't have a concussion," he said, smiling. He gently took her hand away from his face and for a split second he held it before letting it go and standing up. Christine stood also. "I've been hit a lot harder. He threw off my balance is all. Are you going to use that on me?"

She looked down and realized she was still holding the syringe with insulin.

"Sorry," she said. "I grabbed it for Gov — just in case."

"He's been a little more aggressive lately,

I've noticed." He rubbed the back of his neck and head.

"We might need the doctor to adjust his medications." Christine nodded.

Before they could consider the happening any further, Donald, a quiet, easy patient, walked up to them.

"Gov touched me. I think I'm going to vomit. I'm going to vomit. I'm going to vomit." Donald was afraid of touching anyone, no matter if he was sitting, standing, walking, or sleeping. He had his arms wrapped around his body.

"Donald, you're not going to throw up just because Gov touched you," Christine told him as she began walking back to the nurse's office. "You're just fine."

"Nope, nurse, I'm going to vomit. I'm going to vomit," he said articulately.

"Donald, just sit in that chair and don't touch anyone," Eli said. There was laughter behind each word. Christine bit her lip so she wouldn't chuckle when Donald looked at Eli with shock all over his face. He listened immediately and sat, still repeating his words about vomiting.

Eli and Christine looked at each other, trying not to laugh. She was glad that the air of ease between them was returning. And glad she could still enjoy working with him and find comfort in his presence. She replaced the insulin injection in the office drawer and locked the door. She had to check on the patients in hydrotherapy.

"Freeman!" Freddy flew through the day room door, letting it slam against the wall. "Floyd's seizing."

Christine ran as fast as she could out of the day room and into the hall toward Floyd's room. When they reached the room Floyd was facedown on the floor, convulsing uncontrollably. Adkins tried without success to get Floyd on his side. Christine grabbed Eli's hand behind her and pulled him down onto the floor next to Floyd.

"Help Adkins roll Floyd on his side in case he vomits," she said and grabbed the tongue depressor that was attached to the bed's headboard. This was customary for patients on seizure watch.

Eli was able to roll Floyd onto his side without Adkins's help. Christine grabbed the pillow from his bed and put it under his head, then pushed the tongue depressor into his mouth and held his tongue down.

"Come on, Floyd," she whispered.

"How long has he been seizing?" Eli asked Adkins.

"I don't know. I was walking by and noticed it and yelled at Freddy to get

Freeman," he said, breathing quickly.

Suddenly the shaking stopped and Christine began stroking Floyd's hair.

"Floyd, it's Nurse Freeman," she said loudly. "Can you hear me? Try to open your eyes."

His eyes fluttered a little. *Come on, Floyd. Come on.* He opened them. They were sleepy looking, and a smile began forming on his lips when he began seizing again. His eyes rolled back into his head, his breathing slowed, and his lips turned blue.

"Freddy, call for Dr. Franklin," Christine yelled. "I need phenytoin. Eli, in the office you'll see it in the locked cabinet in the corner."

She handed him her keys. Phenytoin was the only anticonvulsing drug they had. While it had been in use for decades, its use wasn't yet perfected, and scientists didn't completely understand how it worked, only that it helped curb seizures in many patients.

"Hurry."

Eli ran out of the room.

"Hopefully the phenytoin will be enough." Adkins looked Christine right in the eyes, then stood and waited. It reiterated how serious this was. Adkins usually never stopped talking and he, for once, was using his words sparingly. Eli ran back in and handed her the vial of medication and a syringe. Christine prepared the syringe, then located the large vein in his arm and injected it slowly. Then she prayed for it to work.

As the minutes passed and nothing changed, Christine's heart dropped. Her eyes locked with Eli's. Tears welled up and she couldn't blink them away. Prolonged seizures could result in a heart attack. Mongoloids often also had heart maladies, which made it worse. Was he going to die right here while she stroked his hair? Why in these awful moments did none of her training matter? If she couldn't save his life, what was the point? Why was she a nurse?

"Floyd, come on." She gave him a smaller dose of phenytoin. Her passion was rising. "Can you hear me?" She didn't hold back her tears anymore.

Dr. Franklin rushed in and squatted down near Floyd.

"Doctor, he's in a status epilepticus. I've administered two hundred fifty milligrams of phenytoin, then a few minutes later another fifty, but it hasn't helped."

The doctor checked Floyd's pupils and his pulse. "If he's non-responsive to the phenytoin, I'm sorry, but there's nothing more I can do," the doctor said, sighing heavily. "You have to understand, Nurse, that Floyd has already lived years longer than the normal life expectancy for mongoloids. I'm sorry, I know how much everyone loves Floyd."

Several more minutes passed and everyone waited. Suddenly he stopped shaking and lost control of his bladder and bowels. He inhaled deeply and exhaled painfully before he went completely still.

"No, no." She held a hand over her face, shielding her weeping from several more attendants and student nurses who had entered the room. Eli covered the hand that still stroked Floyd's hair with his own.

"Christine, he's gone," he whispered.

"No," she cried. "No, it's not true."

She lowered the hand from her face and looked at Eli. Even with her blurry vision she could see his brow warped in sympathy and grief.

"I'm so sorry, Christine," he said, "I know how much he meant to you."

"He never knew his family," she said, "we were all he had. The hospital is the only home he's ever known."

From the corner of her eye she saw the doctor shake his head as he made several notations in a file before he left.

She looked back down at Floyd.

"Come on." Eli put his hand out to her.

She looked into his eyes, which glistened with unshed tears, and put her hand in his. His grip heated her skin. He helped her stand and step over Floyd's body. Freddy and Adkins lifted Floyd onto his bed and began cleaning up the floor where he'd lain. The room was otherwise silent and one by one people left. Even Nurse Minton sniffed away her emotions as she walked out.

"Why don't you get some air," Eli said to Christine. "I'll finish up here."

It was then Christine realized she was not just holding Eli's hand but gripping it as if it was life-sustaining. She reluctantly released her hand from his.

"Will you come with me? I don't want to be alone."

Christine's heart ached at the sight of the empty church. There were no floral tributes for Floyd, no choral music, but most of all, no loved ones. Indignation toward his family, whom she'd never met, grew inside.

"I can't believe none of his family came," she whispered to Millicent.

She shrugged.

"I know you must be shocked," Adkins leaned toward Christine from the other side of Millicent, "but this is normal. It is rare that a patient's family actually attends."

Christine glanced around the church again and found Eli's eyes. He sat a few pews back with some of the C.O.'s. Their momentary connection took her back to the way her hand warmed inside of his on the day Floyd died. The way he'd tried to comfort her. She swallowed hard but kept her eyes on his. He tilted his head toward her and his eyes smiled. A soft smile formed on her lips and she turned away.

Christine imagined the casket being lowered into the section in the local graveyard reserved for the poor and unclaimed dead. It was awful to think that he'd never have a gravestone to mark his final resting place. She'd known this due to the other deaths they'd had, but this was the first funeral of a patient she'd attended. Like a pebble in her shoe, it needled her heart that so many had gone before Floyd. The priest read scripture, recited the creed, offered a benediction, and prayed. He rose from his knees with some strain and walked down the aisle with the crucifer boy. The funeral was over. Before any of them even stood the county gravediggers were there to gather Floyd.

They closed the casket. The hammer banging against nail and wood made her wince. Before she knew it they were carrying Floyd out past them.

"That's it?" she said, disappointed.

"I'm sorry, Christine, but what did you expect?" Adkins said.

CHAPTER 12

It had been two weeks since Floyd's death, and Eli found himself discouraged and tired. Their CPS unit director spoke to them as a group, reminding them of the service they provided the hospital and to not let their motivation wane but to keep their eye on God. He reminded them of the verse that encouraged them to finish the course in strength and faith.

After the talk everyone dispersed and he found a card had been slid under his door. He reluctantly picked it up, knowing it was from Matilda.

It was a piece of cream-colored paper folded in half. On the front Matilda had drawn the shape of that fat baby with a bow and arrows, he didn't remember what people called it. There were red hearts in the corners and Matilda's pretty handwriting along the edges read: *How fragrant is the red, red rose. How beautiful and true. My dar-*

ling, on this Valentine's Day, I'm only thinking of you.

His heart pounded inside. Not for the romance the card was supposed to make him feel, but for the problem he knew he had with Matilda. He sighed as he opened the homemade card.

February 1, 1946

Dear Eli,

Hello to you in the name of our Father in Heaven. Our weather is no better than a typical Delaware winter. No worse either, so I suppose we should be thankful for that. May our thanks to the Lord be ever on our lips.

Happy Valentine's Day! I hope you get this in time. I plan to make a cherry pie for you on Valentine's Day and won't let any of my brothers eat it. I'm going to eat it all myself and while I do, I'll think of us eating one together when you come home.

I thought you'd like to know that Mark and Sylvia have settled well in your old room. I took some pie (a different one than your cherry pie) and bread over, to help out. I know your mother is working herself sick, with the fire and the four new ones living in the house and her Aunt Annie in the cottage across the field. I know everyone wishes the cottage was empty so Mark and Syl could move in. They need more room with the twins. You'd think Annie would just offer to move somewhere else. Surely she could live with another widow instead of burdening your mother.

I better go. It's Friday so I have sewing to do. I'm sewing patches over patches on little boy pants. Had to cut up one of my worn-out dresses for patches. Money's tight right now.

Sincerely yours,
Matilda

Eli's heart moved between sympathy and frustration. She didn't seem to understand that they weren't going steady, which made him feel burdened with the truth. He hadn't been clear enough before he left for the CPS or in one of his first letters. He would have to tell her before he arrived home — whenever that would be.

Her last paragraph made him wince. His parents had also experienced those same hard times for the years before the war. The farm had been close to foreclosure and he'd gone without many times.

Those years had been painful but Eli pretended they never existed. He became the center of attention with his jokes and humor to fill the space in his stomach where he was hungry. His *mem* had let out the hem of his pants to lengthen them since new ones weren't an option. Matilda's family was one of the few who hadn't been able to get back on their feet after the Depression. Though they had only six children, for them money was a constant struggle.

These memories made him long for home again. The open fields, the way the sun came over the hip-roof of the barn, and the smell of his mother's food. He wasn't close with his best friend, Henry, ever since he'd left the CPS for an army enlistment, and all his other friends were married with children. Why had he wasted his youth? Why had he waited so long to see his folly would never make him happy?

"What's going on?" Eli asked. He'd heard a ruckus in the common room of their building and had come out of his room to investigate.

"We're leaving," one of the C.O.'s said and passed him by. "I'm going to go write my wife."

"Leaving?"

189

"Our unit is going to be disbanded in April, which means many of us will be going home in a little over a month." The C.O. looked as if he'd been handed his life back. His eyes bright and mouth wide in a smile. He'd been one of the unfortunate men who had been on CPS duty for nearly four years. "Home. Can you believe it? Home!"

The man patted Eli on the shoulder and moved by him quickly, also heading toward his room.

"Home," Eli whispered.

In that moment, it was like something nudged inside his chest. Christine. While he hadn't wanted anything more than to go home for so many months, now he didn't want to leave Christine. He'd fallen for the wrong girl again. And what about the way he'd lost his temper with Rodney. He hadn't really changed after all, had he?

February was coming to a close but Christine's mind constantly replayed the events of New Year's Eve. Jeanne hadn't brought it up since their one and only conversation soon after it happened. Jack had not written or tried to contact her since the flowers he'd sent.

In a strange way, Floyd's death gave Christine some distraction from Jack. But in the weeks that followed her life still wasn't returning to the *normal* she longed for. The winter seemed endless and March was still ahead of them. The patients had been restless with no outside time, and bouts of illness had plagued the ward. She herself had also gotten ill and, though she'd only vomited a few times, the lingering nausea was bothersome.

She'd also stopped attending church with her parents to avoid her mother's inquisition, so she offered to work every Sunday. Christine was simply exhausting herself. She lay awake for hours on end. She would teeter-totter between praying and cursing God. Resentment and anger overwhelmed her. But when comfort rested upon her, and briefly brought her out of her misery, she knew it was God.

When she closed her eyes she could feel Jack's hands on her. Her shame covered her. Humiliation grew just at the memory. Then her stomach would spin in nausea, and she would find herself over a toilet minutes later.

Christine's face in her small mirror was moist and pallid. Her lips were barely pink and her stomach was swirling inside. She'd been awake since three-thirty that morning and that was only after having restlessly slept for a little more than two hours. How much longer could she go on like this?

She forced herself to rush through her days. Eli was suspicious, however, at her behavior. When his eyes were on her and his smile so comforting, she thought she would nearly burst and tell him everything.

When she worked with her patients, she envied their ability to separate their minds from reality. Their sedation mocked her. *Barbital.*

The medication bottle grew warm and inviting in her hand. It was used to induce sleep, especially if patients were agitated or needed therapy. Would it help her? The thought of this made her breathing hasten. Was she as crazy as the patients she cared for?

For days every time she handed out the medications and organized them neatly, then recorded the dosages in the logbook, she considered how it might help her. Was she even considering this? Stealing? Stealing in order to keep her secret seemed worth it, but the idea of getting caught? Her heart pounded. She couldn't do that.

Maybe just two or three good nights of sleep would help her past the restlessness and nightmares and she would begin to sleep like normal. Gov had been additionally restless one day. He had no more cigarettes and no one would sell him any. His moods were becoming extreme. Dr. Franklin suggested some barbital for the night, when he usually slept fine. Her heart pounded heavier against her chest. Taking out a few extra pills would go unnoticed. She was sure. They simply fell into her pocket like they didn't even exist. It seemed almost too easy. The relief over having two pills to rescue her lightened the heaviness she carried around. The anticipation of a night of restful sleep lifted her spirits.

Once she was in her apartment she immediately pulled the two pills from her apron pocket. Tears burned her eyes when she considered that she was no different from her patients now. Undeterred by that reality, she popped one pill in her mouth. It was bitter. She swallowed it down with a gulp of water and wasn't sure if she was relieved over it or ashamed of her sin.

For several minutes she lay there. It was about twenty minutes later when the sensation of Jack's too heavy body on top of her forced her to breathe quickly. Air was trapped in her lungs. Her chest was heavy. The room spun. Fear branded her mind. She saw her mother, her mournful patients, Eli smiling at her, then Jack reaching for her. Her head tingled and cooled. Her eyes drooped. Her mouth went slack. The tension in her neck released and her shoulders rested heavily against the bed. Christine's hands stopped shaking. Everything went from light to dark.

CHAPTER 13

The next morning her legs hit the floor heavily at the side of her bed, like firewood being thrown into the woodstove. Her eyes moved faster, almost ahead of her body, but her mind was behind, not processing everything at the same speed. The lure of a full night's sleep, however, made her consider taking a dose the second night.

There was a strange sensation when she watched her hand reach for a patient's arm. Like it was detached. When it reached him, his arm reminded her of the play dough her mother used to make when she was a child. Malleable. Her eyebrows joined, furrowing.

"Stand up," she told the patient. Her voice sounded unfamiliar in her ears. She shook her head.

He stood, unaware of her state. His eyes were distant and his motions were slow. Was he feeling like her? Fuzzy. Unsettled.

"I'll take him." Eli's voice came from

somewhere far away. She looked up, finding his face closer than she anticipated, and reeled backwards, falling back into a chair.

"Are you all right?" Eli looked over at her. "You're pale and — are your pupils dilated?"

"What? Are they?" She fiddled with her glasses then giggled and tried to throw him off. When she looked back up at him, his face was serious. Christine was a terrible actress. She shook her head and jolted herself back, forcing the dizziness from her mind. "I'm really tired. I'm not feeling well."

The second night on barbital her sleep was haunted, but she couldn't wake herself to get away from her tormentor. He was holding her down and she was clawing at him. He was so much stronger but she kept fighting. Everything around her suddenly chilled her. Even with closed eyes bright lights bothered her and unrecognizable faces came in and out of focus. Voices spoke but she didn't understand anything that was said.

No, they were saying her name.

"Christine, open your eyes."

Was someone telling her to open her eyes? But they were so heavy. It was too hard. She didn't want to open her eyes.

It was a different voice now.

"Open your eyes, Christine." It was Jeanne's voice. Why was Jeanne there? But where was she anyway? Was she working? No. Her mind worked against her grogginess and tried to figure out the last thing she remembered. There was a low groaning in the room. It distracted her from remembering where she was and why Jeanne would've been there. And who was that other voice?

"Christine, this is Dr. Norton. Open your eyes. Now."

Dr. Norton. He was a doctor that she'd worked with during nursing school. Why was he in her apartment? Yes, she was in her apartment at the hospital where she worked. Right? She was so tired and confused. Couldn't he ask another nurse for help with Gov's barbital? Barbital. Yes, she'd taken some for a second time. Her throat tightened and her hands rounded into fists. She had to wake up. She couldn't wake up. She couldn't breathe. The groaning she heard had stopped and now there was coughing and gasping.

"Christine," Jeanne's voice was worried. Was she crying? "Wake up."

She was awake, wasn't she? She was trying to talk but nothing would come out. Panic rose. Maybe she was still asleep. What if she never woke up? Was this what her patients experienced when they were sedated?

A horrible smell suddenly filled her senses. Her head moved back and forth to get away from it. What was it? It was strong but fishy. She needed to take a deep breath but didn't want to breathe in the odor.

She gasped a large breath, filling her lungs, and opened her eyes.

"Christine, I knocked on your door and you wouldn't wake. I had to get Phancock to unlock your room. Neither of us could wake you so we called for the doctor."

"What?" She tried to get up but was pushed back down. That's when she realized she was in an examination room. How had she gotten there? "How did I get here?"

"We had you brought down," Jeanne said gently.

"Brought down?" She turned to see Dr. Norton. Why was she in an examination room?

"Nurse Freeman." Dr. Norton's deep voice resounded against the walls of the small square room. "May I speak frankly?"

Christine looked at Dr. Norton then over to Jeanne's panicked eyes. They knew about the barbital, didn't they? Lying at this point wasn't going to work and her conscience wouldn't allow for it.

She only nodded, not trusting her voice. Her eyes were dry, as if she'd been holding them open too long but couldn't force herself to blink. If she closed her eyes at all she might drown again in sleep.

"First, I'd like to ask you some questions." He raised his eyebrows.

Christine nodded her head.

"Do you remember fainting?"

"No," she whispered and tried to keep her chin from quivering.

"Your pupils are dilated and your blood pressure was very low. I hesitate to ask this, but Nurse Freeman, did you take something? A sedative, perhaps?"

This was it.

"I haven't been able to sleep lately and I've been nauseated because of it." Her voice got shaky. "I just needed some rest. I thought maybe if I had a few nights of real sleep I would be able to sleep on my own after that. I never thought —"

"Did you talk to a doctor about this?" he asked, interrupting her, his voice still gentle.

She shook her head and mouthed the word *no,* but her emotions had taken her voice away.

"Did you take something from the medicine cabinet?"

Her eyes filled with tears and a hot stream trailed down both sides of her face. The room sighed, or so it seemed.

"Barbital?" Dr. Norton asked.

"Yes," she whispered. "I'm so sorry — I took two pills. I didn't want to steal, only I was too ashamed to ask for help."

Without a word the doctor began performing a basic physical examination.

Christine simply pretended she was someone and somewhere else. Dr. Norton checked her pulse, her eyes, looked inside her ears and mouth. He had Jeanne check her blood pressure again and said it was getting better the more the barbital wore off. The doctor palpated her abdomen and asked her questions about dizziness and nausea.

He marked his clipboard occasionally and when he was through he took her hands and helped her sit up.

"Nurse Freeman — Christine," he said, looking at her over his glasses, "how long has it been since you've had your last menstruation?"

"What?" She'd never spoken about her menstruation with anyone, not even her mother. "What does that have to do with anything?"

The doctor cleared his throat and pushed

his glasses up as he documented something on the clipboard he carried.

Christine looked over at Jeanne. Her friend's face was sallow and she bit her lower lip.

"Christine," her friend's voice was like that of a small child. "Have you had the curse recently?"

Jeanne stifled a sob.

"But I have missed *them* before." She looked from the doctor to Jeanne and back again. "When I've been ill or overworked. During my final semester, I missed two months in a row. That's all this is."

"I'm afraid not," the doctor said, pursing his lips and looking at her over his glasses. "I've examined you and you are expecting a baby."

His eyes were kind when he spoke, only there couldn't have been worse words to hear.

"Do you really mean that I'm . . ." Christine couldn't finish her question. She looked at Jeanne and gripped her friend's arms as she spoke. "I didn't mean for it to happen. He was just too strong. I didn't . . ."

It was true, wasn't it? She was pregnant. How had she not realized this? She was a nurse. The nightmares, exhaustion, Floyd, and even Eli. His watchful eye comforted and cursed her. She hadn't realized that she hadn't bled since the middle of December. It was nearly March.

"No, no," she started crying. She wanted to scream but didn't have the energy. She looked over at Jeanne who was also crying.

"I told him no." She wept as she spoke.

"Did someone harm you?" the doctor asked with concern written across his brow.

Her silence was an answer to the doctor.

"I see." He cleared his throat. "I'm sorry to say that I will have to report your condition to Mrs. Phancock, but I will not reveal the barbital. I think you might have enough to deal with already."

She nodded and gave a half-hearted smile of thanks. "That's very kind of you." She did her best to regain her composure.

Christine heard only parts of what the doctor said after this. Something about rest and if there was someone they could call. He said that the baby seemed fine, but not to do anything strenuous. Mostly, however, she heard the rush of guilt, like floodwaters, drowning everything around her.

Calculations and dates ran quickly through her mind as she lay in bed the next day. She tried to push all thoughts away, filling it instead with once-upon-a-time memories from years gone by, pleasant memories. Her grandma's lap when she was six. Fresh baked bread. Christmas. But that wasn't her reality.

Christine was pregnant and unmarried with no prospects.

Jeanne knew. Her mother did not. Jack did not.

Jack had violated her — but only after she'd carelessly flirted with him and let him believe she wanted it. She lay holding her abdomen. Inside she carried a baby. It seemed no one but her cared. Did she even care? Didn't she have to now? No one but her knew it was her fault. She'd provoked Jack. He was a man and men weren't always able to control their needs. Wasn't that what her mother told her when she was fifteen?

Christine was to blame. This was her fault. She lay awake in bed agonizing about her life. Once the doctor told Nurse Minton she would lose her job. She would have to move back home with her parents. She would have a child. Could she and Jack find a way to work it out?

What else could she do?

The second full day in bed was too much for her. She needed to see her mother. She wore her brown dress and buttoned her sweater and winter coat. She wore a scarf over her head and tied it under her chin.

Lastly she wore her sunglasses — claiming even to herself that it was because her eyes were sensitive to the white light of late March sun. If she was truthful, it was simply to be less recognizable.

She jogged off the hospital campus and then walked the rest of the way, glad to be bundled. Spring was on the other side of the chilly weather, but it didn't excite her like it usually did. The fresh air, however, had helped calm her nerves. It wasn't long before she was walking up the street in front of her parents' picket-fenced house. There was another car in the driveway and Christine's heart sank with the thought that her mother wasn't alone.

"Mother?" she said, sticking her head inside the doorway.

"Christine?" her mother said, wearing an ivory apron over a floral dress. Her hair and makeup were immaculate, making Christine feel a bit self-conscious. Once she took off her headscarf her hair would be mashed and untidy. "What brings you here? You're supposed to be working, aren't you?"

They met eyes and she could see her mother's confusion despite the smile on her face.

"Kathleen is here. She wanted to hear all about Doris and Lewis."

She followed her mother into the living room, where one of her mother's closest friends sat. Mrs. Kathleen Berryhill was the most active woman Christine had ever met. She was a part of nearly every committee and club at church, at school, and in town. A busybody if there ever was one.

"Hello, Christine." Mrs. Berryhill stood and gave Christine a stiff hug. "I was just leaving."

"Oh, please stay," Margie nearly pleaded.

"I don't want to intrude on mother and daughter time, Margie. Besides, I promised to go to the church and start planning the Missionary Ladies luncheon for next month." With a rise in her chin Mrs. Berryhill was gone.

"Where's dad?"

"Napping, of course. It's about all he does these days."

Christine didn't respond but just stood in the living room still with her scarf and coat on.

"Well, take off your coat if you are able to stay," her mother said. Christine did so.

Her mother began tidying, picking up the tea service and jellies. Christine picked up a plate of biscuits and cookies and followed her mother into the kitchen.

"Just set that down there," her mother

said, then continued to busy herself and chat as she usually did. "Well, Kathleen had to come over and hear all about Doris and Lewis. They had another date on Saturday night, you know."

"No, I don't know. Who's Lewis?"

"I must have missed telling you. Well, his name is Lewis Roush and he's perfect for Doris. He visited in February for an interview at the bank and they hired him on the spot, said he's a responsible young man. He moved here right away and even bought a house. Isn't that just great? He bought a house."

Christine wasn't sure how to respond so she remained silent.

"He's twenty-five and has a college degree and he's a decorated soldier."

"And he likes Doris?" She found her voice. Margie spun around.

"Christine, you make it sound odd that someone likes Doris."

"Mother, she doesn't talk to anyone."

Margie turned back around and began scrubbing the already clean countertops.

"Anyway, Lewis likes her and you should just see them together already. Doris smiles and Lewis is just such a gentleman."

Her mother washed the counters clean as she spoke, though they hadn't looked dirty before she started. Suddenly, however, Margie paused and turned to look at Christine. Their eyes met for several long moments before her mother spoke again.

"Christine, what's the real reason you didn't tell me that Jack drove you home on New Year's Eve?"

Christine needed to tell her now, before she lost her courage. The image of Jack and his electrifying grin made her shut her eyes to her own memory. How many girls had he taken advantage of? Her lungs burned from holding a breath, she let it out evenly but couldn't find the words to speak.

"Ma, you don't really want to know why." She stuttered as she spoke.

"Christine, I simply do not understand you." Her mother turned and smiled. "For months I've tried to stay out of it and not play matchmaker, but here you are ruining your chances with the best, most handsome man around here."

"He's not the best man around here. You don't know him." The words slipped from her lips before she could trap them deeply behind her heart.

"Well, I heard that you chased after him at the party — chased him —" she repeated. "Really, Christy, I thought you had more self-respect."

"He was upset and I thought I could help. I wasn't chasing him. I was checking on him. There's a difference."

"A grown man doesn't need to be checked on. What else happened? Obviously something did for him to not ask you on a real date after."

"He did, Ma. But I said *no*," she blurted.

"What?" Her mother's eyes rounded and she took hold of the countertop as if she were going to fall over. She pulled out a chair and sat down, then pulled out the one next to it and gestured for Christine to sit. "Now, start from the beginning and don't leave anything out, young lady. I deserve an explanation."

Christine sat down and suddenly covered her abdomen in some maternal way of protecting the baby inside from the anger she already sensed from her mother. What would she do when she learned the whole truth?

"Did he kiss you? Or maybe you didn't let him? I know I've told you that you shouldn't kiss on a first date, but this is different. This is Jack Delano."

Christine rolled her eyes.

"What, that's a valid question. I am trying to figure out where you went wrong so maybe I can help you fix it."

"You can't fix what's wrong this time, Ma." Her voice was low.

"It can't be all bad."

"It is." She looked up at her mother. "Yes, he kissed me that night. I kissed him back."

Her mother sucked in a deep breath. "All right. Then he likes you. He wouldn't kiss you if he didn't like you."

"A lot more happened, Ma. A lot more than kissing."

Christine watched her mother's face move from confusion to the dawning of truth.

"More? Do you mean you . . ." Her mother's hand covered her open mouth. "Christine Freeman. Have you disgraced yourself and your family?"

Christine nodded silently, unable to speak.

"Who else knows?"

"Jeanne." She didn't think mentioning the doctor mattered right now. "Ma, I told Jack no. I promise you I did." She decided against giving any more details about the beer and the whiskey and the way she'd kissed him back before she realized his intentions.

"But the way you were dressed that night — and if you let him kiss you on a first date. What do you think a man's supposed to expect?"

She didn't respond. There was no point in

arguing when there was so much more to confess.

"It doesn't matter now. It's done and I can't take it back."

There was a grating silence between them.

"There's more."

"More? What more? Are you pregnant?"

Christine's eyes snapped to her mother's and it was almost too terrifying to watch the intensity that came over her mother as realization hit her.

"Yes, I'm . . . pregnant." Christine could barely say the word. She looked down and closed her eyes. She took several long breaths in and out, desperate to keep her composure.

"You're pregnant with Jack Delano's baby?"

Christine nodded and looked up at her mother.

"I don't know what to do."

"Have you told him?"

She shook her head. Tears pooled in her eyes.

"And it's for sure Jack's?"

"Ma," Christine said, scowling at her as she held out the "a" sound for several long beats. She stood and paced the kitchen. "You know I haven't even kissed a boy since I was seventeen and that was barely a peck.

Of course, I've never ever been with a man and it wasn't supposed to happen. I told him no."

"I just wanted to make sure; since you're dumping all of this on me at once, I am wondering now what other secrets you might have."

"There's nothing else," Christine assured her.

"How could you get yourself into such a bind. I could hardly get you to go on a blind date and now this? It doesn't even seem possible."

Christine's eyes finally overflowed, unable to keep the tears at bay.

Her mother stood and wrapped Christine in her arms. "Come here, darling. Come here."

Her mother shushed and patted her for several minutes. It was like a protective cocoon inside her mother's arms.

"Okay, let's sit and figure this out," her mother said and directed her to the kitchen chair.

Margie handed Christine a handkerchief and she wiped her face and eyes.

"How are we going to manage, Ma? I won't be able to work like this — unmarried and . . ." She didn't want to tell her that she would be fired within days. "What money are we going to live on? Doris doesn't make enough money to feed a cat, let alone a whole family. The house is going to get taken away from us."

"Let me worry about that." Margie tapped her mouth. "First, you have to go to Jack and tell him. If I were a betting lady I'd say he'll marry you."

Her mother almost looked excited at the prospect, but there wasn't anything about that idea that excited Christine. No one wanted to marry anyone out of obligation, least of all someone who they weren't sure they even liked, let alone loved enough to marry.

"He's not going to marry me. Even if he did, I don't want to marry him."

"Do you want to be an unwed mother?"

Christine didn't answer. Of course she didn't.

"You don't know that he won't marry you, and it's your best option — really your only option. Otherwise you'll have to go to one of those unwed girls' homes."

"What? You're going to send me away? I'm a grown woman, not a high school girl still wearing bobby socks. You can't send me away."

"Darling, what option do you have? If Jack doesn't marry you, then I'll look into a home. I doubt he'll refuse his own child. But come on, Christine, this isn't some fairy tale. This is real life and it would be a real problem if Jack says no."

There was a long moment of silence.

"He forced himself on me. How could I marry a man like that? It wasn't like I asked him for it."

"Did you kiss him and lead him on?"

Her silence was her answer.

"Listen, you cannot stay around here unmarried. You know that. There are too many reasons to list." Margie stood and leaned against the kitchen cabinets. "Oh, Lord. Oh, Lord. Oh, Lord." She repeated in a whisper over and over.

"People judge you by your past and where you come from. I don't want that for you. That's why you have to go to Jack — today. Before you start to put on weight."

Christine shook her head.

"You have that pretty peach dress in your closet. It's a jot humdrum, but I still think it'll brighten you up some. We'll wash your face and get you cleaned up. By the time he sees you on his doorstep, you'll be a knock-out."

"What if he's not home?"

"He is. I heard his mother talking about it at the Ladies Aid."

Over the next thirty minutes Margie dolled Christine up and out of weakness, Christine let her. Her mother was right. What choice did she have? Was marrying Jack worse than walking around with the stigma of her condition? Was it worse than being sent away to a home? These questions were unanswerable. If she were honest with herself, she would have admitted that she found nothing redeeming about Jack. What about her reputation, though? Deep down inside she believed her child should have a chance at a real father. Christine wasn't confident her mother knew what she was talking about, but it was all she had to go on.

By the time she looked in the mirror through her glasses she wasn't sure who she was looking at. She started pulling pins from her hair. She rolled her hair the way she liked it and rubbed off half the red her mother had painted her lips with.

"Well, I'm not sure you should look so plain to see Jack, but there's no time to do anything more about it." Margie sighed. "Now, I want you to go down to his house, and you let him see how pretty you are. If he liked you enough to kiss you and — well, you know — then I know you know how to use your womanly wiles on a man."

Christine nodded, feeling comforted that her mother was taking charge. Maybe she wouldn't have to deal with this alone.

Christine walked down the sidewalk with her arms wrapped around her. She was thankful for the chill in the air. It helped push away the fog that remained in her head, despite the effects of the barbital being gone. She was near the bus stop when she heard the slight squeal of brakes sound behind her.

"Christy."

She turned, surprised to hear her mother's voice.

"I couldn't let you do this alone. Come on. Let's go together."

Her mother chattered the entire drive through downtown Poughkeepsie. Christine was too nervous to talk. She prayed the entire way that Jack was home and not at Columbia. That way she could get this over with. She admitted to herself that she hadn't prayed much over the past few months. Partly she was angry that God had let it all happen but mostly she was embarrassed to ask for anything after her behavior. But this was different. God knew she needed to talk to Jack. This could change everything.

They parked the car and without a word

found the Delano house. They stood in front of the concrete steps leading to the front door and their eyes trailed all the way up the red-brick, ornate row house.

"Just think, you could be living the high life, Christy," her mother said.

"Don't sound so giddy about it."

"I'm sorry, darling. I just am trying to look on the bright side." Margie went up the stairs without waiting for Christine's response.

Christine's mother was right. The Delano home was beautiful. From the lead and stained glass around the double doors in the front, to the peaked tower at the top — everything looked expensive. Heavy drapery hung around the windows that reminded Christine of the Hollywood pictures.

She slowly climbed the stairs after her mother and, with some prodding, found the courage to use the doorknocker.

"Yes?" An older woman opened the door. She wore a black-and-white uniform and sour expression on her face.

"Is Jack home?" Christine was breathless.

"Yes, ma'am," the maid opened the door wider and let her in. "Wait here and I'll get him. Whom may I say is here?"

"Christine — Christine Freeman."

"And Mrs. Freeman," Margie interjected.

"I'm her mother."

The maid nodded and as she left the foyer Christine saw Jack come down the wide staircase in front of her.

"Christine?" Jack looked confused, but he smiled. "Mrs. Freeman."

"Hello, Jack." Margie approached him with an outstretched hand. He took it gently and nodded, but his eyes were on Christine the entire time.

"Hi, Jack," she said, squaring her shoulders toward him.

"Can I take your coats?" he offered.

How was it possible that he was such a gentleman after what had happened between them? Maybe she was wrong. Maybe that night he wasn't who he really was — maybe this was who he was. Maybe he'd just had too much to drink. Maybe it was just because of how upset he was over Sandy's rumors.

The moment she shook her head no she wished she'd said yes. In her nervousness she had begun sweating. She cleared her throat. "I needed to talk with you."

Christine's voice came out harsher than she planned. Her mother's elbow poked into her side. When Jack turned away toward the maid, Christine looked at her mother.

She gave Christine the look that she'd

remembered since grade school. Yes, *be nice,* she reminded herself.

"Mrs. Burns," he said as he walked over to a door that swung both ways, "please, bring tea into the parlor for me and my guests."

Jack returned to them and led them to an ornately decorated room with windows facing the street. Everything was a mauve velvet and brass. She'd hardly seen anything like it in real life. Christine wasn't sure where to sit.

He gestured at a wingback chair and offered again to take her coat. This time she let him, still feeling overheated. His hand brushed her shoulder and she shuddered. How could she expect to marry a man she didn't want touching her, even in a gentlemanly way? Margie was looking out the window, saying something about the view, when Jack's breath was warm against Christine's ear. The heat of his breath on her skin brought more of a chill to her body than the February breeze.

"You look very pretty," he whispered.

Jack pulled away as Margie turned.

"What a beautiful room, Jack." Margie touched the velvet and silk drape. "Really, it's quite breathtaking."

Christine prayed that her mother would

stop but instead she went on and on about everything she loved about the parlor and house. She was glad when the maid came in with tea and interrupted her mother's nervous chatter.

"Oh, how nice." Christine's mother sat at the edge of a wingback chair as if she were waiting to be served. When the maid left she cleared her throat and served herself. Jack and Christine sat down stiffly on the davenport with a wide space between them. All that could be heard for several long minutes were the clinking of spoons stirring sugar cubes into what smelled like peppermint tea.

"So, what did you need to talk about?" Jack broke the silence.

"It's about the night you drove me home." It sounded funny to say it like that to him when he knew better than anyone what had happened in the car was far more than just a drive home.

Jack cleared his throat and put his tea cup down. He smiled at Christine's mother and nodded.

"It was really nice of you to —" Margie spoke up.

"Ma," Christine said. "Maybe you could wait out in the foyer for a few minutes?"

Margie lifted her chin, miffed, but honored her daughter's request. Neither Christine nor Jack spoke until the parlor door shut behind Margie.

"Listen, Christine, it wasn't the way things should've gone. I didn't think you'd still be upset about it."

"Still upset?" Christine set her tea cup down too harshly and the hot liquid scalded her skin. She winced.

"Here, let me," Jack said and scooted over to her. He took her hand lightly and dabbed her hand dry with a rich-looking burgundy linen napkin.

Christine was amazed by his gentleness. She looked down at her hand in his. They didn't even look like the same hands that had hurt her but they were. She pulled them away from him. His touch made it harder for her to talk with him with clarity.

"Christine, don't do that."

"Jack, I just came because we really need to talk." She put her hands in her lap and looked at him. His eyes were as brooding and handsome as they ever were.

"I sent you flowers. You didn't write me and I didn't even see you at church. I figured you weren't interested."

"I wasn't — I'm not — I mean." She stopped and shook her head before she started again. "It's not that simple."

Christine looked up at him. Her hands were clasped so tightly together that her fingernails dug into her skin. She hesitated for several long moments, considering what her mother had said about her womanly wiles. Was she supposed to seduce him or cry all over him to gain his sympathy before she told him? In a few seconds she considered all of this but decided she had to just come out and say it. "I'm pregnant."

Jack's head tilted at her and he cleared his throat. He leaned back in the couch and wiped a hand over his face.

"And you think it's mine?" He smiled.

She nodded.

"I've never —" she inhaled, "— with anyone else. You were the first — only — man I . . ."

Jack stood. "How do I know that's even true? You didn't seem so innocent to me that night with the way you downed the beer and how you, well, everything else. If I remember right, you kissed me first when we stopped the second time."

Everything he said was true. She couldn't deny it. Her eyes went down to her wringing hands before she gathered the courage to speak again.

"All I can tell you is that I know this baby is yours. It's impossible for it to be any other

221

man's. I thought you should know so we can discuss what should be done." It wasn't that she expected him to bend down on a knee and propose marriage to her. Even if he did, she would have great difficulty ever trusting him. But the truth that she'd driven him to it pricked her heart. She would have to say yes and would have to find a way to make this work. It was her fault this happened.

"You're not suggesting we get married, are you?" He began chuckling in a way that clearly explained how unlikely he thought this was. "You can't really mean that, right? We aren't the same, you know."

Again, he was right. How could she refute that?

"Who have you told?" He stood and began pacing.

Christine released a heavy sigh. She wasn't going to entertain his question.

"All I know is that because you are the baby's father, I knew I needed to at least tell you. I thought that maybe —"

"What? Maybe you could get some money out of me? Is that what you want? You and your family are so poor this is how far you're willing to go to get money?" He pulled a wad of money out of his pocket and threw it at her. Bills fell everywhere.

"It has nothing to do with money." She was getting angry. She stood and grabbed her coat. "I just thought you'd want to know that you're going to be a father, that's all."

"Right. You know, you should go down to the slums and let a dirty doctor take that baby out. If it were mine, and it's not, that's all I'd give you money for."

"I would never do that. You're sick!" she was yelling now. "You know that. You're sick."

"Jack, dear." Margie flung the door open and reentered the parlor. She walked up to him and laced her arm through his. Though he didn't welcome it he didn't push her away either. She led him to the couch to sit and sat next to him. Christine was stunned into silence.

"Mrs. Freeman, I don't know what Christine said to you, but —"

"My daughter told me that both of you made some poor decisions that night." She patted his hand and then put her own hands in her lap. "You've always been an upstanding young man, Jack. I know your mother has done a lot for our community and for our church. She just loves to go on and on about how well you're doing in school and how your grandfather has a great job waiting for you."

"Mrs. Freeman, I —"

"Now, I'm sure that you —"

"Mrs. Freeman," Jack said loudly and stood.

Her mother stood also.

"I can't marry your daughter." He looked into Christine's eyes.

"And why not?" Christine could hear her mother's confidence waning.

"I'm already engaged to be married. Besides, it's probably not even mine."

Margie gasped. Christine's knees were weak.

Margie tried to speak, only her mouth gaped open without a sound. Christine grabbed her arm.

"Come on, Ma," Christine said, then looked at Jack. "We'll let ourselves out."

Her mother resisted for several steps but Christine didn't relent. As they left the parlor she looked back and her eyes found Jack's. The arrogance in his eyes reminded her that he wasn't the gentleman that he pretended to be.

Her mother was shaken up and barely able to drive home. The skin over her knuckles tightened as she gripped the steering wheel. Occasionally she mumbled something Christine couldn't understand. Christine looked out the window. As she watched everything pass her by lonesomeness consumed her. This was her life.

CHAPTER 14

Christine returned to the hospital after the failure with Jack. Margie was still in shock when she said good-bye. Christine slept fitfully that night and packed all of her things on Sunday while giving Jeanne the news about her mother and Jack. Monday morning she put her uniform on as always and didn't make eye contact with anyone as she walked to Mrs. Phancock's office. The damp weather crept through the hazy windows and moved inside of her, chilling her, making her shiver. She clasped her hands together, hoping to stay her trembling. Her hand touched the doorknob and turned it quietly. When she stepped inside she imagined her lips going from red to a sick pink and her rosy cheeks becoming gray. Nurse Phancock and Nurse Minton stood at her entrance.

A sympathetic smile crossed over Phancock's face. She had always been a fair administrator, but none of this would be pleasant for either of them. Nurse Minton, on the other hand, had always been difficult to work with. Christine didn't know why she had to be involved with this. She wasn't her superior on the ward, only more experienced.

"Hello, Nurse Freeman," the older woman said. "You may sit down if you like, but this meeting should be brief."

Christine pushed her glasses up. She repeated the movement a few moments later. She was sweating.

"It's so unfortunate that we are meeting today. You were such a conscientious student and you're doing well as a young nurse. We hate to lose you." Nurse Phancock's voice reminded her of rolling hills. The tempo of her speech even seemed to stop on the top of the hill before sliding downhill again.

Despite the head nurse's friendliness, her heart pounded and her lungs began burning. She realized she was holding her breath. She tried to let it out evenly.

Nurse Phancock's hands shook when she picked up a clipboard. Her eyes scanned it.

"Is it true what Dr. Norton reports to us?" Her voice went almost breathless.

"Nurse Freeman?" Nurse Minton pressed, her eyebrow lifting high into her forehead.

"I'm sorry." Her voice wavered. She looked at the carpet beneath her feet. It was flat and a dingy shade of navy blue. She wanted to sink through the floor. She didn't lift her head when she finally spoke. "Yes, I'm sorry to say that it's all true."

"Excuse me? Please speak up." Nurse Minton's clipped words were loud in the small office.

"It's true." She raised her voice a degree and cleared her throat. She lifted her head for a moment, then lowered her eyes back down.

"I still can't hear you." Nurse Minton's mouth was tight as she spoke.

Nurse Phancock put a hand up to quiet the other nurse. Minton closed her mouth and tucked her chin back.

"Nurse Freeman, I know you are aware that this is unacceptable." Her voice was kind, yet firm.

"Yes, I —" Christine began.

"She's a loose woman." Minton's thin lips were so pinched Christine wondered if they would stay that way. "And her condition speaks volumes of her character."

"Ms. Minton, Christine is a skilled and capable nurse. The staff and patients speak highly of her. She has nothing else negative in her file. I have no complaints."

Minton's jaw dropped and her mouth stayed wide and open as the head nurse spoke.

"Nurse Phancock, you would defend a woman like this?"

"Carol, for goodness' sake, will you cool down? She doesn't have to explain anything to us." She looked from the older nurse to Christine.

Hmph. Minton raised her nose, glared at Christine, and walked out, fairly slamming the door.

Nurse Phancock tilted her head as she smiled at the young nurse. She walked over to her and took her hands and led her to sit across from her at the two chairs in front of the desk.

"Christine, dear, do you need someone to talk to?"

The warm, soft hands against her own made Christine break down. After a minute Christine pulled a handkerchief out and wiped her eyes. She took several long breaths and thanked Nurse Phancock.

"I told him no and he didn't listen. I'd flirted with him and led him on. I know it's my fault," she spoke into the head nurse's friendly eyes. They curved downward a few moments after she spoke.

"Oh, that's hogwash. It's not your fault."

She was the first person who had said this.

"But, I let him kiss me and touch me and —"

"Did your mother tell you that men can't handle hearing *no* or that they can't control their *needs*?"

She nodded.

"Last I heard there was nowhere in the Bible that says that men can't control themselves. It does say that a man should respect a woman."

She looked over at the administrator. "You sound like a feminist."

Nurse Phancock's eyebrow lifted. "Maybe I am."

The older woman paused for a moment, then patted Christine's knee and spoke. "You know, I've been almost exactly where you are, only I was seventeen."

"You were? What did you do?"

"The only thing I could do. My parents sent me away and told everyone I was with my great aunt in Ohio."

"You weren't in Ohio?"

"No, I was in Ohio, but I didn't have a great aunt out there. I was at a home for girls who were *in trouble.* I was seventeen and pregnant and I gave birth to a beautiful baby girl and never got to hold her. The nurse wouldn't even let me see her before

230

my baby's new family took her immediately. I still don't know what color her eyes were or if she has my curly hair or crooked nose." She smiled as she sighed. "I don't even know if she's still alive."

"I don't know what to say."

Christine could see in Mrs. Phancock's eyes that she was reliving those moments years ago. The older woman stood and took several steps away and cleared her throat. When she turned back her eyes were glassy.

"My heart tells me that Sarah's okay."

"Sarah?"

"I heard the new mother call her that when she cradled her. I was glad she had such a pretty name."

The women paused for a long moment. Only the ticking of the clock could be heard. Christine's hands moved to her abdomen. Even though she wasn't sure she loved the baby that was growing inside her, the thought of someone just taking the baby away from her the moment it was born didn't sound quite right either.

"Where will you go? I'm sorry to say the powers that be here at Hudson River want you out by tomorrow night."

Christine nodded then shrugged. "My ma insisted I tell the father, hoping he would marry me — not that I actually want to marry him."

"What did he say?"

"He's engaged to be married." She paused. "My ma has already brought up sending me to a home."

"Don't let her send you to one. Don't let someone take this baby from you." Mrs. Phancock squeezed Christine's arms.

"But I can't raise a baby on my own. I don't know what I'm going to do. I have nowhere else to go."

Christine hibernated behind her locked door for the day, not wanting to see anyone. Maybe they didn't know yet. But if they did know, would they shun her or console her? Nurse Phancock's words had been a comfort, but she had less faith in the average person she worked with. Millicent. Gussie. Eli.

It was past dusk when she decided to take a walk along the perimeter of the grounds. No one would be out there and she needed the fresh air in her face. She walked far enough away that the massive Kirkbride building was no longer visible. The wind stirred around her and she closed her eyes. Her heart told her to pray. Her pastor had always told his congregants that God was everywhere. He was there now, in the looming gray sky, in the air she breathed, in the wind. Supposedly God surrounded her, kept her, and loved her. She'd believed this her entire life. Her heart knew that it was still true even now. Christine wanted to embrace it and throw herself at His mercy, but her mind fought it. Her sensibilities told her otherwise.

Where was He when Jack pinned her down? Had He heard her tell him to stop? She shook her head and couldn't think beyond her grief over the death of her career. She stopped walking and wished the wind would pick her up and take her away. But instead her body stood like a fixture, solid and cold. Had she always been chiseled from stone? Had she ever been warm and soft? A flicker of lightning brightened the skyline ahead of her, and when she didn't react she wished she had. Nothing moved her anymore, except when she heard a soft voice behind her. Eli? Yes, she had not the least idea why, but his nearness moved her.

"Christine?" Eli touched her arm then immediately took off his coat and wrapped it around her. Her coat looked thin and she was shivering.

She turned around and their eyes locked.

"Where have you been? The ward is going wild without you. The patients keep asking for you and — well — nothing is the same." Eli spoke urgently and walked her over to a bench near a small clearing beyond the gardens.

Eli could see that she'd been crying, but for the moment her eyes were dry. He wanted to be patient. He'd heard rumors that she'd stolen drugs from the patients, but he couldn't imagine why. Another rumor was that she was expecting a baby, when he'd never even heard her mention so much as a boyfriend. The worst one was the rumor that said the baby was fathered by one of the patients. Disgusting. He didn't believe any of them, but he knew something was wrong. He'd only seen glimpses of her usual self in so many weeks.

"I thought there would be plenty of rumors by now."

"I don't believe them." With each of the rumors came a judgment on her character. He would not believe what Minton said about her. Even Rodney had started spreading things.

"You shouldn't have so much faith in me." She looked away, far beyond the horizon that spanned the distance. "Why are you out here?"

He rocked forward. If he wanted the truth from her, he should tell her the truth.

"I saw you," he admitted with a grin. "My window faces the hill down from Kirkbride and I saw you walking down. I wanted to talk to you before we left, and I didn't know if you'd be back on the ward."

She nodded but didn't say anything right away.

"I won't be back," she confirmed. "So, you're leaving in a few days, right?"

"Little more than a week." He nodded.

"You're going home." Christine smiled at him and then looked away again.

"Home," he repeated.

Home. The word spun around his head. The big white farmhouse came to mind. It all flooded back: the red barns and fields dotted with Holstein cows and the routine of milking and managing a dairy farm. An eagerness suddenly washed over him. Working in the farm air and the sun instead of in the hospital where everything they breathed was medicated and putrid. Yes, he was ready to go home, though his job here was rewarding at times.

His eyes roamed the curves of her face. Her cheekbones were high. She had small rosebud lips above a petite chin. Her top lip folded slightly over the bottom, giving her a gentle pucker. She looked smart in her glasses, and they brought more attention to the depth of her brown eyes. The girls in his community didn't wear makeup, but he'd grown used to seeing the English women wearing it and liked it. She was beautiful and different from any girl he'd ever met.

Christine turned to face him. For a moment their gaze connected and they were lost together.

"Where did you go?"

"What?"

"You just looked like you were somewhere else." He smiled at her.

Her eyes left his and roamed the dead lawn ahead of them. She sighed. "I'm envious of you. Every time you say the word *home* I can almost see those green rolling pastures and smell those famous Amish pies."

"Are you making fun of me?" Eli nudged her. He was cold, but more than that he was glad she was wearing his coat. It ballooned around her. She gave him a small smile.

"No," she said, releasing a chuckle. "It's just that it's obvious how much you love your home."

"You don't?"

"I do. But I don't know if it's really home

236

anymore. Too many things have changed. First my brothers were killed and now . . ." She didn't finish.

What was on the other side of her words?

"I'm not sure I can go home anymore. I was fired today, you know. Has that rumor made it through the ward yet?"

He'd heard this, so he was able to keep any shock from his face.

"I heard."

"Do you know why?" Her eyes grew desperate.

"It doesn't matter. I know who you are well enough. You're a fine nurse and an even better woman."

"But you don't really know," she pressed. "If you did . . ."

Eli shook his head. "All I know is what you're telling me." He paused. "If it's true that you can't go home, then come home with me."

What had he just said? He couldn't bring an English girl home, no matter who she was or how much trouble she was in. He would never regain his reputation if Christine walked off the bus with him.

"What did you say?" She snorted the words and shook her head. "Eli, you don't know what you're saying. I can't go home with you. Be serious."

Eli smiled at her and he considered just how serious he was. If he wanted to retract his invitation, now was the time. He watched as she pushed up her glasses. She was nervous. She'd done it often when they first started working together. It had stopped at some point, but he couldn't recall when. But here she was doing it again.

"I'm not joking." His heart pounded. He was serious, wasn't he? "My home would be a perfect place for you to figure out what's next. Besides, my mom would love to get a hold of you and fill you full of pie."

"Now I know you're joking. Eli, think clearly here. Your parents wouldn't mind their good son returning home after such a long time away with a girl like me? I'd have two strikes against me right from the start."

"It wouldn't have to be for long. Just until you're ready to go back home." He couldn't help but release a short chuckle, imagining her actually going home with him, meeting his family, and roaming the same countryside he knew like the back of his hand.

She stood and he followed. They faced each other. She opened her mouth to talk but nothing came out for several moments.

"I'm not some stray dog that would just follow you home. This is my real life, Eli, and you don't even know why I have to leave. If you did you'd take back your ridiculous invitation."

Eli was disappointed that she didn't see his sincerity. He used to be able to say whatever he wanted, sincerely or not, and girls would believe him. Christine was different though. She was strong-minded and even though it infuriated him it made him want to be around her all the more.

"I just want to help." He took a step toward her and started raising his hand to touch her, then pulled it back. Should he tell her how much he really cared? His heart plunged into his stomach. What was this feeling? Fear? Nervousness? Girls had never made him nervous, but Christine did.

"It would never work. I'm not going to talk about this." She began walking away.

"Christine, please. Don't go." Eli reached for her, gathering a handful of his coat in his hand. She let his insistence stop her and turned. Her brow furrowed. There was something in her expression that was so familiar. He'd seen that look of hurt too often. Usually he'd caused it.

"Let me go, Eli." She wouldn't look at him. He wanted to pull harder but the voice inside him said not to. Was it God talking to him? When his hand didn't let go of the coat sleeve, the nudge from the voice inside him turned into a holler in his ears. He almost wondered if she heard it, too.

"Why won't you let me help you?" His voice was a raspy whisper in his ears, suddenly filled with emotion.

"I'm pregnant, Eli. I'm going to have a baby. I'm not the woman you think I am. And that's not all of it. I stole barbital, too. It's all true. Do you really want to take a girl like me home to your parents?"

Their eyes locked. His heart wilted, leaving pieces like petals falling into the grass at his feet. He let go of the coat and it pained him to take a step back. Christine turned from him and walked away.

CHAPTER 15

"Have you heard from your folks since you let them know you were coming home?" DeWayne asked Eli as they sat to eat their supper.

"*Ja,* got a letter this week. I think they are chippin' the mud off my farm boots right now." He meant it to be funny but it came out with a bitter bite. It had only been an hour since his talk with Christine and he couldn't get used to the idea that some of the rumors he'd heard were actually true. He stuffed his mouth full of too-salty potatoes. He *would* look forward to his mother's cooking.

"I thought you'd be excited. You've said how this time in CPS has made you realize how much you believe in your church and your future in it. You said yourself you were ready to settle down and give up your *vildeh veyah.*"

Eli grimaced. DeWayne was right. "Yes, I

do plan to give up my wild ways."

"Your words, buddy."

The two ate in silence for several minutes until Freddy bounded up and sat down with his usual energy. He stuffed a few mouthfuls of potatoes in his mouth, his eyes wide with excitement. While he was still chewing he started talking.

"Did you hear about Nurse Freeman? Whoa! The attendant that pulled her out of her apartment said she looked drugged. I just never took her as that kind of woman. The rumors are actually true."

Eli put his finger in Freddy's face. "Don't you say another word about her, Freddy Ens. You don't know what you're talking about."

The others around them looked over. His eyes glanced over several of them before returning to Freddy's shocked round eyes. He bit the sides of his cheeks to keep himself from saying something he thought he might regret. He stuffed a few more bites of food in his mouth before he let himself talk.

"Christine is not that kind of woman," he said in a raspy whisper. His eyes darted around them, not wanting others to hear him.

"Eli, she got herself in trouble. What do

you call women like that?" Freddy didn't seem to care that Eli was upset.

"We all know Christine's an excellent and respected nurse and none of us know the whole story. Everyone should just leave her alone. She doesn't deserve our judgment."

"You need to leave her be, Eli. You're getting too wrapped up." DeWayne put a hand on Eli's arm.

"I can't leave her alone, DeWayne. I just can't." Eli shook his arm away. He knew he needed to calm down before his temper got the better of him, but he was too frustrated over the news about Christine. "I asked her to come home with me."

"You did what?" Freddy's voice screeched.

"Sis net wah." DeWayne couldn't believe what he was hearing. "She's not your responsibility." DeWayne leaned in closer to him; the other people around them looked over again.

"You don't know the whole story." Neither did he, for that matter. He was self-righteous in condemning his friends for their judgment when he'd done the same thing the moment she'd told him about the baby and the barbital.

There were a few beats of silence between the three men. DeWayne and Freddy eyed each other.

"Are you the father?" Freddy always did ask questions without thinking.

"What? How could you even ask that?" Eli scowled.

Freddy and DeWayne's eyes met. Eli let out a hefty sigh.

"Look, Christine already said no to me, but I still believe that she needs help, not judgment — from anyone." He was talking to himself as much as his friends.

"Why does it have to be from you? We're leaving in a little over a week — you're going home, buddy. You said yourself that it's time you find a little woman to marry and settle down — make up for your mistakes before you were drafted. How can you do that if you take an English woman who is going to have a baby home with you? Everyone will just believe it's yours."

Eli didn't have an answer. He got up and walked out, leaving his food and his friends behind.

April 2, 1946

Dear Eli,

Blessings in our Holy God's Name.

The weather is getting prettier by the day. The buds are growing and the spring rain isn't so bad. We're even getting into the sixties already. Wedding season is here. We've already had one.

It's all over church that you're coming home. I can hardly believe it. I feel like you've been gone forever. I thought maybe you'd have written to me to tell me, but I suppose you wanted it all to be a big surprise. Mother often tells me that boys don't write so much as girls. It'll be nice to talk with you soon instead of writing, and see you at the Singings.

What day are you coming in? I was going to check with your mother to see if I could ride with them to the station to pick you up. Maybe I'll make sure to have a few cherry pies waiting for you.

Oh, I meant to tell you in my last letter, but I think you'll be happy to hear that your brother Mark and Syl's burned house and land sold to some Englisher. I guess he's going to tear it down and put up a corner store. Can you believe that? Your dad parceled out some of his land for them to buy and rebuild. Thought it would be easier since he's so involved with the farm. It's the lot of land with that big oak tree that we all used to climb when we were children and church was at your house. They will start building this spring. You'll be here just in time.

Sincerely yours,
Matilda

Eli crumpled up the letter and threw it against the wall in his room. How could his father have done that? He had promised Eli the parcel of land with the oak tree. He was the oldest son and had planned on taking over the farm. Now Mark was stepping in and taking away his future. Maybe he should just stay away. Maybe he shouldn't go home. He could go back to Iowa with DeWayne. He could be a Mennonite easily enough. He could farm or do carpentry. He paused. He could work with a doctor as an attendant. He was good at his job.

And Matilda. He had to deal with her, also. He had every intention of writing her to remind her that they were not a steady couple, but he'd put it off so long and now it hadn't gotten written. He would have to talk to her as soon as he arrived home. Home without Christine. He would probably never see her again.

He slouched down on his bed and rested his elbows on his knees. Instinctively his head went into his hands. Now, when he finally had the motivation to return home and get his life back in order and stop his immature ways, everything was caving in. He didn't want to leave Christine. He knew returning home with her could be the worst decision he'd ever made. But did it matter since everything else was going wrong? His father had just sold his parcel of land to his brother. Learning this made him want to throw all of his respectable intentions away.

God, why? I thought things were going to be better when I got home. Just when I thought my life was getting on track . . .

CHAPTER 16

For the rest of the day Christine remained in her room, waiting for Byron and Jeanne to drive her out to her parents' home with all of her belongings after their shift ended. She replayed the conversation with Eli. She had seen his compassion in the warmth in his eyes and in the way his head tilted as he smiled at her.

Her door pounded and she heard Jeanne's familiar voice on the other side. She'd refused to open the door for anyone else. She opened the door just wide enough for her small friend to fit through.

As they were preparing to go Jeanne pointed at Eli's coat.

"Whose coat is that?"

"Eli's," she said. "I saw him yesterday when I went for a walk. I told him."

"You told one of the C.O.'s?"

"We've become friends." Admitting this settled the fact in her heart. "I trust him."

Jeanne nodded. "He's the handsome Amish one, right?"

Christine couldn't help but smile. "Yes, Jeanne, that one."

"But, really, why did you tell him? It doesn't seem like something very proper to talk about."

"Proper? I'm pregnant and unmarried, Jeanne. I don't think I'll ever be proper again."

"So you're keeping the baby? Even after Jack . . . Do you think he'll change his mind?"

"I'm not sure it matters. I don't know if I could after everything. He told me to have an abortion."

Christine and Jeanne were silent for a moment.

"Eli asked me to go home with him. He said that his community would take care of me."

Jeanne turned to face Christine. "What?"

"It was really before he knew I was pregnant. I think the invitation was retracted once he learned the rumors were true. I think he had more of a short break in mind, not hiding a pregnant woman."

"So, what will you do?"

"My ma has some unwed mothers' home she wants me to go to." She thought of Mrs.

Phancock's story about when this happened to her and winced. "I'll just stay at my parents' house as long as possible. Then maybe find a boarding house."

"No one is going to board or lease an apartment to you. You know how people feel about these situations. They'd never lease or give room and board to an unmarried woman expecting a baby. I wish I had a house. I'd let you live with me. I'd take care of you and your baby."

Christine swallowed the lump in her throat while she forced a smile. Jeanne was right about the apartment. She also knew that if Jeanne could, she'd take her in for the rest of her life.

"Maybe you should take Eli up on his offer. Surely it wouldn't be worse than a boarding house." Jeanne chuckled cheerfully before fading away with a sigh.

Christine smiled. Jeanne's reaction was correct. The thought was nearly laughable, only she was too burdened to laugh about it. She'd seen his eyes when she said she was pregnant. Disbelief. Disappointment. He would never want her near his family in her condition.

The last of her things were taken down to the parking lot and Christine was alone.

She stood in her room and breathed a last

sigh. Her hand went to her abdomen. She wasn't ready to be a mother. She wasn't ready to not be a nurse. She swallowed hard in order not to cry. It was time to go. She grabbed Eli's coat from the bed and caught a glimpse of an envelope in the inside pocket. Instead of stuffing it further into the pocket, she pulled it out. Curiosity suddenly overtook her.

March 20, 1946

Dear Eli,

Praise be to the Lord. He is good to us.

We are having a beautiful spring. You are going to be returning to such a busy time. We are happy that your service is finished in only a few weeks. Life can return to normal when you come home. Dad sure is ready for your help again.

Just let us know when you'll be arriving. We'll pick you up in the open buggy unless it's raining. Of course, in order for everyone to come your brothers will have to drive their buggies also. We'll look like a buggy parade going through town. Won't that be something? I might leave the girls home though. Sylvia or Aunt Annie can take care of them.

Matilda wants to come, too. I told her it was fine. I can see she's excited to have you back as well. She has really been faithful in writing you.

Christine stopped reading. She shouldn't have read that much. She put the folded letter back in the envelope and stuffed it back into the coat. The coat appeared worn but it was well made. She'd never sewn anything in her life, but it was clear that the coat was hand sewn. The dark denim was plain but very warm. Without thinking, she brought the quilted coat up to her nose and breathed it in. A light scent of aftershave lingered. Had Matilda done the same thing when Eli left — try to memorize Eli's scent? It reminded her of the way her mother hadn't moved or washed anything after her brothers left for war. Why hadn't Eli ever mentioned to her that he had a girl waiting back home for him? Why did that bother her?

Once she left the Kirkbride building she took in the view of the misty morning. The sun was bright and shining and it seemed spring had arrived overnight. There were buds on the trees. A light chirping of birds chorused around her. This beauty conflicted with the storm inside. Her ward in Edgewood stood beyond in the distance. How were they getting on? She wouldn't even be a passing memory in the minds of the patients whom she'd cared for.

Byron was leaning against his light-blue Chevrolet when she got down to the parking lot. He had his arm around Jeanne's waist. The two looked so nice together and they looked as young as a high school couple. His sandy hair slicked back, he was wearing a waist coat unzipped halfway, and she had a ponytail and a wide skirt. Their happiness pleased her and brought a wave of sorrow.

Christine told them it would take but a moment to return Eli's coat. She tried to step quickly as she walked through the courtyard and down the back section of the lawn to the C.O. boarding house.

"You need someone?" one of the young men asked, opening a nearby door.

"Eli Brenneman."

A few minutes later he opened the door. His large build filled up the doorframe. His eyes landed on her quickly and he trotted out to her. His mouth angled in the grin she'd grown so accustomed to. Her heart thudded in his presence; she was sad to say good-bye.

"Your coat." She handed it to him.

Eli took it, his eyes not leaving hers. "Hi," he said simply.

She nodded.

"So you're leaving." he said.

"So are you — soon," she reminded him.

"Won't you reconsider my offer?" His low voice was as soft as velvet.

His idea of her going with him to his Amish family just seemed impossible. She didn't really know anything about their community, but by the sounds of it, her going home with him could cause him a variety of problems. She wasn't Amish. She was pregnant. And what about the girl his mother mentioned in the letter, Matilda? Besides, her mother said she would figure everything out.

"Eli, I can't. You know that's a terrible idea."

"Why? I know my mother will know what to do. We wouldn't turn you out. You'd be safe with us."

"You make it sound so easy, but this is my problem," she said, her eyes leaving his. There was a sudden realization that her hands covered her abdomen; she dropped her arms. Her unconscious act of nurture toward the unborn child peeved her. Christine fiddled with her glasses. "Ma and I will figure things out. There are these homes where girls like me can go."

"Homes?"

She nodded. "They help you with — everything — and make sure the baby goes to a respectable home. A Christian family. That's all I know right now. My ma said she would figure something out."

"You want to give your baby away?"

"Do you know any women with children and no husband — and I don't mean widows?"

When he didn't respond she decided to drop the subject.

"I better go. Jeanne and Byron are waiting for me." She pointed a thumb over her shoulder.

"This is for you." Eli quickly handed her a folded piece of paper. She reluctantly took it but didn't open it. "I just want you to consider my invitation."

"And what about Matilda?" She lifted an eyebrow.

"Matilda?" he questioned. "How do you know anything about Matilda?"

She sighed heavily. "When I had your coat, I found a letter from your ma. I know I shouldn't have read it, but I did. When I came to my senses I put it away, so I didn't read all of it. Why didn't you tell me you had a girlfriend?"

Eli chuckled. "Are you jealous?" His chest puffed.

She put her hands on her hips. "No. But I am curious."

"She's not my girlfriend. But I still think you're jealous." His chuckle smoothed into a wide smile and he winked at her.

"I'm not jealous." Her eyes narrowed but couldn't resist the smile that played over her lips.

Eli exhaled. "The truth is that Matilda's just a friend who has been writing me while I was away. Nothing more."

"The truth?"

He raised his hands as if in defense. "Promise."

Her gaze lingered on him before she looked down at the piece of paper he gave her and read it to herself. It was his bus schedule.

"You have a few days to think about it," he said.

She looked at him and wished she could explain how much it meant to her that he cared. But the right words didn't come to her.

"Your hair's longer than usual," she pointed out.

His eyes looked up toward his hair. "I skipped my last haircut." He shrugged and met her eyes. "It's better for going home."

She nodded. Of course, he was Amish, she reminded herself.

"I hope you make it home safely, Eli. You've been an enjoyable attendant to work with — able and caring." She paused. "And certainly a good friend. I really mean that."

Eli took a step closer to her and put the palm of his hand on her shoulder. His thumb rubbed against the fabric of her dress, comforting her. His eyes were fast on hers — the usual clear blue appeared stormy, like the wind turning over the water of a placid lake. In that moment she could see that he cared deeply for her — too deeply. The thought frightened her and even though the warmth of his touch filled her soul, she stepped back, losing his touch.

He lowered his hand and cleared his throat.

"Just go home and move on with your life. Forget about me."

With that she handed the bus information back to him.

Only her first night home and Christine's mother had concocted a plan.

"Now, we are telling your father and Doris that you are going to be working out of state. You are home for a few days or a few weeks and then you'll be away for several months. Like a nurse exchange program. They won't know the difference."

Christine gave up. More lies. She sat with tea at the kitchen table when her mother came over with her cup and handed Christine some official-looking papers in her hand.

"Here," she said.

Christine took them and flipped through them. It was a two-page letter explaining the purpose and benefits of sending your daughter to a home for pregnant unwed girls. The name Stony Creek Ladies Home was in bold at the top. She glanced over them before looking back at her mother.

"Only a bus ride away, huh? Where do you even get this kind of information?" The weight of the two pages were heavy in her hands.

"If you look in the right places, you'll find them. I think it sounds quite nice. It's on a dairy farm where everyone works to keep the home running. Everyone has a job to do and they have nurses, doctors, and midwives there. You might enjoy it since you are a nurse. Did you see that you could learn to cook?" Her mother's face was so full of hope Christine hated to disappoint her.

"I just don't know," she said. She flipped

through the pages again. "I will read it over but I cannot promise you anything, Ma."

It just didn't feel right. For some reason she could not get Eli's ridiculous offer out of her head.

"I want you to really consider what I'm telling you. You know I love you but I have to think about the whole family," her mother began. "If you decide not to go to a home, you cannot just stay here. I cannot have our family gain a bad reputation, and it's not what I want for you. After all of this is through, the child will be with a nice family and you can return to your real life. There aren't enough people who know about this to make that impossible. You can work again or find a nice young man to settle down with. If you keep the baby — and I cannot understand how that would work — your life is over."

Her mother looked away and blinked rapidly, clearly to keep tears away.

"I know with Jack I may have seemed brave and strong." Her mother looked back and patted Christine's hand. "But you don't know how hard this is for me."

Christine took her mother's hand. "I'm so sorry, Ma."

"I just love you and want what's best, darling." The two held hands across the table but only Margie wept. Christine wasn't sure she had any more tears.

"I know you do." She let go of her mother's hands and looked at the Stony Creek letter again.

CHAPTER 17

The last week was the longest Eli had experienced. He said his good-byes to De-Wayne and Freddy at the hospital, as their busses were not leaving until later. As he sat alone at the bus station, he looked out toward the road. Even though Christine had given back his bus information, she had read it. Would Christine come? His heart waffled between wanting her to come, since he wasn't ready to let her go, and knowing that it would be easier for him to return without her.

He watched as several other C.O.'s stepped up onto the bus. They also still wore the hospital uniform, almost like soldiers who returned home wearing their uniforms. He knew his homecoming would be vastly different though. He just didn't want to travel in his Amish clothing. He had gotten used to blending in with the non-Amish. For the first time in his life, he had learned that sometimes it was good to go unnoticed.

Eli heard a woman's voice around the corner; she was talking to her children about being quiet on the bus. Several more people boarded. The bus driver came down from the bus and stood in the front. He looked at Eli. The man wore a nice smile and his eyebrows lifted when he spoke.

"Are ya comin'?"

"I'm waiting for someone," he said.

"I can only give you another minute, son," the driver said and then returned to the bus and sat down.

He looked up at the station clock. The second hand spun around. His shoulders got heavier with each passing moment. Though his life could get incredibly complicated if Christine did come home with him, and even though it might not have been a good idea for him to have even invited her, he wanted her to come. He had grown attached to her smile and kindness. She had great loyalty to her family and worked almost solely to serve them. He didn't know how she'd gotten into trouble, but he trusted her in a way he'd never trusted another woman before. Her strong opinions and independent ways sometimes got on his nerves, but as soon as they were apart, he wanted to be with her.

"Eli." A voice said behind him.

He turned. Like a dream, Christine stood there. She was bathed in the sun that snuck down between the building and the bus. She was wearing her hair back, like she had at the hospital, but fancier, somehow, and was wearing a beautiful yellow dress. Her lips were red and her cheeks pink. She was a vision of beauty.

"Help me with my trunk?" She shrugged her shoulders with a heavy sigh and a quiet smile. She held a bus ticket in her ivory crocheted-gloved hand. They didn't speak a word when the driver helped them with her luggage and they stepped onto the bus. Even as they sat on the hard, uncomfortable bus seats they didn't speak. Their arms touched lightly and after ten minutes of silence Christine spoke.

"Thank you, Eli." She took his hand and looked up at him.

He only smiled at her, unable to find words to express himself. Eli squeezed her hand in return just before she removed it and put it back in her lap, clasping her other hand. This reminded him that she wasn't his and that her coming brought great responsibility to both him and his family. And his journey had just begun.

It didn't take long before Poughkeepsie was in the distance behind them. Christine laid her head back on the bus seat in an effort to momentarily forget the hospital, forget Jack, and forget that she was still deciding on whether or not to go to one of the homes. She couldn't run away from the baby growing daily below her heart. A baby she still thought of as a medical diagnosis. The letter from the *maternity home* was folded neatly in her purse. After days of considering and remaining undecided, leaving with Eli temporarily seemed like the best option. It would give her time to decide what to do without the pressure of her hometown staring at her soon-to-be-growing abdomen.

Christine exhaled.

"Are you okay?"

Christine was startled to hear Eli's voice. She opened her eyes and looked right at him. He'd been so quiet since they sat on the bus, not having said more than, "This seat all right?"

"What?"

"You sighed and I was wondering if everything was okay."

264

She only nodded. Nothing she could think to say sounded right.

Eli gave her his crooked smile and she smiled back but returned her gaze to the passing fields and occasional small town. She wasn't sure how to answer him. No. Of course, everything was not okay. In a matter of a few weeks she had been found unconscious, fired from her job, realized she was pregnant, rejected by Jack, encouraged to go to a home by her mother, and then, at the last minute, decided to flee to an Amish community. It was odd and peculiar how she had gotten to this point. She shifted in her seat before her backside became numb. The bus was all but comfortable. The seats were stiff and her ears rang from the loud engine.

She turned back to Eli. He was looking down at a periodical in his hands — some dreadful pulp magazine. She thought about Wally and how he and Eli had become friends over reading those stories. She surveyed the cover: a soldier on a horse, his spear aimed at some shirtless man wearing war paint. Why would anyone read such rubbish? Especially a pacifist. Her eyes journeyed to his chiseled face and she could tell he hadn't shaved that morning. There was a subtle shade of blond covering his jawline. He swallowed and his Adam's apple bobbed. Eli's eyes peeked over at her and a smile crossed his lips.

"I'm sorry, I didn't mean to stare." She pushed her glasses up. "You actually like those magazines? I thought you read them only for the patients."

He shrugged. "I guess it passes the time."

"That cover looks awfully violent — I'm surprised your church lets you read fiction like that."

Eli raised a single eyebrow. "Are you baiting me?"

"I'm just curious. Why is it okay to read that garbage when you don't even believe in fighting?"

He looked away and inhaled. Christine had gotten to him. Though she hadn't meant to start something, she wasn't being very kind, challenging him the way she did. But it was a true curiosity. How could you stand up for what's right without fighting for yourself? How did the Amish expect to keep their way of life in the changing modern world without defending themselves? He didn't answer her but he didn't continue reading the pulp fiction magazine either. He folded it and stuffed it into the small bag at his feet.

As the morning crossed into afternoon

266

and neared supper-time they talked about everything impersonal. They talked about their patients, the weather, and where they had traveled to in their lives. Christine had learned that besides his CPS service, Eli had only been out of Delaware for funerals and weddings in Pennsylvania, Maryland, and Ohio. She told him how her father had done door-to-door sales for years, then factory work until his previously injured knee had gotten so bad he couldn't work.

"What will your family do now? Since you're not . . . ?" His words faded off.

Christine swallowed before she answered. "Doris has a job that pays some and I think my ma will have to take on sewing or baking. She did this off and on when I was a child for extra money. I'm not sure how she's going to explain it to her friends, but everyone knows my dad can't get a job with his handicap."

"What about your church?"

"What do you mean?"

"Won't they help your parents? That's what our church does. There's a fund the Amish have for those situations, when there's a family in need. We've helped pay for surgeries, build a new barn or house, or pay for travel when a church member needs to get across the country quickly for a family emergency. I'm surprised that your churches don't do the same."

"We support missionaries and send money to the hungry in Africa," Christine responded.

"But what about church members who are hungry?"

He made a good point and left the question unanswered. She was nervous and excited to meet this Amish church he spoke of. Was it as quaint and magical as he made it sound?

"I think, for a city girl, you'll enjoy the countryside. We don't have the same conveniences, but we don't need that much. We grow our food and try to be neighborly."

"It's not like I don't know about gardens, Eli. My ma had a garden for most of my life." She elbowed him.

He smiled at her out of the corner of his eye.

"You do have me curious though," she said. "What about stores? Do you go to grocery stores?"

"There's a small store a few miles away at Crossroads Corner. It doesn't have much, but it'll have some of the extras that we can't grow, bake, or can."

"And you ride a buggy out there?"

"*Drive* a buggy." Eli winked.

Christine smiled. "No radios?"

He shook his head.

"No telephones?"

He shook his head and pursed his lips. "Just the one at our neighbor's house." Was he stifling laughter?

She paused for a moment when a thought occurred to her. Where would she get clothing as she grew out of her own wardrobe? Her hands rested on her lap, close to the babe that grew inside her. The urge to press her gloved hands against her abdomen rushed through her like water over a cliff. Still she fought it. What would she wear once she grew too large for her regular clothes? Her cinched-waist dresses and skirts were not going to last long in her condition.

"What about clothes?" Her voice was quiet.

Several slow beats passed and Eli moved his hand over hers. He met her eyes and his gentle smile was like a gift.

"We'll figure it out."

Would they? She'd seen pictures of Amish women. If those were the kind of dresses that they would want her to wear, she would be better off at a maternity home.

Christine continued to listen to Eli as he told her about his five brothers and two sisters, who were twins. His one brother was married and living with his parents because their house had burned down. They had a big dairy farm.

At some point, Christine slept on and off for several hours. As the bus made stops and picked up and dropped off more passengers, she lost track of time. On several occasions she found her head resting comfortably on Eli's arm. Even when she woke and realized where her head was she pretended to sleep longer, relishing in the simplicity and comfort of the moment. When his body stiffened only moments later she sat up. Roadside signs pronounced that Dover was just ahead. They were nearly there.

The sun was starting to set when the bus finally stopped in Dover. Eli got up and walked down the aisle; when she didn't follow he stepped back and put his hand out to her. Their eyes met but no words were exchanged. Christine let go of his hand when she was safely on the concrete sidewalk at the bottom of the steep bus steps.

"There they are," Eli whispered. "There's my family."

Christine looked where his gaze landed and inhaled deeply. A woman was in the front of a small group of people. She wore a

270

heavy black shawl and bonnet. Below the shawl was the skirt of her navy dress, down to mid-calf. She wore stockings and black, sensible shoes; she walked quickly toward them. All of those details came in a short beat of her heart, but then her eyes landed on the woman's face. In the distance Christine could see that the woman had a furrowed brow. When her arms reached out toward them, she stepped faster, and her mouth began to quake. This was Eli's mother.

Eli broke his solid stance and made several great strides toward his mother. She wasn't short, but next to Eli she appeared small. He took her in his arms and the woman wept. Christine wiped tears from her own eyes. Her eyes scanned the rest of the crowd — it really was a crowd.

An older man stood with his chin up a smidgen more than Christine thought right. He had the same icy, clear eyes as Eli. His beard was nearly white and small tufts of hair could be seen beneath his wide-brimmed black hat. He nodded at her and she froze. The man's eyes returned to Eli and his mother's embrace. Christine was thankful. Near him stood Eli's brothers. The one who appeared to be the oldest of the brothers stood slightly behind the others.

His eyes were brooding. He was a slighter version of Eli, with subtly rounder features in his face. A young woman then walked from around the back and stood nearby with her eyes trained on Eli. She had large eyes and a perfectly rosy complexion. Her pretty face was stretched in gladness. She wore a similar dress to Eli's mother, though she was half her age.

Was it his brother's wife or was this Matilda? His *friend*.

A few moments later Eli and his mother separated and his father stepped toward them with an outstretched hand. There was one solid shake and a few claps on their forearms. The two men were equally large and their smiles mirrored each other's.

A deep, resonant voice escaped the older man and Christine couldn't understand the words. Each of the boys moved toward Eli and shook hands; all shared the same shy smile she'd seen on Eli the first few times they met. They all wore the same black hats in a variety of sizes just like their father. They all spoke, none of it English and none of it to her. Eli tipped the hat off the smallest boy; a messy mop of blond hair fell around the boy's forehead.

The little boy spoke and pointed at his mouth. He was missing teeth. Eli pretended to pull more out, sending the boy into a fit of laughter.

Neither the oldest brother, nor the young woman who stood with the unfaltering smile on her lips had approached Eli. Then, the small crowd parted and he walked with several strong strides with an arm out to his brother.

"Mark," he said.

At least names sounded the same in English and their language. What had he called it? Pennsylvania Dutch?

Eli's hand hung, waiting for several long moments before Mark uncrossed his arms and took his hand. Neither had a smile on their face and it was clear to her that Eli was on poor terms with his brother. The men released their hands and Eli turned toward the young woman.

"Matilda," he said nicely, though after working with him for a year Christine sensed something other than excitement in his tone.

"Eli," she started, and Christine couldn't understand anything else she said. Matilda's voice warbled and she appeared jittery as she blinked excessively. After they shook hands she wrung hers together. Eli spoke back and his words fell heavy in Christine's ears, unable to understand any of it. She suddenly realized that everyone else was watching her, while she watched Eli and Matilda. As she looked around at all the faces, her body heated and the dampness under her arms increased and stung. Christine pushed her glasses up.

Eli's conversation finished and he turned toward her and smiled. He walked to her and whispered.

"It's okay."

She nodded and tried to smile but when her lips shook, she stopped and pursed them instead.

"This is Christine Freeman. She's one of the nurses that I worked with, and —" he paused as if trying to find the right words, "I asked her to visit with us for a while."

Visit for a while. What did that even mean? She pushed up her glasses and made a second attempt at smiling.

"Hello," she said, her voice shaking. "I'm happy to meet all of you."

She realized after she spoke that she was talking loudly in broken syllables.

"They can understand English," Eli said. A smirk crossed his lips.

"Of course." She nodded, her nerves tightening further.

"Welcome, Christine," Eli's mother said and stepped toward her with her hand out.

"I'm Eli's mother."

"Nice to meet you, Mrs. Brenneman." Christine smiled and took the older woman's hand. Her arm jerked with the strong handshake.

"Please, call me Sarah. We are just simple people 'round here." The older lady smiled as she spoke, then stepped aside for the next person.

"I'm Eli's father, Mark David." He shook her hand in the same fashion.

"I'm David," a tall young man said, followed by Moses, Abe, and Enos. Each jerked her arm with a single shake. Christine's shoulder stung.

"I'm Mark," the second oldest son stepped forward. His shake was weak and when he met her eyes, she saw hate and bitterness.

Christine's lungs burned. She exhaled the breath she'd been holding. She turned toward Matilda and held out her hand. Matilda put a hand to her mouth and let out a single whimper and muttered something she didn't understand. She turned and walked back the way they came, only much quicker this time. Everyone stood and watched for several long moments.

"I think you've upset her, Eli. Not sure what you expected." Mark spoke in English. His accent was stronger than Eli's. He nodded his head toward Christine but his eyes were locked on Eli. "You bring your English girlfriend home for your Amish girlfriend to meet? You ain't changed a bit, have you?"

Mark looked over at Christine then back to Eli then turned on his heels and walked away.

"Christine's just a friend." Eli's voice was a fading whisper. "And so is Matilda." He faced his parents and repeated himself. He looked defeated.

Even if Christine could've found words to speak, she decided her silence was better than anything she could say.

A long stream of words came from Eli's father's mouth. He pulled at the shirt Eli wore that was clearly not like the shirts his father wore and gestured at Christine, but his eyes stayed on Eli. Eli spat his own words back. His mother splayed her hands out with her eyes darting between both father and son. Even though Christine couldn't understand her, it was clear she was trying to defuse the situation. This was all her fault. They were talking about her fate in another language. Everything was collapsing in front of her. The least they could do was speak English.

Christine wanted to tell them that she was leaving and go buy a bus ticket to anywhere else. It wasn't too late for her to go to the maternity home. Unfortunately, there was no reserve of courage left in her heart. She could only stand there, her mouth agape. Now what was she to do? Eli said that Matilda was only a friend, and she'd never known him to lie to her. It was clear, however, that Matilda was more than a friend, which meant he would have some explaining to do to both of them. He should never have invited her if he and Matilda were a couple.

Ever since she'd taken the time to get to know Eli she had wondered how a man like him could be unattached. He was handsome and so kind and easy to be around. He never met a stranger and always had a smile around the corners of his eyes, if not on his lips. Christine had grown so fond of him, but she was angry he put her in such a precarious position with Matilda. Even though they were supposedly only friends, he should have thought of how this would affect the girl who had clearly been waiting anxiously for his return. And, by the sounds of Mark's attitude toward him, Eli already had quite a reputation, and her presence was not helping.

The silence froze everyone for what seemed like an hour but really was only a few, long, uncomfortable moments.

"Well, Christine, let's go find you some-place to sleep tonight. I am sure you're tired after such a long journey." Sarah Brenne-man motioned for Christine to walk with her. Christine gave Eli a glance over her shoulder as she passed him. The farther away she was from him, the more her isola-tion grew. The brothers picked up their lug-gage and chattered in their language behind her.

Eli's father drove them back to their farmhouse in an open buggy with three benches. Eli said it was called a Dearborn. She sat next to Eli on the second bench while his parents occupied the front. They followed two other buggies, the black kind with the roof. No one spoke the entire drive and while it seemed to be such a slow way to get anywhere, the rocking movement relaxed her.

They passed farm after farm. The road ahead of them was so flat and the fields seemed endless. It was greener there than back in Poughkeepsie and Christine enjoyed breathing in the cool, spring air. The horses got them to the Brenneman farm just before sundown.

The rest of the evening was a blur. The large farmhouse, the red barns, and the way

Matilda ran off crying when they returned to the Brennemans'. Eli called Matilda's name but she did not stop. His face was labored with burdens. Still he wrapped his hands around Christine's waist and helped her down as if she weighed nothing more than a doll. When her feet landed on the ground their bodies were close and, for one simultaneous inhale and exhale, they didn't move.

"I don't think this was a good idea, Eli." He looked into her eyes for a brief moment before looking away. "Why didn't you tell me the truth about Matilda?"

"She's not my girlfriend." He inhaled and the veins in his forehead pushed against his skin. "She really is just a friend."

"Then why is she so upset?"

"Eli," his mother called. Again the rest of what she said was unknown. Christine looked at the woman on the porch of the large white farmhouse. Two little girls bounced around her. Both of them wore their hair tightly pulled back, one was blond and one was dark-haired. They wore plain blue dresses and no shoes.

"Come meet my baby sisters. I left when they were only about six months old and tomorrow they'll be two." His voice was excitable and his eyes bright. He didn't wait for her but ran up to the porch and put his hands out to his sisters.

Christine watched and while she couldn't understand the words he said his body language said it all. He was asking for a hug and the girls sucked on their lower lips and looked at each other before squealing and running away. Eli growled as he chased them down to the corner of the porch. After a few moments of more giggles and growls he came back with a girl over each shoulder. Their fat legs kicked as they laughed.

It was like the weight of the lines on his brow had vanished, and Eli looked happier than Christine had ever seen him.

CHAPTER 18

Eli's welcome wasn't exactly what he had imagined. Of course, his family was glad to see him. His mother held him for a long time, her grip as tight as it ever was. Her eyes looked older, however. Her hair had gone from a rich brown to nearly salt and pepper. She still looked healthy and merry, which he was glad about. His dad appeared slightly hunched, but his eyes were clear. His hair had been white for a while but his beard was longer than Eli remembered.

But the look on Christine's face said it all. She was lost. It wasn't just their language, but their entire culture. The way she looked at his mother's clothing and how she tucked in her chin as she took in the full view of his father's wide hat. His father was an imposing man. Everyone always mentioned how Eli and his father were so alike: white-blond, tall, broad, and thick. Naturally his parents were glad he was home; but Mark, on the other hand, could've done without him. He clearly was not impressed with his service or his return to the family.

Now they sat at the table preparing to eat their evening meal. Eli's eyes had to adjust to the dimly lit house after over a year of electric lights. To make Christine feel less uncomfortable he decided not to change into his usual Amish clothes. Besides, Mark and Sylvia were staying in his room. He didn't want to make Sylvia feel uncomfortable by going into the space she and his brother shared. It just didn't seem right to him. Sylvia helped his mother prepare their supper but hadn't said hello or even made eye contact with him. It was awkward that his most recent ex-girlfriend was now married to his brother. Then, with the confused circumstances with Matilda and Christine, there was part of him that wished he was still at Hudson River.

His mother and Sylvia brought all the food to the table then sat quietly at the table. His father put his hands on his lap as he bowed his head, closing his eyes. Eli followed suit except he didn't close his eyes. Christine sat next to him and he saw her look around before lowering her head also. He closed his eyes before he knew if she had.

Almost no one spoke during supper, except when Christine loudly commented *good gravy* when the spread was all laid out on the table. His brothers sniggered but no one else commented or spoke. Had it been this way while he'd been away? When would the healthy chatter return? This wasn't common for his family, who were usually always talkative at mealtimes. There was so much he wanted to talk about, so much he wanted to say, but he didn't want to bring more attention to Christine or to what his life had been like during his time away from the church. He wanted to explain that for the first time in his life he realized that not everything was about him. How in the gray halls of the hospital with patients like Wally, Floyd, and Gov he'd found himself. He'd learned that just as he wanted to be accepted as a conscientious objector he needed to value patients who no one else cared for. He wanted to show them that he was better than the person he was before his draft.

"Eli, did you hear what I said?" His mother repeated.

"What was that?"

"I was saying that I think Christine will be very comfortable with Aunt Annie."

Eli looked over at Christine, who held a

bite midway to her mouth. Their eyes connected. Her small ivory gloves lay next to her on the table and her dainty hat hung tilted over the back of the chair. A woman of her culture had never been in his family's home before.

"What?" Christine said when Eli didn't say anything for a suspended moment. There was an edge to her voice that spurred him to speak.

Eli cleared his throat.

"Aunt Annie lives just across the field." He pointed with his fork ahead of him. "She has an extra room."

After the supper was cleared from the table and cleaned, Sarah gestured for Eli and Christine to follow her. They walked together on a trail through the field, single file, with his mother leading the way with a flashlight.

"Annie? Aunt Annie?" His mother called as she knocked on the door.

Several long moments later an old woman opened the door. Annie was a cute, small woman, with a ready smile and pure, white hair. Eli vaguely remembered meeting her years ago.

"You must be Eli," she said in English, eyeing Christine up and down as she spoke.

"Sure am," he said and smiled. They

shook hands.

"Who's this pretty girl?" Aunt Annie put her hand out to Christine, who took it hesitantly.

"Christine Freeman," she said with a breathy voice. Her eyes darted between Annie's and Eli's. "Pleased to meet you."

"Call me Aunt Annie. Everyone does."

Christine nodded and pushed up her glasses. When his mother and his aunt walked away for a moment, Eli could hear them talking about him and Christine.

"You're going to be fine here. Aunt Annie will take good care of you." Eli pushed his hands deep into his pockets and rocked back on his heels. "I think it's for the best, don't you?"

"You regret it, don't you? You wish you'd never invited me." She spoke in a rushed, whispered voice. "I think I should go. I can leave right now for one of those homes for girls like me. I have the information right here."

She held up a small floral purse with a dainty gloved hand.

Eli looked over her shoulder, to where his mother and Annie were speaking. He took Christine's hand and led her outside. Once the door was latched behind her and he knew they wouldn't be overheard he spoke.

"I don't regret it, but that doesn't mean I don't think it is better for you to live here with Annie than over at the farm." An unyielding pull ran through his heart — his nerves catching up with him. The melding of his two worlds wasn't going as he'd first anticipated. All that had been going through his mind when he invited her was that she needed help and the Amish were always willing to help. But this might be stretching the ability of his church and especially his family. "I know this looks bad — with Matilda and the rude things Mark said at the station . . . but I don't want you to go. I want you to give my family a chance."

When she was silent he decided to add another thought.

"If you stay here no one will take your baby away from you."

She swallowed and looked down at her feet.

"I'll be over first thing in the morning." He wanted to touch her face but he didn't let himself. "I promise I'll work everything out — and I won't tell anyone anything until you're ready."

"Thank you," she whispered. "I do appreciate what you're doing for me. I know me being here makes things more difficult for you."

Eli shook his head.

"Don't take all the credit." He winked at her.

Sarah Brenneman came back outside and Christine went inside. Without another glance, Sarah walked back to the farmhouse. Eli walked behind her, his heart drumming. She didn't say anything until they were on the front porch. Sarah pulled her black shawl around her and she avoided his eyes.

"What's the real reason you brought *sellah maedel* home?" Of course, she deserved to know why he brought that girl home, only he couldn't tell her the whole truth yet.

"She's a friend and she didn't have anywhere to go."

"But why here? Doesn't she have other friends, her family, or cousins perhaps? Englishers don't understand our ways, Eli, this will only end in hurt."

"*Mem,* I —" he started.

"*Liebje sie?*"

Sarah had never asked Eli if he'd loved a girl. He didn't know how to answer. His lungs were tight and in the coolness of the evening he was sweating.

"I — um," he cleared his throat, "I care about what happens to her." That was the truth.

His mother nodded then opened the door

to the house.

"Eli." She turned around. "Please, let her go back to her world and her own life so you can move on with yours."

He had nothing to say in return and just followed his mother into the house. An hour later he was handed a stack of clothes and a blanket by his father.

"You can sleep in the loft in the equipment barn. It's warm enough with the straw. I'll be ready for your help before sunrise." His father's hand clapped his back, declaring the conversation was over.

Eli knew this wasn't personal. Mark and Sylvia and their twins needed somewhere to stay. Growing up, he'd often slept in the loft when they had company. He and Mark both would. They would crack jokes about their fat Aunt Bertha or the way their cousins got whipped for not sitting still at supper or in church.

He trained his eyes on the small cottage across the field, noticing a small glow in one of the windows. Was Christine still awake? The way she looked at him when he was leaving almost broke him, especially with the way she said she could go to a home for unwed mothers. Her pretty brown eyes had been round and glassy. The responsibility that weighed on him because of her presence was heavier than he imagined it would be, but his motives were pure. But it also allowed everyone to still see him as the flippant person he was when he left for service. The expression on Matilda's face stacked atop his burden. Both girls had looked at him in desperation for completely different reasons.

He sighed and looked at the ceiling of the barn as he waited for sleep. Neither was his girlfriend. Both had a unique attachment to him that he hadn't expected. Christine was the girl he could easily love, but he couldn't let that happen. Matilda was the girl he should love but never could.

"Eli," Enos called up to the loft. "Breakfast is ready."

He sat up. Where was he?

A beat later he remembered that he was home — in the loft in the small barn. His back creaked and he groaned. The loft was worse than the thin cots he had slept on for over a year. Then he realized what Enos said. *Breakfast?* He had slept through dawn and all the way until breakfast? His dad and brothers would already be through with morning chores. He readied himself quickly and burst through the front door. No one moved from their bowed positions and he stood and bowed his head as well. When the prayer was through he walked over and slid into the small space left for him on the bench. Mark was sitting at Eli's position at the table, at the foot of the table, but he did his best not to let it bother him. He was the one who had been away for eighteen months. His littlest brother, Enos, elbowed him in the ribs and smiled, but no one else made a move to say good morning. This was his family, so why did he feel so pressured, so judged, and so unprepared for it.

"I'm sorry for sleeping through chores. I guess I —"

"I expected this," his father said, chewing on honeyed bread. "You haven't had to work for eighteen months — not hard work like we do here on the farm, that is."

He couldn't respond for several beats of his hammering heart. The sting from his father's words heated his own tongue. "You weren't at the hospital. I know all about *hatteh avet.*"

"Hard work? Giving grown men baths and feeding them like babies?" Mark sniggered.

Eli's hands grasped his knees and he forced himself not to tighten his jaw and show his frustration. He wanted to stand up and put his finger in Mark's face and tell him he didn't know what he was talking about. He could explain the horror that his patients lived in — that few of them knew any measure of love or even the most basic genuine care. There was so much that Mark couldn't have fathomed, such as the overwhelming pity in Eli's heart for grown men who'd known no other life. Unless you worked at a hospital like Hudson River there was no way to understand how it was possible to have failure and reward become the two halves of the same heart. Visions of his patients dragged like sandpaper across his memory. His jaw tightened along with his fist.

Sylvia's brow grimaced when she looked at Mark.

"Boovah, nah schtopes." Sarah scolded her boys and told them to stop. She eyed both Eli and Mark equally. Then her face altered when she looked back at Eli. Her warm smile reached across the table and comforted him. "I think a break the first morning you're home is just fine. Especially on our off Sunday."

"Dangeh, Mem." After releasing the breath he was holding as invisibly as possible — not wanting anyone to see how angry he'd become — he didn't just voice a thank-you but let a thankful gaze fall upon his mother. While he knew she didn't approve of Chris-

tine coming home with him, her tenderness touched him. It was clear, however, that this didn't seem to be shared by the other adults in the room.

The rest of breakfast was at least as uncomfortable as supper was the night before. Eli couldn't wait to leave the house and run over to see Christine. His knee bounced during the Psalm and Proverb reading and prayer after they were finished eating. This reading was customary on every other Sunday, when they didn't have church. An entire Psalm and an entire Proverb. When they got to Psalm 119 they divided the 176 verses among the three meals of the day.

Today's reading was from Psalm 143, and Eli's mind wandered until he heard his father say, "Teach me to do thy will; for thou art my God: thy spirit is good; lead me into the land of uprightness." The words squeezed his heart. It was what he wanted. It was what he'd learned and practiced during his service. Now that he was home he wanted to show his family his devotion to God and the church, only with Christine there, it likely proved the opposite. But, she was now, in part, his responsibility as long as she was in Sunrise.

He only had a minimum of chores to do,

since it was Sunday, so he had a bit of time away from his usual duties. The silent looks between his mother and father when he left the house to go see Christine forced him to fight feelings of indignation toward them. They weren't even trying to understand. Of course, they didn't know Christine's secret. They may never have to know if she left for that unwed mothers' home. He knew it would be better for him in dealing with his family if she didn't stay long, but the thought of her handing her baby to a stranger made his stomach turn.

Eli tried to rid himself of his worries as he ran through the field to Annie's cottage as soon as he was able. He was out of breath when his great aunt answered the door and told him that Christine had gone for a walk. She pointed Eli in the right direction and he had a hard time not running. He hadn't gotten there first thing in the morning like he told her he would.

"Christine," he called when he saw her bending toward the ground. Was something wrong? Was it the baby? He ran faster than he knew he could. "Christine, are you okay? Is there something wrong?"

"Eli?" She looked up into his face. "I was just picking some flowers."

Eli wished his heart would stop pounding

so hard and that she wasn't so pretty. The sun was shining on Christine's face, making her glow even though she wasn't wearing makeup, or maybe very little. She was wearing her hair loose and untamed. It flitted around her face in the breeze. He'd never seen her hair completely free of the rolls she wore in the front. Her beauty struck him, making him stutter when he spoke.

"You scared me. You were bent over and I thought something might be wrong."

Christine smiled. "Oh, I'm fine." She walked by him. Eli couldn't tell if she was angry with him or not.

"I'm sorry I wasn't up sooner. I would have slept clear through breakfast if it wasn't for Enos." He stayed in step with her.

She stopped and gathered a bunch of weeds in the ditch next to the road. Flowers?

"It's okay." Christine arranged them in her hand and walked leisurely, taking in her surroundings. "Aunt Annie made a delicious breakfast for us."

Her mood was calmer today — so much so that he wasn't sure how to take her. This was new territory for him on several fronts. Spending time with Christine away from the hospital was already proving to be vastly different. The burdened lines across her forehead were weakened and a smile bloomed across her face. But still, in this moment, he couldn't tell if she was angry or not with him for not having arrived first thing in the morning.

"Your aunt is a sweet lady. She smiles a lot."

"I'm glad —"

"Why do you Amish pray silently?" She kept walking with a slow gait as she spoke but the question came like a shot.

"Well, I — the thing is —" he stammered.

"And why can't the women ever have their hair down? They even wear some type of sleep bonnet, don't they?"

"You know —" He tripped and barely caught himself from falling.

Christine stopped walking and turned toward him. Her eyes squinted and her finger bounced up and down at him.

"And, tell me why you all are so religious but you don't have church every week? My community church back home has services every week and a prayer meeting on Wednesdays." She tilted her head and her hair fell down the side of her shoulder. The orange sun shone on her head, and her caramel hair appeared even more golden. Their eyes locked. *What had she asked him?*

Eli wanted to kiss her. The frankness of his own thoughts and desires scared him and he stood straighter and cleared his throat. He started walking slowly again and she continued with him.

"Well?"

"I'll answer your questions. The silent prayers are so that no one gets prideful over their personal prayers in front of others."

"So, it's like praying in your closet instead of on the street corners like the Pharisees?"

"Yes, exactly." Why was he explaining this to her when she seemed to be doing just fine with it herself? "And the hair is an issue of modesty. I know it's somewhere in the Bible. You'll have to ask Aunt Annie or my mother about that. I try not to get too involved with those lady issues."

Christine stopped and with her free hand grabbed his forearm. Her delicate hand squeezed harder than he expected. She was standing close and looking up at him with those beautiful brown eyes. The fresh open air wrapped around them, energizing him.

"But you should know these standards, Eli. Someday you'll have a wife and maybe some daughters, and aren't you going to want to understand why they can't wear their hair down?"

He nodded and tried not to laugh but

couldn't keep it in. He loved her chatter and how serious she was about her interrogation.

"You're laughing at me?" She grinned back.

"No. But since you're full of questions, I have a question for you, too." He didn't wait for a response. "Yesterday you were a frightened cat and today — what changed?"

Christine's soft face looked far into the distance. She inhaled deeply and exhaled slowly.

"There is something about being out here, away from the rest of the world that comforts me. I know this feeling won't last forever — I have a lot of decisions to make, but for now — for today — I want to enjoy all of this."

"Because you won't be here long?" Could she hear his heart pounding?

Her head jerked up for her eyes to meet his. Her countenance had shifted. "I don't know. I don't feel like I know anything yet."

Eli was angry to have taken away her lightheartedness with his comments. He wanted her to be free here — to be at peace. But, how could he offer that to her when he didn't have it for himself?

CHAPTER 19

It didn't take long for Christine to learn that the only thing that she could do as well as the Amish women was make a bed. Her nursing career made that possible. Her bed was adorned with a beautiful star-patterned quilt in teals, reds, blues, and greens. The iron bed was common enough, but the quilt made her feel as if she were sleeping in the best bed in the house. Her bedroom at home had been simple, and while her mother was an amazing cook and sewed clothing, she didn't quilt.

Christine ran another hand over the pattern before she decided it was perfect. She pulled out the mirror from her bag and propped it up against the oil lamp. It was so small she didn't know how in the world she would do her hair. The first night she was there she peeked around every corner of the house when she thought Aunt Annie wasn't looking and didn't find a bathroom anywhere. The sweet old lady was laughing at her when she pointed to the outhouse outside.

Outhouse! Of course Christine knew this, but it hadn't occurred to her when it was late and she was tired and ready to go to bed.

"Is there a mirror out there?"

"Nay, mei maedle," she smiled as she shook her head. "Don't you have a hand mirror?"

Christine nodded her head.

"Just use that." Then Aunt Annie had gone to tidy the kitchen before she retired to bed. The kitchen looked spotless to Christine, but somehow the woman still found something to clean.

Christine suddenly became aware of her own vanity and primness. And what was she saying when she called her *maedle*? She was too embarrassed to ask.

So here she was with her small mirror propped up as best as she could get it.

"Oh, Christine, your hair," she talked to herself, trying to fix her pin curls. She pulled out the pins and put them between her lips. She finally did roll it on one side and let the rest of it fall down in waves. Surely that would do. In the small bit of reflection she noticed her earrings. Should she take them out? No one else was wearing jewelry. Her fingers spun one around in a circle as she thought, then she decided to keep them in.

Eli was going to come to see her sometime today, but she wasn't sure when. The previous day he came in the morning and she had gone back to the farm with him for most of the day. He showed her just about every corner of the entire farm amidst the distraction of his siblings, who constantly stared at her. At least they smiled. Sarah and Sylvia both were very friendly, but naturally neither understood why she was there and probably wished she wasn't. The very presence of Mark was what made things the most uncomfortable. This made mealtimes awkward. No one spoke and the tension was obvious. How would they feel if she stayed long enough for them to learn that she was expecting a baby?

Christine pulled out the paper from her clutch purse.

Your daughter will be given a new identity while at our home. Here she will receive instruction on how to live a clean and pure life. She will not be idle but will practice good Christian servitude while doing light farm work or cooking for her fellow house-mates. This will provide her with skills she may not already have and a reformed heart when she returns home. The child she carries will be placed with an approved Christian family. You must not concern yourself with the documentation, as all of this will be sealed and filed away. No one will even know it exists. Your daughter will be returned to you in a condition that is proper and respectful.

She couldn't read any more. She folded the paper crudely and stuffed it back into her clutch. The thought of it brought on nausea, and she rushed to the outhouse in just enough time to retch. By the time she returned and looked at her reflection in the small, round mirror her kohl was smeared and her face pasty, in spite of the rouge. She realized, however, there was no one who cared how made up she was. Aunt Annie certainly didn't care.

She patted her face to encourage the blood flow and walked out into the kitchen.

"Now, don't you look nice. What a pretty dress," Aunt Annie said. "Just a shade darker and the girls in Ohio would wear that color."

What Ohio girls? Christine looked down at her green dress. She'd picked it out because it was on the plainer side, though she'd never have thought that the grassy green color wasn't allowed.

"They dress real nice in Ohio. That's where I come from. The bishop lets them wear more colors, not just navy blue, black, and maroon. Their sewing is perfect, too. Not like here where hems aren't straight and —" Annie interrupted herself. "Would you like to help me bake some bread?"

"I don't know how. My mother said I'm hopeless."

"What about pies?"

She shook her head.

"No." She winced. She was useless to Aunt Annie.

"Nonsense. Anyone can learn. If Rudy's Laura, who's as simple as potato soup, can learn, anyone can learn. Trust me. Would you like to?"

"Learn to bake bread and pies?"

"What else are you going to do?"

Christine's eyes surveyed the house. There were only four rooms: a small kitchen with a table, a slightly larger space for the living room, and two bedrooms. She had no patients to tend. Even if she wrote letters, the only people who wanted to hear from her were her mother and Jeanne. Even still, it wouldn't take her all day to do that. She

302

really should fill her time doing something useful.

"Why not," she said, trying to hide her reluctance.

"Let's get started on the *brote* — that's bread. Next week we'll start working on our garden." Aunt Annie stood from the chair and began pulling her sleeves up to her elbows.

"*Our* garden?"

"We'll have a large one so we can do a lot of canning. We'll give most of it away, of course. Some people never did recover from the Depression — worse here than Ohio." She paused for a moment looking at Christine up and down. "You have an apron?"

She thought of her nursing apron that hung in her home in Poughkeepsie. She shook her head.

"Well, use that one over there." Aunt Annie pointed near the woodstove where an apron hung on a drying rack. "Oh, and pull those sleeves up, too. You don't want to get your pretty green dress dirty."

Christine did as she was told and kept listening as the older woman told her about all the vegetables they'd plant. Apparently, Aunt Annie expected her to be around for a while, when Christine was wondering whether or not she should go to the maternity home. Did she really have a choice? It was clear to her that she was only causing problems for Eli and she'd only been there for a few days.

Over the next several hours Christine did her best to help Aunt Annie. After showing her the process of mixing, rolling, and laying out piecrust in the pan, Annie told her to try on her own. What she wouldn't give to have her nursing notebook handy to take notes. Couldn't she just sit and watch?

"What's all this?" Eli walked into the house without knocking.

Christine's chin dropped against her chest. At some point in the process Annie had wrapped a cloth that looked a lot like a handkerchief around her hair, but strands had come through and stuck to her sweaty face. How was it that she was sweating at all? It was only mid-April.

"Pie?" Christine said, wincing. Her hands were covered with dough and flour.

She caught Eli glancing over at Aunt Annie, who was smiling brightly as usual. He walked over and pushed the hair from Christine's face. He tucked it carefully in her head wrap and pushed up her glasses too. A shiver went down her spine. She cleared her throat.

"Christine's pie isn't quite ready to take

visiting yet, but it was only her first try." She giggled.

Christine knew she was only teasing, though she completely agreed. Her crust looked like the crudely sewn face of Frankenstein from the picture she'd seen years earlier. The pieces appeared misshapen, malformed, as if they didn't belong together.

"Ah, well, we'll take a few of mine instead. I know Truman's Marianna is not well, again, and I know she loves peach pie. I think it'll be lovely for Christine to get out and about."

Christine shot Eli a look of panic. She couldn't go visiting. What would people think of her?

"I'm sure she'll make an impression." Eli winked at her.

An impression?

"Can I steal Christine away for a short walk?"

"Surely, surely." Aunt Annie patted Christine's arm as she gently nudged her away from the dry, pieced together crust. "I'll see what I can do with this. Go wash up outside. Eli can help you with the pump."

Once they were outside, Eli pumped the water and she did her best to wash the flour and pastry dough from her hands and arms.

"I don't know how your aunt bakes without making a mess. I'll never manage." She dried her hands and arms with the borrowed apron and with a sigh let it fall back down over her dress. It was a mess. How would she wash it? She didn't have the laundry service at the hospital to depend on.

Eli leaned forward with a smirk. His hand rose to her face. His fingers brushed against her skin as delicately as a butterfly. He had never touched her quite like that before. A tingle raced down her spine. She didn't want to have a rush from his touch. She wasn't available to him or to any man.

"Flour." His eyes twinkled and Christine couldn't help but laugh. "And I like the head scarf. Royal blue is your color."

"You." She poked his chest. "You'll never let me live down the disaster you just witnessed, will you?"

He shrugged.

"I will if you make me a tasty cherry pie. If it tastes half as good as my mother's I'll spread the news all around the district."

"A harrowing task." She sighed and began walking down the field toward his farm. "I'm not sure I'm up for it." A breeze picked up and she rubbed her hands together and then hugged herself. "Aunt Annie is darling, really, and I'm just a dunce in the kitchen. I'll never be good at it."

"How do you eat?"

"Well, as a girl my mother made everything and at the hospital I didn't have to prepare anything."

"You weren't going to be there forever. What were you going to do after you got married someday?" He winked at her.

"Is everything a joke to you, Eli?" Christine didn't realize her frustration until she heard her own voice.

"I was only picking a little, Christy. I didn't mean —" He turned to face her. Even though she didn't meet his gaze, she could see him smiling at her.

"Forget it." But she couldn't. "And besides, you know my situation. I'll never be married. And don't call me Christy."

Eli cleared his throat and she could see him look at her out of the corner of his eye. They walked quietly for a few paces. A breeze picked up and her hair blew, exposing her neck, giving her a chill.

"It's cold out here. I think I'm going to go back. Can we just talk later?"

She couldn't meet Eli's gaze; instead she looked over his shoulder. The field behind the farm stretched far before the tree line was visible. The other way, toward the country dirt road, stood his house. She watched the activity, people going in and out of the barn with wheelbarrows, and the laundry being taken down from the line. His little sisters teeter-tottered and the younger boys ran around them. They all chanted something she couldn't quite hear and then the girls rushed off and ran around as the boys jumped on. Giggles abounded. Christine didn't belong here.

"I can't stay, Eli." She blurted it out before she even considered her words.

"What?" His brow furrowed. "Christine, please —"

"I stick out like a sore thumb. No one is going to really accept me this way. In just a few weeks this dress won't fit me. I'm not going to be able to hide my . . ." she paused, "my condition for very long."

"You don't need to *hide* here." Eli was handsome when he smiled — very handsome. She was still getting used to seeing him in his Amish clothing. He looked different wearing a hat on his white-blond hair. The loose-fitting shirts and homemade pants with suspenders gave him a boyish look instead of the sharp, professional look of his attendant jacket.

She tilted her head at him in disbelief.

"Come on, Eli, open your eyes. I don't fit in. No one will like me. I'm not perfect like everyone here."

Eli started laughing.

"You think we're perfect?"

"There you go, laughing at me again. Can you ever be serious?"

"I'm not laughing at *you,* I just don't see how you think we're perfect. That's funny." His voice grew more passionate than she was accustomed to.

"But you all are perfect. Your district, that is." She eyed him sharply. "I'm a Christian and have gone to church my whole life and know a lot of highly regarded church members and most of them, maybe all of them, would never understand my — situation. They send their girls off and make them give their babies away. And your church is even stricter and has more rules than any church I've ever known. Of course no one is going to understand me and what I'm dealing with."

"You know my sister-in-law Sylvia, right?"

"Yes. She seems very sweet."

"Anyway, you probably should know that before Mark and Syl were together, she and I dated for a short time. Mark's still sore over it even though they're married."

"You and Sylvia?" Christine reflected on that.

"I only dated her out of spite because I

knew Mark wanted to date her."

Christine shook her head. "Why are you telling me this? What does this have to do with my situation?"

"Sylvia and Mark were expecting the twins before they got married."

"They weren't kicked out?" Christine was shocked.

"We don't just kick people out," he said, lowering his chin. "The preachers and the bishop always give members several chances to make things right. Always. They get plenty of opportunity to decide if they want to make a confession and stay with the church — or not."

"They had to confess their personal affairs in front of the church?"

"That's not the point I'm trying to make. What I'm trying to say is that it happens here, too. None of us are perfect. We all make mistakes. I've made a load of them, and there's no one better than any other here in our community. That's part of what makes our church so unique. We don't expect perfection. If we did why would we need a system for confession and forgiveness?"

"But they didn't have a baby like this." She pointed at her abdomen. The words scraped against her throat. "Did Sylvia yell at Mark? Did she tell him to stop or cry in pain when he wouldn't? Did she despise herself knowing that it was still all her fault?"

Her heavy breaths were all that could be heard for several moments.

"None of that is your fault, Christine," he said and took her shoulders in his hands. His face was tight with intensity.

She gently pulled out of his grasp and continued walking. "You don't really know me. If you knew how I'd acted that night." She shook her head and looked away past the empty field into the line of trees along the horizon. "I'm as guilty as —"

Christine couldn't say his name.

"Was it that Jack-fella that you had the New Year's date with?"

Her head snapped over and they eyed each other for several long moments.

"Sorry, I heard you and your friend," Eli admitted.

"So, as you can see, Mark and Sylvia's situation was completely different from mine. I don't even know why I'm talking with you about this."

Eli raised his hand and hesitantly touched her cheek. His warmth was like protection and safety. In these moments she was afraid she had told him too much. He wasn't, however, like anyone else she knew and especially not like Jack. Telling him reminded her of standing under a large awning in the midst of a thunderstorm. He was a comfort to her. The problem was she was afraid he loved her.

"I'm so sorry, Christine," he whispered.

She looked up into his eyes and for a moment let herself get lost in his sky-blue eyes.

"Eli," a deep voice called from behind.

Eli's hand dropped and he turned around abruptly. It was his brother Mark. The brothers locked eyes. Heat circulated around them. Mark looked over at her and shook his head when their eyes met.

"Whatcha need?" Eli said in English, before sighing audibly.

"Dad's having problems with the bull, we need your help. If it's okay with your *friend*?"

"Don't be rude," Eli bit back. "Christine hasn't done anything to you."

Christine's heart pounded loudly in the silence that hung between them.

"You're right, *she* hasn't done anything to me." Mark stepped closer to Eli.

"You want to talk about it right now?" Eli closed the gap between them.

"I don't think we can talk it out."

Eli's and Mark's hands were clenched at

their sides. Their faces were taut and their chests out toward each other. The hatefulness turned her stomach. She had to leave.

CHAPTER 20

Christine wasn't sure the brothers noticed when she walked away. She accidentally slammed Aunt Annie's door and leaned against it. Eli and Mark's animosity toward each other brought visions of her brothers to mind. But they had been best friends. Her brother Peter, with his dark features, always drew in every girl from miles around. Nathaniel's features were more like Christine's, with caramel hair and brown eyes behind glasses. Peter wanted to be an engineer. Nathaniel wanted to be a teacher. Now they'd never be anything but dead. It made her sick the way Eli and Mark treated each other.

"Oh, you're back." Aunt Annie came out of her bedroom and spoke to her unconsciously. "I'm sorry to say that I couldn't repair your pie. I added a few oats to the mixture and made it into a bit of a peach crisp. The dough doesn't have to be smooth and put together for that. I think we could go down to the farm and see if they have any cream for us to —"

The older woman stopped and just looked at her. Her face sagged from its usual smile.

Aunt Annie walked toward Christine and said something in Pennsylvania Dutch that ended with *mei maedle.* It didn't matter that she couldn't understand any of her words, Christine didn't need a translation. Of course, the older woman was asking what was wrong.

Christine just shook her head and willed the surfacing tears not to fall. She swallowed and blinked them away.

"Nothing, I'm fine." She stood straight.

"Fiddlesticks. *Schvetz* — talk," Aunt Annie urged.

There were several moments of quiet between the two. Christine sniffed and decided against confiding in Aunt Annie this soon. The last thing she wanted to do was talk about Jack and the baby again. She swallowed down the remainder of her emotions and shook her head.

"Can you teach me how to keep the fire going in the woodstove so I can be more helpful to you?" Christine changed the subject.

Annie narrowed her gaze onto Christine.

"Well, if you wish." She waved her over to the woodstove.

Christine watched carefully as Aunt Annie showed her how to make kindling from the box of papers and small trash pieces behind the woodstove and how to layer it just right to build the fire. She showed her how to stack the wood and that just a small splash from the kerosene was all she needed. Christine laughed that the kerosene was in a squeeze container like you'd see ketchup in at a diner.

"Make sure you keep your hair back," she said to Christine as she tossed the ties of her translucent bonnet over her shoulder. "Sometimes the flame bursts up a bit."

Christine watched carefully and jumped when she threw in the match and the fire started just as the door flew open behind them. They both turned around to find Enos, the youngest Brenneman boy, standing there, red-faced, huffing and puffing.

He started talking in Pennsylvania Dutch. Annie gasped.

"What? What's happened?"

"It's Mark, he got struck by the bull's horns, and he needs your help," Annie translated for her.

"My help? What's the matter with calling a doc?"

"You're a nurse, right?" Annie grabbed her own coat off the small hook near the door and pushed Christine out the door.

"Sure, but I don't have any equipment," she said, splaying her hands.

"Are they calling the doctor, too?" Annie asked Enos.

He nodded yes and said a few Amish words.

"He said that they are going to call Dr. Sherman but the phone is down the street, so it might take a bit for him to get here."

"Aunt Annie," Christine resisted but Annie held on to her arm and wouldn't stop pulling her. "I will need some cloths, and he might need stitches. If he's bleeding really badly, he might faint or go into shock."

"Christine," Annie stopped walking and shook Christine's forearms. The woman was easily eight or nine inches shorter than Christine but the strength in her hands shocked her. "Don't worry, I'll help you."

"Do you know anything about nursing?"

The older woman pursed her lips. "I've been a midwife for decades. I know more about babies and birth than wounds, but I will be more help than any of the other women. They're probably in shock already."

"You're probably right about that."

Christine's confidence rose as they ran through the field, heading for the barn. Before they got there she could hear Mark yelling. She couldn't see anything with all the brothers standing in a circle around him. Eli's mother was crying and trying to make the twin girls turn away. Sarah pointed to the swing set and said a few words in their language and the girls ran. Christine's head began spinning until she heard Mark cry out again. She took a deep breath and gathered her wits. She put a hand on one of the boys and he led her through the group. His eyes were as big as saucers.

The vision of Mark sitting with his back leaning against a post was graver than she'd imagined. Sylvia stood near Eli but looked as pale as her white covering.

"Eli, I'm here," Christine said, squatting next to him.

"What do I do, Christine? What do I do?" Eli was breathing so quickly she was afraid he would hyperventilate. His hands shook and his sleeve was torn and he was pressing it against the wound. His knuckles were colorless. The cloth was soaked and blood dripped through his fingers and onto the dirt floor of the barn.

"Good gracious, I've never seen such a —" she stopped herself. She could feel eyes on her from every angle. The gash on Mark's midcalf had opened all the way up to his knee. "Okay, Eli, just don't panic. I need to examine the laceration." She didn't want to see it. Eli lifted the soaked sleeve, his breathing almost as ragged as Mark's. She tried not to gasp when she saw parts of the bone of Mark's kneecap. The bleeding was getting worse. She pushed Eli's hand down on it again, pressing it hard. Mark yelled. "You're doing exactly what you should be doing. We need to try and stop the bleeding."

"Sylvia, I need more cloths! Thicker ones."

Christine stood and saw that Sylvia was in near shock. The woman didn't seem to know that Christine was standing in front of her. It was the first time Christine noticed how young she was, younger than herself, and pretty — dark hair and dark eyes. But her olive skin tone was growing grayer by the minute. Why had she bothered with her when Annie was right there?

"Annie," she turned further around, "I need clean cloths. I saw diapers on the line earlier. Gather up several of those and bring them to me."

Annie ran in the direction of the clothesline. Sylvia and Sarah were both useless and Christine really couldn't blame them. If it weren't for her training, she would be also. Christine took both of their arms and moved them back. Hovering over Mark wouldn't help. Neither of the ladies seemed to notice.

She went back to Mark and squatted.

"When the rags come, I am going to pack the wound and continue direct pressure to stop the bleeding. But I need you to keep his vitals, Eli." She stopped talking for a moment and looked at Mark. "Mark, stay with us. I want you to keep your eyes right on Eli."

Mark nodded slightly and his eyes went from hers to his brother's. His jaw was tight, showing Christine he had some strength left. Eli kept his brother's wrist in his hand and she could tell he was counting. She couldn't have been more thankful for his learning some of the basics at the hospital. Annie handed Christine several clean line-dried diapers.

She took away the bloodied cloth. Christine did it too quickly and Mark yelled. She apologized. Mark's dark-blue pants were shredded and pieces of the fabric were stuck in and throughout the wound.

"I'm going to clean your wound a little, Mark. Just keep looking at Eli."

Her hand was steady as she gently pulled

the shredded pants away from the wound, taking pieces of skin along with them. She kept apologizing to him but worked carefully and quickly.

"How's his pulse, Eli?"

"Stable but a bit weak."

Mark's face had lost even more color. His jaw slackened, his skin was damp with sweat down to his chest. The palms of her hands touched his face and neck.

"He's freezing," she said. "We need to warm him up."

"David, go get a buggy blanket," Eli yelled over his shoulder.

Christine took a diaper and packed the wound. She leaned into it, adding pressure. The bleeding began to slow but it was still urgent. He must get to a doctor immediately.

"Get me something to wrap around his leg," she said to Annie. "Wide strips of cloth, like bandages would be best."

"Would twine work?" Mark David asked. He had been a silent observer until then, with his hand on Mark's shoulder. His shirt was covered with blood splatters.

"Yes, that will be just fine," Christine said quickly.

He jumped up and pulled a spool from a nail on a post near them. His hands quaked when he handed it to her. She took his hand instead of the twine.

"Mark David, everything's going to be fine," she told him, fighting against the desire to speak more formally and call him Mr. Brenneman. "But keep praying anyway."

He nodded at her. Even though he kept his eyes on his son and didn't say a word, Christine could feel his prayers as she wrapped the other diaper around Mark's leg first, then bound it with twine. His eyes began diverting from Eli's, which concerned her.

"How far is the doctor's office from here?"

"Not far," Mark David said.

Behind her she heard the open buggy against the gravel drive. The horse seemed as riled up as everyone else. She saw one of the brothers driving. Moses, she thought. It infuriated her that they didn't just ask a neighbor to drive them. It seemed so much faster than the buggy would be. But in the moment, it didn't matter. Mark just needed to get to the doctor as fast as possible.

"Can't we get an automobile — maybe a truck with a bed in the back?" Christine suggested harshly to Eli.

"Neighbors aren't home and none of us can drive even if there was a car or truck available," Eli told her.

Of course she hadn't thought of that. She couldn't drive either, for that matter.

"Our English neighbors let us use the phone when they aren't home as long as we write it down for them. The rest around here are Amish," Eli said breathlessly. "This is the best we can do."

David came, and she grabbed the blanket and draped it around Mark's shoulders. He was limp — his weight dead in her hands.

"Lay him flat," Christine said. "David, take Eli's place on his side. You and your dad are going to hold hands underneath Mark's back. Eli, come down here and wrap your arms around his legs. Lift when I say."

The men repositioned themselves and when all of their eyes were on her, she told them to lift. The small crowd of people divided, letting them through. She guided them to the open buggy bed and climbed in. She grabbed the blankets in the corner and layered them.

"Mark, are you with me?" she said, hovering her face over his.

Mark didn't say a word but gave her a slight nod. His teeth began to chatter and she reassured him they would be at the doctor's office shortly.

"Sylvia, do you want to ride up front or

next to Mark?"

The young woman's eyes grew. She shook her head and stepped backward away from the open buggy.

"This is your husband. Get in." Christine grabbed Sylvia's arm. Eli helped Sylvia up on the bench seat. Christine grabbed another blanket and roughly handed it to the young wife who was shivering wildly from adrenaline. "Here."

Eli told Moses to get off the bench so he could drive. As they started out the jostling made Mark call out. Christine saw that as a positive sign. He was still responsive to the pain. She kept her eyes on Mark and when he opened his eyes she spoke.

"The doctor will know exactly what to do."

"I thank you, Christine, but don't think this changes anything," he said between chattering teeth. "Between Eli and me."

She didn't know what to say. When Mark's well-being was on the line he chose now to still speak ill of his brother?

"If you were smart, you'd stay far away from him."

"What?"

He winced and groaned loudly, but he wouldn't stop talking. "Actually, when you leave, why don't you take him with you?

Nobody wants him around."

Then he lost consciousness. The doctor ran out to the wagon when they arrived.

"His color was getting better but he just lost consciousness and he appears paler again. His pulse is stable, however. Bull accident. Deep laceration on his right leg. The bleeding appears to be slowing down."

"Who are you?"

"My name is Christine Freeman. I'm a nurse. I'm staying at the Brenneman farm temporarily."

"Nice to meet you, Nurse Freeman, I'm Dr. Sherman. Let's get him inside."

Dr. Sherman, Eli, and an attendant carried him inside and got him onto an examining table. Another nurse was there immediately, so once Christine knew Mark was safe, she backed away and sat in the waiting room. She leaned over and put her head in her hands — there was too much to take in. Eli returned from the examination room behind her.

"Where's Sylvia?" Eli put a hand on her shoulder.

Christine looked up and around the small room. "She must still be out in the wagon."

"I'll go get her." Eli walked out.

A few minutes later Sylvia came in with the blanket wrapped around her shoulders.

Her face was still blank with shock. Christine didn't often deal with the family of her patients since so few families visited the hospital. She stood and put an arm around her, deciding she needed to relate to her as a woman rather than as a nurse.

"Come, sit with me." She guided Sylvia to a nearby seat and they sat together quietly.

After more than an hour the doctor came out. He nodded and smiled at Christine. "I think you might have saved Mark's life. I was away when my wife got the call and just returned. He might've bled to death by the time I got out there without your quick action. It is a very deep wound, and wide. Nice job, Nurse Freeman."

Christine sighed and pursed her lips. Maybe she could ask about working for him. She needed to do something besides baking terrible pies.

"I think anyone would've done what I did."

"Sometimes when it's a family member, it's difficult to keep calm. Well done." He nodded and offered his hand.

"Thank you, Doc," she responded and shook his hand. Though it had only been mere weeks since she was fired, being recognized as a nurse and providing help brought a sense of self-worth to her.

Eli put an arm around Christine's shoulder then wrapped her in his arms for a few brief moments until Christine pulled away, feeling uncomfortable.

"Thank you," he said, looking into her eyes.

"I'm going to check on Sylvia. She's had such a shock." She walked away from Eli.

Christine sat next to the young wife as the doctor told her that he needed to keep Mark overnight. Sylvia had a hard time leaving Mark but the doctor reminded her she could come tomorrow. Christine put an arm around Sylvia's shoulders as they walked back to the buggy. The two women's eyes met; a bond was forming.

As they sat in the back of the buggy while Eli drove them home Christine realized that she hadn't eaten since breakfast. With her adrenaline now gone she suddenly grew so hungry she couldn't control her shaking.

"Are you all right?" Sylvia asked her.

"I'm just hungry," she said simply.

"I'm sure Sarah will have food ready for us when we get back."

Sylvia's brow knitted together but neither of them spoke again until they reached the farm.

"Thank you, Christine." Sylvia's eyes were puffy from crying. She put her hand out.

Christine took the young wife's hand and shook it. It wasn't like the handshakes she had gotten up until now. This one was gentle and friendly.

Sylvia smiled at Christine and let go of her hand then scooted off the bed of the buggy and straight into a hug from her mother-in-law.

Everyone rushed out of the house and barns, wanting news. They all turned to Christine for information. Christine told them everything the doctor had said. She'd assumed that on a farm they would have experienced wounds like this in the past, but apparently they'd been spared such injuries. Christine made sure to explain that as long as there was no infection he shouldn't lose his leg and he would be just fine — but he wouldn't be on his feet for weeks.

"Christine saved his life," Eli added.

Christine hesitated to accept the compliment, embarrassed at the attention, but she didn't know what more to say. She lowered her eyes to her feet. First, Mark David went to her with his hand out to her and said thank you. Then followed Sarah and the rest of the family. While the simple act of shaking her hand didn't seem like such an outpouring of thanks to those in the outside world, it was to this family and also to Christine. Annie skipped the handshake and pulled her in for a hug. Her heart swelled and she found herself desiring their acceptance more than ever. Even Enos, with a toothless grin, shook her hand and said something in Dutch.

Everyone laughed.

"What did he say?" She looked at Eli.

"He said he's never seen a girl run as fast as you did." Eli smiled and winked at her. "Come on, let's get something to eat."

Somehow the terrible accident had broken the ice with the family and even though it was well past lunch and not quite supper, they all sat for a meal. During the silent prayer Christine knew what was on the hearts of everyone around the table. For the first time since her arrival she joined in. Today, she thanked God for showing her how to help Mark and for the beginning of a friendship with Sylvia, who she kept an eye on throughout the night, given the shock she had experienced.

After another few hours Eli ran to the neighbors and called the doctor. Mark was doing well. Christine accompanied Eli as he went out with his brothers to do chores. They even spoke in English for her sake. When Enos asked Eli what *real-life crazy people* looked like, she burst into laughter.

Later Eli walked her home. Annie had gone home earlier. Sarah gave Christine a coat to wear since it had cooled off quite a bit. The bulkiness of the coat was awkward but the gesture warmed her more than the quilted denim coat did.

"They like you," Eli said, nudging her shoulder as they walked side by side.

"Hmm." She agreed nearly silently and decided to take in the sunset ahead of them. "Do you think you could drive me out to Dr. Sherman's soon so I can ask about a job? Or maybe a neighbor with a car could take me?"

"But why? We can take care of you."

"Not forever. I'm not used to not working. I've been working since I was fourteen. And, maybe . . ." Christine wasn't sure she could finish her thought. Getting a job meant she'd have some freedom to care for herself and a child. But who would take care of the baby while she worked?

"If you want, I'll help you." His brow furrowed and his hand went to her arm.

Eli's touch was so warm and suddenly, more than anything, she wanted to throw herself into his arms. She looked up into his eyes and his intensity startled her.

She slowly pulled her arm away. Nothing

330

could happen between them. She would ruin his life like Jack ruined hers.

"Good night."

Christine didn't look back until she reached her new bedroom; there she watched him through the slit of the curtain. He still stood there, then kicked the dirt beneath his feet and walked away. Her eyes followed his silhouette until she couldn't see anything but the darkness that consumed the night.

That night she wrote a letter to Dr. Sherman, asking for a job. She couldn't remember the last time she was excited about something in her life. Though she didn't know what to do about the baby she carried, if she could continue as a nurse she would at least feel like a valuable member of the community. This could be a new start for her.

CHAPTER 21

By the time Sunday came rumors were going wild about the new girl. Eli was not
surprised that people were more curious
about meeting her than welcoming him
home. After Mark's accident his parents had
warmed up to Christine. Sylvia seemed
especially friendly with her, but not toward
Eli. He didn't blame her. While everyone
was getting used to one another, he was still
the outcast. Hadn't they worked as a team
with Mark's wound? Hadn't he been attentive and sensitive toward Mark?

Mark came home the day after the accident and had been on bed rest ever since.
His wound was going to take quite a few
weeks to heal. Dr. Sherman told him if his
leg wasn't taken care of and he got an infection he could lose it. All of this didn't just
mean that Mark would be bedridden
through the spring, but also that their house
wouldn't get built until he was on his feet

again. Eli would be stuck in the loft even longer.

He hitched up a horse on the Dearborn instead of his own buggy that he'd let Moses borrow while he was away. The Dearborn was big enough to take two additional people, Christine and Annie, to church, whereas his two-person buggy was not. Annie and Christine were waiting for him as he pulled up, and he took in the view. His small aunt wore heavy Amish clothing next to Christine's light spring dress. Christine's hair glowed in the morning sun and her lips, though not red this time, still shone brightly.

For a moment Eli wished Aunt Annie had her own way to church so he could steal a few moments alone with Christine. He watched her as she walked out the door. She seemed completely unaware of how pretty she was. He leaned over to help his aunt up and she sat on the second bench. He was surprised how spry she was. He helped Christine next and she bounced up, better than the first time just over a week ago. Had it only been a week since they'd arrived back in Sunrise? Just over two weeks ago he was still an attendant in a mental asylum. It had been like a completely different life and if it weren't for Christine being with him here in his small community, it would have almost seemed that it never happened.

Christine wrung her purse with her hands. He wanted to hold her hand and put her at ease. He winced at the thought. He pushed it away and tried to think about something unimportant to talk about.

"You look nice in your suit," Aunt Annie said. "Good thing you're growing a beard. In Ohio you might get away without one for a spell, but not here."

He rubbed his jaw.

"Any young man who is a member of the church is supposed to grow a beard," he said to Christine, leaning toward her.

"Then why didn't you have one while you were at the hospital?"

He chuckled.

"Don't you like it?" he asked.

Christine shrugged. "It doesn't matter what I think, only what the church thinks."

Then she dismissed him and she spoke to Annie, asking her why things were different in Ohio. Annie explained to her how each district was similar but still had their own set of standards. Some were more lenient in some areas and stricter in others. Christine didn't talk to him the rest of the way to church but chewed at the side of her mouth and pushed her glasses up every few minutes.

They arrived at the house where church would be held and everyone around them watched as he helped Christine down. Her dress was blue with bright pink flowers. She wore a knitted beige cardigan over it. Everything about her clothes stuck out against all the navy blues, maroons, and blacks. The brightest color he saw that day otherwise was the royal blue that was usually worn by a bride on her wedding day and the newly married wives.

Eli watched as Aunt Annie stood and walked at Christine's side. He wasn't sure at first but after some observance he recognized his aunt's expression to be pride. She appeared proud to be the one living with this new, unusual addition to Sunrise. He nodded his head to many people as they passed, and a few of the younger men and boys came to shake his hand and get a closer look at Christine.

One of the younger boys jogged up and offered to take care of his horse and Dearborn. Usually he would do this himself, but it seemed there was some excitement over his homecoming.

"You'll sit with me," Aunt Annie said as they walked toward the crowd of people.

She looked at Eli. "Will you sit with us, too?"

"No," he said quietly, leaning toward her ear. "The men and women sit separately. I'll see you sometime during lunch."

Eli looked for her as they lined up to enter the church. He could see Christine's light hair and English dress stick out in the sea of Amish colors. The line of unmarried girls was ahead of him. Some had really grown up while he was gone. He noticed how the girls wore a *schnupduch* folded in a triangle in their waistline. As if they would ever use those hankies to wipe their noses. It made him smile that these hankies in their waistlines were considered fanciful in their community.

"*Sis zeit,*" said a voice behind him telling him it was time.

He turned to see Danny Yoder and the lineup of other unmarried young men stretching back.

"*Vas?*"

"You're the oldest now, Eli," Danny said. "Larry and Junior married while you were away."

Eli was the oldest among the unmarried, which meant he would lead them all to sit at church. Having forgotten this rite, it stung to learn the truth. He walked into the house and sat in front of where the young women were. Behind him was Bertha and next to her was Matilda. Giggles and teasing commenced between the two groups throughout the service, quietly and secretly. He was given dirty looks for not participating.

Eli had forgotten how long church actually was. Sitting still on backless benches for two hours was harder than he remembered. Maybe it was because he was out of practice, or maybe it was because his thoughts were on Christine. She was sitting through the service just like him but didn't understand anything that the preacher was saying. How much would Annie be able to translate even? It would be too distracting for those around them.

By the time the service was through and it was lunchtime his eyes roamed the sea of people, looking for the bright blue of Christine's dress.

"Where's Christine?" he asked Aunt Annie, who was dishing out potatoes for lunch. He was going up for seconds and no one else was in line at the moment.

"She said she needed some fresh air," Aunt Annie said, winking at him as she gave him an extra spoonful.

After he finished his meal he spotted

Christine sitting with a circle of completely ancient women and Aunt Annie. He recognized all of them and he couldn't help but smile considering what conversation she must be listening to, if they were speaking in English, of course. She was sitting in the midst of the hen house. They were known in the community for being the Amish telephone, relaying messages and stories quicker than you could say *bawk-bawk.* He walked toward them to save her but was cut off before he got to her.

"Eli," Matilda stepped in front of him.

"Matilda," he said. His eyes went just above her and briefly caught Christine's eyes. He returned his eyes to Matilda. *"Vee bish?"*

"Do you really want to know how I am?" she asked, looking him directly in the eyes. "And why did you ignore me during church?"

She was pretty with deep brown hair, fair skin, and brown eyes.

"Maybe we could go and talk somewhere," she suggested.

He led her to a corner of the living room, where long, backless benches were still set up. Most of the people were mingling in other places of the house or were outside.

They would be able to talk somewhat privately.

"I'm really sorry about the other day. I didn't mean to upset you."

"After all our letters, you brought that girl here, Eli. How do you think I would feel?" Matilda's lip quivered.

Don't cry, Matilda.

"Christine is a friend." He sighed. "She had no place to go."

Matilda raised an eyebrow. "Well, doesn't she have any other friends?"

Eli clenched his jaw instead of rolling his eyes.

"Listen, Matilda, remember what I said about us also being friends?"

"Didn't you like my letters? I wrote you sometimes twice a week." Matilda avoided his question. Her shrill voice nagged at his ears and pride. They were getting looks from those who mingled in and out of the room.

"Of course I did."

There were tears in her eyes. How had he gotten himself into this mess?

Christine tried to focus on the conversation between the older ladies. She found herself wishing for only one thing: somewhere to lie down. Her stomach had been turning in circles for most of the morning, but she hesitated to say anything to Aunt Annie, afraid she would figure out she was expecting. Sure, everyone would find out eventually, but not now, not here, and not yet.

The older ladies were all holding or feeding babies — their grandchildren — except for Aunt Annie. Christine watched as she looked lovingly at the children and reached out and stroked the softness of a plump cheek or arm. Where were Aunt Annie's grandchildren?

Since Christine's arrival at the Amish community she hadn't seemed to go more than a day without learning something new about their ways. Today had been no exception. Besides the entire church service and routine, she learned that women did not talk about pregnancy. In her own society, naturally, they wouldn't talk of this in mixed company, but among other women, it wasn't completely unmentionable. Christine learned that Sylvia was expecting in the most roundabout way. Sylvia was about a month behind her. The older women talked about a number of people, but she only recognized a few names.

They couldn't believe the misfortune of Mark's being laid up for maybe more than a month while his leg healed, and so soon after he and Sylvia had lost their home in a fire.

"Sometimes you wonder why two people have to be so burdened with several hardships when others don't have a care in the world." A woman named Rosella looked at the other three women, skipping Christine, as she spoke, thankfully, in English. When Rosella leaned forward as if she had a secret to share, Christine found herself leaning in as well. "I've always said, the sins in your youth will punish you later in life."

"They were hardly youth, they were already members, when —" Rebekah stopped midsentence. "Well, everyone knows what happened."

Three of the ladies — Rosella, Rebekah, and Mandy — all looked at one another with raised eyebrows and tucked chins. Then they looked at Annie, whose face carried a disinterested expression.

"You think the fire and the accident with the bull were because they made a mistake before they were married?" Annie questioned them.

The ladies looked at one another as if they were shocked this was being questioned. Of course, Christine knew better.

"Every sin has a consequence," Rosella stated, setting her jaw.

"So what was my sin? I've lost all three of my babies." Annie looked into each woman's eyes before standing up and walking away.

"Nah, Annie," Rebekah said, but Annie was already gone.

The ladies switched over to Pennsylvania Dutch as Christine stood and followed Aunt Annie. The conversation bounced around inside her mind. Aunt Annie had lost three babies? Their talk of consequences for sin stung her heart as she contemplated them. Her own guilt pummeled her like being hit in the head. Memories from that night flooded her — feeling heady from beer and whiskey, flirting too much — letting him touch her. She brought her hand to her forehead and put her other hand against the wall, leaning against it.

"Christine?" Aunt Annie turned and put a hand on her back. "Not feeling well?"

"I don't feel well." She shook her head.

"After that conversation, neither do I. Come, *mei maedle*. Let's go."

The older woman led her to one of the bedrooms, where they both gathered their things. Annie covered her *kapp* with the black bonnet and pinned the shawl around her shoulders. Christine's turning stomach got worse by the moment. She breathed evenly, trying to keep her nausea at bay. Her mind wandered to what the women said about Annie and her losing three babies. It was unimaginable.

"Enos," Aunt Annie called through the screen door as they walked toward the porch. She spoke to him in their language and her ears perked up when she heard her name in the middle of the sentence. The older woman then looked back to Christine. "Come on, let's go to the buggy. Eli will meet us there."

"But he's talking with Matilda. Maybe we shouldn't . . ." Christine didn't finish the sentence.

"Oh, Matilida." Aunt Annie waved her words away. "She likes to make her belt so tight because it makes her breasts look bigger."

"Matilda, don't cry." Eli touched Matilda's arm, trying to calm her, but feeling awkward, he pulled away only to have her grab his hand and hold it in her lap. His face grew hot.

"It was really hurtful that you brought her here and you haven't tried to reach me since you've been home." Her grip was tightening.

"You heard what happened to Mark. Things have been —" he searched for the right word, "busy at the farm."

"And you're spending time with her, aren't you?" Matilda's face was red and puffy. "It's all over the community how much time you spend with her and all the long walks you take."

"Mat—"

"How do you think that makes me feel?"

"I'm sure —"

"It's embarrassing. That's what. Leah and Kibby Miller heard from Mariellen Peterscheim that she saw you holding hands while you were walking to Aunt Annie's cottage. Right by the road for everyone to see." Both of her eyebrows went up this time.

Eli winced. Had anyone read his thoughts, that would've been true, but they hadn't held hands on their walks. Any number of buggies may have passed them, catching them during a walk, though. But he hadn't noticed, his attention focused solely on Christine. He began pulling away only for her to grasp his hand with both of hers. He cleared his throat.

"Is she coming to the Singing tonight?" One of her hands let go of his and brought a tissue to her eyes, wiping them.

Eli hadn't even considered it. He hadn't planned on going himself. If he did, he couldn't imagine that Christine would want to attend or that the church would approve of it. Everything was so foreign to her; even coming to church was a bit of an experiment. He was itching to talk to her about everything and here he was with a crying Matilda. Her eyes looked up at him, pleading.

"Listen, Matilda," he said, pulling his hand away and clasping it to his other, hoping it would deter her from grabbing his hand again. "I never meant to hurt you by bringing Christine here. We don't need to keep talking about her because she's not my girlfriend."

"Well, of course she's not because I am." She sat up straight and puffed herself up like an angry hen on the farm.

He opened his mouth to talk. "What?" He nearly choked on the word.

"Eli." Enos jogged up to him. "Aunt Annie told me you need to come. Christine isn't feeling well and you need to take her home."

Instantly he stood and looked past Enos, trying to find Christine. Was she okay?

"Eli Brenneman."

Eli turned to find Matilda standing with her hands on her hips.

"I have to go," he said dismissing her.

"Meah sin en schvetzah."

345

"*Ja,* I know we are talking, but I have to go. You heard him. Christine's not feeling well." Was it the baby? Was it that she just wanted to get away from the church members, was it becoming too much for her?

Tears welled in Matilda's eyes.

"Will I see you tonight? We need to talk." Her voice reminded him of how his mother used to speak to him and his brothers when she expected something from them.

"Maybe," he said, still wincing at her confused pronouncement that she was his girlfriend. "Listen, Matilda, we aren't together like that."

"But now that you're back?" she said, smiling at him coyly.

"No, Matilda." Without thinking, he said it too loudly. "Listen to me: we are not a couple."

Matilda set her jaw as he told her that he had to go.

He didn't look back as he walked away. He would have to deal with her later. All he could think about now was Christine. By the time he made it to the Dearborn the horse was already hitched and Christine and Aunt Annie were waiting for him. Christine looked waxen and tired.

"What's wrong? Is there anything I can do?" Eli asked, hopping up into the buggy.

"It's nothing." She waved him off.

"Nothing?" Annie piped up. "She's turning green. Look at her."

"Your stomach?"

"It was the ham." She eyed Eli, not wanting to reveal more in front of Aunt Annie.

"The ham?" he questioned.

"Sorry, I could see you were in the middle of something." Christine cleared her throat and pushed her glasses up.

"I told Enos it didn't matter. Matilda has been assuming too much ever since I moved here." Annie snorted. "Did I tell you that she started visiting me and asking about how long I planned on staying? She was looking around my cottage like she was planning to move in."

"What?" Eli scowled.

"And I don't think she was thinking of moving in alone." Aunt Annie crossed her arms in a huff.

"Well, everyone knows that she's Eli's girlfriend," Christine said over her shoulder to Aunt Annie, then caught Eli's eye, smirking.

He forced a smile back, more frustrated than humored.

Eli's grip on the reins got tighter. How had this happened? Matilda had marriage on her mind and was plotting to get the cot-

tage for the two of them. With his exasper-
ated energy fueling the horse, they were
home in no time.

CHAPTER 22

"How is Matilda doing?" Sarah Brenneman asked. They arrived at the farm within minutes of each other. "Her *mem* told me she cried for two days after you returned."

"*Mem,* I'm not dating Matilda."

"Well, you definitely have made her feel that you are through all those letters you wrote her."

"She wrote me. I wrote her back every few weeks because I didn't want to be impolite." His voice rose. "In one of my first letters I told her that I appreciated her friendship, that's it. I told her that all I wanted was a friendship."

"She's a nice girl. A good girl. You really need to think about settling down. She would make a fine wife."

Enos and Abe were listening and started chuckling behind their hands. Eli rolled his eyes. He wasn't humored by the conversation but he couldn't do his usual thing by making a joke and waving off his parents' comments. It wasn't that simple anymore. He had to face this issue with Matilda.

"I saw her just before we left and she's expecting you tonight."

"I told her maybe." He didn't want to tell his mother he also told Matilda that they were not a couple.

"So the CPS made you too *hohe* for Singings now." His father did not say this as a question but as more of a declaration. The use of the dialect word for *high* that they used when referring to the English was a slap across the face.

"Of course not. But I'm not a young boy who wants to play all those silly games and be chased by ridiculous girls anymore."

"It wasn't that long ago that those silly games and girls were exactly what you liked. Too much, I might add. We may have stayed quiet, but we've heard plenty of stories about your ways, Eli. Mark also feels that you've put your morals and those of the family into question. I would suggest that you make up for lost time and start showing the proper behavior from now on." His mother's voice was as firm as he'd ever heard it when she returned to the room without the twin girls. "How else do you think you are going to find a wife? Tell me."

Eli ran a hand through his hair. He hadn't realized how short his hair actually was until today, when he had been around all his friends who had much longer hair than his own. He knew his parents were disappointed in him with the way he'd avoided settling down, but they'd never talked about it.

"You've made some very questionable choices for years, Eli," his father began. "We've stayed quiet about them — as your mother said — and just prayed you'd come back ready to finally get on track. Then you bring that girl home."

"That girl?" Eli was dumbfounded. They had been so accepting of Christine since she saved Mark's life.

"Why can't you just stop playing around with that English life and just settle down like a proper Amishman? Matilda would be an excellent wife for you. That Christine's a nice girl, but she's not one of us. She's not right for you."

"I didn't bring her here to marry." He was yelling now. His heart was pumping fast and he couldn't believe that after all the work he'd done on his temper that here he was again, yelling and getting angry. He breathed evenly, trying to compose himself.

"Then why did you bring her here?" his

mother asked. "Why can't she go home to her own parents?"

"Because she's going to have a baby, that's why! Her mother wanted to send her to a home where they take your baby away after it's born. She has no one else that could help — no one but me."

Eli was breathing heavy by the time he was done, and he looked back and forth between his mother and father, their eyes round and shocked.

"Boys, go outside to play," his mother said to Enos and Abe.

"But it's Sunday," Abe said.

The look their father gave them brought instant obedience. They left the living room and Eli imagined they were likely standing on the porch near an open window, listening to everything being said. He couldn't believe he had just blurted out Christine's secret.

"Is it your baby?" his father asked.

"Of course not," he said. "Do you think so little of me?"

"It happened to Mark and he was never as wild as you," his mother said. Her eyes were filled with tears.

"The baby is not mine," he said so forcefully the muscles in his throat tightened. When his parents didn't say anything for several long moments it was clear that they didn't believe him or at least needed more of an explanation. "It doesn't matter that you don't believe me. I know the truth. Christine knows the truth."

Eli walked to the front door then turned around. "I'm not the same as I was before. Leaving for the CPS and being away for so long changed me. I don't want to be that wild son you had before, but I also can't be who you want me to be and just marry Matilda. When I marry — if I marry — it will be for two reasons. Because I will be ready to love the woman for the rest of my life and because I know God has set her apart just for me."

His parents looked at each other then looked back at him again. Eli realized he didn't think he had ever mentioned God in any conversation before. He had always been looking out for his own happiness, the futile, immediate kind, but he knew better now and he meant what he said.

After his parents didn't respond for several long moments he decided to leave. He didn't stomp off or slam any doors like he'd done many times before. He would show them he had grown. He would show them he was different.

Moses arrived home and unhitched his

horse just as Eli pulled out his own horse and hitched him up to the same buggy.

"What are you doing?" Moses asked.

"I'm going for a drive and then — I don't know." Eli didn't look at his brother. He had told Moses he could use the buggy while he was away since he hadn't saved enough money at the time to buy his own.

"What am I going to use? I have a date tonight."

Eli shrugged. "You'll have to take the open Dearborn I guess. That's what I had to use this morning. I'm home now, Moses, I need my buggy back."

He heard his younger brother let out a frustrated sigh and kick the dirt. He mumbled something under his breath but Eli didn't care. He just needed to get away.

Several hours later he found himself walking into the house that was hosting the Singing. Eli couldn't believe he was there. It was really the last place he wanted to be. He couldn't help but wish Christine had come with him. But she wasn't there. She was still at home, maybe still feeling sick. He did know that attending the Singing was what his parents wanted from him. And getting their acceptance and approval was what he wanted.

Attending a Singing after so long gave him

the sense of getting younger. Joining in the singing portion didn't bother him much — he actually enjoyed singing. His harmonica was in his pocket and he wanted to pull it out, but thought better than to draw more attention to himself. He didn't, however, want to play the games. He gripped the bench where he sat. Walk-a-Mile, Love in the Dark, Pleased and Displeased — there were several others that their district played regularly. It gave them all the chance to mingle and be social. Tonight thankfully there was only time for one game and he had almost made it through the entire game of Pleased and Displeased until he was called on.

"Matilda," Simon, who was running the game, said. "You and Eli will have a date tonight. Pleased or displeased?"

Matilda's eyes nearly fell out of her head. Eli started groaning, then turned it into clearing his throat. It wasn't unheard of for whoever was running the games to set up a date without permission. Up until now, just like church, the boys and girls had been kept separate. He hadn't had any interaction with Matilda, except for avoiding her eyes on him.

"Pleased!" Matilda hopped up like a piece of popcorn.

"Come on, Eli," Simon waved him up. "Games are done."

He stood, grabbed his hat, and stuffed it on his head. Eli knew it would be too hurtful to turn Matilda down in front of everyone, and it wasn't the way the game was played. Matilda was at his side, reminding him of a barn cat that wouldn't leave him alone. She grabbed his hand and wrapped her arm around his. She led them down the porch stairs and around to the side of the house where the lineup of horses and buggies were hitched up at the fence near the barn.

"It's so nice to have you home, Eli," she said. Her voice made him wince. She was using a childlike voice that irritated him. "There's no one else in there that I would have been *pleased* with like I am you. But you already know that."

"Matilda, this is just a game. We are just friends." If he pushed too hard, everyone in the community would know their business by morning. He didn't need more rumors spreading around about him.

He pulled his hand away. The dull thud of the horses beating their hooves against the spring-soaked ground mixed in with the sound of distant thunder. Like a flashlight, the sky filled with lightning and the breeze

356

picked up. The chilled draft blew through his loose shirt, refreshing his sweaty skin. He hadn't realized how hot the *haus* had gotten. The crisp air brought some clarity to his situation with Matilda. He looked down at her. She looked at him with sparkling eyes.

"Listen, Matilda, I know that I'm supposed to take you home because of the game." He stuffed his hands in his pocket and walked slowly to his buggy, trying to avoid looking at her. "But, like before, this isn't a date. We are just friends."

"Eli, I just do not understand you." Matilda's voice shook. He could see from the corner of his eye that she had wrapped her arms around herself. "We can talk about it on the drive."

He turned to face her only to find that she was jogging toward the house. He backed out his horse and buggy and Matilda was ready to hop in by the time he had it on the drive behind a few others. Without a word or a smile she got into her place on the buggy. He got in next and they both remained uncomfortably silent even when they reached the road and the horse started to canter all the way to her house a few miles away. Still neither of them spoke. Eli hadn't even known it was possible for

Matilda to stay quiet for so long.

"Here we are," he said, pulling into her driveway. He could see an oil lamp in the front window, but otherwise the house was dark.

"Aren't you coming in?"

"I think I should go home. I really don't want —" He stopped talking when he could see her eyes glisten even in the darkness of the buggy.

"I didn't date anyone the entire time you were away. I was waiting for you. And now you just want to go home?" Thick with emotion, she hiccupped when she spoke. She turned her face to look through the front of the buggy. "I have your favorite pie waiting."

Another rumble of thunder rolled above them. Eli looked up and though his eyes only met with the buggy ceiling, he imagined the black clouds turning over the navy blue sky.

"I can't, I don't want you to get the wrong idea," he said. "Besides, I have an early morning now that we have to pick up Mark's chores, too."

"Everyone's already in bed. So we'll have time to ourselves."

"No, Matilda." His voice was harsher than he'd planned. "I'm sorry."

Repeating what he'd told her from the beginning, that they were just friends, seemed useless. Small pellets of rain dotted the windshield and drummed atop the buggy. She choked on her emotion and Eli turned toward her. As soon as their eyes met in the darkness she started crying and left the buggy.

His lungs squeezed in guilt as he watched her walk through the rain to her front door. He sighed when she struggled to open the door and looked over at him as she finally stepped through. When he was sure she was safely inside he left.

Eli pulled up the windshield as he pulled out of the drive then paced his horse. Eli loved the fast, smooth gait. The rain hitting him was refreshing and brought a smile to his lips.

"Come on, Billy," he said to his horse, named after Billy the Kid when he bought him during his early *rumschpringa* years. Had Matilda gotten the message? Eli wasn't sure.

Billy pushed himself faster. Eli hollered into the rain. With Matilda behind him and the fresh air and a fast horse and maybe real love ahead of him, his true self was returning.

Christine's sudden nausea had only been induced by the smell of the ham at church. She was glad that bacon didn't have the same effect on her when she woke to Annie's breakfast the next morning. Not to mention all the food Annie prepared for the two of them for lunch and supper as well. Aunt Annie was such an excellent cook that Christine was glad to eat anything she made. Unfortunately she realized that she was beginning to gain weight fast, and it wasn't just the growing baby.

It was late and the oil lamp glowed. She undressed but before she pulled on her nightgown she took in her reflection in the window. Her dresses would soon no longer hide an abdomen that seemed to expand daily. Though it didn't look like a pregnant belly yet. She remembered her mother saying that she never looked with child until she was nearly six months. What would she do when she could no longer keep her circumstances from everyone around her? That's when she would have to make a real decision about the maternity home or staying in Sunrise. Either way, her life was going to change forever.

Christine moved her hands down the small bulge and imagined she had a husband who would put his ear to her belly and swear he could hear the baby's heart beating. He would look up at her excitedly and they would dream of a house full of children. Just thinking about this made her face grow warm with embarrassment. She slipped the nightgown over her body quickly, not wanting to see her shape anymore. It hung loosely around her, hiding her shame, but her guilt would never be buried.

Past her window reflection she could see Eli's house and the barn where he was still staying. There was a dim glow through the small window near the loft where he was sleeping. She had only seen him for a few brief moments since yesterday. He'd been busy on the farm with Mark still in bed. He still jogged over each day after supper to say hello and good night, if Christine and Annie hadn't eaten with the Brennemans.

"David's wedding banns are being announced soon," Eli told her one evening after supper as they sat on the porch swing hanging from a nearby tree.

"Wedding banns?" Her bare toe dragged against the grass before she pushed against the ground, keeping the swing moving.

"Their wedding announcement, which usually happens about three weeks before the ceremony. In our language we call it *aus ruffah* — which means *to call out*."

"Sounds romantic." She pulled her legs up onto the swing and faced him. The breeze lifted her hair from her shoulders. She'd been wearing her hair more simply since being there, rarely pin curling it. She'd been bathing in a basin instead of showering, using an outhouse, and learning to cook on a woodstove. Life seemed slower and more relaxed in Sunrise and the perfect hairstyle was becoming less and less important. Wearing it long and loose or in a ponytail was more normal.

"Really, you think so?" He grinned, his blue eyes twinkling. "Here I thought English girls would find our ways too simple."

"Not too simple." She shook her head. "Don't get me wrong. Every girl I know has dreamed of the man she loves on bended knee and a pretty lacy or satin snow-white gown on her wedding day. Pretending you don't know that the man you love has already asked your dad for your hand in marriage, practicing your vows and the wedding kiss . . ."

Christine inhaled the cool air. She was talking about dreams that would never happen. The words from the maternity home letter crossed her mind. She would be returned to her family *in a condition that is proper and respectful.*

Impossible.

After breakfast a few mornings later a knock resounded at the door. Christine was sitting at the table writing a letter to Jeanne.

"Come on in," Christine called out before she thought to consider who might be standing there. Usually Eli was the only one who visited.

"Sylvia?" Christine waved her to come inside. "Come on in. I hope Mark is doing well. Has he been able to sleep? I heard he was complaining about being tired still."

Sylvia nodded and smiled shyly. The two of them hadn't spent any time alone together since the day in the back of the buggy. She bit her lower lip as she stood there. Her abdomen pushed against her brown dress in the shape of half a cantaloupe.

"Oh, Mark's fine — but you're right, he does complain a lot. I just came over to see if you wouldn't mind helping us again." Sylvia sat at the kitchen table with Christine.

"What's that?"

"Dr. Sherman is busy today and can't stop in. He asked that maybe you could check on Mark's leg for him — but only if you're up for it?"

Being useful in this way brought her a thrill. "I'd love to." She hopped off the chair and grabbed her coat before Sylvia could even say thank you.

They walked over in silence and entered the small bedroom.

"Syl?" Mark asked, followed by several Dutch words that Christine didn't understand. Sylvia sat down on the edge of the bed and spoke back. Christine realized scolding sounded the same in Pennsylvania Dutch as it did in English.

Mark's eyes darted to Christine and then back again.

"I'm just here to help," Christine interjected.

Mark let out a loud sigh and his arms went down to his sides, surrendering. His face went to the window opposite Christine.

Sylvia looked up at Christine and smiled. She moved away so Christine could get to Mark's leg. She used the supplies that Dr. Sherman had left and cleaned and redressed the wound.

"It is healing very well, Mark," she said, standing.

"Really? See Mark. We'll get the house up

before the heat of the summer hits."

Christine left them to discuss their plans. When she left the room two ladies were walking into the house with Sarah.

"Christine." Sarah smiled but appeared uncomfortable, her eyes darted between her and her company. "This is Mariellen Fisher and her daughter Amanda."

Christine smiled. "Hi, nice to meet you," she said and put her hand out. She'd learned a hearty handshake went a long way in this community. After they shook hands she looked back at Sarah. "I was just checking in on Mark."

The ladies smiled at her and simultaneously untied and removed their black bonnets and unpinned their black capes. Both wore navy dresses and white coverings. The two women looked more like sisters than mother and daughter, blond hair and bright blue eyes. Both had smiles that stretched along their faces.

With a nod she walked through the living room then down the porch steps when Sylvia called her back.

"Christine. Wait."

She turned around. "Did you need something? Does Mark need anything?"

Sylvia shook her head. The women both stood at the bottom of the steps in an awkward moment of silence.

"I just wanted to say thank you for helping."

"I'm always willing to help. Being a nurse is actually something I'm good at," Christine said, chuckling.

"Sorry that Mark's so ornery. I scolded him."

The women laughed.

"Don't be too hard on him. I've had a lot worse patients than Mark. Eli and I both have."

She wished instantly that she'd left Eli out of it since Mark and Eli were so hateful toward each other.

"I'd love to hear your hospital stories sometime."

"Really?" Christine let out a measured breath and smiled.

Sylvia nodded and her mouth formed a quick grin.

"I'd love to visit with you more. Would you stay now?"

"Sarah has company. Maybe today isn't a good day."

"Mariellen and Amanda are here to talk about the wedding," Sylvia said in a whisper. "Since it's still a secret you'll get to hear the plans before anyone else."

Sylvia looked at her with hopeful eyes.

"Okay," Christine said.

She followed Sylvia into the house and pretended not to notice when the other three women went silent.

"I asked Christine to join us."

"Can you crochet doilies?" Mariellen asked, eyebrows up.

"No, you don't want me to do that. Annie says she's planning to teach me though."

"You'll want to learn to soon, right?" Amanda asked.

Sarah eyed Amanda, then changed the subject. "Why don't you slice the cherry pie for us?"

Christine pushed her chair away from the table and did as she was asked. She took out a butter knife, having learned where Sarah kept her kitchen items. The butter knife in her hands hovered over the pie for several long moments before she replayed how she'd watched the other ladies cut into pie.

"I'm surprised that cherry pie didn't get eaten for breakfast," Mariellen said.

"Oh, I have to hide it from the boys otherwise it's gone *before* breakfast," Sarah added.

"Especially with Eli, so I hear. Matilda said cherry is his favorite," Mariellen said with obvious intention behind her words.

"She baked one for him when he drove her home from the Singing."

"Oh, he's not even my worst, it's Enos. He sneaks under the porch with pie, brown sugar, and just about anything else sweet that you can imagine. But, *ja,* cherry is Eli's favorite."

The conversation continued in Pennsylvania Dutch and Christine's heart hammered in her chest. Her nerves made her stomach turn and she breathed evenly to push away the discomfort. She shouldn't be feeling this way about Eli but his smile was engraved in her mind. Did she have real feelings for him? She made the last cut in the pie carefully.

"Sell gookt gute," Sylvia said, standing next to her. She smiled. "I said that it looks good."

Christine smiled back. "Think so?"

Sylvia nodded. "I'll get the plates and forks."

Christine set the pie on the table and the conversation returned to English. She ate a piece of pie in silence and learned that since the war rations had been lifted they were planning a bigger spread than the weddings during the war. She excused herself in the middle of their wedding conversation, needing to get some air.

"Annie is expecting me for lunch. I better go," Christine told the women. As she left the farmhouse she heard Eli's booming baritone coming from the barn. She decided she had a few minutes to say hello. When she got closer she heard a non-Amishman's voice.

"How did you like the camp life?" the man asked when she was still a short distance away. She could see the non-Amishman leaning against the wide-open door of the barn and assumed Eli and his brothers were inside.

"Oh, it wasn't so bad. I learned a lot at the hospital job." Eli's voice brought a smile to her lips.

"You didn't have anyone shootin' at ya, did ya?" the man asked.

Christine slowed her pace. Maybe she should turn around and leave. This man was clearly baiting Eli. She ducked behind the outhouse near the barn, too curious to stop listening.

"Come on, now, Bucket, you know how I feel about that." How could he keep his voice so calm? And, did he call the man *Bucket*?

"You mean what your church believes. You shot lots of guns when we were growing up," Bucket was badgering Eli.

"We were hunting," Eli's voice grew louder.

"What about that time you got me in the back?"

"That was a slingshot, not a gun, and we were ten. If I remember, we were playing cowboys and Indians and you got me back."

"Coward."

Christine quietly gasped and her hand covered her mouth.

"What did you call me?" Eli's voice was steely.

"Hey, Bucket, when did you get back?" Christine recognized Moses's voice.

"Got back a few weeks ago. Got a purple heart."

Christine could hear the clap of hands joining in a strong handshake.

"Gettin' married next week," Bucket said. Christine breathed a sigh of relief. For now the other man was leaving Eli alone.

"Is that right," Moses said. His voice wasn't as deep as Eli's.

"Eli here's gonna be getting married soon, too. Ain't that right, Eli?"

Christine's gasp was almost too loud. She put her back against the outhouse. The air warmed around her and her underarms tingled with sweat. Eli was getting married?

"Moses, drop it," Eli said.

"Who's the lucky girl?" Bucket asked.

"Well, I think he's got his pick. He's taking Matilda Miller home after the Singing and then sitting on a porch swing with the English girl through the week."

So he *had* gone on a date with Matilda. He hadn't said anything to Christine about it and she didn't want to ask. It was time for him to move on now that he was home from the CPS, but somehow it still stung her heart hearing he had gone on a date.

"Oh, Matilda's that real small, pretty thing. Kinda mousy though. Who's the English girl?"

"Moses, Bucket, stop. I mean it."

"Christine's a pretty little lady. He brought her home from his fancy hospital job."

Christine grew hot. What was Moses saying?

"An English girl. Maybe I need to take a look at her."

"Oh, no, you won't want to. She's already all used up. I think Eli's gonna be a daddy."

Christine's gasp was more of a cry. She stepped away from the outhouse wall and looked at the three men. Bucket turned and she could see the scars that ran the length of his face. His hair was cut like all the soldiers. He was tall and thin. Moses's face grew red and Eli's hands clenched but his eyes locked on her own.

"Eli, you promised," she muttered. Beginning to cry, she ran as fast as she could through the field and toward the cottage.

"Christine!" She could hear him step toward her but then all she could hear was the sound of her own sobs.

CHAPTER 23

Eli had lied to her. He had told his brothers that she was expecting, and they thought he was the father. He'd promised her that he wouldn't tell until she was ready. He had been so good to her — so kind, and so sure that everything would work out. Now everyone would know that she was *all used up*. She closed the front door behind her then ran to her room, slamming the door. With her back against the door she slid down and sat, pulling her knees up. The very action of this made her feel how her belly was growing. The bulge pushed against her legs and told her that her secret was going to get out any day now anyway. She leaned her head forward, not quite on her knees, and cried.

Christine had been in Sunrise for less than a month and she thought things were going well. She and Annie had an instant connection and even Sylvia was becoming a friend. But now that her disgrace was known, this arrangement would never work. Christine would have to write to the maternity home and buy a bus ticket as soon as possible. Then she'd give the baby up for adoption. No one would ever have to know.

"Christine?" Eli's voice came from the other side of the door.

"Go away, Eli."

"Christine, please. Open the door. We need to talk."

She didn't answer. Her anger was nothing compared to her hurt.

"I didn't tell Moses. I promise you." After several long moments he sighed deeply. "I had to tell my parents and he overheard. Please, Christine," he whispered.

Christine could feel his heat through the door. She could always feel Eli's heat when they were anywhere together. It was always something that bothered her in the beginning but the more she got to know him and the more she had grown to care for him, she began craving the heat. It energized her and made her believe that she could trust what he said.

Christine scooted away from the door, lifted her hand, and turned the key under the door knob. The click was loud in the quiet of the house. When the door moved open she saw Eli standing there. His face

374

was in a panic and his knuckles bloody.

"What did you do?"

He looked at his knuckles then back at her. "Punched a wall."

"Why?"

"Because I knew I couldn't hit Bucket or Moses."

"Come on." She pulled him into the kitchen where there was a basin of water. She took his bloodied hand and dabbed it with a wet cloth.

"I really am sorry, Christine." He put his other hand on hers. She looked up and inhaled. He was so close. She wanted to forgive him but her hurt was too much. She looked down and he pulled his hand away so she could continue cleaning the wound. She couldn't let his gaze penetrate her too deeply. He'd lied and betrayed her confidence.

"I'm going to —" her voice quivered as she spoke. "I'm going to write to that maternity home. I can't stay here. I need to go. You know that I'm right."

"Please. Don't go." Eli took his wounded hand from her, put both of his hands on her waist, and pulled her closer.

Christine held her breath.

"Christine, look at me." The heat grew — her body was on fire. She closed her eyes for a long moment before she opened them again. She couldn't trust her instincts. She had trusted Jack and look what had come of that. Now Eli had disappointed her as well. She saw Annie walking toward the cottage through the window.

"I can't." She gently pushed against his chest. "I want you to leave."

"Christine," he whispered and leaned closer in to her.

"You need to leave," she whispered back and let her eyes find his. She saw in his eyes what she imagined was in her own — disappointment, fear, and maybe even some self-loathing. As she tried to blink away her tears several slipped down her cheek. Eli's shoulder sagged and his hands dropped from her waist. She clenched her jaw in order to keep herself from crying.

"Hi, there," Annie strolled in, walking through the kitchen without really looking at them. "Walked down to the Peterscheims for coffee." She took her coat off and looked over. "Oh, Eli, I didn't notice. Do you want to stay for lunch? I've got some friendship bread cooling."

Eli stepped away. Their eyes met again.

"I need to get back to work," he said.

Christine didn't watch him leave but when she heard the front door close she leaned back against the kitchen counter and for a moment thought she would collapse. In a few moments Annie stood in front of her.

"Do you want to talk about it?" the older woman asked.

Christine sat down in a kitchen chair as her answer. Annie put some water on for tea then joined her at the table.

"When are you due?" Annie asked.

Christine's head snapped up, looking at her.

"How did you find out? Did Eli tell you, too?"

Mei maedle." Annie patted Christine's hand. "I've known since the first day you were here. Then when you were suddenly sick at church. The ham."

"How?"

"Listen. I delivered my first baby forty-four years ago. I know a baby's on the way before the mothers do. It's just something I can sense after all these years."

"Why didn't you say anything?"

"I figured God would tell me when."

They were both quiet for a few moments. The wall clock clicked loudly and she could hear a storm brewing.

"Eli said he didn't tell Moses but he found out and then this boy Bucket was there and —"

"Christine, what's really the problem? I don't really think it's Moses or this *Bucket* you're talking about."

Christine contemplated what Annie was getting at.

"But Moses said I was *all used up.* It was terrible and humiliating and . . ." She couldn't finish.

Annie took her hand this time.

"Those Brenneman boys are all pretty spiteful against Eli. Now that he's back I think they might do whatever they can to make things tough on him."

"It's because of Mark, isn't it? Why?"

"You know, a lot of people think that old folks like me don't know or see anything. I've been living here since December and I've seen a whole lot. More than what anyone thinks I do. Mark just likes to stir things up, mostly just petty things, and I think all the other boys are taking Mark's side."

"Before I got here I thought that all of you just always got along. I mean, you pray twice for meals, before and after. That's pretty religious. Then you wear your bonnets or *coverings* and it means you can pray all the time since your head is covered. And your families are so big and everyone takes care of one another. Like this house, your family is taking care of you, right? So how is it possible that Eli's brothers don't even like him? I've begun to wonder if they're right about him."

Annie leaned back in her chair. It creaked even though she was so small. There was a smile on her face as she began speaking.

"We're Amish, Christine, not angels."

"I didn't mean . . ." She paused.

"You're not alone with thinking we are *angels*. People often confuse the two. Less so since the war started. It brought up a lot of judgment that we've all tried to forget since the beginning of the First World War. When our boys didn't sign up to fight I think our churches were seen as more than just different on the outside from all the other American boys. We seek peace but we still have problems like everyone else. We separate ourselves from the world because it's the best way we know to be close to God. But that doesn't mean we don't still have our fair share of problems." She paused. "Give Eli a chance to explain. He cares for you."

"He shouldn't care for me. This is not his baby," she clarified. "This baby doesn't have a father."

Annie leaned forward and took Christine's hands and squeezed them in her own.

"Everyone has a Father."

Christine didn't want to talk about Jack. She wanted to change the subject and thought of Aunt Annie's babies.

"The first Sunday I went to church with you I heard you say that you've lost babies."

Annie's face twitched and she squeezed Christine's hands before letting go. After a moment she nodded.

"Can I ask what happened?"

"We really don't know why. I lost three beautiful babies. But they weren't miscarriages; two were stillborn and one was born alive."

"I'm so sorry. Couldn't the doctors do something for you?" Her hands went to her abdomen as fear coursed through her heart. What if that happened to her baby?

"Oh, they just rattled off some highfalutin words that I never understood." She sighed. "Joyce, my third, lived the longest. Two hours and eleven minutes."

Annie's eyes were so sad. Christine reached a hand out to Annie only to pause suddenly for the stirring that grew within her. It puzzled her and slowly her hand returned to her stomach. The fluttering sensation was the baby.

"What is it?" Annie asked and sat a little taller.

"I think I am feeling the baby." Her voice was laced with wonder and shock.

"May I?" Annie asked. Christine nodded.

Annie leaned over and put her hands on Christine's small stomach.

"Does it feel like a feather just brushed up against you?" the older woman asked.

Christine nodded. "Is that normal? Everything's all right, isn't it?"

"It's like a secret between your baby and you. No one else can feel what you are feeling. Your baby wants you to know that he's there."

"He?"

"I could be wrong, but I think this babe's a boy."

Instead of mirroring the storm that was brewing outside, a calmness poured over Christine with Annie's hands warm and comforting on her abdomen. A boy.

"Can I ask you a question?"

Christine nodded.

"Let me be your midwife. Let me take care of you."

"But I don't even know if I'm going to stay. I think I should leave. There's a home —"

"Don't go. If you go your child will surely be taken away from you. Is that what you really want?"

Christine shrugged. "I don't know. I could start over again, right? And the baby would have a mother *and* a father. Isn't that what's best?"

"Just don't make any hasty decisions. There's plenty of time." She patted Christine's hands. "I have a feeling this baby was conceived in fear and pain, but don't punish the babe. I just know things will work out."

Hot tears trailed down Christine's face. "I hate his father and I feel very angry with Eli also. I'm afraid God isn't very happy with me right now. So, how do you know that things will work out?"

"I know because I know our Father. That's the only way you're going to heal. If you decide to go to this home, just don't shut God out of your life or your plans."

While all Eli could think of was the day's events with Christine, he was still obligated to join the Millers for supper. Eli had heard Matilda was spreading rumors about him eating a whole cherry pie she baked for him. He needed to clear everything up and finally put Matilda behind him. The weeknight invitation wasn't common for the young people. They usually had to depend on Sunday church services and Singings. Since

Eli had been away for so long, it was natural that he would get some supper invitations. He figured it would be better to deal with Matilda at her own home instead of at another Singing, since she hadn't gotten the message at the last one.

All through the drive Eli thought of Christine and their argument. In a different way from Matilda, he'd let himself get in too deep with Christine also. If she stayed or left, nothing would be easy.

The evening drive was warmer than expected and somehow Eli believed that the comfortable temperature would make his words to Matilda less biting. Matilda bounded out of the house when his horse and buggy pulled into the gravel drive. He sat in silence, giving himself a few long moments before attempting to break up with a girl he wasn't dating.

Eli hopped out and Matilda's brightness nearly blinded him. He inhaled deeply and diverted his eyes to the tree nearby that blew softly in the spring breeze. He couldn't put it off any longer. Eli leaned against the buggy and cleared his throat. How to start?

"We've been cooking all day. *Dat* said to pull out the canned venison for a hearty stew and I baked another cherry pie — just for you."

"Because I ate the last one all by myself?" He raised an eyebrow as he looked at her.

Matilda shut her mouth and her face turned red. She looked at her feet.

Eli stood and walked a few paces over to her. He saw her younger siblings looking through the window and for a moment thought he saw her mother slipping casually out of view when he caught sight of her. He looked back at Matilda who hadn't raised her lowered chin yet.

"Eli, I just know that we're right for each other," she squeaked.

"You need to stop spreading stories. We never dated and we aren't going to date."

Her glow diminished to a dull reflection from a tin plate. Was she going to cry now or just stomp off? Would she slap him across the face? All of those things had happened to him with other single girls and he had no idea how Matilda would ultimately react.

"It's that Christine girl, isn't it? I don't believe the rumors that you're the father of her baby."

Was she serious? He shook his head, disturbed at the way this conversation was going. "This isn't about Christine, Matilda, it's —"

Eli was caught off guard. She lunged at him, wrapped her arms around his neck and pulled him down. Next thing he knew her lips were atop his. She made *mmmm* sounds as she kissed him. Her eyes were shut. His were open. He pulled her away and set her firmly down on the ground. Enough. This needed to end now.

"Now, please stop all of this," he spoke clearly and directly, looking right into her eyes. "We were never a couple. We will never get married. It is time to stop this nonsense and move on with your life."

In slow motion her face sagged and a loud wail escaped her mouth. Her sister came out and wrapped an arm around her and led her inside.

Eli let out a sigh as he returned to his buggy. He hoped he had not been too harsh with her, but at least this madness was finally over. What would the reaction be among the youth? He knew they would believe Matilda's story and he would once again appear to be the wild, noncommittal, single man. It was too late to stop by Christine's place as he drove home. It infuriated him. He needed, more than anything, to talk with her.

As he drove home that night all he could think about was how it would be so much easier if he just left.

CHAPTER 24

A week after her argument with Eli, Christine saw Dr. Sherman's car pull into the farm drive. He hadn't contacted her about the job opportunity she had inquired about yet, but perhaps talking in person might urge him to make a decision.

"Annie," she called out, "I'll be right back."

Christine didn't wait for a response from Annie but walked briskly over to the Brennemans' house. Dr. Sherman was with Mark for about ten minutes. The rocker on the porch was a pleasant place to wait, and she stood as soon as she heard the doctor step through the hardwood-floor living room.

"It's looking just fine, Sylvia," Dr. Sherman said. "I'll come back again next week."

The door opened and the doctor replaced his hat on his head when Christine stepped toward him.

"Dr. Sherman." Her voice sounded eager and her hands were wringing.

"Nurse Freeman, right?" he said, smiling.

"Yes, that's right. A few weeks ago I wrote you about a job."

"Yes, I remember." The doctor gestured for her to follow him down to his car. "I was ready to give you the opportunity, but was advised otherwise."

The doctor inhaled and pursed his lips. He opened his car door and placed his black bag inside.

"May I ask why?"

"Nurse Freeman," he began, "the truth of the matter is that I really could use a nurse with your skills in my practice, don't get me wrong. It's just that —"

"Because of the baby," Christine whispered. He was only doing what any other employer would do in his shoes. No one wanted their business to become a place of scandal.

"I am sorry, young lady, I wish things were different." He lifted his hat as he nodded at her and then climbed into his car and drove away, leaving Christine to stand in the drive alone.

Over the next few weeks Christine sequestered herself from the Brenneman family. Her life was a glasshouse. The knowledge of her condition had reached the good Dr. Sherman so quickly. The disappointment with Dr. Sherman brought the burden over her argument with Eli to the forefront of her mind. She had hurt him by not listening to his side of the story. The shock in his eyes and the way his shoulders slumped as he walked off bound her heart in guilt. Her talk with Annie had made her realize that her baby wasn't to blame, whether she kept the child or not.

Finally, after a week of staying away, her guilt could stand it no more. Christine would have to find Eli first thing in the morning. She had already lost too much time with her friend. Was he just a friend? She'd missed Eli far more than she cared to admit to until now.

Before the sun was up she was dressed and walking down the well-worn path to Eli's barn. The morning mist hung around her and she could feel the dampness on her skin. He would be waking soon or already up, and she would be waiting. She opened the barn door carefully, not wanting to wake him herself. The squeal of the door, however, made her wince. If he wasn't already awake, he would be now.

A rustling from the loft sounded.

"Eli?" She spoke softly. "It's Christine."

There was more rustling but he didn't answer. After another minute he climbed over the side of the loft and down the ladder. His suspenders hung down from his homemade pants and he wore an undershirt that seemed a bit small over his chest and arms. She cleared her throat and pushed up her glasses.

"My clean shirts are in the house," he said quietly and rubbed his face.

Eli was more handsome than she was prepared for. His long mussed hair hung over his forehead.

"I'm sorry for waking you, Eli," she said. Christine had the sudden urge to push his hair away from his eyes and touch his face. How dear he really was to her. "I needed to see you."

Eli sat on a rough-hewn bench against an age-beaten stall and gestured for her to sit next to him. She did and tried not to wring her hands. His closeness made her nervous. It would be too easy to let her feelings get the best of her. Despite what they both said, they were more than just friends.

"I really am sorry the way it all came out. Not long after you got here I knew my parents needed to know — it would help them understand why you were here," he said, placing his elbows on his knees and looking over his shoulder at her. "I really didn't tell Moses. He admitted to me that he overheard my conversation."

He shrugged.

"You know the rest. Moses should've come to me first but he's headstrong and stubborn."

"Sounds like it runs in the family." A smile crept on her lips before she could stop it.

Eli smiled back but it didn't linger.

"You can imagine how the news spread after that."

He took her hand and Christine let him. His touch was honest and natural. They weren't dating and for several weeks they seemed barely friends. When their hands joined, however, it boasted of safety and value — she was cherished. The opposite of how Jack had left her. Eli was like the dawn's green grass and prism raindrops after a thunderstorm. But even with her hand in his, she was still stuck in the blackness of the night, and the glimpse of the morning was a fleeting sight.

"I hate this for you because I know what the Amish telephone is like. I've been the brunt of it many times."

"The Amish telephone?"

"That's what we call all the gossips. We

don't need your kind of telephones, believe me."

Their smiles were mirror images. She pulled her hand back to her lap but regretted it as soon as she did.

"It was my fault. That's why I'm here." She turned toward him and touched his arm hesitantly. When the warmth of his arm was beneath her fingertips her blood rushed hot through her body. She kept it there. "I never should've made you keep my secret. It's made things way too difficult for you. I don't want to make things more complicated for you."

"Are you coming to tell me that you're leaving?" He looked over his shoulder at her. Christine could see fear in his eyes.

"Not yet. Annie convinced me to stay."

Eli sighed heavily, then leaned back against the stall wall. His movement forced Christine to release his arm. She put her hand in her lap. How had she come to care so deeply for him without realizing it? This was a dangerous place to be. His family was so important to him; she couldn't ask him to give up his future for someone like her.

"I'm glad." He inhaled and stood.

Eli put out a hand for hers. She took it. He pulled her closer to him. Their bodies were nearly touching. Christine knew he wanted to kiss her, but she also knew it couldn't happen — or shouldn't anyway. They were from two different worlds — not to mention she was expecting a baby.

"Eli, I can't," she whispered.

He traced his finger down her jawline with a resigned smile.

Christine released a small gasp. She took a step back and brought her hands to her stomach.

"What is it?"

She giggled and smiled. "It's the baby." She looked up at him. "Kicking."

"Really?" His eyes beamed as if he were suddenly wide-awake.

"Here," she said, holding her hand out for his. She took his hesitant palm and put it on her abdomen. His eyes went from her stomach to her face, locking eyes for several long moments, then back to her stomach.

"Oh, I felt it." He chuckled as he spoke.

"Him," she said. "You felt him."

"Him?"

"Annie said I'm having a boy."

A son, he thought, then reminded himself that this child was not *his* son. But how he loved her. How he wanted to tell her. How he wanted to kiss her. He didn't just want to hold her to console her through disappointments and fears, but to hold her in that way that makes the rest of the world fall away. He wanted her to see that no one ever meant to him what she meant to him. Eli wanted to make Christine happy and to take care of her for the rest of their lives. He wanted to be a father to the baby.

This could never be.

He removed his hand from her abdomen and put his hands gently around her fore-arms — keeping her close.

"Let's just leave and make a life some-where else," he blurted out, shuffling away his former thoughts on how this could never be.

"What? Eli?"

"Why not? No one wants me around here. Mark is making my life miserable. We could be happy. Let's just run away from all of this. I'll take care of you. I'll take care of you both."

Christine's mouth was open but she didn't speak any words. Eli bent down and she tilted her head toward him. His heart raced.

"Just like I told Dad." Mark pushed through the barn door. "I knew you couldn't be trusted. You haven't changed a bit, Eli. Just leave before you hurt Mom and Dad even more."

Mark walked away before either of them

could respond.

They hadn't even heard him approach.

CHAPTER 25

For the next several mornings Eli made sure he was out in the field ahead of everyone else — hoping to avoid Mark as much as possible. Mist hung around him as he made tracks against the long, dewy grass, steering the cows toward the barn for their milking. The chill of the morning woke him and it was the only time of the day where he could sense God speaking to him and where he could speak back. The cows didn't mind his easy, whispered prayers.

Most of the time he didn't even know what to pray for. He and Christine continued their easy conversations at the end of the day. Neither of them had brought up their discussion about taking off together. What would've happened if Mark hadn't interrupted them? Would they have kissed? Would she have answered him, and would they have made a poor decision or the right one? Which was the right one?

One morning a man with two children trailed into the farm and leaned against the milk house. Eli could see the man was neatly dressed, but his pants were too short and his children weren't wearing shoes. His brothers were ahead of him and he watched as Moses and David walked into the barn and Mark walked toward the man and his children. The limp from his leg injury was still distinct but improving.

He couldn't hear them talking so he jogged up next to Mark.

"Good morning, I'm Eli, can we help you?"

"I'm handling this," Mark looked over at him, his arms already crossed over his chest.

"A neighbor down the road said you used to give out some free milk — you know, to needy families? My name is Lawrence and this is Mae and Larry Junior." The man wrung the hat in his hands as he introduced his family. "I'm a war vet, and when I came back my wife passed away and we're just struggling to make ends meet."

"We sure —" Eli started.

"No, we haven't done that for a while. I'm sorry," Mark said, eyeing Eli.

Eli grabbed Mark's arm and pulled him aside.

"We are going to give them as much milk

as they need," Eli whispered loudly.

"We stopped doing this just after you left. We had families come by who weren't even needy. They just wanted a handout. *Dat* put me in charge, Eli, not you."

"Then you can blame me. I'm giving them some milk."

"*Dat*'s used to you not listening to him anyway." He shrugged. "Why do you think he gave me the best property and didn't make you manager again?"

Eli shoved Mark — not hard enough to hurt him, but enough to appease his frustration. Mark put his hands up in surrender.

"Some things never change, Eli."

Eli turned to the man and his children. They stood further back then, and the father had his hand stretched out in front of his children. Their eyes were round as they looked at him.

"Sorry about that," Eli said.

"We don't mean to cause a fuss."

"Why don't you go sit over there and I'll have bread and milk for you in a few minutes."

Eli went to the house and got a loaf of bread from the breadbox and a glass bottle of milk. A moment after he handed it to the man the children were devouring the food and milk. He couldn't stand to watch and walked away. Less than an hour later the family was gone and the milk jar was sitting empty next to the milk house.

"You might think this makes you such a good guy, but I know the truth about you, Eli. Especially about you and that English *frau*. I told *Dat* that you'll probably leave with her any day now. So if you want to be a man of your word, you better follow through."

Eli hadn't seemed like himself for weeks. After Mark had caught them in the barn together, he avoided being alone with her. Christine understood, but missed him. He wore his customary brilliant smile, but it didn't reach his eyes. What was going through his mind? Was he even happy in his community?

Despite missing time with Eli, she was happier than she had been in months. In the past few weeks she and Aunt Annie had grown closer and the community around her began to reach out and befriend her. Sylvia visited almost daily and they received company several times a week just to sit and have tea. Though most of these visits were from other widows or elderly women in the district, she welcomed them. With Aunt Annie's encouragement, she even attended their every-other-week church services. She still couldn't understand what the preacher was saying. Annie interpreted enough of it for her on a notebook during the service, writing out key phrases and verses.

The world's glow is a mere blur in comparison to the radiance of the Lord Jesus. Be firm in your commitment. Be steadfast in the hope He brings. Blessed are the meek, for they shall inherit the earth.

Christine relished the peacefulness she experienced while sitting there. Spring was in full swing and summer was around the corner. The windows would be opened so that the congregation could catch a breeze and the scent of flowering trees. The music of birds whistled through the houses they met in.

Though she didn't help with the noon meal after service, she was greeted with smiles. The young mothers with their babies and the women who were very visibly expecting would invite her to chat in the large bedroom where some of them would sit during the church service. They spoke in English and chatted amongst one another about what new thing their babies were doing and what was going on around the community.

While they didn't ask her any personal

questions, she imagined they wanted to. She respected the restraint they practiced in an uncomfortable situation. Annie had made her three new dresses; a yellow one, a blue one with lighter blue polka dots, and a tan and cream one. She'd made them with simple patterns and did her best to make them work for now and later as her stomach continued to grow. Christine was fascinated by the design, the way it wrapped around her waist and could adjust to her size. They weren't as unadorned as the Amish dresses, but they were simple enough and she liked them a lot.

The baby continued to kick, getting stronger and stronger. She wrestled with the guilt over trying not to love him — or her — but found herself wrapping her arms around her belly and poking back when the baby kicked. She'd giggle and poke again. Often she would fall asleep comforted with the baby moving around, feeling less alone.

June approached and Christine found herself running through the cow's pasture like a young girl. She had a letter in her hand and a smile on her lips. Joyful news came so unexpectedly these days. Eli had to be the first to know.

"Eli?" she called into the barn's opening. "Eli."

"He's out in the back field. A few cows got loose," Moses told her.

"Thank you," she said. She hadn't spoken to Eli's brothers much over the weeks since Moses had ridiculed her. Mark had begun working again in the last few weeks, though he was still taking it easy and not putting in a full day's work. He continued to let Christine check his leg but made no move to be friendly to her. Sylvia remained pleasant and sweet, however. Her belly was larger than Christine's even though Sylvia wasn't due until a month after.

"I look like a dairy cow next to you," she said once and turned bright red. They had both giggled over it.

Christine walked through the barn and made her way into the field. Since living at the farm she'd learned that the Holstein cows ran from her if she walked through the field. They were far more afraid of her than she was of them. She didn't run, afraid she'd step in manure, but she wanted to. Eli's large frame was up ahead, and he was pulling a few cows through a downed-fence area. In the distance she could see how his hair had gotten even lighter — though she hadn't known it was possible. The sun was orange and hot; Christine wished she'd

401

brought a glass of water or lemonade for him.

As she got closer she could see that his shirt was stuck to his chest and back with sweat. His skin had begun to bronze and she'd never seen such strong hands. When he turned to look at her, her heart leapt, shocking her. He gave her a real smile and the sensation stirred through her as they walked toward each other.

"I don't want to disturb you." Christine pointed at the cows.

"They are all in now." Eli's chest rose and fell from the hard work. He wiped his brow with the back of his hand, sending his now-longer hair off to the side. His beard had also grown and was as white-blond as his hair. They were silent as the few stray cows ran toward the group deep into the pasture.

"I should've brought you something cold to drink," Christine said. Why was she nervous? She was sweating more than she should be and all she could think about was his smile and the way he lit up at her presence and, for the first time, the way her heart raced at seeing him. What had changed?

"I'm okay. Just a little hard work." Eli waved her over to the downed fence. She watched as he nailed an extra piece of wood to hold the pieces together. "Looks like I'll need to rebuild this soon, maybe before it gets hot."

They laughed as he grabbed his tools. They walked together toward the barn. Christine didn't want their time to go quickly.

"I got a letter today," she said after walking in silence for a few moments. "That's why I came out to find you."

Eli's head jerked over to look at her. She saw fear in his eyes just before he looked away. He was trying to hide it.

"Oh yeah, who from?"

"From Jeanne." Christine saw relief cross over his eyes. "She and Byron are getting married in a few weeks."

He smiled at her. His eyes twinkled. "That's wonderful. She's a nice girl."

"She's been my best friend for years. I was at her first wedding and with her when she had her memorial for her husband after he was killed in the war." She ached inside, wishing she could go to the wedding. "I can't believe I'm going to miss this wedding."

"Why don't you go to the wedding?"

"You know why. I can't go like this."

"Let's go together," he suggested. "I wouldn't mind some time away."

"But look at me." Her hands were splayed over her abdomen and her eyes grew larger. "This is when I realize how sheltered you've been in your community. Women like me don't just go out in public where people can see them. Not without a ring on this finger."

She wiggled her fourth finger at him.

"Where's the wedding?"

"The hospital courtyard. They want all of the children they work with to be able to attend." Christine opened the letter and glanced over it. "She didn't invite the usual high school crowd since this is her second wedding. But I just know I'd feel so ashamed to walk back onto that property and see the nurses and the aides."

"There's so many children at the hospital we could easily get lost in the crowd. Let's go together."

"I would love to visit with my ma."

Christine looked up at him and they held their gaze for several long moments, and Eli even moved forward before he pulled back, remembering their visibility. This wasn't what was supposed to happen. He dropped his hand from her arm and continued walking. They walked side by side the rest of the way and discussed how it would be possible for them to go.

Two weeks later she was packed and ready to go. She smiled when she saw Eli walk to meet her in the field.

"I like your hat." He smiled into the bright sun behind her.

Her gloved hand went to her yellow hat. "Thanks."

"You look so different. More like the Poughkeepsie Christine than the one that's been here in Sunrise. It's been nearly two months, you know." He winked at her.

She was glad to see her hair rolled nicely again, feeling more like herself. The length of her hair swam in waves around her shoulders and her neat rolls framed her face, which was slightly more rounded than usual. Her lips were bright and she was wearing earrings. Even Aunt Annie had commented on how pretty she looked.

Their hands touched when he took her suitcase from her. The electricity between them coursed through her. She couldn't let this go further. She'd imposed on his family and his life long enough. She would have to make a decision. It wasn't just a decision about whether or not to keep her baby but also about Eli. If she stayed there was a strong chance she would ruin any chance of him having a relationship with his family. Her presence wasn't fair to him.

CHAPTER 26

Riding the bus together brought back memories of when they left Poughkeepsie. Christine couldn't believe they were going back. Like the gray exhaust of the bus, the chance to change her mind was behind them.

Eli pulled out the newspaper he'd grabbed in the station. Christine glanced over, catching a few article topics: a US Supreme Court ruling on segregation on buses, the first one-day transcontinental flight between California and Maryland, and the prison sentence for a Dutch Nazi. She didn't want to be reminded of the war and turned away. Instead she got lost in the passing landscape only clouded by the cigarette smoke coming from the Hollywood-looking blonde behind them.

They arrived after supper and Freddy, who had returned to work at the hospital after his service, gathered them from the bus station. He was proud driving in his black Mercury. He looked smaller than normal behind the large steering wheel. It was strange to see the Kirkbride building again. Its green, pointy hoods cut into a perfect summer sky. It appeared more menacing than she'd even remembered.

Jeanne hugged Christine in the parking lot and then rushed her away to her new home. Christine would be staying overnight in Jeanne's new house on the grounds of the hospital while Eli was with Freddy.

Annie had made a dress for Christine that would hide her burgeoning midsection. She made the waist higher and added fabric that would float right over her front. Since she was only six months along, this hid her belly almost entirely. The following day was filled with curt nods and hellos from the staff. Some were cold enough to usher back the winter weather and others were warm and friendly. She wasn't sure whether or not people noticed her small bulge, but everyone was shocked at her arrival with Eli. In the chairs near the courtyard gazebo sat Jeanne's parents and siblings and what looked like Byron's parents. Behind them was the crowd of hospital children that Byron and Jeanne cared for. Christine stayed around the edges of the patients during the wedding, and even though she couldn't enjoy it like she would've liked, she was glad Eli had talked her into attending.

Jeanne was every bit as beautiful a bride as she was the first time. The desire to be like her — as happy — and rid of this scandal burned her heart. She took it in as if it were the last of all joys she would see in her life.

The wedding ceremony was interesting to Eli. He'd never been to an English wedding before. He watched Christine, who stood next to him as the couple repeated vows to each other, and saw how she seemed to hang on every word.

He listened to the words. He loved how Byron vocalized his promise to love, honor, and cherish Jeanne. The intent was the same in their Amish weddings, but hearing the English words spoken aloud struck his heart. His eyes shot over to Christine, who was dabbing her eyes and smiling. He wished he could stop loving her and move on. But moving on meant continuing on alone. He wasn't sure he would ever find the right girl in his church. Christine was the only woman who was right for him. Maybe he could be with Christine. Maybe it was possible. Maybe he would never go back.

Eli pushed those thoughts from his mind as the wedding concluded and he offered to help return the institution children to their building.

"Pretty wedding, wasn't it?" Christine walked up to him as he exited the children's building.

He nodded. "Yeah, it was."

They stood in silence for a while. The chairs where guests had been seated were already removed and the courtyard didn't look any different from how it usually did. Jeanne and Byron mingled with a few people.

"She didn't wear white. Don't English brides wear white?" he asked.

"Usually, but since this is her second wedding she decided to wear her favorite color instead. Besides, she looks beautiful in baby blue." Christine sighed and smiled. Her hands reached around her stomach and for a moment she cradled the baby inside — Eli's eyes trailed down to her hands and she pulled them away. She pushed up her glasses and cleared her throat. "Let's take a walk."

They walked back toward the garden and watched as the patients and employees worked in the sun then sat at the bench they'd sat at months earlier.

"I think I need to sit," Christine said, breathless.

"Sure. Maybe the walk was too much for you."

She let go of his hand and patted it. "No. The fresh air is nice."

Eli nodded. Several jokes ran through his mind about putting her to work on the farm chasing after the cows and mucking out stalls.

"Your beard and your hair, they're shorter again. Looks like your Gillette's gotten some use." She smirked at him.

He rubbed his smooth chin. "I just cleaned myself up a bit. Didn't want to come looking like some — farmer."

"I don't mind you looking like a farmer."

Eli gave her a weak smile.

Christine elbowed him. "Are you all right? You have something on your mind, don't you?"

The leaves rustled and the warm breeze folded itself around them. Their unspoken words seemed to float alongside the cottony clouds that moved past.

"No, I'm not all right," he said, lowering his head into his hands, then sitting up and looking at Christine he took her hands. "Being here right now with you — away from the farm —" He couldn't finish.

The silence hovered over and around them. A few green leaves fell in the stiff wind that came upon them. It lifted Christine's wavy locks that lay loose around her shoulders. He let go of one of her hands to touch her loose tresses. They felt like silk between his fingers. He had to tell her that he didn't want to go back. He had some money in the bank and they could start a life together.

"I've never seen you like this. What are you thinking?"

Eli sighed and smiled at her. She didn't ask him why he had worn his English shirt with his Amish pants to the wedding. Everyone at the hospital knew he was Amish. It would've been fine for him to attend in his Amish clothing.

"I heard that Matilda is finally moving on."

"If you call spreading rumors about how I went back on my promise to date her when I returned moving on. I guess it's better than her spreading that we actually were steady."

"Just add her to the list of girls who have fallen for you, Eli." She elbowed him, trying to loosen him up.

"Yes, my life has been one mistake after another." His voice was raspy and loud.

Christine jerked back at his intensity.

"Don't be angry. I was only teasing. I really only wanted to lighten the mood. I don't think I am doing a good job at it."

"But you're right. The rumors are true. I dated a lot of girls and broke a lot of hearts. I haven't been very upstanding either. Now when I'm trying to be the right kind of man and do the right things, no one sees it. All they see is my past. I just want it to be worth it. I don't want to waste my life somewhere where I don't matter or where the only thing people see in me is everything I've done wrong."

"You matter, Eli. You just have to show them who you are. I see it and I know others will see it."

Eli glanced over at her. She couldn't tell what he was going to say.

"I know I've brought a lot of this on you. I just —"

"I love you, Christine." His whisper interrupted her. "I love you and I don't want to go back to Sunrise where I can't have you. I want to leave with you — go anywhere — and be together."

Her breathing quickened and she couldn't

speak. When he began leaning toward her she inhaled but didn't move away. For months she'd considered what it would be like to kiss him. The back of his finger traced her jawline then cupped her cheek. The roughness from his hard work played against the softness of her skin. An eternity before his face was close enough to feel his breath, and then his lips touched hers. There was gentleness and passion mixed together. The kiss only lasted for several perfect moments, but the heat from it circulated through her entire body for much longer.

Christine longed for more when he pulled away. His face remained near hers for several long moments. Her baby kicked wildly, reviving her senses. She moved toward him and kissed him back, the passion heightened until she pulled away.

"You can't leave your home." Her words were breathless.

"But it's the only way I can have you."

"Who said you could have me at all?" Christine knew her resistance toward him was weakening.

Eli kissed her again. This time with more passion and energy, taking her very breath away. She pushed him aside.

"I'm sorry," she said, breathing fast. "I

won't let you leave your family."

"But why? You see what's happening there. I'm stuck. They don't want me there."

Christine imagined what this meant. Leaving Sunrise — together — starting a new life. She would have the baby soon and he would be a great father. He would be a great husband. They could make a life together.

It wouldn't work though, not like this. She could admit that she cared for him, but if they were together that meant he was abandoning his family. She couldn't let that happen.

"No, they don't want *me* there. If you leave Sunrise because you want to run away from your problems, then you're not the man I thought you were. You are not the man who I've learned to trust and respect. If you're really the good man that I know you are, then you will return to your family."

A flash of something passed over his eyes and he walked away, leaving her alone.

CHAPTER 27

Christine didn't see Eli for the rest of the evening and stayed alone in Jeanne and Byron's new home, since she and Byron had taken a few days away to honeymoon. When she entered she flipped on a lamp and a giggle escaped her mouth. It was childish to get excited over an electric light, but she didn't restrict the idle joy. The art deco-furnished home was so different from the Amish homes Christine had spent so much time in recently, lonesomeness consumed her. The brown, wooden radio caught her eye and she turned it on, hoping an evening show might cheer her up. All the radio-theater she could find was about war or romance, but she was pleased to find Glenn Miller and his band playing. She found Jeanne's crochet hook in the middle of what looked to be an afghan. She pulled it over to a rocking chair and continued where she must have left off. In a matter of minutes she was humming and tapping her foot. She'd missed music, she realized. She'd also almost forgotten how convenient indoor plumbing and electric refrigeration were.

When she finally went to bed Christine's restlessness returned. She found herself tossing and turning the entire night. In between waking she dreamed of Eli. Eventually she would have to say good-bye to him, and the time was growing closer every day. This reality, along with choosing whether or not to go to the maternity home, consumed her. All of this made her see that she was utterly alone.

Christine was glad when morning came, not just because she could get away from her recurring dream but she would get to see her mother. After showering and repacking her clothing she did her hair in victory rolls. It was strangely awkward to use such a large mirror rather than her small, hand-held one. Her breakfast only turned her stomach and after dropping a juice glass, she finally admitted to herself that she was more nervous to see her mother than she had expected. She was supposed to meet her in the parking lot at seven. With the glass cleanup behind her and all the lights off she put a thank-you note that included an apology for the broken glass on the kitchen table and left the house.

Christine saw the older model Ford in the corner of the lot. There was rust around the wheel wells that she hadn't noticed before. Her mother got out and her long, lean body looked thinner than Christine thought was healthy. Her golden hair looked grayer, and it hadn't even been two months. She put her bag on the pavement of the parking lot, only then realizing that the straps had been pinching her skin the whole time.

"Oh, look at you," she said. They hugged and Christine saw how her mother looked down at her abdomen when they parted and again when she offered to put her bag in the backseat when they climbed in.

"Aren't we going to go to the house?"

"I'm sorry, sweetheart. We don't have the house anymore."

"What?" How could her mother not have told her about this sooner?

"We sold it and we bought a much smaller house. I had to tell your dad and Doris about —" She gestured toward Christine's belly. "Otherwise they wouldn't understand why."

Christine almost asked how they had reacted but decided against it. She didn't want to know what her dad or Doris thought. It was too painful to consider.

"I'm so sorry, Ma. That must have been awful for you. You raised us in that house." She squeezed her eyes shut. "This is all my fault."

Her mother sighed.

"Christy, let's not dig this all up now, all right? We don't have a lot of time before your bus leaves. I have news for you."

"News?"

Margie pulled out a paper from her pocketbook and handed it to Christine. She read it then and shook her head, not understanding.

"It's a list of names and addresses. What does it mean?"

"I wrote to that maternity home and asked them about couples who want to adopt. They gave me this list. They didn't provide their last names, for privacy, but just look at how many lovely Christian couples are ready to adopt a child."

Christine looked back down at the paper.

"The home wrote that there are even more families waiting for children that aren't on the list."

"I know I should go but —"

"Is it because of that Amish boy?"

Christine didn't answer.

"That's why I think you should go to the home. You don't need to get involved with anyone before this baby is born. Once it's all over then you can start your life again. Just like that letter said, it would be like it never happened."

Her mother had a point. The more attached she grew to Eli, Annie, and Sylvia, the harder it would be to leave. The sooner Christine left the better. She would be saying good-bye to all of them along with the baby. At the home she wouldn't even be Christine. She would just be another face in the crowd. No one would remember her, she would leave, and it would be all over.

"Okay, Ma. I'll make the arrangements." She saw Eli waiting for her on the other side of the parking lot near Freddy's car. She looked at her wristwatch. "I have to go."

"Is that him?" Her mother's eyes spotted Eli. "He's handsome."

Christine could only nod, unable to find her voice. The memory of his arms around her body and his lips on hers — she loved him. Admitting it to herself for the first time brought her new resolve. Because she loved him, she had to leave him. She would have to go to that home. There was no other way to make sure she wouldn't ruin his life.

"One more thing, Ma," Christine said, "have you heard anything more about Jack? Is he married already?"

Her mother huffed and bristled at the mention of Jack. "I saw her. He brought her to church, if you can believe it."

Christine nodded. "It's not that I think about him that way. He's not a nice or respectable man. But I guess I still wonder what it was about me that was so awful."

"No time for a pity party, Christy. This is your burden to bear."

"You're right," she said, reaching over and hugging her mother. "Thank you for helping me. I'm so sorry about the house."

Her mother squeezed her as hard as Christine had ever remembered. She heard her sniff and clear her throat. They parted but continued to hold hands.

"Don't you worry about us. We'll get by. I'm taking in some sewing and taking some baked goods to the market." Margie nodded and whisked away tears as she spoke. "Write to me when you settle at the home?"

Christine bit her lip as she nodded. Then she left the car and carried her suitcase over to Freddy's car. Her eyes were on Eli as she walked. He leaned against the car. Neither of them smiled. Too much had happened between them the day before.

As they reached the bus station Eli looked at the list of cities they could travel to.

Everywhere looked brighter than the journey from Poughkeepsie to Dover. But he bought their tickets back home to Dover and the quiet of Sunrise, a fresh and heavy burden atop his shoulders.

Christine slept against his shoulder most of the trip, giving him a lot of time to think — spinning through the different scenarios of where his life was going. Committing to leaving or staying; whatever he decided, he needed to follow through instead of waffle back and forth. The driver he'd arranged for dropped them both off at Christine's cottage. Eli paid him and by the time he turned around Christine was already inside and the door was closed. He let out a heavy sigh as he walked away.

Eli stepped into the house, and his parents turned from their letters to look at him. Eli was glad to see that no one else was in the living room. His father stood. His jaw so set Eli could see it bulge from across the room.

"Eli, you're back," he said.

"I am." He tried to keep his voice even. His dad had every right to question his commitment, he knew. "I'm sorry that you question this, but I am going to buy the land on the east side of the farm and I'm going to build. I know I haven't given you very much confidence in my decision making but

I want to change that."

His dad shook his hand and nodded his head a few times.

"All right, son," he said. "Let's parcel it out."

CHAPTER 28

Mark, Sylvia, and their twins were in their house less than a month after Jeanne's wedding. Christine had never seen anything like it in her life. The look on Sylvia's face when she showed Christine around her new home warmed her heart. She'd been living in Eli's bedroom for so many months. She said the house was even bigger than the one that had burned down. There was so much hope for the young family's future. It was almost too much for Christine to handle.

Eli didn't move back into the house, but the day after Mark's house was done, he started surveying his own land to begin building. She'd watch him walk out to the eastern property, behind the cottage, and work between his chores at the farm and then again late into sunset. Her prayers were more frequent than ever before. She prayed to be healed. Less from the pain of rape and the guilt — those feelings slowly faded away as her heart made room for Eli.

Christine found the courage to write the Stony Creek Ladies Home to see if they had room for her. After the letter was written it still took her several days before she put it in the mail. It was June and her small bulge suddenly had become much larger, and she was constantly hot.

Her mother and Jeanne wrote to her every few weeks. Her mother never mentioned any of their money problems, which concerned her. Was there more than just selling the house? Jeanne, on the other hand, sounded happy in her new life. She didn't say so, but Christine could hear that they were hoping to start a family. In one moment the thought that perhaps Jeanne would be willing to adopt her child crossed her mind and in the next moment she knew that wouldn't work. It would be one thing to give her baby to a family she didn't know from the maternity home, but a completely different thing to hand him over to her best friend. She would have to watch her child grow up right in front of her, but not be his mother. Her lungs tightened.

What were the chances that an Amish family would accept her child into their culture? She wouldn't have to go to the home at all. She would just move away after the birth, maybe back to Poughkeepsie, and never come back to Sunrise. The countryside brought her such peace — she could imagine her own child growing up and roaming the same fields that she was growing attached to herself. He could watch the sunrise over the tree line then catch the sunset on a fishing hook after a day at a nearby pond or stream. He would never have to learn of his true beginnings. That was a comfort and a curse to Christine.

As she carried the child below her heart, she was the only person that mattered to the baby. When she imagined him growing and never knowing her, never knowing how she loved the kicks and stretches, and even in her darkest moments somehow found the light he brought from within her, it crushed her. But what option did she have? Women didn't raise children on their own, and if they did they were considered outcasts from society. She didn't want that for her child.

It seemed there was a natural pace to her life in the Amish community. There was less than three months left. What happened after that was a mystery. None of it added up to her being happy. In every scenario there was loss and failure. Each time her reality left her desperately alone.

"Mail's on the table," Annie told her one

afternoon after a visit with Sylvia.

When Christine picked up the envelope a shock ran up her arm. She had waited for several weeks to hear back from the maternity home.

"Excuse me," she said quickly and closed herself in her room.

Dear Christine,

Thank you for your letter. We are sorry for your circumstances, but this does not have to be the end of your life. There are many families waiting to care for a child like yours.

We are currently full but would be able to accept you into our home by August. According to your letter you are due in early September. We will write to you confirming when a bed is available.

Sincerely yours,
Linda C. Mathers
Stony Creek Ladies Home

CHAPTER 29

"Ready?" Sylvia asked, calling from the open buggy.

Sylvia, Annie, and Christine were attending a quilting. It was tedious work in the heat of early August, but Christine was glad to go. It broke up the routine of the day and would give her mind something else to think about other than Eli and the baby.

The hosting woman was one of the elderly ladies, Ellen. All of her nine children were married with children. She had over fifty grandchildren and more on the way. Her husband had a large construction business but only worked a few days a week since his sons had taken it over. They were one of the wealthier families in the district. Christine had often heard of the beauty of their home but had yet to see it. These were the things the women talked about at church and other events.

Sylvia parked the buggy and a young boy,

no older than ten or eleven, unhitched the horse and walked him away. It didn't matter that Christine had seen this since her arrival in April, it never ceased to surprise her how capable these young children were in handling what she saw as adult responsibilities.

When she walked up to the front of Ellen's home, the wide wrap-around porch was filled with several small quilting racks. The hum of the women's voices and the scent of fruit-filled pies enlivened Christine's senses. The three of them received waves from several women, and Christine waved back. Ellen's large frame came through the open front door and walked down the front steps. She was a rosy-cheeked woman with a genuine smile.

"Welcome," Ellen said with a loud, song-like voice and a touch on each of their arms. "I am so glad you've joined us."

"Now this looks like a party," Annie said, giggling.

"I had no idea her house was so large and beautiful. I didn't know any of the Amish had money for anything like this."

Sylvia whispered in Christine's ear. "They have eight boys and one daughter. Imagine how fast they can build a house with that many boys. They already have some grandsons working on the crew and employ other men as well. They have traveled all around the eastern states building houses because of their speed and craftsmanship. When you go in her kitchen, you'll see. Their cabinets are the most beautiful I've ever seen. Mark calls it vanity."

Christine's eyes were wide as she took in the scene. She and Sylvia were separated from Annie, each sitting with women their own age. Christine had practiced small straight stitches, but this was her chance to sew a real quilt. It made her nervous and excited all at once. She concentrated as the women spoke. They quilted without thought.

"Christine, your stitching has really improved," Sylvia commented. The other four ladies all took note, leaning over. "Annie and I both have been teaching her."

"You didn't grow up quilting?" Ida May asked. She was expecting her third child.

"Oh, no," she shook her head. "My mother sews but doesn't quilt."

"Do you sew like your mother?" Sylvia Miller asked. Sylvia was a common name in the community, though Christine hadn't known any before moving there. This Sylvia often went by Sylvie, which made conversations easier. Christine shook her head. "I'm getting better. My ma tried to teach me, but I wasn't any good. Annie has taught me a lot though."

"How did your appointment go with Dr. Sherman, Sylvia?" Ida May asked.

"Es wah gut." Sylvia nodded and put her needle down as she spoke. She eyed Christine, who responded with a nod that she understood her brief words but Sylvia continued in English anyway. "He said that everything looks fine. He knows I lost the last baby and I'm nervous."

Christine had heard all about her early delivery and Sylvia's anxiety over this pregnancy. Her twins had been born at home with a well-liked midwife that many of the Amish used, but after her second pregnancy ended at six months in her bedroom with only her husband at her side and a tiny unmoving figure laying on bloody sheets, she was insisting on having her next baby in the hospital. She declared it was the only way she would feel safe.

"Are you also going to Dr. Sherman?" Sylvie asked Christine.

Christine was sure her face was blooming into a bright red. Though she'd been accepted well among the women in the community, she hadn't been asked about the pregnancy by anyone except for Annie and

Sylvia. She shook her head no.

"Oh, I thought since you were a nurse you'd feel better with a doctor." Sylvie continued to sew as if she didn't know how uncomfortable the conversation was for Christine and likely everyone else around the small quilt. Sylvie was eighteen and old enough to understand tactfulness but often acted even younger. "Then how do you like Suzie Klein? She's been delivering babies for years around here."

"I am not going to have Suzie Klein," Christine said in a low, quiet voice.

"Well, then who is going to deliver your baby?" Sylvie's voice was shrill and the circles of women around her looked over. Ida May elbowed the younger expectant mother. Sylvie looked undeterred and unaware.

Christine inhaled and cleared her throat.

"Aunt Annie," she said. Of course, she'd likely not be in Sunrise anymore and be far away in the maternity home. "Since we live together and she delivered hundreds of babies when she lived in Ohio. It just feels like the best decision."

"Oh, I could never do that." Sylvie shook her head then leaned forward toward Christine. "She's not even a mother. You know that, right?"

"She's had *three* children." Leaving behind her humility, her words were instead quilted tightly with the rough-hewn fabric of indignation.

"But it's not the same. I wouldn't feel comfortable. I want someone delivering my baby who knows what it's like." She said it in such a simple and light-hearted way it made Christine more infuriated.

"Last I heard Dr. Sherman never had a baby either. He's never been *pregnant* and he's never been a mother," Christine said with a stealthy quiet. Then she stood, careful not to upset the table with her protruding belly. "Excuse me for a moment."

Christine heard whispers behind her and footsteps. Sylvia strode up next to her with a giggle bursting out as soon as they were side-by-side.

"*Sis ken fashtant,* Christine."

Yes, Christine couldn't believe what she'd said either. She almost wanted to repeat the expression she heard multiple times a day from Annie.

"You have more nerve than my Uncle Perry at a quilting bee," Sylvia finished.

She laughed again, breaking Christine's dark mood, making her chuckle behind her hand.

"Sylvie has always been that way. Her

mom is the same. She asks the queerest questions and doesn't know that half of what she says isn't very nice. They're not trying to be mean, I hope you know that."

"Well, by the time its church Sunday everyone's going to know that I said the word *pregnant* and that the most well-liked doctor has never been a mother."

Both the girls got as far as the line of buggies and laughed until they cried behind one of them. They held their bobbing bellies.

"I am going to miss you, Christine," Sylvia said, wiping her laughing tears.

"But it's so hard to be around everyone like this."

"I remember feeling so self-conscious when Mark and I were first married. I know how people stare." She leaned against a buggy and cradled her belly.

Christine nodded. Sylvia had never brought up the fact that she'd been expecting before she was married. They'd accepted her like family and she was starting to feel like a part of the community but that was exactly what she couldn't let happen.

"I know if anyone understands how I'm feeling, it's you." Christine found Sylvia's hand and squeezed it for a moment.

"You've been avoiding Eli ever since you

came home from your friend's wedding."

Christine leaned against the opposite buggy from her friend but didn't look at her when she spoke again.

"I'll be leaving in August."

"What? Where are you going? Aren't you due in September?" Sylvia's brow was laced with concern.

"There's a home that my ma has wanted me to go to since the beginning." She started walking toward the garden and Sylvia fell in step next to her.

"A home?"

"For women like me. Women in trouble. They'll have room for me in August. I think it's for the best."

"For who?" Sylvia asked quietly.

Christine didn't answer.

"I just want to make sure my baby has a proper Christian home."

"You just told us that Aunt Annie was going to deliver your baby. But you're leaving?"

"If I don't hear back from the home Aunt Annie will deliver the baby. I won't have any other options," she said, narrowing her gaze at her friend. "But the director of the home said they will let me know in August. I think that being at this home might just make it easier for me to move on with the rest of my life."

She looked past the perfect rows of the large garden to the red barn beyond, past the field of black and white cows even farther away. She found comfort in the vision in front of her. How would she leave this, when had she grown so attached to country life — *Amish* life?

"Eli told me he loves me." Christine kept her eyes trained on the distance.

"*Vas?* I mean, what?"

She nodded her head. "He did."

"I've known a lot of the girls he's dated, I don't think he's ever said that to anyone. You're telling me the truth that he said he loves you?"

Christine could hear his voice in her ears and the way her heart pumped harder and faster when he was close. "He did, and it breaks my heart. I can't be around him. It's too hard to bear."

"Why? Because you don't love him?"

She didn't answer right away but let her eyes roam until she found a place far off in the distance, past the buggies, barns, the small pond ahead of the fields, all the way to the horizon with a lining of evergreens, their tips like arrows pointed to the heavens. She inhaled before she spoke. "No, because I do."

They heard the laughter from the porch filled with ladies behind them. They both turned and began walking back.

"But there is one thing maybe you haven't thought of," Sylvia said.

"You're right — I haven't had the courage to talk about it yet." The words Christine was about to say made her stomach lurch.

Sylvia stopped and looked at her, almost like she knew Christine was about to say something important.

"Would you and Mark consider adopting my baby?" It was an idea Christine had been pondering, but hadn't voiced.

"What?" Sylvia's eyes were large and round.

"Wasn't that what you were going to say?"

"No," Sylvia said, her voice carrying the shock as obviously as her mouth which remained open until she spoke again. "I was going to suggest you marry Eli and stay here."

Eli couldn't bring himself to face Christine. But he still didn't want her to leave. It was August and he was afraid the month would fly by as fast as July had, then September would bring the baby and she'd be gone forever. He'd done his best to focus on finishing Mark's house, then starting his own, and forgetting his love for Christine. The first two seemed almost effortless, but the latter was impossible.

He crawled out of the loft and walked to the milking barn. It was still dark at only four o'clock. Even without the moon's glow his feet knew the way to the barn. His prayer this morning was the same as every morning.

Lord, give me the wisdom and patience You promise in James. The faith you show in Hebrews. Show me how to abide like John fifteen. Help me love like First Corinthians thirteen. Forgive me for failing with Mark and help me not hate him. Give us reconciliation. And Christine.

That's where the prayer always abruptly ended. He never knew how to pray about Christine.

Why hadn't he understood the importance of depending on God before his time in the CPS? His communion with God had become real and comforting. But now, as he forged ahead with life, probably alone, the peace in his prayer was all he could hold on to.

"Did you hear that your girlfriend Christine told that snippet Sylvie off at the quilting?" A cow mooed after Mark spoke and Eli chuckled. He decided that was enough of a response.

"She told Sylvie that she's going to let our old aunt Annie deliver that baby. That is, if she stays."

Eli ignored him, remembering what he'd just prayed for.

"You going to be pacing the kitchen outside her room when it happens? Or did you want to pretend that none of it exists anymore now that you have your piece of land?"

When Eli didn't respond Mark baited him further. "I guess you lost your tongue as much as you lost your girl?"

"I'm not going to argue with you. Say what you want."

Mark began walking away.

"Calving season is coming soon. Do we have everything we need?" Eli asked, changing the subject and following after him.

"*Ja.* I might only be *Dat*'s second choice, Eli, but I know how to run this farm better than you. Of course I'm ready for calving season."

Eli's broken relationship with Mark bit at him like the horn flies on a cow's ears — unrelenting and diseased.

"*Dat*'s second choice? Are you sure about that? You're the one he put in charge now that he's only working a few days a week.

You got the land he promised me, and then for your birthday he gives you his best hunting rifle. The one we all learned on. The one he knew I wanted." He strode toward Mark and was close to his face. "You don't think that it would've meant a lot to me, his eldest son, to have gotten something like that from *Dat*?"

Mark shrugged and lifted his chin.

"I got a pat on the back and a new shirt," Eli said. "Who do you think is *Dat*'s second choice?"

CHAPTER 30

Dear Christine,

We have a bed available for you. You may come at any time. The family at the top of our waiting list has been contacted and knows that they may have their baby very soon.

When you arrive, please call yourself Edna. This will keep your real identity confidential. Please call us at the number listed on the letterhead to let us know when you will arrive. We will send a car to pick you up at the train or bus station.

Sincerely,
Linda C. Mathers

Christine folded the letter and tucked it under her pillow with the other one from the Stony Creek Ladies Home. It was already the third week in August. It was time for her to gather her wits and decide what to do, and she couldn't do that without Sylvia and Mark. She would talk with them later tomorrow.

Annie walked into Christine's room.

"Why don't you lay back and let's check on that babe of yours," Annie said, motioning to the bed.

Christine did as she was told and Annie hovered over her. Her small hands touched and pressed over her now very large, round belly. Annie's face was serious with concentration when she sat down next to the bed.

"All is well," Aunt Annie said, smiling. "You have a strapping baby boy in there."

Christine looked down at her belly and she resisted smiling at the thought.

"I know you don't want me to give him up, but do you understand why I have to?"

Annie sighed.

"All I can imagine is giving up one of my own — willingly. If any of them had lived I don't think anyone could've ripped those children out of my arms without killing me first."

"But you were married." She paused and changed the subject. "I heard from Stony Creek Ladies Home. If Mark and Sylvia decide they can't take the baby I'll be leaving soon. The home has a family ready."

"What if the baby was his?"

"Whose?"

"Eli's. I just mean, what if the baby was Eli's? Would you give him up?"

Christine couldn't answer that aloud. Of course, she could never give up Eli's baby. But Eli would never have forced himself on her, and she wouldn't be doing this alone. He would never have belittled and violated her. If she were in this condition with a child of his, it would be because they were married. The mere idea of that was like something out of a fairy tale.

"Eli isn't the father. I cannot be an unwed mother on my own. If Sylvia and Mark don't say yes, I have to go."

"But you could stay." Aunt Annie raised her eyebrows. "If you married Eli."

"I don't want him to give up this life."

"He wouldn't have to. You could give up yours."

"Syl?" Christine knocked on the door.

"Come on in," her friend said. "I'm in the kitchen."

Christine walked through the mud room and through the living room and into the kitchen. It was hotter than normal. She was baking bread.

"Can I help?"

442

"Why don't you grease those pans?" She pointed at the bread pans on the counter.

"How are you feeling?"

"Huge."

The two giggled.

"Besides that."

Christine shrugged. "Annie said that everything looks good and considering how hot it is, I feel fine."

They worked in silence for a few minutes.

"So, have you and Mark made a decision?" she asked quietly.

"Christine." Sylvia turned from kneading the dough to Christine. She grabbed a towel, wiped her hands, and let out a long sigh. "I don't know. Mark is real reluctant and I just don't know if it's a good idea. I just don't think I could take your baby away from you."

"It wouldn't be like that."

"And what about my baby? I'm due a month after you."

"You've had twins before. If you can't take the baby, I have to leave right away. The home is ready for me."

Christine's lungs squeezed her. This conversation wasn't going as planned. Everything she said sounded like she was trying to force her baby on Sylvia like it was a stray dog. It wasn't right. This meant only one

443

thing. She would have to leave. There was no other option.

"I'm sorry, Christine," Sylvia said. "I just don't think I could take someone's baby away from them."

The farm work was done for the day and Eli ate his supper quickly, leaving his family still sitting at the table so he could go out to his property. Moses and his dad helped him a few times a week, but the progress seemed slow and endless. There was, however, such reward in it. This was his home.

He picked up his tool belt and filled the pouches with nails when he heard the voice he heard every night in his dreams.

"Eli."

He turned to find Christine, beautiful and glowing, standing behind him.

"Christine." His voice barely left his mouth. "I've missed you."

She looked down at her belly. Eli's eyes traced down her body. He smiled at the great roundness of her midsection. A small chuckle released.

"What? I know, I'm as big as a house."

"You're beautiful."

He unbuckled his tool belt and set it on the ground. He took her hand.

"Come, let's sit." He led her carefully

through the construction site and they sat on what would be the first floor of the house.

"What's over there?" She pointed.

"It's the front door." He smiled at her.

She nodded but didn't say anything. The nature around them was like music. His body was on fire with having her near him. It took all of his strength not to pull her into his arms. All those prayers asking God to provide wisdom when it came to Christine and here he was with no more answers than ever.

"I need to tell you something."

"What's that?"

She took a deep breath and exhaled slowly.

"I'm leaving, Eli. I'm going to the Stony Creek Ladies Home. I'll be there this time next week."

His lungs deflated. He knew this was a possibility but still it came as a shock.

Lord, what do I do?

"I need to call them tomorrow and let them know my travel plans. Will you take me to the neighbor's phone?"

Eli inhaled deeply then nodded his head. He couldn't speak. He stood and put his tool belt back on. It was too painful to sit there with her.

The next day he pulled his buggy up to

Annie's house. He couldn't believe that he was actually helping her leave Sunrise. She stepped out of the cottage wearing a pretty yellow dress. Her hair was up on top in the rolls he loved seeing on her. He noticed, however, that she only wore lipstick and he'd never seen her look more beautiful. Her simple beauty was breathtaking.

"Here, let me help you."

"You might need some type of catapult," she said, laughing.

He helped her up on his seat and turned the buggy around in the drive and headed out on the road.

It took fifteen minutes on the bumpy dirt roads to get Christine to the neighbors. He helped her out again and walked up to the house with her.

"Hi, my friend Christine needs to use the phone. I'll make sure to pay for it," he said to the farmer's wife.

"Over there," she said, and pointed to the phone on the stand near the kitchen table.

He noticed that when Christine walked her hand cupped her stomach in a different way from before. She breathed more when she pulled out the chair and sat down. Her hands dialed the operator and she was connected quickly.

"Hello, this is *Edna.* I just wanted to

confirm that I will be there by Wednesday. My bus arrives at five-thirty in the evening."

She was listening to the other end.

"I am due next month."

She stuttered trying to talk.

"I know, I should've come sooner." Christine turned away from Eli.

The farmer's wife listened in and watched the clock the whole time.

"Yes, thank you. I will see you on Wednesday."

She put the phone down carefully and her face was stricken when she walked past Eli as if he weren't even there. He thanked the farmer's wife and followed after Christine.

In a few minutes they were on their way back to the cottage with a wave of discomfort moving between them. Neither of them spoke.

Several nights later Christine dreamed she delivered her baby. She yelled and yelled to see him, but the doctors, with pale masks covering their noses and mouths, didn't seem to hear her. She could hear her baby cry but couldn't see it. She awoke in tears.

Christine wrapped a bathrobe around herself and walked out of the cottage. Tomorrow she would go. She would get on a bus and never return to Sunrise. Once she got to the home she would be called *Edna,* and when her baby was born a doctor or midwife would deliver her baby and give it to another woman.

The morning air filled her lungs and she resisted yelling when she exhaled. This wasn't supposed to be her life. She had walked farther than she realized when a pain radiated through her stomach. It stopped her where she stood. She squeezed her eyes shut and held her breath until it was over. This couldn't happen now. The pain was gone as suddenly as it came and she started walking again.

The next one was harder and longer, about a minute later. She walked over to the side of the grassy trail and leaned on a tree stump. Between each contraction she took small, quick steps back toward the cottage.

As she began walking the pain was so severe she fell to all fours. Christine rested her head against the tops of her hands when the pain diminished. She tried to get her breath back and stood. She'd stood too quickly and the green world around her spun. She squeezed her eyes shut until her head stopped swimming in the morning air.

Christine had to get home, that's all. Annie would have it under control then. But this was not the way it was supposed to happen. Maybe Sylvia and Mark would still be able to take her child or maybe Stony Creek would still be able to take the baby even though she didn't deliver it there. She leaned against a tree and panted through another pain. Eli's house was nearby now. The cottage wasn't far off. The contraction faded and she walked on. She heard someone whistling, the sound getting closer.

"Eli," she shouted.

"What are you doing out here?" He came running to her.

"It's time. The baby is coming." She started crying. "Please take me to Annie."

As soon as he lifted her, she went limp. She couldn't respond and all that mattered was that he was there. That was all that mattered in the moment. Her head fell onto his chest and she could feel his heart beat against her ear. He was warm and strong and she loved him. In her mind she told him so but she didn't have the energy to speak it.

His voice was labored as he jogged, holding her. What was he saying? It wasn't in English, but the words made sense in her ears.

At first she recognized words from the Lord's Prayer.

Unsah Faddah im himmel. Our Father, which art in heaven.

Dei villa loss dedu sei. Your will be done. He repeated this phrase four times. Didn't he remember the rest of the prayer?

Then he stopped moving. His breathing anguished and labored.

O, Gott, gep auf juh sie. Oh, God, take care of her.

Macht des babeh tsunt. Make the baby healthy.

Ich liebe sie. I love her. *Ich liebe des babeh vie sis meine.* I love this baby like it was my own.

He loved her. He loved her baby. Then she didn't remember anything but him laying her down in her bed. Oh, she didn't want him to let go. Why did he have to let go?

"Christine," Annie said, smiling as she spoke. "Don't you worry. I'll take care of you."

Her words were in Pennsylvania Dutch. Christine's eyes opened to see her speak them. Her ears heard them and she was able to pick up enough words to understand.

Sis nah zeit. It's time.

"I'm not ready," she said. Her dizziness was subsiding now that she was still. Being with Annie comforted her. "It's not time.

450

I'm supposed to leave tomorrow for the home."

"*Aesh bisleh frie, mei maedle.*" Just a bit early, my girl.

Christine nodded to the old woman.

She looked up at Eli, whose face was ghostly pale.

"Eli, *nah geh.*" Annie pushed against his chest toward the door. When he still resisted, her voice became firmer. "*Grick deh* Sylvia." Aunt Annie told him to go get Sylvia.

"*Les meh mit sie sah.*"

Hot tears streamed down her face as she understood his words, telling Annie that he wanted to stay with her. A contraction surfaced and she bit her lip. When it wasn't enough she yelled.

Annie soothed him with comforting words, reminding him that it had been like this since the dawn of time. Had it comforted Eli? Somehow in the moment, it wasn't comforting to her.

"Please, go get Sylvia. This is her baby. I know she and Mark will agree once he sees the baby," Christine said as a contraction left her body.

"*Vas?*"

"*Geh.*" Annie pushed him out farther and closed the door in front of his face.

Christine found her strength returning.

Annie helped her peel off her dress and put on a light nightgown. Her calmness was returning. When a contraction came she leaned over her bed, making the pain bearable, and she wondered how her body knew how to react. She had never seen anyone in labor.

Annie left for several minutes and returned with wet cloths, towels, and a small black bag that reminded her of a doctor's.

"What's in there?"

"Just things we will need once the baby's here. You don't need to worry. Right now your body will do what it's supposed to do. I'm just here for comfort. You can do this."

"It hurts."

"And it will get worse before it's over, but I can see it in your eyes, Christine, you're strong and ready. You can get up, walk around, or get in just about any position that helps. Your body will know what to do. The Lord will bring you and your baby through." Annie brushed away the sweaty hair from her face and Christine believed her.

Sylvia arrived soon after that, out of breath with her own belly leading the way. She embraced Christine. They both had tears in their eyes that ran down their cheeks.

"What can I do?" Eli asked, standing in the kitchen where Christine had been pacing, also breathing heavily.

"You need to go," Annie said, pointing toward the farm.

"Can I stay outside at least?"

Annie looked at Christine. Christine looked at Eli and hesitantly nodded yes. Eli let out a breath he'd been holding. Before walking out he went to her and took her shoulders and looked into her eyes.

"Please, don't give this baby away."

A contraction came over her and she pushed him away. All she needed to do now was focus on making it through the delivery. She heard Sylvia walk him to the door and tell him everything would be fine.

Annie was right. Christine's labor did move quickly. In just over five more hours it was nearly time. She closed her eyes as she hunched over the bed. She could hear Annie and Sylvia whisper to each other. Words all in their language, but still she understood.

Macht the kessleh vassa heis. Heat up the water in the pot.

Deh schah ist gabuztd. The scissors are clean.

Doh kompts babeh. Here comes the baby.

The elation of delivery overwhelmed

453

Christine. The weight of her body changing, her organs shifting, and the courage it
had taken overtook her. Like a glass that
even when full was continually filled again
and again, there was so much to take in all
at once. The baby's cry filled the room —
filled the world, even. He was strong and
loud. Sylvia helped her clean and get comfortable in the bed. Annie was next to her,
cleaning her very chubby baby boy. It was
no surprise that Annie was right about the
baby being a boy.

"Look at him," Sylvia said, sitting on the
edge of the bed.

Christine looked away from the baby and
instead through the small slit in the window
the other way. The curtains were drawn but
through the two she could see Eli pacing.
Had he been there the entire labor? Her
hands went to her abdomen and even with
the sheet and thin coverlet over her, it was
empty in the space where the baby had
been. The feeling of loneliness panicked her
and for a moment her vision was clouded in
gray with only a tunnel of light. She begged
God for numbness, blindness — anything
to keep her from experiencing the moments.

The baby grunted and cried, bringing her
back though she couldn't force herself to
look at him.

"Christine," Annie's voice was more serious this time. "Look at your baby boy."

"I can't." Her face fell into her hands and she wept.

"You must. He needs you. You're his mother."

"I can't give him what he needs. Sylvia, please take him. You need to be his mother. I know you said you can't but you have to." She looked up at her friend, their eyes connecting. "Take him," she whispered.

"I can't, Christine." Sylvia shook her head, her eyes filling. "He's yours."

Sylvia regained her composure and diverted her eyes from Christine. She sniffed a few times then she looked down. From the corner of Christine's eye she could see the squirming pink-skinned baby Annie had wrapped in a sky-blue blanket. Sylvia reached for the babe and lifted him and held him close. She laughed through a few tears. Christine continued to look the other way but was relieved and burdened to see that Sylvia had finally listened.

"Doh ist dah glennah booh." Here is the little boy.

Her voice was almost like a song when she spoke, lilting in the air around the baby, instantly filling the room with love. Her friend would love her son. She couldn't fight her instincts any longer and looked at Sylvia and the babe just as he was lowered into her empty arms.

"The best thing I can do right now is refuse to take your son. He's yours."

Christine's arms wrapped around him and her weeping turned from sorrow and pain to the freedom of loving the innocence she held. His eyes were squinty and his lips were full and pink. He had a head full of chestnut-brown hair and the roundest face she'd ever seen. He was hers. God was not punishing her, but rewarding her with a beautiful son. He had been there all the while. God had always cherished her as His own. She wept, chose to let go of her shame, and keep her child.

"Peter Nathaniel," she said after a few moments. "Your name is Peter Nathaniel after your two heroic uncles."

He let out a loud cry and the ladies all giggled. How was it possible the circumstances that caused the greatest pain suddenly were worth every moment of it? But how would she do this? How would she manage?

"Tuesday's child is full of grace," Christine whispered the line of poetry to her son.

Annie helped her nurse for the first time and after he was finished gave her a quick

456

lesson on burping and diapering. She'd done little with babies until now, but everything came to her as naturally as any mother would pray for.

"*Kann Eli nah kumma?*" Sylvia asked if Eli could come in.

Christine nodded. She wanted Eli to come in. Baby Peter was sleeping, heavy in her arms, and she couldn't believe that he was hers. How could she ever have thought to give him up? Tears hovered inside her eyes when she heard a light knock against the doorframe.

Eli filled the doorframe when he walked in. To look at him one would've thought that he'd gone through the labor instead of her.

"You look terrible," she said to him.

"I was so scared for you, Christine," he said, kneeling next to her bed. His eyes filled with love and longing.

"Women have babies every day."

"You're not just any woman." He covered her hand with his.

Christine took in a deep breath but didn't respond to him. She didn't know what she was supposed to say.

"Meet Peter Nathaniel."

Eli smiled. He looked at the baby then back at her. "Your brothers."

She nodded.

"Can I hold him?"

"I don't know if I can let him go, but I want you to hold him. You've done so much for me — for us." She handed him over to Eli and he pulled up a chair to sit on as he held the baby.

"He's beautiful, Christine," he said, not taking his eyes off of Peter. He began to sing. *"Homleh moo moo moo, shippleh bah bah bah . . ."*

Her baby fell into slumber listening to a silly lullaby about barnyard animals.

"I can understand most of what you are all saying," she admitted. "I think I have for a while, only I didn't realize it."

"What?"

"When you carried me here I realized I could understand what you were saying. Not every word, but enough to know what was being said."

He looked back down at the baby and rocked gently, smiling.

"You heard me then — understood what I said?"

"When you were praying?"

He didn't look at her but nodded.

"I did."

"I meant every word of it and I want to be your husband and Peter's father."

"Eli," she breathed his name. "We've been

458

through this. I won't let you leave."

"Why don't you stay instead?"

"Me — be Amish?" She imagined it. No electricity for the rest of her life. Outhouses. No cars. No jewelry. No makeup. Plain dresses and hair pulled back under a covering. "Eli, I can't. This isn't my real life."

Eli handed Peter back to Christine.

"If this isn't your real life, Christine, what is?" he whispered to her gently with his hand on hers, then he walked out of the room.

CHAPTER 31

It was a mild September day. Christine stood at the bus station doing her best to shield three-week-old Peter from the exhaust. The sidewalk below her feet had brush marks where it had recently been swept. The waning summer sun hung high in the sky, not hot, but somehow she was still sweating beneath her blue dress, that while awkwardly outdated for the world, it was too modern for her life in Sunrise.

She shifted Peter in her arms and checked her hair again with the palm of her hand. She wasn't wearing a hat. On an important day like today, she should've worn a hat. Her new responsibilities as a mother, however, had caused her to be distracted. The hat had been left behind. Her purse was hanging on her arm and feeling heavier by the moment. She eyeballed the wooden bench against the brick building but there was a young family sitting on most of it. A perfect *English* family — something she'd never have.

Christine looked at the bus ahead of her. It wasn't the right one. There was one up ahead, heading into the station. She moved onto her tiptoes as if to try to see farther. Its flat nose was dusty when it stopped a bus length away.

"The bus should be arriving shortly." Eli walked up next to her.

"I think that's it." She pointed.

"Are you ready?" Eli swallowed hard.

"I'm not sure it was altogether a good idea that you come with us." Eli had spent time with Peter daily, but didn't talk much to Christine. She'd hurt him by turning down his marriage proposal, but how could he expect her to convert and be Amish?

"I didn't want you to come alone. That didn't seem right either."

"I had the driver — there she is." She wanted to run, but she was holding Peter. Carefully handing him to Eli, she turned back and let her feet carry her quickly into her mother's arms.

"Oh, my darling, Christy." Her mother's voice was gentle and sweet and like a medicine to Christine's soul. "Let me look at you."

Margie took her daughter's hand and

461

turned her about.

"You should be wearing a hat, but other than that I can't believe it's only been three weeks. Look at you, my girl."

"Mother, I can't tell you how glad I am that you're here." The two looked more seriously at each other. There was so much she could say, but it wasn't the time or place. "Come, meet your grandson."

Her mother bit her lower lip and inhaled deeply. Christine took her arm and pulled her toward Eli. Eli was wearing a new, deep teal shirt that Christine had sewn — another insistence from Annie. His black hat set off his blond hair that had grown as long as the other Amish men's. His light beard set off his tanned skin. He was as handsome as any man ever was. Though she'd refused to marry him, she still cared. She couldn't have him excommunicated from his family and it didn't make sense for her to become Amish either. It was one thing living among them for six months, it was entirely different leaving her real life forever.

"Mother, this is Eli Brenneman."

She looked up at him with a smile. "I would shake your hand but I see you're holding my grandson."

"Yes, Mrs. Freeman, your grandson." Eli leaned forward and laid the babe in his grandmother's arms. His wide blue eyes looked from Eli's face to the new woman smiling at him.

"Peter Nathaniel. Oh, my dear boy. It's like Peter and Nathaniel aren't as gone as they were before, isn't it?"

"He has Nathaniel's cleft chin," Christine said.

"And yours," her mother interjected. "Peter's lips. And he's already smiling. You smiled the first week you were born. You were my most smiley baby."

They were silent as they watched Peter move around. He found his mother's face and smiled.

"But still, he looks like Jack," Margie whispered.

Christine stiffened.

Nothing more was said as they walked to their hired driver and rode back to the cottage. After some tea with Annie and after Peter was fed, diapered, and laid down to sleep, Christine walked Margie to meet Sylvia and Sarah and then around the farm. As they stood against the fence, the black and white cows moved around the field gracefully in the light breeze. Eli was ahead rebuilding the lean-to that had blown over from a recent storm.

"That Aunt Annie is as sweet as pie, isn't

463

she? What is it that she calls you?"

Christine smiled. "She calls me *mei maedle*. It means *my girl*."

"Oh," was all her mother said for several long moments. Christine looked over to find tears trailing down her mother's face. Her mother had this amazing way of crying and looking beautiful. Her skin stayed as porcelain as always, and her eyes didn't grow bloodshot. It was just such an honest emotion.

"Mother? Annie's very special to me, but she's not you." Christine took her mother's hand.

"I wrote Jack," her mother looked off into the field as she spoke. "He needs to see his son."

"Why?" Her exacerbation surfaced.

"Maybe he'll change his mind once he sees Peter."

"But I don't love him, and he rejected me. Remember?"

"Peter is his son," her mother insisted. "If he doesn't want to see him, then that door will be closed, but if he does, you need to let him."

A day later Margie brought up the topic of Christine's future again.

"Aunt Annie," Margie began, having taken to Annie as quickly as Christine had, "don't you think Christy would be better off marrying Peter's father?"

"Mother," Christine spoke harshly.

"It's all right." Annie lifted the palm of her hand gently toward Christine. "I'd like to share my thoughts."

Margie nodded at Christine.

"I believe God has it all in His hands. We don't know what will happen next week or tomorrow or tonight even. Just trust, Christine. That's all I can say. Trust."

"But she cannot live like this," Margie exclaimed. "It's not proper."

The rest of the supper was eaten in silence, and for the next few days Christine and Margie chose to forget the uncomfortable conversation and live in the world of accepting what they could not change. Margie cried when she kissed Christine and Peter good-bye. Christine stayed next to the bus until it pushed out of the station. She waved until she couldn't see it any longer. The relief of reconciliation with her mother was layered with the dread of not knowing what her future held.

Peter was a month old when Christine saw a familiar black Cadillac parked at the farm. Jack?

Though part of her wished she could run

away, she strode through the field as if Peter's life depended on it. As she rounded the side of the house, completely out of breath, she saw him on the front porch with Sarah. He was wearing a black suit and tie, and even from the short distance she could see he was impeccably manicured; his hair slicked and dark. He hadn't noticed her yet and the smile on his face as he spoke with Sarah appeared disingenuous: it was too large; his teeth sparkled in the September sun.

Christine turned to look past the field toward the cottage. Though she couldn't see it closely, she was sure that the lilting breeze pulled the blue curtain out from the inside. Peter was inside their room sleeping. Her imagination went wild and imagined Jack running in, grabbing him, and taking him away. Her breathing increased.

"Christine?" She turned toward Jack's voice. Their eyes met and Christine's hands went to her heart. She didn't want to see him, but there was still something that drew her to him. "There you are, my darling."

"Would you excuse me, please," he said with a nod toward Sarah and stepped across the porch and down the steps.

Sarah's and Christine's eyes met. Christine's breath continued to be labored after running over and from adrenaline and with Sarah's eyes on her, defeat plunged into her heart. Sarah broke their trance on each other with a glance toward Jack before walking into her home.

Jack reached Christine and stood incredibly close. His gaze was too intense. Goose bumps formed on her arm.

"Your mother told me. I decided I should come." Jack smiled as he rocked on his feet nervously.

Christine's heart pounded.

Over Jack's shoulder she saw Eli in the distance. The milk truck was here to swap out the empty milk cans from the previous day for the full ones from today. *Look over here, Eli.* The breeze blew and his face turned. Their eyes, even with the space between them, met. Christine could see his face in a matter of moments turn from confusion to recognition. Like a strong wind, he ran toward her.

"Christine." Eli's voice alone was a refuge. Their eyes joined for a long moment.

"What are you doing here, Jack?" Christine found her voice.

"I came to see my son." His voice softened to Christine's great surprise. "I probably should've let you know I was coming."

Christine looked from Jack to Eli, whose

eyes were like flints. Her mind spun between ordering Jack away and understanding that he was Peter's father and surely that meant he had the right to see his son. Wasn't that how it should be? But his manners and his composure — they were different.

"Come with me," she said quietly.

Jack walked smartly just behind her and Eli came in step with her.

"No, Eli," she said then looked at Jack, then back to Eli. She patted Eli's arm and then began walking again with Jack at her side. When his hand went to her elbow it was like a hot coal on her skin. She was too stunned about it all to pull away.

"This is where I've been staying. Where Peter was born." Christine opened the door. "Annie?" she called when they stepped into the cottage.

The older lady stood from the kitchen table with eyes widening by the moment when she saw Jack. A smile crossed over her face slowly. Christine made introductions and they shook hands.

"Annie's been taking care of me — and Peter." Christine's voice was formal in her own ears. "Jack would like to see Peter. Would you mind pouring some lemonade or iced tea?"

Annie nodded and busied herself.

"Wait here," Christine told Jack.

Christine went into her room and closed the door behind her. She sat on the bed and breathed slowly. In, then out — several times. Her hands clasped and she looked at the ceiling. Where could she begin in speaking to God? That Jack was the same cruel monster he was before and would leave her and Peter alone? Or that he really was a good man and wanted to be a family? And what about Eli? Where did he fit in? She'd refused his proposal but loved him regardless. Only without answers she lived in limbo.

Peter stayed asleep when she picked him up. She held him close to her chest and even in his rest he rooted at her breast. She giggled.

"Always hungry."

His mouth went slack and he returned to deep sleep. She exhaled to calm her nerves and walked out of her bedroom.

"Is that him? Is that my son?"

Christine had never seen Jack nervous before. He was blinking excessively and he pushed a hand through his pomaded hair, something she'd never seen him do.

"This is Peter Nathaniel." She nearly tacked on the words *your son,* but she couldn't.

469

He looked at the baby and smiled.

"He's got my eyes, right? But why did you name him Peter and why's he wearing a dress?"

"The Amish put blue dresses on all their babies since they are much easier to sew than tiny pants for the boys. And it's much more convenient when changing diapers."

"But you're not Amish, Christine, and neither is my son," he said sharply.

"Jack —" she started.

"He does look like me, doesn't he?" Jack smiled. "Can I hold him?"

Christine looked at Peter's face then back at Jack. She nodded.

"Okay." She handed Peter to Jack and swallowed down her tears.

"This is my son. I can't believe it — I'm a father."

The two of them were silent for several minutes. Jack gently bounced Peter and smiled when he grunted and squirmed. Jack looked up at Christine.

"We need to talk."

The house rumbled in the booming thunder. It was like God set the thunder upon the clock of Eli's frustration. Christine and Peter's safety was all he could think about. The wind picked up outside and it began pouring. He had to go over there. Whatever Jack's intentions, he didn't like it.

He was drenched in minutes as he ran over to the cottage. He hadn't finished the broken down lean-to, however, and hoped that what he had built was stable enough to resist the winds that were growing stronger. He held his flashlight with one hand and his other was formed in a fist and filled with his hate. He barely knocked as he pushed his way in. He was dripping everywhere. He hated making a mess for Annie.

Jack stood and stepped toward him when his and Eli's eyes met.

"Where's Christine?" Eli asked.

Jack nodded toward Christine's room. "Putting our son to sleep."

Eli stared at Jack. He wasn't what he expected for Christine — all starched and angular. His eyes were analytical and un-friendly. He didn't smile.

"Haven't you done enough?" Eli asked Jack.

"What? You think you're better than me?"

The muscles in Eli's hand were painfully tight.

"Better for Christine and Peter. You better not touch her."

Jack smirked when he eyed Eli's clenched hands. "Well, aren't you as hard-boiled as

I've ever seen?"

"Listen, Jack, I don't want any trouble. I just want Christine and Peter to be happy." He knew he should've stepped back, but he didn't.

"You don't think I could make them happy?" Jack sniggered. "Is that what you're saying, *Mr. Amishman*?"

"Don't call me that." Eli's heart beat against his chest and it took every bit of self-restraint not to go at Jack with both fists.

"What's happening in here?" Christine whispered loudly when she came out.

"You can't be serious letting him see Peter and letting him sit down like he's a welcomed guest in your home. He hurt you, Christine."

"Is that what she told you?" Jack cackled. "Come on, Christine. Are you still spreading that story? Did you also tell him that you came to me after you found out you were knocked up and begged me to marry you? Even brought her mother with her."

"What?" Eli's brow furrowed when he looked at Christine.

"And you rejected me because you were already engaged to be married."

"Just stay away from her," Eli spoke through bared teeth.

"Don't tell me to —"

"Listen!" Christine put a hand against Jack's and Eli's chests. "None of that matters now."

"You're right, Christine," Jack said, his voice growing soft. He took the hand from his chest and held it. "It doesn't matter now. I came here because I want us to be a family."

"What? But you were . . ." She couldn't finish her thought.

"Sabrina and I split up." His eyes diverted from her, then back again. "I came to say that I'm ready now. We can get married and raise our son."

Christine stood stunned. Her mouth hung open, yet she could find nothing to say.

"I'm staying in a hotel in Dover. I'll come back tomorrow night for your answer." He bent down and kissed her cheek then he grabbed his coat and left.

Palpable silence filled the cottage. This wasn't what she'd expected.

"Christy, what are you doing?" Eli whispered. "Please tell me that you're not going to marry that creep. Have you forgotten how he hurt you?"

"He was drunk, Eli. Maybe he wasn't himself." The excuses were bitter in her mouth, but there was something about Jack that weakened her. "He's Peter's father, Eli. Don't I owe it to my son to try?"

CHAPTER 32

"Where's Aunt Annie?" Mark pushed himself through the door. He looked at Christine, ignoring Eli standing there. "Sylvia's in labor and she's scared. She needs Aunt Annie — and you, Christine."

"What about Dr. Sherman?" Christine asked as she headed for the bedroom to gather Peter.

"The roads are flooded from the storm."

"What? But Jack just left."

"He won't get far." Mark shook his head.

"Let him go, Christine," Eli said, still angry.

"Eli, *vachts uh,*" she spat back, telling him to grow up.

"I'm ready," Annie interrupted the argument. She was already dressed and had her bag with her. "I suspected this might happen. Let's go."

In a few minutes Christine had Peter wrapped closely to her body, and she and

Annie held an umbrella over them as they walked across the soaked field, with water up to their ankles. Mark ran ahead of them and Eli came from behind. When they arrived at the farmhouse Christine found Jack, who was staring out at the road from the covered porch. He asked Christine politely if he could stay. Eli cringed. How could she let him stay?

"Eli, please ask your mother if she could keep him for the night."

"But, Christine," Eli said. This man was manipulating Christine. Why couldn't she see that?

"Please, Eli." He couldn't say no to her.

He nodded and watched her run toward Mark and Sylvia's house.

"You're not going to push me out," Jack said. "I'm going to raise my son."

With the eyes of God watching him and His strength coursing through his veins, Eli listened to Christine and left Jack alone.

Sylvia was crying when Christine and Annie entered the house. Rachel, Sylvia's sister who was tending to the twins, rushed to them and helped them with their umbrellas and coats. They both went straightaway to Sylvia's room. She was laying in the fetal position on the bed. She cried out as another pain came and didn't even notice they had walked into the room.

"All right, Sylvia, I want you up." Annie winced with every movement. Her small but strong hands pulled Sylvia up into a sitting position.

"Les mich geh." Sylvia pleaded to be left alone.

"Come on, Syl, you're going to have a baby. Remember how you helped me. Now it's my turn. Everything is going to be fine."

Over the next several hours the two women served Sylvia's every need and encouraged her to keep moving around. They made sure she was as comfortable as possible as she labored. Though she'd never helped a woman through labor or delivered a baby, it was more natural than any other nursing she'd ever done.

Sylvia repeated over several times that it was too early, and Christine had to remind her that it wasn't. Christine knew Sylvia's last experience had traumatized her.

Annie said Sylvia was having one of the worst labors that she had seen in a long time. Annie's knees were swollen and hurting from running over, and she could do nothing more than sit in the chair in the corner and instruct Christine on what to do.

After fourteen hours, Sylvia said she needed to push. Christine looked at Annie as Sylvia's breathing sped up.

"Just like you knew when it was time, so does Sylvia," Annie said, her eyes droopy with tiredness but she had a smile on her face. She pointed at the cloth on the dresser. "Under that towel are a few things you're going to need. Tie off the cord with that small string and then cut it. But wait until the cord stops beating like a pulse. Wrap the baby up in that blanket and give him to Sylvia to nurse. Just like Peter. Everything is going to be fine."

"I need to push," Sylvia said again.

It seemed all it took was a few contractions and suddenly Christine held a slick-skinned baby boy in her hands. He was pink and chubby. She handed him to Sylvia first, who looked at Christine with elation and exhaustion.

"It's a boy, Syl," Christine said, laughing.

"A boy," she whispered and smiled as she looked down at her baby who didn't cry much but looked up at his mother.

"Davey, his name is Davey," Sylvia said to Christine. "Davey and Peter are going to be best friends."

Christine smiled at her friend. How was this going to be possible? Jack wanted to marry her, and if she did marry him she and Peter would have to leave Sunrise. But she would have a proper family. If she didn't marry Jack, what would she do? She couldn't stay in Sunrise forever. The only way Davey and Peter would be friends was if she stayed in Sunrise and married Eli.

Later that night a knock sounded. Christine opened the small cottage door and Jack stood there. He raised an eyebrow.

"Is that angry *Mr. Amishman* here again?" He cleared his throat. "Or will we be able to have a civil conversation?"

"Eli's a good man, Jack." She stepped aside to let him in. "He stood by me and helped me when you wouldn't."

Where had her courage come from?

"Are you always going to throw that in my face?" Jack asked, raising an eyebrow. "Where's Jack Junior?"

"Jack Junior?" Christine questioned.

"Listen, if he's going to be a Delano, he's going to be Jack Junior."

"*Peter's* asleep," she said, putting her hands on her hips. "And Peter's not a Delano, he's a Freeman."

"Well, if we're alone." He stepped toward her and rested his hands on her hips.

Christine froze. His breath came closer. She could smell a subtle hint of beer. Before she could resist him he kissed her. For a brief moment the magic of their first kiss returned. The intensity of the rest of the night intruded and she pushed against his chest. He responded by putting his arms around her back and holding her tighter. She scratched the skin at his neck so he would let go. When he did, anger laced his face. His lip curled and his brow lined deeply. Then the burning sting of his hand scraped against her cheek. After the shock, the fear came.

"Jack." She held her cheek. "You hit me."

Jack's eyes grew larger and he rubbed his hand, the same one he'd used to hit her, over his face. He pulled out a flask and took a swig, and strangely it seemed to bring him back to reality.

"I'll leave for now, but this isn't over. I'm coming back for him. He's my son." He pushed by her and Christine watched as he ran across the field. A few minutes later she heard his engine rev and saw him spin out of the driveway away from the farm.

Christine knew that no matter what, Jack meant what he said.

CHAPTER 33

The sun rose the next morning as if it should have been a good day. Jack's threat, however, hovered over Christine like the worst kind of storm. The last thing Christine wanted was to be alone with Peter at the cottage when everyone else was going to the Sunday service. There wasn't anything safer that she could think of than being with an entire Amish community.

Eli jogged up to Christine, Peter, and Annie when he saw them approach the Peterscheim farm, where church would be hosted. It was a neighbor's farm, just over half a mile's walk. Christine was wearing the dress she'd worn the first time at church, blue with small pink flowers. He didn't take his eyes off her until he lined up and went to sit with the single men.

Christine hadn't told anyone about the night before. All she could think about was getting through church then telling Eli everything. She didn't want him to believe that she would marry Jack. She had been thick for considering it at all.

She did love Eli, on the other hand, and it was time she admitted it out loud.

Eli fixed his mind on the words he sung. His fear had startled away the peace he longed for. Christine was out of his reach. He'd done everything in his power only to realize that he had none. He prayed the words of the hymn and let them sink within his soul, pleading with the Lord for wisdom.

As always the second song they sang was a favorite among not just their community but among the Amish everywhere. *Loblied.* It was a Hymn of Praise.

O may thy servant be endowed with wisdom from on high.

After several more songs the preacher took his place in the middle of the crowded home. Not a moment later a man's voice came yelling from outside and a fourteen-year-old boy, Mervin, who was helping with the horses, ran through the door, his eyes wild.

"*Sis ein mahn en yollah dat drass.* He wants that English girl to come out and to bring the baby." The boy told everyone that there was a man yelling outside.

Eli stood and looked around for Christine in the rows of women. She was easy to pick out since her head was the only one uncovered.

"Christine," he said. Everyone turned to look at him, then her as she stood. "Jack."

"Vas ist letz?" The stooped bishop asked what was the matter. *"Vas vit des mahn?"*

Yes. What did Jack want? Eli wished he had an answer. He made his way up to the front of the house where the boy still stood breathless and the bishop stood near him with confusion in his eyes.

Christine's eyes were saucers when she reached Eli. Beyond her a sea of eyes stared at them. Everyone was watching. He couldn't make any mistakes right now. Eli gestured for Christine and the bishop to go into the bedroom just off of the main room. Coats and purses lay all over the bed.

No one spoke until they were behind the closed door.

"The man out there is my son's father," Christine said. Her voice wavered and her hands shook. The bishop nodded his head at her. "He cannot be trusted."

By the time Christine spoke the last word they heard Jack yelling again.

"I'd like to talk with the young man," the bishop said. Before Eli or Christine could stop him he opened the door and the three of them walked to the front door. The bishop opened it and walked out to the front porch.

"Young man, we don't want any trouble. We ask you kindly to either join us inside and listen to the truths of the Scriptures or calmly leave the property."

"I'm not going to listen to you, old man, I want you to send out Christine and my son."

Eli and Christine looked at each other. The frail-looking bishop seemed to try his best to stand taller. They couldn't see Jack from their vantage point but could hear him. Jack hollered again but this time Eli couldn't understand anything he said except for several profanities. The bishop returned inside looking pale and deflated.

"The young man is indeed troubled. I believe he has some strong drink with him."

Several of the young women began ushering the children upstairs, and many of the remaining members gathered in small groups.

"Mervin, run to the neighbors and have them call the police," Eli said.

Mervin looked at the old bishop. Christine knew that they didn't often — if ever — involve the law with the church.

"He's an Englisher and he might be

dangerous," Eli suggested. "Go out the back and he won't see you."

The bishop nodded yes to Mervin who was out of the house only a moment later.

"I need to go out there," Eli said.

"Nah, Eli, we don't want no trouble." The bishop spoke in English in front of Christine, then turned to Eli and began in their dialect. "We don't want a mark against our church's testimony. Let someone else deal with this man."

Eli inhaled. The bishop didn't trust him.

"I won't let him hurt Christine or Peter. His fight is with me."

"No, you can't go out there," Christine piped up. "He thinks you're getting in-between him and me."

The bishop's skin-sagged eyes nearly burst from his face.

"I'm the only one who can get him to leave." Christine's bravery reminded him of the grit she had at the hospital. She flung open the door and ran across the porch and down the steps. He took a short step only to have his father grab his arms from behind.

"No, let her talk to him, this should be her fight, not yours," he said, tightening his grip.

■ ■ ■ ■

"Christine." Jack's voice was raspy and strained. "Where's my son?"

"We can go somewhere to talk," she suggested. "We shouldn't disrupt their church service."

"Go get me my son!" He walked closely to her and put a finger in her face. His face was red with anger.

"I think it's time for you to go, Jack." Eli stepped between Jack and Christine.

It took but a moment for Jack's fist to connect with Eli's gut.

"Eli," Christine said breathlessly and instantly bent over to help him. Eli took a few moments to catch his breath and then straightened his back, shielding Christine.

"Eli, he's not worth it. Just go."

"Yes, Eli, why don't you go? You're yellow, ain't ya? Yellow about the war and yellow about fighting me."

"It's time for you to leave," Eli insisted, rolling his shoulders back.

The smack of Jack's fist against Eli's face was loud enough to make Christine scream. He nearly fell to the ground but caught himself. She took his arm and tried to pull him back.

"Leave, Jack," Eli said. The skin on his cheek broke open and blood began to drip slowly down his face. "I will not fight you, but I will not leave."

"Bring me my son!"

Jack landed another blow to Eli's stomach, doubling him over, then Jack kneed him in the face. Eli groaned for several long moments while the sound of Jack's laughter boomed against the trees that lined the property. Eli's nose was bleeding along with his cheek and though he stood less straight this time, he still managed to get back up.

"Leave, Jack. Get out of here." Christine's voice scraped against her throat like sandpaper.

"You ever kill anyone, *Amishman*?" Jack paced. Without waiting for a response he went on. "Yeah, you haven't. I have, you know. I killed all sorts of Nazis. Didn't even feel bad about it. I kind of liked it. Once you get that power in you, it's hard to let go." He mimicked pulling out a gun from a holster and pointed his fingers in the shape of a gun at Eli. The smile on his face was maniacal. He pretended to fire the pretend gun and laughed. "Just like that. Now, you gonna fight me like a man or do I have to kill you with my bare hands?"

Eli still didn't say a word but stood just a

measure taller.

This time when the blow came it was swatted away. It was his brother Mark. He pushed Jack away then stood next to Eli. Shoulders wide, he stood tall next to his brother. After him came Eli's father, Mark David, and two other men. Then David came out with three other young husbands; then Moses and a few of the single men. All of them stood shoulder-to-shoulder in silence.

"Leave my brother and Christine alone," Mark said, his voice resonating like an echo in Christine's ears. "Leave."

"You're a coward, man, a coward. You don't fight because you're a coward."

The door kept opening and more men poured out of the house. Christine was overwhelmed.

Eli's face was like a statue of bravery. Unflinching and relentless. He would stand in the gap between Jack and Christine no matter how many times he was hit. He was protecting Peter, who wasn't even his son. Where had he garnered such strength? Christine knew it was God. His strength kept Eli standing. But for how long? When would this end?

Then more came, one by one, building a wall in front of Christine and the house.

Who were these people who stood to protect her?

Eli's chest swelled as he stood with the men positioned alongside him. His arm went to his ribs but he managed to roll his shoulders back and look Jack in the eyes. Jack pulled out his flask and emptied it in one big swig. He looked at the lineup of men and threw it at them. With the madness in his eyes, he looked as if he were ready to take on every man that stood before him. But when the sounds of a speeding vehicle with gravel flying from the driveway behind him were heard, Jack paused.

"This isn't over," he spit as he took off toward the woods.

With Jack in the wind, Eli staggered and his brother's arm kept him from crumbling.

For several moments, his vision was foggy and he could only hear murmuring from the crowd and not real words. He could hear Christine crying but couldn't move to help her. Mark kept him from falling as the men filed over to Eli and shook his hand or patted his arm. His dad looked older as he turned back to the house.

"*Dangeh,* Mark," Eli said, when everyone else was gone. He cleared away the hitch in his throat leaving it as rough as gravel.

"We're brothers, Eli."

Mark helped him up to the porch swing so Christine could tend to his injuries. When he finally walked away, Eli knew nothing more would need to be said between the two of them. He had his brother back.

Christine hovered over Eli and dabbed his cheek with her *schnupduch* — her Amish handkerchief. Though tears fell from her jawline onto Eli's shirt, mixing with the drops of his blood, he couldn't help but smile at her. Eli found enough strength to put a hand on Christine's cheek. He'd been frightened for her. How could he tell her how much he loved her when he couldn't fathom leaving the community that had just put its life on the line for her?

They looked at each other for several long moments.

"He's just like all the men we worked with at Hudson River. I'm afraid this isn't the last we'll hear from him," she said, worried.

"He's not going to hurt you ever again. I won't let him. I promise."

"How can you promise me that? You don't know what my future holds."

"Marry me and let's find out together."

"But, it wouldn't be right for you to leave

the church. Look what they did for you today."

"What they did for me? Christine, they did this for us."

"I know that." Christine looked around then her eyes settled back onto Eli's. "I don't know why it's taken me so long to realize that this is my home — here with you."

"Christine?" Was he hearing her right?

"Yes, Eli, I'll marry you."

CHAPTER 34

Seven Months Later

Christine woke to a warm breeze pushing past the curtains that hung in the windows, matching the sky. The June morning sun lit her face and she smiled. She looked over and found the space next to her empty. Where had he gone?

Even though they'd only been married for three days she'd already grown accustomed to having him near her when she fell asleep and when she woke. Since that day at the church Jack had been arrested, convicted for assault, and given up the legal rights to his son. Christine was happy to resign the trauma with Jack to her past so she could look forward to her bright future with Eli. She learned more about the new life she'd chosen for her and Peter every day. Having gone through baptism classes while their *haus* was being finished and then the anticipation of their wedding to be announced in church, life had not slowed down since the day she'd finally told Eli *yes*. She'd also helped Annie with four more births in the community and had more scheduled.

She sat up in bed and stretched. The six o'clock sun lit up the room. Her feet moved into slippers as she stood and walked through their bedroom. As she passed the closet, which didn't have a door yet, she touched the sleeve of the royal blue wedding dress she'd worn a few days earlier.

"That dress is made just as neat as the Ohio Amish. It's just perfect," Christine had heard Annie say to Rosella and Rebekah. She tried not to feel some pride in it, but couldn't pretend she hadn't heard the compliment.

She walked into the living room, still not seeing her husband. Where was he? He told her he wouldn't be at the farm until Monday and today was Sunday, not to mention an in-between Sunday, which meant they had most of the day alone together with only the essential chores around their own *haus*.

She peeked into Peter's room and saw he and her mother were still sleeping. She had come back for the wedding and was staying for a few days. When Christine explained that the Amish don't go away on honeymoons, Margie insisted on being on night duty so if Peter woke he would not disturb the newlyweds, as she called them. Margie had embraced her role as a grandmother. Christine smiled at the thought of her newly married sister, Doris, and Lewis expecting their first child as well. As if an answer to prayers, Lewis loved her parents and was happy to help support them.

What her mother did not know was that the Amish community encouraged newlyweds not to view consummation as the goal for their first few days. This was not just another way for them to demonstrate that their love was more than physical, but a spiritual act in dedication to the Lord. Of course, this was a personal decision. Christine would never tell.

"Christine." She heard Eli's voice behind her, but before she could turn, his arms wrapped around her. Her first instinct was to try and cover up. She was wearing the thin, white nightgown he'd bought for her and given to her on their wedding night. It was dainty and simple. She didn't ask if this was a typical gift among other Amish couples, but accepted it with joy.

She turned and put her arms around his neck, gazing up at him.

"Where were you?" She flirted with her eyes.

"I want to show you something." He kissed her before continuing. "Come with me outside."

"I can't go like this."

"No one can see. The trees hide us, you know that."

Christine considered this and decided she would trust him. She let him lead her through their *haus* and back behind it where half of a barn was up. Behind that was a field of tall grass where she imagined her garden would go or just a place where their children would run and play in the sandbox or on the swing set. Eli stopped and turned toward her holding both hands. He was so handsome. The sun lit his hair, making it even lighter. His eyes were clear and gazed into hers.

"Will you take your hair down for me?" Eli asked, letting go of her hands.

"What do you have up your sleeve?" She took out the few pins that held it up and let the breeze carry it away, her caramel locks fell long against her back.

"I wanted to see you like this."

"What? In my nightgown and hair everywhere in the wind?"

"I know you gave up everything for me."

"But I have you and Peter has a father. I don't feel I've given anything up; I've gained so much more than I ever imagined."

"Remember when we went to Jeanne and Byron's wedding back at Hudson River?"

She nodded. Where was he going with this?

"It's the only English wedding I had ever been to and I realize you gave that up for me, too. The beautiful white dress and even the spoken vows that were so memorable."

"We said our vows on Thursday. I loved our wedding."

"But I wanted you to hear the vows in English, like I know you've always dreamed of. I bought this white nightgown for you — I thought you'd like the lace edging — I wanted you to have something pretty to wear, and I wanted you to wear your hair down because it reminds me of how you came to me that day when you let me hold you for the first time."

He faced her and took her hands.

"I, Eli Brenneman, take you, Christine Freeman, to be my wife, to have and to hold from this day forward, for better or for worse, for richer, for poorer, in sickness and in health, to love and to cherish; from this day forward till death do us part."

Christine's heart swelled and with tears of joy spilling from her eyes she repeated the vows to Eli.

"I, Christine Freeman, take you, Eli Brenneman, to be my husband, to have and to hold from this day forward, for better or for worse, for richer, for poorer, in sickness and in health, to love and to cherish; from this day forward till death do us part."

"And I have one more thing for you."

Christine wiped a tear away. "What?"

"This," he said, digging into his pocket and pulling out what looked like a ring. "With this ring, I thee wed."

Christine held her left hand out which trembled with emotion. He placed a small wire ring on her finger. Upon inspection she could see that he'd fashioned the wire into a heart at the top. While she wouldn't be able to wear it when others could see it, it was no less valuable to her. The Amish believed that it was best for the community to be uniform, so not to cause animosity in those without and pride in those with.

"It's the most precious item anyone has ever given me. I will treasure it always." She took in her gift for several long moments. "You're not done yet. You have to pronounce us."

He took her hands again.

"I now pronounce us husband and wife," Eli said loud enough that his words danced in the warm breeze around them, in the

497

trees, and as high as the birds in the sky.

"You may now kiss your bride," she finished.

ACKNOWLEDGMENTS

To the first, middle, and last of all time, my Savior. You shelter me under Your wings. Your faithful promises are my armor and protection. *Psalm 91:4*

To my amazing husband, Davis. You should put together a "Help, I'm Married to a Writer" kit and sell them online. You'd make a fortune. I love you forever!

To my sweet girls, Felicity and Mercy. I don't think there are two girls more excited about deadline week: Netflix marathons, take-out Chinese, and fewer baths. You two are amazing. My heart is so full of love for you both.

To my outstanding agent, Natasha. You're a miracle worker and I'm so glad that I have your number on speed dial. You always have the right words for me. Love and gratitude to you.

To my hard-working editors, Beth and Amanda. Meeting you at the writing conference was a highlight for me. Thank you for your patience on this journey of the publication learning curve. I couldn't have done this without you. You're both always so encouraging and confident in what we are doing. I appreciate you both beyond measure.

To Howard's genius art director, Bruce. Thank you for all the work you put into this cover. I love it, love it, love it!

To the entire team at Howard Books and Simon & Schuster. I sincerely thank you for the work you've put in on behalf of this book.

To my dramatic and dynamic family: Mom, Dad, Johannes, Emmalene, Joseph, Brandalyn, Celine, Madeleine, Sophie, Phoebe, and Joseph. Each of you fills my life with laughter and insanity and my belly with the best food ever (a.k.a. best lemon pie ever). Love to each of you.

To my sweet Mammie, Lydia. I hope you feel Daudy in the words of this book and are reminded of the service we can honor him for. I love you!

A big thank you to my amazing friend, Linda Attaway. A cheerful heart does good like a medicine . . . love you!

To *the little town that could,* the community of Springport, MI. I was a cheerleader for the Springport school system for six years as a student and now you are cheering me on. You humble me with your encouragement.

To the Hudson River State Hospital Nurses Alumni Association, namely Jeanne Wiley. Your willingness to share your experiences at HRSH as a nurse made all the difference. You are truly appreciated.

And last but not least, to my fabulous readers. Your reviews, emails, cards, Facebook messages, and hugs . . . it all means so much to me. I truly hope you enjoyed *Promise to Cherish*.

■ ■ ■ ■

PROMISE TO CHERISH
READING GROUP GUIDE

INTRODUCTION

Christine Freeman is a nurse at Hudson River State Hospital in the mid 1940s, during which the effects of World War II rage on. She has lost both of her brothers to the war and works tirelessly, serving patients at the ward. Worlds collide when conscientious objector Eli Brenneman comes to work at the hospital. Despite, and even in the midst of, differences, Christine and Eli begin to develop a friendship.

Christine becomes pregnant when things with her crush, Jack, go too far. Now, as an unwed soon-to-be mother, she must decide what is best for her and the baby she shamefully carries. Uncertain of her future, she joins Eli to find refuge in his Amish community until she can decide what is next. But with the passing of each week and her growing belly, she cannot ignore her growing feelings for Eli.

With the birth of Christine's baby boy, Eli confesses his love to Christine and begs her to stay. Jack too comes to visit, pleading with Christine to win her back. She must make a choice. Though she loves Eli, how can she remain in a culture and town so different from her own? How can she marry an Amish man and ignore the promise of a future together that Jack has now made to her? In *Promise to Cherish,* the conflict of World War II brings two people together to wage their own costly battle for love and discovery of self.

QUESTIONS AND TOPICS FOR DISCUSSION

1. Eli views the opportunity to join the Civilian Public Service camp for conscientious objectors as a way out of his hometown. He was not seeking "to make a change" or to "leave the Amish for good, but he did need to get away, even if just for a short spell of time" (p. 11). Can you relate to this desire to escape your present circumstances, but not out of a desire to change? What were your primary reasons for seeking time away? What change(s) did you experience during this time away or break from routine, if any?

2. Christine serves her family for years by working at Hudson River State Hospital. She did not want to work there, but "her family needed her to work . . . their very survival depended on it" (p. 18). Knowing that her mother made ends meet once Christine left, do you believe it was right for Christine's family to depend on her the way that they did? What reasons, emotional or financial, did Margie have for depending on Christine's income?

3. The reader is privy to Eli's thoughts on his first day at Hudson River State Hospital. "He'd never been a crying man, but there was something so desperately sad about the men in this room" (p. 76). What is revealed about his character here and in the way he interacts with Wally later?

4. In chapter 5, Christine and Eli argue over a conscientious objector's position toward war. Christine argues that wrongs should be righted and freedoms defended. Eli argues that the cost of war is too high, basing his beliefs on Christ's example to seek peace and love one's enemies. What do you think? Do you think Eli's beliefs would have been the same had he experienced the loss of loved ones as a result of

war as Christine did? Explain.

5. Jack tells Christine, "You wanted this to happen and now you're just pretending it's entirely my fault so you don't have to take any of the blame" (p. 144). Christine believes it: "She'd let his hands roam. . . . The only person she could blame for this awful night was herself" (p. 150). What do you think about the situation? In your opinion, was Christine raped? Who do you hold responsible?

6. Eli receives a phone call one day notifying him that his sibling's house burned down. His younger brother tells him "Everybody sure wants you home . . . because we need you" (p. 161). Based on this statement, were you surprised by the type of welcome and treatment Eli received once he returned home? Apart from Christine's joining him, what other reasons do you think the family had for treating Eli the way they did? Describe how you would feel if you were one of his family members.

7. Margie's response to her daughter's pregnancy likely depicts the social norms of America in the mid 1940s. She holds

Christine responsible for leading Jack on and provides an immediate solution for the pregnancy: Christine will either have Jack marry her or she will go to an unwed girls' home. How do present-day norms influence your judgment of Margie, if at all? Do you think Margie's response toward her unwed, pregnant daughter resonates in today's society? If so, in what ways?

8. Nurse Phancock is the first person to tell Christine her situation with Jack is not her fault. She bases this comment on her understanding of scripture and concludes that "nowhere in the Bible" does it say "that men can't control themselves. It does say that a man should respect a woman" (p. 230). How does scripture inform your beliefs and decisions? How do you believe Christine's relationship with God impacted her decisions in the weeks surrounding the situation with Jack?

9. The following comments about sin are made by women at church one Sunday: "sins in your youth will punish you later in life" and "every sin has a consequence" (p. 341). Aunt Annie's response indicates her adamant disagreement when she asks

them what her sin was since she lost all three of her babies. How does her background minister to Christine? To what extent do you agree with the comments made by these women? What informs your belief?

10. Aunt Annie recounts the ways that Amish people have been judged for their ways. Specifically, she speaks to the way they have separated themselves "from the world because it's the best way we know to be close to God" (p. 379). Regardless of whether you agree with their conscientious objector position, what benefits can you see in this level of separation? What negative consequences can you see in it?

11. Eli informally proposes to Christine once she has her baby, Peter. "I want to be your husband and Peter's father" (p. 458). She imagines the Amish way and declines his offer with the statement that "this isn't my real life." Identify the reasons Christine may have still felt this way, declining the gift of a man she loved in a community that she had come to enjoy.

12. When Eli is frustrated for the way the

hospital patients and staff view him for being a conscientious objector, his friend DeWayne responds with the following: "If you know who you are, you can't ever really lose yourself. You might stray a little from time to time, but you don't lose yourself — unless you just don't know who you are" (p. 81). How does this statement play itself out in both Eli's and Christine's lives throughout the novel? How have you seen the truth of this in your own life?

13. How does Matilda symbolize the person Eli was before he left the Amish community?

14. Discuss how the brother in the story of the prodigal son (Luke 15:11–32) is similar to Mark.

15. Describe how the theme of God's redemption characterizes Christine's and Eli's journeys.

ENHANCE YOUR BOOK CLUB

1. Hudson River State Hospital faced hardship. Workers were few and their supplies and funding were low. Additionally, support was little: families did not visit their

patients and the town wanted little to do with the institution. Consider the institutions or nonprofits in your area that receive little support. Decide how your group could meet one of their needs and develop a plan of action to do so.

2. Homes for unwed mothers were a national trend from the beginning of the twentieth century until the 1970s, when use began to decline. Research and discuss the historic and present-day types of these institutions. Be sure to elaborate on both their positive and negative influence. For an in-depth account, read *The Girls Who Went Away: The Hidden History of Women Who Surrendered Children for Adoption in the Decades Before Roe v. Wade* by Ann Fessler.

3. As Aunt Annie says, the Amish have chosen to separate themselves *"from the world because it's the best way we know to be close to God"* (p. 379). This month choose one way you can separate yourself more from "the world" in order to be closer to God. Share it with the group and ask for accountability.

4. Eli prays the following: *"Lord, give me the*

wisdom and patience You promise in James. The faith you show in Hebrews. Show me how to abide like in John fifteen. Help me love like First Corinthians thirteen" (p. 437). Select one of the passages that Eli may have been referring to and read it aloud. Share with the group what those verses mean to you in this season of your life. Commit the scripture verse(s) to memory.

- James 1:5–6 "If any of you lacks wisdom, he should ask God, who gives generously to all without finding fault, and it will be given to him. But when he asks, he must believe and not doubt, because he who doubts is like a wave of the sea, blown and tossed by the wind."
- Hebrews 11:1, 6 "Now faith is the assurance of things hoped for, the conviction of things not seen. . . . And without faith it is impossible to please God, for whoever would approach him must believe that he exists and that he rewards those who seek him."
- John 15:4 "Abide in me, and I in you. As the branch cannot bear fruit by itself, unless it abides in the vine, neither can you, unless you abide in me."

- 1 Corinthians 13:4–8 "Love is patient and kind; love does not envy or boast; it is not arrogant or rude. It does not insist on its own way; it is not irritable or resentful; it does not rejoice at wrongdoing, but rejoices with the truth. Love bears all things, believes all things, hopes all things, endures all things. Love never ends."

5. Author Elizabeth Byler Younts has also written an Amish memoir titled *Seasons: A Real Story of an Amish Girl.* This is a story of her grandmother Lydia Lee Coblentz, who grew up in an impoverished American family through the Great Depression. Read this memoir and discuss how this book differs from *Promise to Cherish.*

A CONVERSATION WITH
ELIZABETH BYLER YOUNTS

Have you always wanted to write?

I'm told that even as a child as young as three I was writing my stories in small notebooks before bedtime. My mom was not surprised at all when around eleven I started talking about becoming a writer.

Praise the Lord she and my dad nurtured my love of writing and books.

Describe your favorite writing location or room.

I just moved from the south to the north and into a new house. I love my house. It's not perfect — but it has the best sense of home. I usually write either in our home-school room in the basement near the windows or next to the fireplace that opens up into the great room and kitchen.

How do your two young daughters influence your writing? Are there specific lessons in the Amish culture that you hope they learn?

As I write about the Amish way of life I long for the slower lifestyle. I wrote a blog post about a vintage lifestyle and how captivating it is to think about — though there are realities of vintage living that has its disadvantages, I understand. But I don't want my children to be addicts to technology and require constant, entertaining stimulation. The best way to do this is through the example of my husband and myself and accessibility. I don't do this perfectly and pray for better consistency.

My husband and I strive to provide our girls with the best possible childhood that resembles the best part of our own. Quality time is important to us, and we like simple, home-cooked meals, and healthy conversation around the table. We have a lot of time together with homeschooling, and we are planning a garden this year. We believe it's important to be a part of a community of people whom you can care and pray for and who do the same for you. Our faith is built on the Bible. We teach our children that everyone needs a Savior — no one is perfect. Accepting the gift of Christ's sacrifice allows the Bible to unfold with the most amazing wisdom. I pray my daughters learn that they have to work hard for what they want and need — real living does not come through being spoon-fed.

It seems your own *Daudy* was an inspiration in writing this book. He was a conscientious objector in World War II and worked at a mental hospital during that time. How were his stories passed down to you? At what stage in your life did his service truly impact you and draw you in with a desire to learn more?

Yes, my *daudy,* Freeman Coblentz, has

definitely inspired this book. I can't remember learning his stories; I feel like I've always known them. I used to be bothered by the fact that he was never recognized for serving in the way he knew how to serve. Now, with this book I can honor his service in a way that I think would've pleased him if he were still alive. I feel like I understand his stance so much better now and believe very strongly that our country is better for having conscientious objectors who, when given the chance, will help the country in a way that does not disrupt their faith. After World War II there was also a movement of pacifists who went overseas to help those who lost so much during the war. Some went right from the CPS to this work. While my *daudy* did not participate in this, I am so thankful for the pacifist movement that was willing to prove its beliefs through real action.

This story also blossomed through the experience of one of my first cousins. He fell in love with a young woman outside the Amish faith. You'll be happy to know they married also and have a house full of beautiful children. She embraced her new life because of her love for my cousin.

The story of *Promise to Cherish* is steeped in the history of World War II. What was your research process like? What resources were particularly helpful in studying the culture of unwed mothers and conscientious objectors?

Researching as many details as possible was very important to me. There wasn't a specific website I used for unwed mothers but doing research online makes this process accessible. I went to www.civilianpublicservice.org for the CPS and the mental hospitals research. This was where I began the research for this entire series. I also used several books: *The CPS Story: An Illustrated History of Civilian Public Service* by Albert N. Keim, *Service for Peace* by Melvin Gingrich, *Acts of Conscience* by Steven J. Taylor, and *Detour . . . Main Highway: Our CPS Stories* by the College of Mennonite Church. These books were incredibly helpful.

Promise to Cherish does not even touch the tip of the iceberg with how life was in the institutions or the CPS wide. It would bring many to tears. The men and women who worked in these institutions during those years when it was especially difficult, and I don't just mean the CPS workers, deserve medals.

6. In your *Letter to the Reader,* you note that you are a "proud military wife with an ancestral line of Amish conscientious objectors." What are a few things you respect about *both* of these groups of people?

I'm so proud of our military. I believe a current statistic is that only about 1 percent of Americans will serve in the military in active duty. During World War II the percentage was closer to 9 percent. There are really so few people who fight for the freedoms of the 99 percent. Truly, hats off. The sacrifices that come with that responsibility are many — the greatest being putting your life on the line knowing your family could lose you. My husband is now in the Air National Guard after eleven years in active duty, and I'm as proud of him as I ever was. I stand by the hard work that our military does and their committed and loyal spouses and their "brats" who have to take on every new home, job, and school changes, and make new friends every few years and so much more with courage and grace. This is not an easy way to live, though it can be very rewarding.

As I look back at my ancestry and the lineup of nonresistant men and women, I'm also proud. I respect that they followed through with their beliefs and didn't just do what was popular or acceptable. In World War II the pacifists were hated and despised yet they stood for their right to be a C.O. Consider how difficult this would've been for them. I'm proud of my present and my ancestry because in both I see a resolve to follow one's conscience, no matter how difficult. Both require a strong-willed spirit and perseverance.

The reader follows both Christine and Eli on a spiritual journey. With which character can you relate the most, speaking in terms of your own spiritual journey? Why?

I think maybe pieces of both. Christine and Eli, in different ways, saw their spiritual value in how people perceived them. This is not where our value lies. No matter how much good people see in you or if you are someone easily judged for wrongs . . . your value comes from God. This is such a hard concept. This affects not just how we view ourselves but how we make friends and our sense of belonging.

I am constantly reminding myself that what truly matters are God's wondrous thoughts toward me. I fail so often but God reminds me that He knows the number of the hairs on my head, that He knit me in my mother's womb before the world was set in motion, and that He would've sent Jesus to die even if I was the only person who needed a Savior. My life has value to the Lord and He cherishes me. Ultimately, this is what Christine and Eli needed to learn. They are worth loving and cherishing no matter the mistakes they have made or the opinions of others.

Who is your least favorite character in *Promise to Cherish*? Why?

I really enjoyed these characters. I had several that could make this list but because I see redemption in them, even Jack, I think my least favorite would have to be Nurse Minton. My reason for this is because she let her circumstances make her jaded and harsh. She couldn't see the humanity that was within the walls of the hospital anymore. The years of hard, thankless work had crushed her spirit. In writing that, however, it makes me sad for her and I wonder what her story was.

I also didn't like Bucket, a very minor character, at all. I believe the vast majority of our heroic World War II soldiers would've disapproved of how he belittled Eli.

The reader is challenged to consider how World War II demanded change from the lives of conscientious objectors. Their financial climate was altered. Expectations were redefined. Loved ones spent an indefinite amount of time waiting on their conscientious objectors to return home. And when these individuals _did_ return, they themselves were different. What do you hope the reader gains by considering how conscientious objectors sacrificed for the war as well?

All I can truly hope for readers to gain is what I've gained myself. It's important to see a new and untold perspective and that everyone has a story to share. I'm learning not to condemn the decision not to fight but to be thankful we are in a country that allows for personal freedoms with regards to faith and conscience. Their sacrifices were different from soldiers — true, but they still sacrificed. Just because it wasn't dangerous or didn't cost their lives doesn't mean it's a sacrifice that should be forgotten.

With *Promise to Cherish* now complete, what are your plans for future writing?

I am currently writing the third book in the series. It is tentatively titled *Promise to Keep.* Esther Detweiler was brought up knowing too much about abandonment and broken promises. Through a fear of rejection and an independent streak she has rejected the concept of love and marriage. When Esther is asked to care for a little motherless English girl while her father, Joe, goes off to the Pacific in World War II, Esther's life changes. The real complications start, however, when Joe returns from war four years later.

Once this book is finished I hope to write many more stories that challenge our thinking and provide readers with an ear to the past.

The employees of Thorndike Press hope you have enjoyed this Large Print book. All our Thorndike, Wheeler, and Kennebec Large Print titles are designed for easy reading, and all our books are made to last. Other Thorndike Press Large Print books are available at your library, through selected bookstores, or directly from us.

For information about titles, please call:
    (800) 223-1244

or visit our Web site at:
    http://gale.cengage.com/thorndike

To share your comments, please write:
    Publisher
    Thorndike Press
    10 Water St., Suite 310
    Waterville, ME 04901